Joy Eramian

THE AGHA'S CHILDREN

A Cypriot Armenian Dynasty

Copyright © 2006 Joy Eramian
kay.joy@btinternet.com

All rights reserved. No part of this book may be reproduced
or transmitted in any form by any means,
electronic, mechanical, photocopying, recording, or otherwise,
without the prior written permission of the author.

ISBN 9963-9218-0-9

Design and typesetting by Toby Macklin
Printed and bound in Cyprus by Imprinta Ltd.

Contents

Preface 7
1768 Sunset at Tersu, Dawn at Deftera 9
1798 A Stone for Hanemie 29
1825 The Wise Woman 45
1850 The Italian Painter 59
1858 The Owl and the Moon 75
1859 Caterina's Voyage 89
1884 Monkey and the Poet 107
1885 The Hermit and the Hunter 129
1891 The Choosing of Elise 139
1892 The Judge of Boursa 151
1896 The Boy from Zeitoun 159
1897 Carpe Diem 173
1899 The Diplomat and the Hodja 185
1910 A Man's World 191
1914 The Constant Lover 203
1915 Hasmik and the Death March Major 217
1918 A Place of Refuge 235
1924 Mustafa the Assassin 243
1930 Irini's Revenge 255
1940 In the Midst of Life 267
1942 Boghos and the Thief 275
1946 The Little Pasha 281
2005 Respect 295

*With heartfelt thanks to David Hessayon
for telling me to stop talking and start writing,
and in affectionate memory of
Joan Hessayon, author and friend,
whose kindness encouraged me to believe I could do it.*

Preface

This book was originally written solely for the 300 cousins descended from Boghos-Berge Eramian, the family of my Armenian husband, but as it developed and I showed parts of it to people whose opinion I valued, I found that many of my friends knew little or nothing about the tragedy of the Genocide carried out in Turkey under the Ottoman administration, and I decided that I would like it to reach a wider audience.

It changed from a fairly basic recounting of facts to something more readable and hopefully more enjoyable, but this necessitated considerable dramatisation of the older stories, and the inclusion of some which are not verifiable, or vary in major details when told by different branches of the family, and it has resulted in a work which is neither wholly fact nor completely fiction.

There are tales of family ancestors who showed astounding bravery, dignity, and resourcefulness in enduring and overcoming great cruelty and brutality. Their descendants have only loving admiration for them, but they have asked that some names and events should be changed, and I have done so. There are also stories of cousins who lived in happier times, and here the names are their own.

I ask my wonderful cousins to forgive any mistakes I may have made, and I hope that they will enjoy the book, which is intended to celebrate the extraordinary courage and indomitable spirit of the Armenian people.

Joy Eramian
January 2006

The ancient, mountainous, stark, and unforgiving homeland of the Armenians lies across the Silk Road, the route from Europe to the East, and so, century after century, one marauding army after another has passed through it. Their culture has grown strong in overcoming the hardships caused by these frequent invaders, and though it has not been able to flourish and blossom as easily as those of more fortunate lands, it has tenacious roots which have grown in stubborn defiance of the many conquerors who have tried to destroy it.

The first of the Eramian Aghas to settle in Cyprus came to the island from Turkey, a land in which his people had lived for centuries, long before the Turkish hordes invaded and conquered it. They had been there for so many generations that they thought they were part of it, and that they had a right to a place in its future, but they were tragically wrong.

The story of this young man has been told from generation to generation. He was born in Izmir in the middle of the eighteenth century. His name was Boghos-Berge.

HERE BEGIN THE STORIES OF THE LIFETIME OF
BOGHOS-BERGE ERAMIAN AGHA

1768

Sunset at Tersu, Dawn at Deftera

STEPAN AGHA and the Vali Hassan Karim Bey had been friends for many years. The Bey was old and tired and today he was in a great deal of pain, but in the name of this longstanding friendship, he rose from his sickbed and went to give Stepan the news that would change his son's world for ever.

It was nearing the end of a long, hot, and seemingly ordinary day, and the sunset was truly spectacular. The enormous crimson disc was slowly disappearing behind the plane trees which Stepan's great-grandfather had planted in the fields along the river a little way from the house, and it cast a warm light on the whitewashed walls of his office.

Stepan had moved this office from its original site in the basement to a room on the ground floor at the back of the great house, so that he could look out over the wide sweep of grass and trees to the fields at the other side of the water. He had only to raise his eyes from his ledgers or stock books to see this lovely view, and he had watched the sun go down from his comfortable chair many times in the years since he had succeeded to his father's honours. Today, he had been working since dawn with only a short break at midday, and he and his estate manager had just agreed that it was time for coffee and a *nargileh* when a servant knocked at the door and announced that the Bey had called on him, and was waiting in the drawing room.

That morning, the man he sent to Hassan Karim's house to enquire after his health had returned with the news that His Excellency was still very ill, and was as yet unable to leave his bed. This visit was therefore most welcome, though somewhat surprising. Relieved that things were not as bad as he had feared, Stepan sent his manager off to a solitary refreshment and hurried to meet his guest.

He went into the drawing room smiling and holding out his hands to greet this most pleasant arrival. "Exalted Bey!" he exclaimed, "this is the most delightful of surprises, old friend! Your man sent a message that you were so ill that you were confined to bed."

Hassan Karim Bey was seated in a high-backed chair by the tall window, and he turned his head towards the door but did not rise. He had been a big man when young, taller even than Stepan, who was himself above average height, but now he was bent and he had lost weight during his illness, so that his clothes hung loosely. He was dressed with his usual care and elegance in a formal gold-embroidered jacket and black fez, but his face was pale, with an unhealthy greyish tinge, and his voice was weak as he began their customary greetings.

"Noble and illustrious Agha, forgive me for remaining seated. The pleasure of your august company should of course be sufficient to make one leap with joy from a death-bed in any circumstances … but unfortunately, this is now my situation in truth, and I am feeling the weight of my years."

At once, Stepan abandoned their enjoyable game of endeavouring to outdo one another with fulsome and courtly compliments. The Bey was obviously far too ill to have called on him for some trivial reason. He seated himself opposite the old man and dismissed his own manservant, but he signed to his visitor's man to stay. The Bey's *ushak* was a deaf-mute and he went with a soft tread to his accustomed place behind his master's chair, where he stood watching for any sign that the Bey needed help.

"You should have sent for me to come to you," Stepan chided. "We have known each other so long that you must know that I would have come at once, and I can see that you should not be away from your rest. What has brought you here in such a state?"

The Bey looked at him sadly. "I have good reason, my friend, and I know this will be my last visit to your home. Our doctor says that I must prepare to give my account to Allah, and indeed I had resigned myself to it, until this morning. I have come to you because I have received a most disturbing message from the Vali whom the Sultan has chosen to take my place. It has meant that I still have one last thing to do – and that I must also ask a favour from you."

"Anything," Stepan offered at once.

"Don't be so hasty to grant it untold," the Bey protested, but he smiled appreciatively. "This is not a request for myself, however. I must ask you to give your protection to someone, now that my own patronage will soon count for little. I have a young groom among my servants. He is one of your race and he has been badly beaten by this new Vali's men, and then mutilated for good measure. Our *Hakim* believes that he will recover more quickly among his own people, and that he should be cared for by those who can speak to him in his own language and who know his customs." Hassan's breathing became laboured and it was a moment or two before he could go on. "Also, I very much regret to inform you that your new Vali will be Selim Achmed Bey."

This was very bad news.

Selim Achmed was a fanatical believer in Islam, and his cruelty to non-believers in his present province was well known. His servants called him Sheytan Selim, though never to his face, for he seemed to take a devil's pleasure in his relentless harshness towards those he considered infidels and who, since they denied his beliefs, were unworthy of mercy.

"The poor lad nearly bled to death before he was returned to us with the Vali's compliments," the Bey said. "As you know, the law against *Giavour* being allowed to ride horses has never been enforced by me, but on his way here Selim Achmed saw my boy exercising one of my greys and decided to make an example of him as a message to me. As a result, my groom has lost his left hand, and he will bear the scars of the whip on his face and body for the rest of his life." He shook his head and frowned. "I do not understand the cruelty of such men."

He gestured with an elegant, manicured hand, and his man hastened to uncap a small blue bottle and hold it to his master's nose. The pungent smell of the salts seemed to help his breathing, and he leaned back in his chair and closed his eyes.

Stepan waited silently while the Bey recovered. So, a new Vali had already been appointed, and his old and cherished friend was now without office and power. The poor young groom had suffered so that a message might be sent to himself, as well as to Hassan, and that brutal act meant that the new governor intended to observe and enforce the Law in every respect, and that the power, influence and wealth of the Armenian Agha would not help him in any way.

He bowed his head as he remembered what he had heard of this Selim Achmed Bey. The man was feared and hated in his previous province, and with good reason. Extortion, injustice, flogging and humiliation awaited the unlucky new subjects of this dangerous and cruel man. It would be very hard to be in the power of such a tyrant after so many good and happy years of prosperity under the benevolent rule of Hassan Karim Bey, and Stepan did not think that his sons would easily tolerate such oppression. He feared that they would not be sufficiently humble to survive. Inevitably their accustomed freedoms would be curtailed and they would react with outrage, surprise and anger. He was particularly concerned about his youngest son, Boghos-Berge, who was full of the sudden intensity and energy of youth and who would not willingly bow to such a man. With sorrow, the Agha realised that it would be extremely unwise to remain at Tersu.

He could see no alternative. The family must leave the lovely old house with its mellow stone walls, its large and graceful rooms. The peaceful gardens and the well-tended and fertile acres which surrounded it must be sold. The great estate, named by Stepan's remote ancestor for the abundant sweet waters that made it so green and beautiful and which generations of Eramians had loved and cherished, would pass from their ownership, and with it the home in which their children had been born for more than two hundred years.

Ostensibly, the Bey's groom had lost his hand because he was riding a horse in the presence of the Vali, but there was very much more to the matter than that. The *Giavour,* a term which included Jews and Greeks as well as Armenians, were forbidden to ride horses and permitted to use only the humbler donkeys and mules, but there were other humiliating laws which also applied only to them and which a Vali may enforce or not as he chose. The strict enforcement of these could make life unbearable.

Under Selim Achmed, taxes would be as high as the *Giavour* could pay, and there would be no redress. There would be no justice from the courts, where the word of a Muslim with his hand on the Qur'an would be accepted without question before that of a non-believer, and there would be no protection from this Vali against the general theft and abuse which was temptingly possible within such a law. *Giavour* must be very humble and must behave with respect in the presence of a Muslim; there were clothes they could not wear and employment and official positions they could not hold. A wealthy *Giavour* Agha would be nothing more than a provocation and a tempting target to Selim Achmed.

It was a very, very bad thing to be in the power of such a man.

The Bey's injured groom was named Garo. He was still unconscious when four of the Bey's *syces* brought him into the house on a litter, taking great care not to jostle or jar the boy as they set him down. Stepan's two sons, Artin and Boghos-Berge, were waiting for him. They had been told of his arrival and the reason for his injuries, and they reacted with shock and anger as they saw his cuts and bruises, the dreadful marks of the whip across his face, and the bloody, bandaged stump of his left wrist.

"The new Vali is an animal!" Artin exclaimed in a horrified voice. "This is only a boy, he looks about the same age as my brother. Is this Selim Achmed some kind of madman?"

"You must be careful where you say such things, my son. That is now a very dangerous remark, and if such a speech as yours were to be reported to the new Vali, you would die." Stepan was standing behind them, with his arm supporting Hassan Karim. The two young men greeted the Bey respectfully. He was a frequent visitor to their home and they were glad to see him.

"Didn't you wonder why our friend came in person to bring the boy to us, when he is so ill?" Stepan went on, "And why he is attended by a deaf-mute? With the arrival of Selim Achmed Bey, the good days here are over. From now on, you must mind what you say, what you do, and even what you wear. The serpent has arrived in Eden, and now we must remember that even the oldest and most valued friend, the truest and most honest of men may do a foul thing for a large reward or to secure the safety of his family, and that the bravest and most trusted retainer would say anything once he is in the hands of the Bey's torturers. I believe they are well practised and expert at their business."

Artin and Boghos-Berge fell silent. The young groom groaned softly in his drugged sleep, and they watched him with pity and horror, but also with a dawning realisation. They shared their father's quick intelligence and they were already following the same train of thought to its inevitable conclusion. It was hard to believe that they might have to lose Tersu.

When he had seen that Garo was settled as comfortably as possible, Stepan left his sons to sit with the boy so that he would have someone to greet him in his own tongue when he woke, and he walked slowly with Hassan to his carriage.

The Bey's *syces*, six matched running-retainers in white and gold tunics and crimson turbans, turned to their master as he approached, and they bowed to him, saluting him with the gilded and lacquered rods they used to clear the roads. The lamplight glinted on the scabbards of their long, curved swords and the hilts of their silver-bossed knives as they trotted in perfect unison to their positions at the front of the horses. They moved with a strange and distinctive high-stepping, backward-kicking gait, and they halted as one man, grounding their staffs to stand as immobile as statues, waiting for the carriage to leave.

The friends took one another's hands for the last time.

"You will leave Tersu very soon, I hope," Hassan said, softly. "Your sons are more important than even this lovely and cherished home of yours, or any other of your possessions. You have taught your heirs to be men, and they will not tolerate a yoke such as that of Selim Achmed."

"We'll go back to our house in Izmir." Stepan told him, "Tonight I'll send my wife ahead of us with an escort, and she will have everything ready for us there by the time I have chosen and packed the things I wish to take with us. I'll be quick about it, and gone before Selim Achmed takes his place in your house and turns his attention towards Tersu."

They were reluctant to part. Their friendship crossed many years and they both knew that this would be their final meeting.

Stepan returned Hassan's embrace. "Thank you for these few days' grace, my friend," he said. "I will never forget you. I shall miss you and think of you often. May God be with you…."

He watched the carriage move away behind its high-stepping runners, and stood there till it had passed through the tall iron gates and the light of its lamps grew fainter and disappeared.

The Agha's Children

The return of the Eramian family to Izmir before the end of summer caused an interested stir in the houses of the Armenian Quarter, but everyone except Boghos-Berge settled quickly back into the normal routines of city life. His brother and father enjoyed the dances, dinners, amusements and entertainments the city could provide and he himself was much courted by hopeful Armenian matrons with marriageable daughters. Though it was rumoured that he was betrothed in childhood to a cousin of the family, they nursed the hope that such an old promise might be forgotten in the present charms of their elegant, perfumed, coiffed, demure and delicate daughters.

Boghos-Berge doggedly did his duty and raised hopes in many a matronly and ferociously-corseted bosom as he obediently danced with the Armenian community's most eligible maidens, bending his handsome head to pay a gallant compliment as he and his partner circled the floor in the scandalously intimate waltz which until recently had been considered too 'fast' for respectable ballrooms. Now, however, it was accepted by even the most particular and careful of hostesses, and young people were allowed to hold each other in quite shocking but delightful proximity.

In the next few months Boghos-Berge changed from a rather awkward youth into an assured, polite, tall and presentable young man with crisp black curls, fine dark eyes and, at last, a respectable moustache, and his flawless manners and engaging smile featured largely in the dreams of several young ladies. He was refreshingly unaware of this distinction and would much rather have been out in the fields, walking and riding in the open air and helping with the business and management of the lost estate, instead of making polite conversation in elegant reception rooms.

He missed his friends among the estate workers, most of whom had been with his family from time out of mind, and he wished for all the familiar daily activities of the well-run farm, and for the wonderful variety of the seasons. In Izmir, only the heat or cold, the dust or mud in the streets, and the trees showing leaves or bare branches gave an indication of the time of year, and he became very weary of the dirty streets and the stuffy enclosure of the town houses.

There was nowhere in the world like Tersu, the place of sweet waters.

Izmir was like any other major city or great port, inhabited by people of many nations, grimy and splendid, dangerous for the unwary, a place of opportunity for the bold and intelligent, and at the same time beautiful and sordid. A great deal of its charm or unpleasantness, glamour or danger, depended on the observer's prosperity and point of view.

The city had one of the largest safe harbours in the Mediterranean, and it was crowded with houses, from the humble mud-brick homes in the suburbs to the imposing three or four-storied stone-built mansions in the wealthier quarters. Great ships and merchantmen from all over the world jostled for space at the wharves where sailors, porters and labourers argued, shouted at each other and bargained using an ingenious lingua franca, and there was bustle and noise at all hours.

The unpaved streets were filthy, reeking, unsanitary and noisy. They teemed with people and horses, carriages, porters and hawkers, and everywhere there were little stalls and push-carts selling sesame bread, *lahmajouns*, and a hundred other sweets, pastries and delicacies. There were water sellers bent under their ornate brass canisters, all hung about and chiming with metal cups on chains, there were sherbet vendors, and small boys dashing between the crowds, calling their unmistakeable high pitched warning: "*Chai, Chai, Chai,*" and holding high their miraculously unspilt trays laden with small, waisted glasses of hot sweet tea. No transaction could politely be concluded without this drink, or equally tiny cups of thick black coffee.

The merchants offering carpets, clothes, jewellery, shoes, leather goods, brassware and a thousand other necessities accosted passers-by loudly in all the tongues of Europe and the Ottoman Empire, and the air was full of the smells of roasting coffee and the apple and vanilla-flavoured tobacco in the smoke which bubbled up through the cooling water of the *nargilehs*.

Meanwhile, Boghos-Berge pined for the fresh, sweet air of Tersu, and the streams and fields where he had spent the happy days of his childhood, running and playing among the fields and trees, fishing in the streams, talking to the herders, ploughmen and labourers, watching and taking part in the work that went on from month to month and quite naturally learning over the years the management of its land and industry. He was stifled in the city and unable to settle to any of the opportunities it offered.

He spent many hours with the boy whom Selim Achmed had mutilated and sent as a warning to his father and the kindly Hassan Karim Bey, reading to him at first and later teaching him the beautiful script of their language which, as he told him, was invented for his nation by a saint. The language itself was eloquent and wonderfully versatile, and Garo already spoke it like a gentleman.

During these months when he was slowly healing and becoming accustomed to his new scarred face and missing hand, he developed his lifetime's devotion to Boghos-Berge and made his solemn vow that he would die before he allowed any danger to harm him. As time went on, he became Boghos-Berge's *ushak,* his personal valet, and soon people became used to seeing this dark and silent shadow a step or two behind his young master.

Garo went to forbidden schools of fencing, shooting and unarmed fighting along with the sons of *Giavour* aristocracy, and his single-minded attention to the lessons quickly made him a competent bodyguard. The smith who had been brought from Tersu made him a small double-hook which attached to the end of his left arm with cleverly contrived straps, and he practised constantly with this until his skill gave him the ability to do many more things than people suspected. A second, razor-sharp attachment provided a deadly weapon which could be fitted to the hooks in seconds, and he kept this in a sheath strapped to his forearm, and concealed under his shirtsleeve.

Garo applied himself to the lessons with such diligence that Maitre Letissier offered him private tuition, and taught him some most unsporting techniques to deal death quietly and effectively. "You have an advantage given to you by the Vali who took your hand away and forced you to replace it with this hand of metal," the Maitre told him. "You may catch a sword-blade with these hooks and take no harm, and with a twist you may disarm your assailant, so!" The diminutive Frenchman took Garo's hook in his hand and guided him through the movements, patiently repeating them until he had them by heart. It took only a few lessons. Alone at home the young *ushak* practised these, too, until he was adept and the moves were natural to him, and very quickly he was able to use the double-hook for a sudden and unexpected deflection of a thrust, and then catch and raise his attacker's guard to score with the point of the sword in his right hand.

Maitre Letissier was pleased. He replaced the fencing foils with heavy sabres, and took Garo through some unusual defences against the edge of the blade, using both sword and hooks. "No one will expect you to take a stroke and block it in this manner," he said, with a smile of satisfaction. "Keep this ability as covert as these lessons, *mon ami*, and it may save your life one day." And he graced this most apt student with an approving salute of his sword, a rare and appreciated gesture from this extremely exacting master. Garo treasured it secretly. He did not care that none of the others had seen the accolade.

His expertise with a blade was soon noted by certain of the other *Giavour* pupils, sons of wealthy fathers with various reasons for ill will against their Ottoman masters, youths sworn to a Brotherhood of Honour which promoted violence and armed resistance against the humiliations of the unjust laws. Garo declined their advances as courteously as he was able, saying that he was the sworn retainer of the Eramian family, to whom he owed a debt of honour, an excuse which could be accepted by the young bloods without loss of face on either side.

The two young men went together everywhere, and Garo was *ushak* in public, and a friend at home. He always dressed modestly in black, wearing close-fitting breeches and boots, with a short jacket over a loose shirt. These were clothes which he found most comfortable, which were no impediment to fast movement, and which could hide a secret blade.

Boghos-Berge, unable to shake his resolve to be so drably dressed and self-effacing, gave in eventually and had his friend's clothes specially made for him. Although they were plain, they were of the finest quality, the jackets embroidered modestly with fine black silk at collar and hem, the breeches tailored snugly to his long legs and the expensive boots finished with a fashionable high polish and decorated with a small pendant tassel, Hessian style. Garo wore a black fez and cut his curly hair short in the European manner, and his modest demeanour and reticence made him an object of speculation among the gently-reared maidens of the salons where Boghos-Berge was a frequent though unwilling visitor. The *ushak* had an air of mystery and a most intriguing scar which gave him a sardonic twist to his mouth, and which some of the bolder ladies admired and found quite devilishly attractive. When he and his tall, equally interesting, and extremely eligible master walked the *rambla* along Izmir's fashionable boulevards, or trod the expensive Turkish carpets which graced the salons of the city's grande dames, heads turned to watch their progress.

Meanwhile, the Agha had finally to accept that his second son had no aptitude or liking for trade, and that he would be happiest running a country estate like their much-missed Tersu. Boghos-Berge had presented his father with a problem. He detested the offices, salons and smoky coffee shops where business was done, and he was not interested in the day to day minutiae of trade. He would not spend hours in pleasant conversation leavened with a little enjoyable bargaining, and the necessary conventions of polite society with its etiquette and silly customs exasperated him. Also, Stepan suspected that the boy was keeping dangerous company.

His suspicion was correct. One night Boghos-Berge and Garo were returning home from yet another interminable ball in honour of the emergence of yet another debutante, and where they had been exquisitely bored for several hours, when they were accosted by a drunken bravo in the company of several similarly lubricated friends.

"Money!" he demanded in somewhat slurred accents, "Spent all mine, an' I need a carriage. Got to get home…" and he pawed at Boghos-Berge's arm.

Garo stepped forward and removed the offending hand, but Boghos-Berge took pity on the befuddled party-goer and gave him a coin. "Go on home, then," he advised, "it's late."

The man staggered happily away, but his companions scented prey, and the two found themselves defending against four attackers, three with swords and one with a knife.

They committed the crime of killing one of them, *Giavour* against one of the Faithful, and they wounded all the others in an unpleasant, bloody skirmishing up and down the narrow alleys. The fight was nothing like Boghos-Berge had expected. It was not exciting, he did not enjoy the fear, and he was sorry that he had been forced to take part in the death of any man. Garo looked on the night's work simply as necessary self-defence and he felt no regret that he had killed a man who was threatening the life of his friend. On the contrary, he was rather pleased to prove that his skills were so effective.

Although what they had done was in self-defence, it would mean a death sentence in an Ottoman court if they were identified and two very subdued young men returned to the Eramian town house that night.

This was when they decided that it was time to join the Brotherhood.

Stepan heard of it from a concerned friend whose son had noticed the type of young men with whom they were spending their evenings, and who had fortunately jumped to the correct conclusion. The Agha was so worried that he sent urgently to his cousin in Constantinople, and asked for Boghos-Berge's fiancée Hripsimé to come a year early to Izmir, in the hope that she would distract him from these dangerous pursuits. She came at once, and the two resumed the relationship which had begun years before, when they were children at Tersu together. Soon they were seen at all the fashionable cafes and dining rooms, they attended soirées, parties, balls and picnics, and rode out in the company of a maid and the unobtrusive Garo. They walked in the parks, attended the theatre, and took tea at the literary salons, where they heard poetry and listened to chamber music, and they danced together beautifully, gazing into each other's eyes. At last even the most hopeful of Armenian hostesses had to accept that Boghos-Berge was no longer on a list of possible sons-in-law.

He duly married Hripsimé, and although this marriage had been arranged when they were both babies, she was his friend and his heart's love.

Stepan decided it would be best if the couple were settled before the children began to arrive, and when a business associate mentioned that there was good land for sale in Cyprus, and that furthermore it was in an area populated by Christian Greeks, he was interested enough to make further enquiries. It seemed that the Turks of the island were comfortingly apt to turn a blind eye to a little flouting of the *Giavour* Laws, and so his son would be safer there, where his pride and self-respect would be less likely to get him into trouble.

The sale of Tersu had brought a considerable sum, and Stepan decided to give Boghos-Berge his inheritance early, so that he could buy the land if he wished.

Boghos-Berge did wish it, with all his heart.

A week after their arrival on the island, he had already ridden once over the land which was for sale. He was accompanied by his exalted father the Agha, and by the landowner, and by attendants carrying umbrellas to keep the Agha from the sun, grooms to hold the horses' heads, and servants to take care of refreshments and drinks.

He needed to go over the ground again, without people deciding for him how this or that field should be planted, where irrigation channels should run, or which would be the best place to build his house. His father would find the idea fanciful, but his future life might lie here and he needed to be alone with the place. He avoided unwanted comment by saying merely that he would like another look at it, and he brought only Garo, whose presence would not intrude.

The property was 500 *donums* of mostly prime farmland lying between the river Pedios and a point just past the Nicosia road at Deftera, which was a small village in the centre of Cyprus. Boghos-Berge had been delighted and overwhelmed by his father's offer to buy it and to give it to him as his portion of the Eramian inheritance, which he sincerely hoped would otherwise be long in coming.

He began his ride at the river. At this time of year it was just a sluggish and muddy stream bordered by reeds and grasses, hardly visible in the middle of the river bed. On the opposite side, towards the Girne mountains, there was a high, stone-studded cliff but on this side the banks rose only gradually to the flat lands which would be his.

On his way here he had passed a cave high up in that cliff, with a well-worn path winding from the road across the river bed and the stony ground to a series of rickety wooden ladders leaning this way and that across the crumbling cliff face. The cave held the shrine of Chrysospiliotissa, where hundreds of years ago an ancient icon of the Holy Virgin had been found. Miracles were worked by this darkened and mysterious image, painted reverently on wood by some long-dead hermit, and the small cave was hung all around with wax and silver images of the limbs and organs which had been healed after prayers to Her. The macabre and touching collection of legs, hands, eyes, bellies, heads and hearts varied from miniature to life-size, tinkling, twisting and swinging in the breeze, bearing witness to the gratitude of men and women for whom even the smallest coin represented long hours of backbreaking labour.

Each year on the day of the Assumption of the Blessed Virgin, the villagers of Deftera held their festival there, and this, with the other high feasts of the Church, allowed them a little respite from their lives of unrelenting and constant toil. Boghos-Berge was pleased to see that his neighbours had built a small stone church nearby, with a single bronze bell in a separate square tower. All his life he had heard the wailing call of the *muezzin*, and it would be good to hear the sound of a church bell. He turned his back to the river and headed his big black mule towards Deftera.

Yesterday, he had ridden a horse.

When he saw the fine bay gelding provided for his use, he raised an eyebrow at his father, who smiled and told him that things were a little different here, and that attitudes to the *Giavour* laws were more relaxed. It was far from the Sultan's capital, and the Vali of Cyprus ruled from his luxurious estate on the island of Rhodes. As long as taxes were paid, this indolent and comfortable man saw no reason to make the journey to Nicosia.

At a short distance from the Pedios, he came to a good sized pool, which was fed by a swift-running stream of clear, bright water. Trees and bushes grew at its edge, and there were little golden-eyed green frogs which plopped quickly into the water as he approached. Dragonflies hovered above clumps of lilies, and while he and Garo stood quietly watching, a small flock of dusty brown sparrows came down to drink and wash, ducking their heads and splashing about in the shallows with noisy banter and argument.

The incoming waters rushed into the large rocky pool, which looked to be about waist-deep, and hurried down a short, steep slope into a pebbly channel, to run swiftly along to the river. Boghos-Berge dismounted and tossed a stone into the water. He saw that the land bordering the far side of the pool was solid rock, and thought it would be a good firm base for a mill. Or a farmhouse. If the stream was still flowing at such speed in September, it would probably run all year, turning the mill and providing plenty of clean water for the house and the animals. He led the mule a little way along the upper part of the stream, looking around him with pleasure.

They remounted, and after twenty minutes at a leisurely pace they came to another spring. The water welled up from a depression below some rocks, and here the channel ran in the opposite direction to the first, towards the village of Deftera, and near to the Nicosia road. There were date palms, walnut trees, acacias and vines, and a truly venerable plane tree with immense branches that gave a wide, dappled shade. It was a beautiful old tree and provided a cool respite from the sun, which by now was uncomfortably hot. This would also be a good place for a farmhouse, near to the stream, the road, and a source of labour. He rode on, with Garo following a little further behind now, aware of his friend's absorption in this place.

Now and then Boghos-Berge stopped, dismounted and took a handful of the soil, crushing it between his palms. The land was good: with irrigation he could grow anything. There could be barley, or any kind of corn, he could farm cattle for meat or milk, and there were date palms and fruit trees by the water. This would be a wonderful place for Hripsimé, and for their children.

She had stayed behind in Izmir while he made this journey, and he missed her, his cousin, his friend, and now his wife. They had been married only a year, and she told him that she would be content to go anywhere that he went, but he thought she would be happiest with him on this land where you could see the ground meet the sky, where you could watch the sun rise in the morning, and see it set each evening.

The wind would race past in the spring, making waves in the young green corn, and great banks of cloud would keep pace in the sky, trailing misty veils of rain all the way from the Girne mountains in the north to the peaks of the Troodos in the west. There would surely be spectacular thunderstorms over those summits, which he thought would be covered with snow well into the spring. This, however, was a clear day, and Boghos-Berge could just make out the white squares of houses in a village miles away on the lowest slopes of the nearest range.

Of course, they would also have a town house in Nicosia, but in the summer the city was unpleasant and unhealthy, a dusty, dirty place where disease spread in from the marshes. He was certain that Hripsimé would spend as little time there as possible, and that she would prefer the beauty and distant horizons of this place.

At present she was living at his father's home in the Armenian quarter. The Eramian residence was crowded about with others equally large, and wishing for the peace and fresh air in the open countryside of her own childhood home, she spent as much time as she could in the elegant little garden at the centre of the house, trying to be content with mosaics, a few jasmine bushes, and a fountain with a tiled pond.

Boghos-Berge truly did not think that either of them would miss the city.

Only one thing now cast a shadow on his enthusiasm for a new life in Cyprus, but it was a serious thing, about which he could do nothing.

Adventurous Armenians had been arriving in Cyprus for more than fifteen hundred years, but there were few on the island at this time, and there was no Armenian community in Nicosia. The family he hoped to found would have no one nearby with whom to speak their language. There would be no school, no other Armenian children for his own to play with, no other women for Hripsimé to visit, no older relations to consult for information and advice, and nowhere God could be praised with the glorious music of their Mass. The little mediaeval church in the city had only one elderly and ailing priest, and there was no choir.

Boghos-Berge was a resourceful and positive man, and as he slowly rode around the boundary of the land on his way back to the river his spirits recovered. They would not always be alone here. He would persuade other Armenians that this was a good place to live, a place with opportunities, a place with greater freedom than Ottoman Turkey, and with a majority Christian population of a similar persuasion to their own. He would win them over, or rather, this good land itself would win them over, and in time he was sure that there would be many more here. First, though, he must build his own house and be able to show a thriving farm to prospective neighbours.

By late afternoon he had returned to the pool with the lilies and dragonflies. As he approached, he could hear the stream rushing and chuckling in its channel as it dropped quickly down to the river and he thought it would be a good sound to hear at the beginning and end of each day. He sat beside the pool while the sun dropped lower in the sky, and imagined a house here, small to start with, maybe with only three or four rooms. It should have the graceful pointed arches sitting on short, round columns ringed at the base, like those he had seen in many places on the island. Even if the rest of the house were to be mud-brick, it should have these stone arches, and they would support a covered veranda in front of the main rooms so that he and his family would be protected from the sun or rain as they moved from room to room, and they could sit outside and be sheltered whatever the weather.

He would whitewash his walls to throw back the heat, and he would roof his house with red, fat-bellied tiles. He would plant flowers and fruit trees and fragrant herbs in the garden, and build extra rooms for his children, as they arrived. Here, one day in the future, he and Hripsimé would sit together and watch the sun go down across the clear, cold waters of the pool. Certainly, the other spot nearer to Deftera and the road would be a more practical choice, and he supposed it would be more sensible to build his house there, but this place was, quite simply, beautiful.

Suddenly he saw how his house should be placed. He would build it *across* the stream, so that the water would flow underneath. The rock was solid enough and would support it well at both sides. The constantly running water would keep the rooms above it cool and comfortable, even on the most stifling of summer days, and the mill wheel would turn behind it. There would be nothing quite like it anywhere else. *This* would be where he and Hripsimé would begin their life together.

Satisfied, he remounted and turned the mule's head toward Nicosia, and as he rode, the setting sun threw a long, long shadow on the dusty road before him.

Boghos-Berge built his farmhouse and the mill and he planted fruit trees and flowers in his garden and barley in his fields. He bought animals for the pastures and hired servants for his house, his farm and his stables, and now began the long and rewarding years of bringing life from the fertile land of Deftera. Even today one can find the places where his daughter Hanemie grew up and enjoyed her childhood. The stepping stones, the shrine, the river, and the field where the travelling puppet masters pitched their tents are still there, but the performers no longer come to delight people with their old, old traditions.

Here, then, is the story of Boghos-Berge's daughter, little Hanemie.

1798

A Stone for Hanemie

H̲ANEMIE'S PARENTS loved their little daughter dearly, but they had hoped for many children, and among them a son. She was their first born and their only living child, as the babies that followed every year lived only a few weeks or a few months before dying suddenly in their cribs, causing such heartache and despair that her mother Hripsimé almost dreaded the signs that she was expecting another child which might raise the same hope and cause the same grief.

When, once again, she realised that a new life was growing in her body she rejoiced and feared in equal measure, but her desperate worry for the baby made her ill. For the first time she suffered badly with the changes of her pregnancy, growing thin, tired and pale, and suffering from dizzy spells and nausea, and she endured frequent agonising headaches. Boghos-Berge cursed his selfishness in having found so much delight in his beloved wife and began to fear that he might lose her as well as the child.

Longing for relief from her almost-constant sickness, Hripsimé burned candles and prayed at the little shrine she had made in her garden for the Holy Mother, and again at the dim and scented cave sacred to Her at the nearby Chrysospiliotissa shrine.

There was still no choir at the Armenian church within Nicosia's high walls, and she found herself dreaming of the transcendent beauty of the music of the Armenian High Mass, which she had not heard for years now. She wished sadly that she could hear once more the lovely words and music composed over five hundred years ago and the sound of sweet voices singing the prayers of her own people in her own language.

In Jerusalem, at the birth place of Christ, the Armenians had built a cathedral which was the object of pilgrimage for all their countrymen. Hripsimé had always wanted to see the Holy City and she began to think that prayers offered to the Mother of God at the cathedral might be more effective there than in any less sacred spot, and she yearned to ask in that holiest of places for the safe delivery of a healthy child, and the gift of a son. The sea journey would be calm and easy at this time of year, her pregnancy was not far advanced, and her husband's brother Artin and his family from Constantinople were visiting Deftera with their children on their way to Jerusalem. It was very much safer and more pleasant to travel in a good sized company, and so Boghos-Berge indulged his wife's wishes and agreed to join his brother's pilgrimage.

Hanemie was nine years old, and she could not bear to be left behind while everyone else set off on this great adventure. She decided she would go with them to see the holy places and to be blessed by the Bishop.

"It's only fair, *Hairig*," she said, smiling as appealingly as possible at her father, "because cousin Mariam is only two years older than me, and *she's* going. I'm nearly as grown-up, and it wouldn't really be fair to leave me behind, would it? And besides, you'd miss me, and I'd be very unhappy here on my own...."

Soon she would put her hair up and let her dresses down and she would be expected to behave like a young lady, putting childish things behind her. She already had a riding habit with a proper train and a loop for carrying it, and a most fetching hat of the same deep blue silk with a very modish feather trim. A ladies' saddle had been made for her, with a velvet saddlecloth bearing her monogram, but she had not yet mastered the knack of reliably staying on it, and if she had her choice she would rather ride astride. Of course, that would be scandalous once she put away her short dresses.

Her face was still rather rounded, but her high cheekbones and full lips hinted at beauty to come. Her masses of thick black hair fell in unruly curls to her waist, and her dark brows gave her a look of serious concentration so that adults sometimes found the child's intent gaze a little disturbing. She was never tired, and hardly ever unhappy, and her father thought she was as perfect as anyone could be, this side of Paradise.

Boghos-Berge and Hripsimé still deeply mourned the sudden, inexplicable deaths of each of their beautiful, dark-eyed, vigorous, and apparently healthy children, and Hanemie was therefore doubly precious. Her father found it difficult to refuse her anything and to be truthful, he would rather have her near him than leave her behind, and so she had her wish.

She much enjoyed the novelty of the sea journey. She was not seasick or bothered by the pitching of the ship, and she was a little unsympathetic with her cousins' disinclination to spend more time on deck with her. After all, the waves were hardly bigger than ripples on the pool at home, and the wind was merely bracing. Other than this, the voyage was surprisingly and disappointingly uneventful. No typhoon or sea monster disturbed the smooth passage of the great wooden-hulled ship, no pirates hailed them and no mermaid sang beguiling songs to them from the waves.

She began to suspect that her cousins had rather exaggerated their accounts of previous journeys.

The visits to the mysterious, heavily scented, shadowy and candlelit churches and shrines of the Holy Land were very exciting, and she felt a proper awe when she stood beside the spot where the Mother of God had borne the Saviour of the world.

Hanemie knew why her mother had made this pilgrimage. She knelt beside her at each sacred place to pray for the souls of her little brothers and sisters whose bodies lay in the peaceful plot of land just outside the City walls at home. The old priest had buried them, chanting the solemn words of the funeral service in a faltering monotone, but her father had promised that one day the row of tiny graves would be blessed for a second time using the lovely, heart-rending prayers for the dead, sung properly in their own language.

Beside the holy shrine in Jerusalem was an ornate and splendid Armenian church, domed and columned in polished marble, and here Hanemie first heard the soaring beauty of the High Mass. The priest slowly and reverently raised the Cup before the massive golden cross which stood on the jewelled altar with its great wax candles and heavy-scented flowers, and his assistants in their princely robes shook the great, glittering discs of the systrums in a sweet, shivering emphasis. A single, sublime soprano voice suddenly soared in joy and exaltation at this greatest and most sacred moment of the service, and Hanemie felt the small, soft hairs on her arms and at the nape of her neck stand on end. She had not known how lovely music could be, and she thought that her soul was rising from her body, borne aloft on the beauty of the anthem.

Beside her, Hripsimé bowed her head humbly.

She could not believe that the Saviour who gave His life for her would condemn any of her babies to eternal fire because, through no fault of their own, they had not been baptised in the rites of her Church. She had come to this most sacred place to be blessed and to be made new, to ask for mercy for her sons and daughters, and to pray to the Holy Mother in Her own land at the place where She had given birth to

Her beloved Son. She pleaded for a miracle, for a healthy baby boy who would live and thrive to cherish the land as lovingly as his father had done, so that their names would be remembered and their line continue in him.

She was given no great sign, no shaft of light, no sudden inner knowledge or revelation, but still she felt comforted, and she was content.

Hanemie's Greek nurse from the village had missed her dreadfully. Like most villagers, she was suspicious of strangers and strange things, fearing the sea, the boat, the foreigners and the heathen customs and outlandish food of these distant lands. She was overjoyed to see her young mistress once more, and she teasingly began to call her Haji'Anna because she had been on a *haj*, a pilgrimage, like their Muslim neighbours. The name was taken up by the villagers and workers around the farm, and she answered to Haji'Anna in the village and Hanemie at home.

At the end of the year, Hripsimé's prayers were answered and her longed-for baby boy was born. His delivery cost his mother many hours of unremitting pain, but she bore it willingly to give him life. This child had not arrived early, and he was delivered healthy and perfect, and they named him Artin Boghos after his uncle and father.

He was a long, thin, dark baby, quiet and solemn, and he seldom cried. His wide eyes observed the world with the same oddly grown-up air as his sister, and Hanemie loved her new brother at once, and dearly. She spent many hours beside his carved cedarwood crib, talking to him and singing softly while she dressed her dolls and showed them to him, telling him the stories she had made up about them. Each of them had their own name, and their special likes and dislikes, and every day they had different adventures, which she related to him with a dramatic flair, taking the parts of heroes and villains, ladies and knights, princes, bandits and intrepid adventurers whose valour always won the day.

Many of her stories were freely borrowed from the tales of the Karagiosi. She loved these travelling puppet theatres, which arrived each year for the festival held for the Blessed Virgin at her shrine in the cliff by the river. On August the fifteenth, her feast day, the miraculous Icon was removed from the cave, passed carefully from hand to hand down the ladders in the cliff and taken across the ford in the shallow, pebbly riverbed. It was slowly and reverently brought with candles and chanting from the river to the church, round which it was ceremoniously carried twice before returning to its cliffside home for another year.

The music and dancing at the fair which followed were wonderful too, and the performances of songs composed on the spot, when the villagers vied with each other in composing scurrilous and hilarious verses about their neighbours and friends, but she waited excitedly for the Karagiosi. She was only briefly distracted by the lure of *loukoumades,* the little balls of crisp-fried dough arranged in hot, tempting heaps, glistening with rose-flavoured sugar syrup, and liberally sprinkled with cinnamon. Even the plates of *shammali* and *mahalepi,* sweet and inviting though they were, failed to delay her for long.

She was always early to take her place on the front row of chairs, always one of the first, and she awaited the beginning of the show with impatience. At last the sun went down and it was dark enough for the performance, the lamps were lit behind the screen and those in the audience were extinguished. The delicate and cleverly-cut puppet silhouettes of the king, the maiden, the villain, the warrior and the dragon danced and flickered behind the gauze screen. The crowd ooohed and aaahed, the lamps hissed and spat excitingly, the puppet masters recited their characters' lines in loud and florid tones, and Hanemie loved every minute. She knew the proper intonation and singsong delivery for all the traditional themes, whispering them along with the stories, frowning at any deviation. It was always wonderful and it was always over too soon.

She could chatter happily in Greek with the villagers and farm workers, speaking it as fluently as the Armenian which the family used at home, but her cosmopolitan cousins from the mainland said she had a barbarous rural accent and teased her mercilessly, so that her father heard them and sent to Constantinople for an Athenian tutor to teach her to speak like a cultured lady. She obediently learned this softer manner of speech, more musical, and almost sensual compared to the villagers' patois, which had diverged considerably from its origins during their long separation from the Motherland. It was used for calling the goats and cursing the birds which stole the seed corn, shouting at children and berating errant husbands, rather than reciting Homer, though indeed there were those in the village who could give the speech of Achilles at Troy or quote Xenophon on the care of horses.

A polite conversation between neighbours was quite likely to sound as if it were an exchange of the sort of insults which should lead to bloodshed, but Hanemie found the villagers' accents familiar and dear to her, and out of earshot of her parents, she spoke comfortably in their own way to her friends in Deftera.

Unlike his tragic predecessors the new baby survived his first year, and after his second birthday, when he had reached the stage of energetically investigating everything around him, Hripsimé and Boghos-Berge began to allow themselves to believe that this most beloved and exceptional child might live.

His first words were greeted with astonishment at his precocity, though Hanemie had been quite as forward in her early development, and his first steps had been the excuse for a celebration and party. His uncertain progress around the house was punctuated with the occasional crash of crockery and furniture, but no one begrudged him the damage, and he was picked up and consoled with kisses and loving words. The villagers called him '*O Bebis*', as if he were the only child in Deftera, and he quite rightly believed that the universe revolved around him.

The house by the pool now had extra rooms for the children and their nurses, a dairy and buttery, and several sturdy new outbuildings. There were yards and walkways, all laid with polished brown pebbles and stones from the river bed so that they would not be muddy in the rain, and the garden was shady with young trees and fragrant with flowers.

There was also a pack of dogs of many sizes and ancestries. Their leader was Ajax, a great yellow-eyed descendant of the famous Molossian breed, whose ancestor's stone effigy could be seen standing guard over his master's tomb in Athens, gazing from the Kerameikos to the misty heights of the Parthenon. Their job was to guard the farm and the family.

An unfamiliar presence in the yards or stables which were the dogs' domain would provoke a riot of snarling, growling, and barking, ferocious enough to terrify the bravest of thieves, but they would not harm Hanemie or Artin Boghos. The baby's experimental tugging of an ear or tail was stoically endured, with only an occasional yelp in protest, and this led the children to assume that any dog was a friend.

As Artin Boghos began to walk more confidently, they would go exploring together. There were sticks and stones to be tossed into the river, trees to be climbed and fields and woods for playing hide and seek. There were leggy foals, wide eyed calves and noisy kids. There were wobbly lambs, ducklings on the pool, dozens of fluffy chicks in the yard, and the children were allowed to help to feed any orphans and to collect eggs, or carry a small pail of milk between them to the buttery. There were always interesting activities going on around the farm and plenty of people to watch as they went about their work, all of whom welcomed them and explained what they were doing when asked, and who let them take part when it was an activity which was safe for them to try. There were butterflies and beetles, insects, birds and flowers, and a thousand new things to see each day.

Hanemie showed her little brother the secret den which she had discovered in the grove of trees by the river, where she could curl up in the shade and dream her dreams of heroes and Kings, of chivalry and high adventure. They would hide there when they were punished, which was rarely, or when they wished to escape adult supervision, which was often.

1798 A Stone for Hanemie

At the crossroads of the village was a kafenion, where the men sat and drank coffee and fiery, throat-stripping *zivania* while their wives made dinner in the evening, or when they had a little leisure. This was solely a male domain, and here women were not welcome. It was strictly, absolutely, unchangeably a refuge for men.

Except for the only concession ever made, and that was for Hanemie.

She had been visiting the kafenion since she was a toddler and her plump little legs were too small to take her any further without a rest. She hoisted herself onto one of the rush-seated chairs, breathed a comical sigh of relief, and politely asked for a drink of water in locally accented Greek.

Charmed by her innocent breach of etiquette, and deciding that she did not yet qualify as a woman, they had allowed her to join them whenever she wished, at the outside tables only, of course. This meant that she was banned from the kafenion for the short Cypriot winter when the men met by the warmth of the fire indoors, and it was another reason to look forward to the spring.

They were chivalrous, those rough-spoken, rough-handed, poor, proud, generous, weather-beaten villagers, and she learned no curses or foul language from their lips, nor anything which could not be repeated to her mother She did learn a respect and affection for them which she communicated to her little brother and it stayed with him all his life.

On her thirteenth birthday, Boghos-Berge gave Hanemie a fine chestnut mare, to go with her grown-up saddle and riding dress. He had not been able to find a pony, but his brother had sent him the lovely little mare all the way from Constantinople.

The mare's name was Anahita, and Garo said she was the most stupid horse it had ever been his misfortune to train. Here at Deftera, Garo could choose his duties and he loved best to work with the horses and riding mules which were stabled at the farm. He was the trusted and cherished servant and friend of Boghos-Berge and now he readily included the engaging Hanemie and solemn little Artin Boghos in his devotion. He was happy and very content with his life in this peaceful place. He taught his young mistress how to ride with confidence on her awkward adult saddle, and he accompanied her on her morning rides, staying correctly a little way behind her and providing the company of the attendant which her father felt was proper now that she was growing up.

She had ridden every horse on the farm since she was tall enough to put her feet into stirrups, except, of course, for her father's big, dangerous stallion. Even with all this experience, it was difficult to ride with grace while managing her skirts, her riding crop, her elegant but ridiculous new posture, and, most importantly, her mount. Nevertheless, Hanemie loved pretty, flighty Anahita, and rode out early every day. She jumped branches and ditches and shadows, and galloped on the grassy side of the river, racing the current down to Nicosia. She thought herself quite dashing and daring and also rather an expert horsewoman.

Garo kept pace behind her on the big, stubborn, evil-tempered mule which only he could ride, and which, unknown to Hanemie, could outrun Anahita with ease if necessary and from there he kept an indulgent eye on both his precious charges.

Hanemie had taken Artin Boghos up before her one day when he put his arms up to her in the yard, but her father lifted him down with a smile and said that he could have his own horse when he was old enough. Till then, he could be put up on Hanemie's dear old Boule if he wished, because the fat old gelding was steady and reliable and it would be impossible to persuade him to proceed any faster than a staid walk. Anahita, on the other hand, was not only rather a silly horse but also somewhat unpredictable. She would take it into her head to be frightened of a butterfly, or shy at the breeze in the grass, and Boghos-Berge did not wish to risk his little son on her back. He had made sure that Hanemie could control the fancies of the pretty but stupid mare, and he was quite content to let his daughter ride out with her groom or with Garo in attendance, but the safety of his son and heir was a different matter.

When Artin Boghos was big enough to manage Boule without a leading rein, he was allowed to join Hanemie's morning outings. He rode proudly next to her, his little legs sticking out almost horizontally each side of Boule's plump barrel, but with his back very straight and his head held high, indicating a deep satisfaction in his achievement.

Garo rode his big mule a little way behind, and kept a careful eye on both of them. He was fiercely protective of both his young charges, and it was not his fault that the accident happened.

The three riders had dismounted at the turning point of their excursion to let their mounts have a very short drink. Allowing the horses to drink at mid-ride was not a good thing, but in the summer months the heat of the sun was hard on them even at this early hour, and when Garo thought it necessary, they were allowed a brief stop.

A little further along the riverbed, four or five scruffy dogs also ran down to drink. They had two half-grown puppies with them, and Artin Boghos called to them, laughing and waving his hands, till they turned their heads and ran towards him, their pink tongues lolling and their feathery tails waving jauntily over their backs. Garo, who had been holding his mule firmly while it drank with the horses, had not seen them, and it was not until the pups were overtaken by the full-grown dogs and were nearly on to the boy that he realised what was happening.

He let go of his mount and reached for the child, throwing him up into Boule's saddle where the dogs could not reach him. He lashed at them with his riding crop, giving Hanemie time to steady Anahita and to get her foot into the single stirrup and her hands on to the saddle. He kicked at the big lead dog, but it caught his boot and held on, while another closed its jaws on his handless wrist. Biting back a scream and slipping on the treacherous, river-worn stones, he looked frantically for his mule, but that sensible beast was already far away, galloping for its life.

Garo knew that he must not fall, for once he was down he would be lost. He reached for a driftwood branch and clubbed the lead dog with it. The big animal backed off, yelping, and the pack circled round him, heads down, the ruffs of fur on their backs standing up while they snarled menacingly. Garo held the branch ready to strike, and kept an eye on the leader.

Meanwhile, Hanemie at last got control of Anahita, who had panicked and tried to follow the mule, and she kicked her nervous mount towards the melee, putting the reluctant horse between Garo and the pack. For once in her life the flighty mare did the right thing. She rolled her eyes, bared her teeth, reared, and lashed out enthusiastically at the snarling and snapping dogs with her iron-shod hooves. Hanemie had lost her stirrup as Anahita danced and slipped on the pebbles, and was barely managing to keep her seat when her little brother brought Boule into the fray. He was only able to make the old pony circle around at first, but after one of the dogs nipped a fetlock, the indignant animal kicked out as willingly as Anahita.

To his immense relief, this allowed Garo to haul himself up one-handed behind Artin Boghos and the two horses at once broke into a gallop. Anahita soon pulled away from the slower Boule with his double load and rounded a bend in the river ahead of them, so that neither was able to tell what had happened next.

Hanemie lay on her back in the river, arched across one of the stepping stones. She had lost her hat in her mad dash and her dark curls had come loose from their pins, so that her long black hair streamed around her in the water, mingling with crimson swirls of blood. When they reached her, Garo saw that her eyes were open, but unseeing, and he flung himself from Boule's back with a dreadful fear. He gave the pony a hard slap on the rump and shouted to Artin Boghos to ride straight to the farm and bring help. They were near enough to the house for the child to reach it safely, and he did not want the boy to see his sister's face.

Help was swift in coming. Hanemie was carried home to Deftera with the greatest of care, but she remained deeply unconscious and there was a little blood in her ears and nose. Garo saw this with further dread, but he held his peace and did not give Boghos-Berge or Hripsimé a greater grief by telling them what such bleeding could mean. While Hanemie still breathed, there was always hope.

Around midday a Turkish doctor arrived by carriage from Nicosia, and did not leave. The hours wore on, with the household quiet and fearful, the servants speaking in hushed voices, and everyone neglecting their duties to stay near her room.

Garo waited anxiously in the courtyard, sitting cross-legged on the stones and looking up at her window. He stayed there, bare-headed in the blazing sun all day, and would not move. He would eat or drink nothing, and he was still there when the sun went down and the lamps were lit.

At last he heard Hripsimé's wild scream of unbearable pain and loss.

He knew at once that Hanemie had died, and he ran from the place where he had found friendship and great contentment, and where, in his own agony of remorse, he thought he had failed in his duty. He went to the stables, saddled Anahita, and rode her away at a reckless gallop.

After a while, Boghos-Berge tore himself from his own grief to do his necessary duties, and eventually he enquired after Garo. He listened to the tale of desertion and theft without comment. It would have been difficult at that moment for him to hear the account of the accident from the trusted friend in whose care he had placed his daughter, but of course he understood that it must have been impossible to prevent. Garo would never allow harm to come to her if he could have stopped it. He did not care about the foolish horse which had probably been the cause of his daughter's death, but Garo was as dear as a brother to him, and he worried that he may come to harm in the grip of such remorse, so he sent men at once to search for the runaways. Though they asked at every village nearby and continued the search further abroad for many days, they could find no trace of him.

In a remote area of Troodos some months later, a ragged, scarred, one-handed, wild-looking man arrived and took up residence in an unused cave which was a little higher up the mountain than the nearest village two or three miles away. It seemed that he could not speak, though he nodded courteously to any who greeted him. He wore torn clothes and half-cured furs and lived off the land, and he went barefoot, even in the snows of winter.

The villagers were at first deeply suspicious of him, as they customarily were of any stranger, but he appeared to be harmless and even pitiable and poorer than themselves, and after a while they became accustomed to his presence.

During the autumn of the second year after his arrival, a shepherd came down from the mountain to spend the winter at his family's home in the village, bringing his flock of sheep and goats down from the summer *mandra*. He told the men at the kafenion that he had made the acquaintance of the mysterious hermit. It seemed that the scarred, speechless stranger was skilled in the treatment of animals, and the yearling lambs the shepherd brought back were fat and healthy and carried fewer ailments than usual. The shepherd said that the hermit made up a drench for them which repelled the disease-carrying ticks and lice, and that his two fierce sheepdogs lay down at the ragged man's feet and behaved like silly puppies in his presence. This last fact had impressed him deeply, as his dogs were trained to be ferocious with anyone but their master, and they had never behaved in this way with any one else.

The healthy lambs were very good news, but what caught the men's attention most was what the shepherd saw when he went past the hermit's cave with his flock very early one morning. He thought he heard weeping and so he crept quietly through the surrounding bushes until he could watch the man unobserved. The hermit was kneeling on the ground, naked to the waist. He was very thin, and his back, chest and arms were covered with old, silvery, knotted scars overlaid with the crimson marks of fresher stripes. While the shepherd watched with astonishment the one-handed man began to weep bitterly, and he flogged himself with knotted strips of leather tipped with iron till his back was torn open and blood ran down to the ground.

They discussed every aspect of this with great interest and awe, and it seemed to them very likely that since he could make the sound of weeping but did not talk, he may be a monk or holy man under a vow of silence. They were very proud to tell the people of neighbouring villages that they had the immense distinction of a saint-in-making living nearby and they regarded him with great respect, and began to think of him as one of their own. They believed that he brought them good fortune, and they addressed him respectfully and with reverence whenever they chanced to see him.

They were desperately poor and their lives were very hard, but they began to leave small gifts of food and firewood, oil, a little grain, olives, bread, or some precious salt outside his cave for him to find, hoping that these charitable acts would gain merit for them in Heaven. He knew how much these little gifts truly cost them and in return he tended their sick or injured animals, and he won their further esteem and gratitude for his skilled care and treatment of their mules and donkeys in particular. They became used to his terrible scars and his gentle ways, and eventually he set their bones, treated their wounds, pulled their teeth and dosed their worms, and he ministered to them as carefully as he looked after their animals. He pitied them their short and harsh existence and he did whatever he could to lighten their burden.

His saintly reputation spread, and when he died of cold and self-neglect a few years later, his bones were reverently buried in the cave, which became a shrine.

In due time, miracles occurred.

Hanemie was buried beside her brothers and sisters in the quiet and shady plot beyond the city walls, and a great stone pillar was laid flat above her grave to protect her for eternity.

HERE BEGIN THE STORIES OF THE LIFETIME OF ARTIN BOGHOS ERAMIAN AGHA

While Artin Boghos grew to manhood in the safety of Deftera, there were desperate uprisings by some of the subject peoples of Cyprus. These were followed by terrible and bloody reprisals against the Greek population in other parts of the island, and the oppression and harsh treatment of the Giavour continued across the water in Ottoman Turkey.

As before, Greeks, Latins, Armenians and Jews were exploited and unfairly treated under the law, and some were sold into slavery for their own debts or transgressions, or those of their family.

One of our cousins was made a slave near Adana. He lived alone in the mountains since infancy, working as a goatherd for his owners, and he spoke not one word of his own language. The poor boy was illiterate and half-starved when he was rescued and brought home, and most of his wits had been knocked out of him along with his teeth. He did not live long to enjoy his freedom, that simple soul.

The heroine of this story touched the family of Artin Boghos with gentle hands.

1825

The Wise Woman

Two turkish merchants found Sofia in the *baraka* which had been built on to the back of the inn stables. This was where she had lived since the innkeeper bought her from the Vali, and she had forgotten when that was, or what life had been like before the misery began. Sometimes when she was in pain, or very hungry, or shivering from the cold, she cried when they locked her in the damp and dirty shed after she had finished her work or provided a diversion for a customer, but mostly she endured her dreadful life with a dull patience.

The traders were from Constantinople and they were watching their mule drivers bring the pack animals into the stable yard where they would supervise the offloading and storage of their goods for the night. They dismounted and tied their horses to the iron rings set into the rear wall of the inn, looking forward to relaxing over a good hot dinner and a cool drink after the long day's ride and glad that they had arrived before nightfall. When they heard the faint sounds coming from the *baraka* they thought that a child might be trapped inside and they hurried to lift the heavy bar on the shed door, finding Sofia huddled in the furthest corner, cowering from the light and making herself as small as possible.

They were kindly men, and of course they could not help every slave, but they found it impossible to leave her there once they had seen her.

Nor could they hide their disgust and contempt for her owner when they bought the little girl from him, and so he charged them extra for their unfriendly words and insulting manner. Even so, her price was a paltry sum for the child was thin, unattractive and uncooperative even after a good beating, and the innkeeper was quite happy to part with her.

They paid what he asked without further comment, and because they encountered no Greek community on their way to their ship, they took the terrified, damaged child with them to their next port of call, which was Larnaca in the island of Cyprus. Here, with some relief, they handed her over to her own people and made a generous gift to the local monastery for her keep.

It was the duty of the Church to take care of waifs and strays, and the Bishop sent her to the mountains, where there was a small establishment run by three elderly monks who had some experience with traumatised refugees. These good old men were sorry to find that she spoke only a vulgar Turkish dialect and remembered very little of her native tongue, but she would soon learn. They were horrified and filled with pity when they realised that she thought her name was *'eshek'* which was what the people of the inn had called her, and at once they chose a proper Christian name for her and gave her a surname to go with it. She became Sofia Adamidou. With this name came a new self-respect and a sense of identity.

She did not know when or where she had been born, but they guessed that she was around nine or ten years old and they assigned her a new birth date, that of her saint's name day, so that she could have a special time to celebrate like everyone else. Obviously she could not live with the three old men, and they entrusted her to the care of a matronly woman who was doing gift-work for the monastery in fulfilment of a vow. Dame Helena took Sofia into her lodging at the monastery's pilgrim-house outside the wall, and her sensible and kindly care brought the brutalised little girl back from the edge of insanity.

Slowly, the thin, starved child with her ragged hair and broken nose began to mend. She put on a little weight, though she would always be thin, and gradually the dullness and misery left her eyes. Her nose would remain slightly crooked, for it was far too late to treat the old break and so her small, pale face was interesting and unusual, but not unattractive. Her roughly sheared hair grew out thick, very dark, and lustrous.

She had a quick and retentive mind and now she thirsted for knowledge, having been denied for so many years. Brother Lazaros, seeing that she needed something to turn her mind away from the past, patiently began to teach her all he knew of his own speciality. This was the preparation of herbs and the brewing of simple remedies for the healing of the sick, and noting that she had an aptitude for herb-lore, he thought that she might later do well in this work.

When she had been with them for two years and no longer flinched from strangers, the good brothers arranged for her to go to Kyria Maria of Deir Menlik, whose house was on the other side of the mountains at a 'mixed' village, populated by both Greeks and Turks. Sofia was still unhappy with strange places and people, but her new mistress lived a little way out from the other houses, and her only immediate neighbour was a deaf and elderly Greek priest of uncertain temper and reclusive habit.

Brother Lazaros knew perfectly well that the Kyria was not exactly orthodox in her ideas and that she was somewhat disapproved of by the Bishop, but he thought that she was the person best qualified to help Sofia at this stage and so it was agreed that the child would do half the housework, help with the gardening and share the cooking, and that she would learn Kyria Maria's skills and arts in return.

Sofia's new mistress was a big, comfortable woman in late middle age. She had several chins, iron-grey hair scraped back into a tight knot, and a competent air. Her small brown eyes were kind and she had smile-lines etched deeply into her sunburned skin. She could not abide dirt, stupidity or laziness, and though she was endlessly patient with frightened children or those in pain, she gave short shrift to superstition, cruelty, wilful ignorance, and husbands who beat their wives.

She made the new arrival welcome, showing her to a clean and simple room. Sofia thought it was luxurious. It was furnished with a wicker-seated chair, a chest of drawers with a mirror, and a wood-framed bed covered with a brightly coloured blanket. There were two matching rag rugs on the scrubbed stone floor, one on each side of the bed, and the door had a bolt. It was the first time she had been given a room of her own, with the option of privacy, and she hardly believed that it was hers. Timidly, she sat on the bed and stroked the blanket, which was soft and clean, and smelt of lavender flowers. Through the window she could see far across the plains of Mesaoria and watch the clouds making patterns on the great expanse of fertile fields, dotted here and there with trees and a few small villages.

With a brisk kindness, the Kyria gave her half-an-hour to get used to the idea of having her own room, and then set her to boiling willow bark.

She was a wise-woman, in both senses of the word. Much of her success was due to her scrupulous cleanliness, both in her own person and in the care of the instruments and dressings she used, and to her insistence that her patients also washed regularly and kept their linen clean, at least for the duration of her treatment. Even after a difficult delivery, her new mothers had the lowest incidence of childbed fever in all of the villages around, and her potions and liniments at least did no harm, and in most cases had some beneficial effect. She was practical, sensible and kind, and she inspired confidence and commanded respect, all of which helped her reputation and her positive results.

In a field by the house she had a cantankerous and noisy white goat with slotted yellow eyes. There were also three graceful silver-tabby cats and a pair of large and menacing black dogs with lean muscular flanks, and great ruffs of stiff fur behind their flat, handsome heads. These she kept partly because she liked them, and partly because they provided company, deterred intruders when she left the house, and made her feel safe at night. She gravely introduced them to Sofia and after they had sniffed the girl's hands and allowed her to pet them, they accepted her as one of the family. She felt honoured.

The Kyria lived in a sturdy thick walled mud-brick house beside the river, which rushed down from the mountain all year round. It reminded Sofia in some strange way of her childhood home, and this was odd because although she must have had one, she could not remember it at all, and the place gave her a feeling of safety which she had not experienced for many years. It had a garden with a well-made stone wall to keep the goat out, several neat beds of vegetables and herbs, and an old vine with a massive trunk, the many twisting boughs trained over a frame to give shade and coolness to the flagged yard at the back. Here, she could sit and rest after work and chores were done, with dogs at her feet and a cat in her arms, and she could doze in the warmth of the evenings or watch the stars move across the sky at the edge of the mountains.

When she asked what she was to learn, she was told that at first she should simply sit quietly in the room with her mistress while she attended to the women who called on her for help, and that she must listen carefully to their recital of their ailments and symptoms. She may be asked to assist with some simple procedures. She was to notice the manner of each patient as they spoke, and she should note the colour of their skin, eyes and nails, whether they breathed easily or with difficulty, and how they moved and walked. Were their legs or ankles or any part of their body swollen, did they move stiffly and did they seem nervous or calm? Did they speak hoarsely, did they sweat or shiver, and did their skin or their breath have an odour. If so, was it sweetish, foul, sour, or acrid? Sofia was fascinated and not at all repelled by the things she witnessed or was asked to do.

Later in the day, she would repeat what she had observed, and would be taught in turn what the various signs indicated about the health of the visitor. In this way, she forgot her discomfort with strangers while concentrating on her duty of observation and memorising their symptoms, and this was the second purpose of her teacher's instruction.

There were expeditions to the mountains, fields and forests to collect, weigh, measure and prepare medicinal plants and herbs. Sofia much enjoyed these outings, and for her they were like the best of holidays with the added special treat of enjoying a picnic meal, eaten while sitting on the grass or rocks and listening to the Kyria's explanation of the many uses of the plants they gathered. Sometimes she would tell Sofia stories of her long years in the village, and the characters and extraordinary events which she most remembered, and what lessons she had learned from them. Sofia believed that the Kyria must be one of the most wonderful people who ever lived.

The skills and knowledge she had already learned from the lessons with Brother Lazaros brought her a rare compliment and with it the new responsibility of making medicines for coughs, colds and minor ailments. She took this new duty very seriously and felt very pleased to have won her teacher's trust. When she had shown that she was able to follow instructions exactly and to measure dangerous items with meticulous care, she was allowed to learn and prepare remedies for dropsy, apoplexy, severe pain and other more serious disorders. The potions could be more deadly than the ailments if not prepared with great attention and exactitude and Sofia knew that this was a further indication of the Kyria's growing confidence in her.

At the monastery she had learned to speak a good plain Greek, free of Turkish words and villagers' patios, but now she was taught to write so that she could keep notes on her lessons. She was well aware that this was a great gift, and she was deeply grateful for it. This was an absorbing and exhilarating time, and work or learning filled every daylight hour.

A week after her arrival, the Kyria had given Sofia a tiny grey-patched kitten of her own, the only survivor of a litter she had found by its mother's body out in the fields. The little scrap of life was fading, but Sofia nursed it with absolute devotion, and in looking after something so helpless and so dependent on her, she learned once again to care. This was the third of the Kyria's purposes. The kitten clung to life, thrived, and grew astonishingly fast, so that by the end of the year he was a big, bright-eyed rough-coated tom and there was an end to the plague of mice which had raided the store-cupboard and which had been studiously ignored by the Kyria's elegant tabbies. Sofia loved him and did not mind that she occasionally had to replace the plants he dug up in the garden, or rescue a bird from his clutches, and she named him Zaki.

After four years of this peaceful and productive life, Kyria Maria judged that Sofia's own illness, which she considered no less important for being an insult to the soul rather than to the body, had improved sufficiently for the girl to make her own way in life when a suitable position could be found for her.

It chanced that the following month, Artin Boghos Agha of Deftera came to the monastery on business, and he mentioned to Brother Lazaros that he needed a nurse to help his ailing wife with his children. The lady Caterina had not recovered well after the birth of her third child, and he was looking for someone who liked children, knew how to care for them, and was also young enough to keep up with their astonishing energy and curiosity. The old monk told the Agha that he knew just the girl he needed, that she spoke her native tongue sweetly, and was clean and industrious as well as a trained herbalist, and furthermore she was experienced in the care of the sick and the very young and very old. He explained to his exalted visitor what had happened to her, and why she was still a little reserved.

The Agha was silent while the old monk related her history. Visibly moved, he took the old man's hand and said that he would be happy to accept her into his household if she would come, and that it seemed to him that she was little more than a child herself.

"She has never had a chance to be a child," the Brother said with sadness, "and that is why I think it would be an excellent thing for her to have the company of yours."

Kyria Maria had become very fond of Sofia and was grieved to lose her, but it was time for her to go among strangers to complete her recovery and to take her knowledge out into the world, where she could do the most good. As long as she lived, there would always be a refuge and home for Sofia at Deir Menlik with the Kyria and her cats and dogs, a place to which she knew she could escape if need be, and she would have this assurance of eventual return in order to give her the courage to leave it.

Sofia was now a young woman. At fifteen years old, she had seen the best and worst of the people who had come to the Kyria with pain, grief, fear, suffering, and often with the knowledge of impending death, and she had learned a great deal about human nature as well as the treatment of the sick. She had acquired her teacher's intolerance of dirt, slovenliness, brutality and laziness, and she was well on her way to being as independent, observant and resourceful as that most extraordinary woman.

She set out for Deftera with the Kyria's second-best set of instruments and a leather-covered box of herbs, potions and tinctures, strapped onto a sway-backed but steady old mule belonging to the monastery. The ugly beast, who was considerably stronger than he looked, also carried a bundle containing her two winter dresses, a petticoat, a spare pair of shoes and some second-hand stockings and small-clothes which had been sent to her each year from the kindly monks. In front of her she balanced a wicker basket containing an affronted and complaining Zaki.

These precious things were all she possessed in the world, and she thought them wealth indeed.

The farm at Deftera delighted her. It seemed like paradise, with its stream and pool and the whitewashed buildings around it. Flowers blossomed everywhere, spilling exuberantly from pottery pitchers and urns, climbing walls and pillars, and crowding each other for space in the boxes placed by the walls in the stable yard. There were lilies in the pool, and there was the splash of fish and frogs, and the lovely sound of water, still rushing along in its channel under the main house. An old and sprawling jasmine bush covered with thousands of fragrant white flowers crept along below the windows, and its intoxicating scent strengthened at dusk and came softly into the rooms on the evening's cooling breeze.

There were fruit trees and date palms in the garden outside the window of her room, and one was a very strange tree which bore oranges, lemons and citrons at once. She puzzled over this for some time, concluded that someone must have found a way of putting the branches from three trees on to one trunk, and made a mental note to ask the gardener how it was done. It was a lovely and peaceful place despite the comings and goings necessary for a working farmhouse, and it showed the care lavished on it by owners who loved and cherished it.

Her new mistress, the Lady Caterina, was at present confined to bed. Her children had been born here at Deftera, away from the dirt, heat and dangerous vapours of the city, and she remained here when she failed to recover properly after the birth of the youngest. She had borne her three children in a very short time, and the eldest, Yeremia, was only three. His sister Hripsimé was two, and the baby Virab was now just three months old.

Sofia suspected that the poor lady was suffering from an infection resulting from her last confinement, but she did not know whether her advice would be welcome. The Lady certainly should not have any more children for a year or two after she recovered. She was small and fine-boned, and her last baby was large. She could lose the ability to carry any more children to term if she went on in this way.

To her practised eye, Yeremia seemed a little small for his age, but he was a most lovable child with a merry little face and an intelligent and curious mind. Hripsimé was quiet and sweet-natured, with her father's large, dark eyes, but the baby was quite simply an impossible tyrant. He cried incessantly, and with a determination, volume and endurance surprising in one so young. Sofia examined him carefully, gave him Kyria Maria's infallible potion for colic, then she picked him up and carried him with her as she went about the house, talking to him and keeping him near her whatever she was doing. With his painful tummy soothed, and his small, lonely self comforted and loved, Virab was silent and contented for the first time in the memory of the long-suffering household. She cuddled the other two children frequently, told them stories, played the childhood games with them which she herself had never had a chance to enjoy, and her heart began to complete its healing.

Lady Caterina showed no improvement as the weeks passed, and the Agha grew more worried and distracted as his wife became thinner and weaker. Eventually, Sofia began to fear for the Lady's life and she felt she could wait no longer. She gathered her courage and timidly knocked on the door of the Agha's office.

Artin Boghos had the reputation of being a rather haughty and intimidating man, but he smiled kindly at his children's nurse, and invited her to sit down. He listened carefully as she explained that she had seen conditions such as the Lady Caterina's when she was studying in the Kyria's house, and that it was curable in many cases with certain medicines, a special diet, and cleansing packs. She begged his pardon for her presumption, and asked if she might speak to her mistress and perhaps examine her.

The Agha had not forgotten that Sofia had studied for four years with the renowned healer of Deir Menlik, but she was only a young girl and he had not thought that her training had been as extensive as it now appeared. His wife's condition seemed to be worsening, however, and Caterina's own father, who was a most eminent doctor, had done all he could. Artin Boghos had an increasing and awful fear that he might lose his vivacious little wife, and he would do anything to prevent it. While it did not seem likely that a hedge-doctor could do anything which a trained European expert could not, there was nothing to lose if the treatment was not dangerous or painful, and the girl insisted that this was the case. He concluded that it would do no harm to let her speak to his wife, and he agreed to her request.

It was as she had suspected. Sofia gently examined the Lady Caterina, and explained her illness to her and what they would need to do to heal the infection and stop the discharge. The Lady was weak and in some pain, but she found the girl's brisk competence reassuring and she recognised the Kyria's mannerisms and common sense in her protégé. She was inclined to take Sofia's advice.

The ingredients were readily available, and Sofia could easily prepare them. The treatment should be applied three times a day and should commence as soon as possible. She hoped she had not left her intervention till it was too late, but there was still a professional etiquette to be taken into account. The treatments would not conflict with the measures prescribed by Caterina's father, but everyone agreed that it would be necessary to ask his permission before commencing them. It was fortunate that Doctor Carletti was an open-minded man and that he, too had heard of Sofia's teacher.

He came the next day to see her and he questioned her at some length about the changes to his daughter's diet, and the herbs and douches she intended to use. Sofia sat in a large, upholstered armchair which made her seem very young and very small, but she was outwardly composed, and gave no sign of her inner nervousness. She was suddenly aware that she was just a rather young girl, who had once been a slave, and she glanced across to where the Agha was sitting behind his great oak desk. He nodded and smiled reassuringly, and she took heart from this encouragement and made her case with confidence.

Sofia answered the doctor's questions calmly and clearly, and when she had finished, she waited while Doctor Carletti considered her propositions carefully. He could find no harm in her remedies and he had also observed that an optimistic attitude on the part of his patient sometimes tipped the balance between a worsening prognosis and a cure, and it seemed to him that these new measures could certainly be beneficial if Caterina wished to try them. He gave his blessing.

When his daughter began to show an improvement, the doctor was greatly relieved and very thankful. He knew well that childbed fever was often fatal, but he had done his best, and he had at least managed to keep her alive. He did not know if Sofia's treatments had helped in the recovery, but he politely asked her to give him the methods for her potions, and decided that he would try them, together with the conventional treatments, in any suitable future cases.

Sofia stayed with the Agha's family for five more years, and grew to love the Lady and her children. Caterina had borne two more babies in quick succession, very much against Sofia's advice, and she now felt able to scold her mistress gently about her lack of care for her health. Caterina said that she and the Agha wanted a large family, but Sofia shook her head, and told her firmly that she must wait at least two years before bearing another child or she would be toothless and bowlegged before she was forty. If she survived to be forty.

She had a real affection for her kind and good-natured mistress, and she helped to nurse her through the resulting illnesses, while pointing out that the Agha now had a good sized family with five vigorous children, and three of them boys. He would not wish her to risk her health and well being in her desire to give her dear husband the children he so wished for, and there was plenty of time. She nursed the two latest babies, who were both a little premature and rather small, and when they were out of danger she felt she could return to Deir Menlik, where Kyria Maria was feeling the effects of old age, and needed her help.

She said farewell to the Agha's children with great sorrow. Yeremia was now a handsome, mischievous boy, and secretly her favourite, but he still gave cause for concern with his susceptibility to every cough, cold or ague at large in the city or the village. Sweet Hripsimé, the dark and lively Virab, whom she called her little jester, and the two new babies were all thriving and she had no qualms about their health in general, though she would miss them all sorely.

She left with gifts from all of them, riding a good strong riding-mule which the Agha had insisted she take, and leading a donkey bearing her luggage. Zaki was once again complaining loudly from his basket on the saddle in front of her, and trotting at the donkey's heels was a big puppy from a litter sired by Sheytan, the Agha's own huge black hound, his ungainly paws and too-large head promising growth to match that of his stately father.

Sofia spent many productive and satisfying years working at Deir Menlik and caring for her much-loved teacher. When the Kyria died, Sofia moved back to Deftera and took up residence in a two-roomed mud-brick house near the river, at some distance from both the farm and the village. She brought the dogs and cats from Deir Menlik and the herbs and plants she would need for the garden, and she lived to be a very old lady, very respected, visited often and loved by the children of the Agha's children, and companioned by the many times-great grand kittens of Zaki and the descendants of the Agha's long-dead hound Sheytan.

At Deftera, all of Artin Boghos's children except little Bedros lived past infancy, which was in no small part due to the teachings of their young nurse Sofia. There were, of course, few Armenians suitable for them to marry, and the Agha arranged a match for his exquisite eldest daughter Hripsimé with his friend Hairabed Melikian Agha, who was nearly the same age as himself. Fortunately Hripsimé was as dutiful as she was lovely, the marriage was a good one, and she was very content with her indulgent and loving husband.

1850

The Italian Painter

Artin Boghos Eramian Agha

CARLO TASHIATZY knew very well that he was no Michelangelo, but he felt that he was at least a competent artist and furthermore, he was managing to make a living doing something he enjoyed. He was born in Florence to an Italian mother and a Polish father, and after they died and his elder brother inherited the family home, he travelled south down the length of Italy, painting a portrait for anyone who would hire him and enjoying the great wealth of art and architecture along the way.

He loved his work, and when he was down on his luck he would paint for his keep and the cost of his materials, but work became rarer as he reached the poorer extremity of the country, and now he had to risk damage to his sensitive hands while working on farms and docks to earn enough to feed himself. In Brindisi, he was lucky to find a merchant who hired him to tally the lading of a ship taking a cargo of wine to Larnaca. Carlo wrote an elegant sloping copperplate and he had been taught that he should always do his best work no matter what the task might be, so his records were beautiful as well as legible. His employer was pleased, and on learning Carlo's real profession he mentioned that an artist should find rich patrons a-plenty in Cyprus. Carlo had nothing further to look forward to in Italy, and so he took the advice.

He worked his passage on the very ship he had helped to prepare, and he left Italy confident that he would find better things at the next port of call. He was quite sure he could flatter some of the wealthy citizens of Cyprus into commissioning a portrait to hang on a wall of their salon to impress their guests. He would persuade them that it would bring them a kind of immortality and point out that the picture would ensure that they would be remembered by their descendants every time they looked at it, and that they might do so for centuries if they took proper care of it.

Besides, the island had been Venetian once, and he hoped that some of that great city's culture would still survive for him to sketch and enjoy.

He was not impressed with what he found on his arrival. No one seemed able to speak his language, even brokenly, and he could only communicate with great difficulty using a mixture of French and Italian, supplemented by simple sign language. The port was dirty and hot, the architecture uninspiring, and the people seemed rough and unfriendly.

Nevertheless, Carlo had an open and sunny nature, and he resolved to make the best of it. Cheerful at heart, he always thought things would get better and he tried to see the good in his fellow man. Had he been more of a pessimist, he would have been less likely to have had his pocket picked and one of his bags swiftly removed when he turned his back for a moment, and he might have been less surprised and angry afterwards.

Shaking the dust of Larnaca from his feet, he moved on at once to the capital, where he hoped that things might be less unpleasant.

Nicosia also failed to enthuse him at first sight, but he found lodgings with a charming Armenian family in a picturesque old house off Main Street, within the old city walls. To his relief, they spoke French. Nishan, the owner of the house, had a tailor's shop nearby and he and his wife supplemented their income by letting the top floor of their home. Here, Carlo rented a small, comfortable suite of rooms with his own balcony over the busy street where he could sit and watch the people passing by. There would be plenty of subjects for his sketch book.

Nishan's wife Repeka was a cheerful, bustling woman who kept everything spotlessly clean, and best of all, she was an absolutely wonderful cook. Within a few days he was introduced to *lahmajoun*, small, tasty Armenian pizzas made with lamb, and later the savoury stews *afelia* and *tavas*. Next, Repeka made the most renowned of all Turkish dishes specially for him: i*mam bayilde*. This was made with plump black aubergines baked with thick green olive oil, onions, tomato and garlic, and it was said to have made the reverend *Imam* faint with delight when his wife first served it to him. Carlo was a gourmand, and it almost did the same to him when it was presented for his approval, accompanied only by Repeka's fresh, fragrant bread and a crisp cold wine. He was ravished by subtle sweets such as *salep* and *mahallepi*, and by the more robust *baklava*, and he hailed Repeka as a fellow artist, a master of Greek, Turkish and Armenian cuisines. He praised each meal extravagantly. He kissed his fingers to his hostess as each new offering delighted his palate, and he counted himself very lucky to have found such a comfortable lodging.

Inspired to even greater effort by her guest's flattering appreciation, Repeka produced *mante*, (which took even this skilful cook a whole morning), crisp-fried *goubes* filled with spiced meat, *avgolemono* soup with lemon and eggs, *pastrma*, and *kokoretsi*. Carlo was ecstatic about everything, except for the *pastrma*, which he felt might be an acquired taste. His eyes watered at the thought of it, and as he passed the corner of the yard where he had furtively unwrapped the pungent, oily slice of sausage from his handkerchief and left it for the local wildlife, he saw that the gelid lump was still there. It seemed that the rats also had too much good taste to eat such a thing. He applauded their discrimination.

The streets of the capital were better than those of Larnaca, but even here the main roads reeked of rotting waste, and were littered with rubbish and the droppings of the many donkeys, mules and horses which passed along them each day. Some of them were cleaned daily by gangs of men hired by the residents, but donkeys and horses are by nature incontinent and the sewer was un unknown luxury, so that matters rapidly returned to their previous noisome condition.

Carlo was glad that he had come at the beginning of summer, when every day was sure to be dry. He would not have liked to walk these streets in his thin shoes after rain, and his sturdy boots had been in the bag that was stolen. He fervently hoped that he would be able to save enough to replenish his meagre wardrobe before he left the country and that there would be no unseasonable storms.

He squinted a little in the brilliance of the early morning sun. Its heat was already baking the narrow streets, and, looking up, he realised that the sky had a clear, bright radiance of its own. This splendid light would be a challenge he would enjoy, and he wished that he might somehow earn enough money to spend a few weeks out in the countryside, and perhaps even travel for a while in the high mountains which he could see from his bedroom window. He knew that he was not a great portrait painter, but he hoped his name would one day be remembered for his landscapes of Italy and now, maybe, for recording the beauty of Cyprus.

He spent the day looking at light and shade on whitewashed walls and tumbled stones, admiring shadows among Roman and Lusignan ruins, and wondering what lay behind shuttered balconies and half-open doors. The hidden gardens and dark, dappled courtyards promised him the mysteries and the enigmas of an exotic and foreign land.

1850 The Italian Painter

He imagined that dusky and beautiful maidens lingered by the pools, that elderly, white-bearded sages in brightly coloured costumes pondered the mysteries of life under the shady trees, and that perhaps in the shuttered depths of cloistered rooms, anguished poets composed odes to the shadow of an eyelash on a rosy cheek. He was a romantic, as well as an optimist.

He finished his expedition at the old cathedral of Saint Sophia, which had once been one of the greatest churches of the middle east and was now a mosque. He washed his face and feet and rinsed his mouth at the fountains placed in the courtyard just outside the entrance for that purpose, took off his shoes, and went in.

Nishan had told him the history of this place, and he found it quite as impressive as he had expected. It was cool inside the vast space of this huge building with its high and vaulted ceiling. Two rows of massive supporting columns marched along the centre, and long shafts of light, dancing with dust motes, slanted across the open area. There were great hanging lamps of brass, and the entire space of the floor was covered with rugs and carpets in many colours. The Turks had converted the richly decorated and splendid mediaeval cathedral into a mosque after they had conquered the city and gave honourable terms for surrender to the defenders' commander. After they had this brave man in their power they changed their minds, cut off his nose and ears, tortured him and finally flayed him alive in public. Carlo saw that they had treated the church with a similar brutality. They had roughly truncated the spires without bothering to even out the shattered stones, they smashed the bright stained-glass windows and the shrines and images of the saints, and they whitewashed over the great frescos of the interior. They melted down the gold and silver reliquaries, and destroyed the crusaders' tombs. Finally, they constructed two incongruous minarets which were completely out of proportion to the rest of the building, leaving the cathedral scarred and ugly, and looking strangely unfinished. Inside, the focus of the once-breathtakingly beautiful basilica was twisted perplexingly off centre, for Mecca was not exactly in the East and the new congregation worshipped while facing to the right of the empty space where the High Altar once stood.

He was thoughtful as he left the courtyard. It would certainly serve to remind the subject races who their masters were, and what they could do if they chose.

Later that evening, over yet another wonderful meal, he asked Repeka and her husband for advice in choosing a patron to approach for his first commission. They gave it a proper and solemn consideration, and there was silence other than the sound of cutlery on plates.

Finally, Nishan had an idea. "You might try Hairabed Agha. He's one of the best-known men of the city. He's a cultured man, he appreciates art, and he has many paintings. And he's very rich, he could well afford to have his portrait painted."

"I've heard him mentioned. He's not Turkish, is he?"

Repeka helped him to another portion of *souberek,* a delicate flaky pastry layered over subtle cheese. "No," she said, "he's Armenian, like us, but we don't know him well, I'm afraid. We don't move in the same company, but we do know his wife." She warmed to her subject. "She's a wonderful lady, generous and kind. She's very beautiful, too. She helped us when we first came here and had nowhere to live, and when we started our business she asked her husband to buy some things from Nishan, so that he could tell people that he had the custom of the Agha. It helped a lot."

Nishan nodded his agreement. "But you'd better call at the house tomorrow, or as soon as you can. Everyone who can manage to leave the City for the summer will set off soon, to spend the hot months in the mountains or the countryside, and it won't be long before the Agha and his family will be away to Konak, their estate in the Pentadaktylos range." He leaned back in his chair and took a sip of his home-made wine, which was a little rough, but quite drinkable and rather potent. Gesturing expansively with the glass, he continued. "It will start to feel as if we're living in an oven here in the next few weeks. You can't believe how bad the heat is in July and August unless you've experienced it, and it's also very unhealthy. Every year malaria comes across from the marshes and many people die. They die from the heat, too, especially the old ones, and we'd leave for the mountains ourselves if we didn't have the shop to run."

Carlo appreciated their kindness, especially as they must have known that if he took their advice and was successful, they would have to find another tenant for their rooms. He promised himself that he would come to their shop with the first money he earned and he would order some new clothes to be made. He had already visited Nishan there and admired his work, so he knew that whatever he bought would be of fine quality and well made.

His kind hostess thought of one more thing that might help his bid for a commission from Hairabed Agha. "Give me your best suit and shirt, and I'll press them ready for tomorrow," she offered, when they had finished their meal and her Turkish maid-of-all-work had begun to clear the table. "You'll want to look like a prosperous man and a successful painter when you call at the Melikian house!"

The polished wooden stairs creaked as Carlo climbed up to his large, cool rooms, and the house smelled pleasantly of beeswax and Repeka's good cooking. He had been most fortunate in Nicosia, after his initial bad luck in Larnaca. He hoped this recent good fortune would hold tomorrow.

In the morning Carlo chose several sketches and water colours from his canvas-wrapped bundle and put them into a blue leather portfolio. He dressed himself in his good suit and a crisp white shirt, both beautifully pressed by Repeka, and went to the mirrored wash-stand to see if he was tidy.

He sat on the hard wooden chair in front of it and looked at himself with a critical eye. He tried to comb his rebellious, dark brown curls into a neater style, but as usual they stubbornly resisted his efforts.

Otherwise, he supposed his appearance was well enough. He was of medium height and slim build, and his narrow face was already tanned by the sun. There was a suggestion of a Roman curve to his nose, his eyes had a candid and open look, and his eyebrows, having met in the sign of Aries, curved up and outwards a little to give him a slightly surprised expression. Their were smile-lines at the corners of his mouth, which would no doubt deepen over the years, and he had white, even teeth. He was only a little vain, just enough to be glad that he was presentable.

His hosts were waiting at the door to see him off. Nishan wished him luck as he left the house, and Repeka gave him a flower for his buttonhole.

It was only a short walk to the lovely mediaeval stone building with its great arched windows and pillared doorways, which was the city home of the Melikian family. He stood in the street and admired it for a moment or two, ignoring the shouts of passing carters and carriage drivers.

It was practically a palazzo!

His spirits rose: these gentlefolk could certainly afford his services.

A servant told him that the master was not at home and took Carlo's card up to Signora Melikian, having shown him to her drawing room to wait. This really was a wonderful place. The wooden ceiling was beautifully painted with flowers, and suspended from it were magnificent and obviously very expensive chandeliers with lovely amber glass globes. More practically, Signora Melikian had frosted glass oil lamps for day to day use, and there was a pretty oak writing desk by the large, shuttered central window. It had the deep glossy patina of many years of polishing and the drawers bore little enamelled handles and a brass lock. Carlo assessed it with a professional eye. It would be a good piece to include in his painting if he could get the commission.

He was admiring a particularly nice porcelain group when he heard the door open, and turned to greet Signora Hripsimé, the wife of His Excellency Hairabed Melikian Agha.

This must surely be someone else. This lady was only in her twenties, and Repeka had told him that the Agha was over fifty. But then, he had heard that the Armenians in Cyprus were few here as yet. Perhaps there had been little choice. And any man would be happy to have a wife like this....

Hripsimé stood watching his confusion with an amused smile. Her heart-shaped face was flawless, and her large and beautiful eyes were very dark, with long lashes. She had soft black hair drawn up into a simple chignon, from which a few rebellious tendrils had escaped to curl around her delicate ears. Her deep rose silk dress was quite plain, high necked, and closely fitted to her slender form, flowing in graceful folds which accentuated a tiny waist.

She wore no jewellery other than magnificent pearl drops in her ears, and an unusual gold ring with a bar of impressively large diamonds, placed at right angles to the band so that it fitted along her finger, rather than across it. It sparkled brilliantly on her slender white hand. A single rose, of exactly the same colour as her dress, was tucked into the narrow belt which encircled that small waist.

Carlo became aware that his mouth was open. He closed it quickly, and bowed.

Hripsimé came towards him and offered her hand. "I think you were not quite expecting to see me," she said, in perfect, unaccented Italian.

He took the proffered hand and kissed it.

"Forgive me, Signora. I was just a little surprised. And now you have surprised me again. You speak Italian beautifully."

Hripsimé seated herself in one of the brocaded armchairs beside the wide window, arranged her skirts, and indicated that he should take the matching chair.

"My mother is Italian," she told him. "She came from Italy with my grandfather, and the family settled here."

She smiled at him again, and waited.

He was struck dumb, admiring her with an innocent and candid appreciation, and after a moment she gave him a perplexed frown, which made an adorable little furrow between her delicate eyebrows.

"Is there something I may do for you?" she enquired, with a slight coolness.

"I beg your pardon once more, Signora." Carlo started, and realised belatedly that he had been rather rude. "... I was just thinking that I would like to paint you. I am an artist and I specialise in portraits. I came here to ask if I might speak to your husband, but since he is out of town, I wonder if perhaps you would consider having your picture painted for your own pleasure, and that of your descendants?"

Laughing, Hripsimé shook her head, but she took the portfolio of paintings and looked at them carefully. "I have only three descendants as yet, and they are too little to appreciate a picture of their mother. But there may indeed be someone else you could paint for me."

She held a picture of Brindisi harbour to the light. "This one is very good. If it is for sale, I would like to have it."

Carlo bowed. "It is my pleasure to give it to you Signora."

"That is most kind of you, but I think it would be best if you would send your bill to me." Hripsimé put the little drawing on the side table and folded her hands, the diamonds throwing a spray of light as she did so. "My father has a birthday soon, and I have so far been unable to choose something for a man who has everything he could possibly need. I think that a portrait would make an excellent gift. Also, I believe that he might like the idea of being remembered by his descendants. I will speak to him about it and let you know if he will sit for you. Where do you lodge?"

"I am staying with Nishan and Repeka Atamian," Carlo told her, hardly able to believe his good luck "I believe you know them."

"Yes, indeed. You chose well, Signor Tashiatzy. Diggin Repeka is an exceptionally good cook, and if I could tempt her to my kitchens, I would do so in a moment. Unfortunately for my family, she is content to keep her talents at home to please her husband, and so you are very lucky to be her guest and enjoy her wonderful food."

It was to be a short interview. Carlo hastily got to his feet as Hripsimé stood.

"I will send to let you know my decision before the end of this week." she told him, as she accompanied him to the door.

He did not quite dare to kiss the hand of this beautiful and self-possessed lady again, and he bowed his farewell.

Outside the little palazzo, standing for the second time in the middle of the dusty street, Carlo looked up at the window where he sat and talked with Signora Hripsimé. He supposed he would not see her again if he was to be commissioned to paint the Eramian Agha. He would very much have liked to see her once more, and for a moment it made him a little sad.

Any negative emotion was foreign to his temperament, however, and his natural sunny optimism soon reasserted itself. He had an excellent memory. He knew that he would never forget her, and he decided that when he had the time and the materials he would paint her portrait to keep for himself.

Carlo heard from the Lady Hripsimé sooner than he expected. To his great delight, a letter arrived informing him that he was requested to paint the portrait of her father, and within the week he was on his way to meet the head of the Cypriot branch of the Eramian family. The Agha was currently at his country residence at Deftera and he had instructed Carlo to paint the portrait at the farm, to which his family had removed for the early part of the summer. They would go on to the Troodos mountains a little later, when even the cool breezes at the farm could not abate the heat sufficiently for comfort at night.

Carlo was not a good rider and given a choice he would have taken a carriage for the journey to the village, but his host had kindly sent a man with a couple of mules to bring him out of the city so he really had no option. At least it would allow him to save the money he would otherwise have spent on hiring the carriage, and this was most welcome as his funds were running dangerously low. He was invited to stay as a guest of the Agha until the painting was finished, and though he was sorry to lose Repeka's wonderful meals, he reflected happily that he would be staying rent-free and enjoying the hospitality of one of the island's richest men, surely an enviable experience. He had heard only good things of Signor Artin Boghos, but he was spoken of with respect and envy rather than affection, and the young painter was already a little in awe of his illustrious sitter.

The road was dusty and rutted, though actually in quite good condition when compared with most of the others he had seen, and for much of its way it was bordered with trees which gave a welcome shade. An infrequent and inexpert rider, Carlo bumped painfully and inelegantly along on the mule with the servant following correctly a short distance behind him. He had attempted to get the man to ride alongside, but had been made to understand that 'the master would not like it,' and the servant had kept to his place, riding along in the dust behind him.

It was therefore a long, hot and uncomfortable ride without even the distraction of attempting to learn a little Greek, and the man's insistence on keeping a correct distance had increased Carlo's nervousness about this commission. After all, in truth he too was little better than a servant.

He need not have worried. The mistress of the house was Signorina Caterina Carletti before she became the Lady Caterina Eramian, and she was delighted with the opportunity to speak her native language with him, to reminisce about places they both knew, and to hear all about his interesting travels in Italy.

She was a little lady, plump, dark and vivacious, and she soon coaxed Carlo into telling her a good deal more than he had originally intended. She learned that he was as yet unmarried, that he missed his brother and his brother's children, who were a mischievous pair of hellions but most beguiling, and that he could sing and play the lute a little. He did not know whether to be pleased or alarmed when she said that this would be a welcome addition to the evening entertainments while he was with them. He also found himself telling her that he thought the local food was absolutely wonderful, especially the sweets, the wine quite drinkable, the language difficult, and the city rather commonplace, apart from the cathedral and the classical ruins. He had enjoyed a Turkish bath and massage very much, but a *nargileh* made him cough, though he intended to persist until he appreciated the habit since so many people took the smoke with such evident enjoyment; and he would like to paint the mountains and her daughter, although not necessarily in that order. Finally, he emphatically did not like *pastrma,* which he suspected may have been invented by a practical joker. She laughed, and decided that she liked him.

Soon he was settled in a comfortable, airy room in the guest quarters and he was given the run of the house, which was quite charming and not as rustic as he had expected. To his absolute joy, the very best materials were provided for him and he gloated over these for a while before he started work. If he was lucky, there may be enough of these wonderful oils left over for him to paint another picture for himself when he had finished.

The Agha gave him a couple of hours each morning, rather earlier than Carlo would have liked, and then was seen no more until the evening meal, when they would be joined by his delightful little wife and whichever of his several children were currently in residence. Most often the party which assembled for dinner included the Agha's eldest son, Yeremia, a handsome, competent young man with the confident manner of an Eramian heir, but he was disappointed to find that Signora Hripsimé had already taken her children to the Melikian estate in the mountains and that she would therefore not be seen at the dinner table.

Carlo was told that in the city the Agha wore European dress, but here in the relaxed surroundings of his country estate and farm he wore a wonderfully embroidered, high-necked waistcoat over a snowy cotton shirt and tailored black trousers. For the portrait, he also wore a finely woven jacket, richly trimmed with fur, and a red fez, all of which symbolised his high estate. He sat completely still for the two hour period, apparently at ease and gave no sign that he felt the increasing heat of the day, dressed as he was in clothes more suitable for a cooler season. He seemed quite relaxed, occasionally turning the beads of a fine amber *omboloi* in the blunt, capable fingers of his right hand, and he surprised Carlo by conversing politely with him in excellent French on all manner of subjects. Carlo had expected a cool, high-bred silence.

He learned that the Agha's father had built the original farm buildings, which comprised the veranda with its red tiled roof and the three pointed arches with the rooms behind them, and that his present employer had added to them considerably over the years until the estate had a residence worthy of its size and prosperity. Carlo had the impression that the Agha was immensely proud of Deftera beneath his reserve, and that this was where he felt really at home. He could understand that. He was enjoying his stay very much.

As the days went by and Carlo spent more time with his sitter, he thought that he had seldom met a man more completely in control of himself and his environment, and he found himself thinking that it would be a very serious mistake to cross him. Even so, he grew to like the Agha greatly, this man who took the trouble to set an unknown painter at ease, and who also arranged that he should be comfortable and happy for the short time their paths would meet.

A month later, as he laid down his brush for the last time, Carlo was quite pleased with his work. He was aware that the finished painting was not one of great artistic merit, but he had caught the cool, direct gaze of this strong, intelligent man, and the level regard of the portrait's eyes under their bold brows seemed to follow the viewer wherever he went.

Artin Boghos humoured Carlo and agreed not to look at his portrait until it was finished. When he came to see it, Carlo waited, hardly daring to breathe, while his patron stood in front of the canvas without speaking.

At length, to his great relief, the Agha nodded and said, "When you proposed this commission to my daughter, I think you told her that this is how my descendants will see me."

He smiled. "I like that idea."

Carlo was paid a handsome bonus over and above what he had asked, the Lady Caterina commended him to various of her friends and acquaintances, and he received a further assignment to paint Signora Hripsimé's husband, Hairabed Agha. He spent one more extremely happy year in Cyprus, painting other notable men and attempting to capture the astonishing light in his landscapes, and when he returned to Italy he was satisfactorily solvent.

He did not see Signora Hripsimé again, or have the opportunity to paint her picture, but later, back home in Florence, he did paint her portrait from memory as he had promised himself. He never sold the painting, and all his life he cherished the memories of the time when he was an impressionable and optimistic young man trying to capture the wonderful light of the bright and lovely island of Cyprus.

The painting was in his room when he died, still unrecognised as a great landscape artist, but sincerely mourned by his children and his children's children.

Yeremia was the eldest of Artin Boghos's seven surviving children. Despite Sofia's fears for his health during his childhood, he grew tall and well built, with the disconcertingly direct gaze, large dark eyes and strong, curly black hair of his father and grandfather, and he had a lively intelligence, though perhaps also rather too much levity of spirit to suit his reserved and exalted father.

Yeremia was rather irreverent and inclined to make jokes about the Bishop. He was not at all superstitious.

1858

The Owl and the Moon

YEREMIA TOOK his wife's hand and walked with her in the moonlight. It was a harvest moon, huge, yellow, and mysterious, just clearing the horizon and slowly rising over the August fields.

Their baby daughter Huliané was sleeping in her bedroom back at the house, watched over by her nursemaid, while the two older infants, Hagop and Mariam, had at last settled down in the nursery. There were plenty of people to look after them, but Negdar loved to be with her children and would not leave all their care to the maids. She had begun the habit of singing to the two oldest children when they were put to bed, and saying their prayers with them before they went to sleep. They all enjoyed this special time together at the end of the day, and Yeremia had waited patiently till they closed their eyes and she was ready to leave them.

Here at Deftera it was less humid than in the city, and though the night was still hot it was much more bearable than during the day, when everyone sweated at the slightest exertion. As they walked, Negdar loosened her blouse and shook it, fanning herself with her straw hat.

Her waist was just a little thicker than when they first married, as could only be expected after bearing three children in as many years, but she was still slender and supple. Her long legs matched his stride easily, and she was nearly as tall as he. They were a handsome couple.

Negdar was not beautiful in the style of his sister Hripsimé, but then, few women could match Dudu Kadin. Negdar had clear, golden skin, fine, strong features and an open, level gaze. Yeremia loved her high cheekbones and her slightly slanted, wide-set eyes, which gave her a somewhat exotic look, and he jokingly called her his Amazon.

He also loved the way she teased him: she had never been impressed by his wealth or family, and from the first moment they met, she called him 'exalted Agha' in tones of deepest reverence whenever she thought he was being a little too grand. Her brothers and sisters, cousins and parents all shared this disgraceful lack of respect and a joyous outlook on life, which made their family gatherings a great deal of fun. He loved her, he admired her parents, and he was immensely fond of her self-confident, practical and outgoing family, and he counted himself a lucky man to have won this wonderful wife.

Negdar's healthy young body thrived during her trouble-free pregnancies and she produced big, strong babies, who never gave her a moment's worry. She joked that they could populate the island with their offspring, given a few more years, and indeed Yeremia would welcome and cherish every child she gave him.

They were out into the fields now, and no one was about at this time of night. She reached up and pulled the pins from her waist-length hair, shaking it loose with a husky murmur of pleasure. It was a night-time sound, intimate, deeply personal to the two of them, and it made him catch his breath and miss his step. She laughed delightedly, outlined dramatically against the moon as she twisted the dark, silky mass and pinned it loosely in a knot at the nape of her neck. She caught his hand again and swung it as they walked on.

"And what is this surprise, O secretive one?" she asked, "Is it far?"

1858   The Owl and the Moon

"O my Negdar, Negdariné, Negdarinik ... have patience, impetuous woman!" he retorted, neatly avoiding her play-punch at his chest.

After four years with his beloved wife, he was still puzzled that his father had acceded so readily to his carefully worked out and much rehearsed plea to win his consent to their marriage. Yeramia was thirteen years older than Negdar, and a great deal more experienced.

The Eramian Heir had plenty of pleasurable reasons to delay marriage, most of them elegant, beautiful and expensive, and he had left it late. Had he not met Negdar, recently returned from school in Lebanon, he might still be single. She had conquered his bachelor's reservations with a single laughing glance, and was thereafter in sole possession of his heart.

Four years ago, he was prepared for solid resistance from his father, but when he gave Artin Boghos the news that he was at last ready to continue the Eramian dynasty, he found that his carefully worked out arguments were not needed. This marriage would be even more important to their father than those of his brothers and sisters, because Yeremia was the Heir and must produce children with a wife from a good family, and so he had expected to encounter a straight and non-negotiable refusal, to be followed by another holiday in Izmir or Constantinople where he would meet a procession of eligible maidens presented by hopeful mamas for his consideration. Of course the matter would be arranged with somewhat more tact than the bald facts suggested.

Artin Boghos may have been rather awkward and a little stiff with his offspring, but he cared deeply for them all, and most especially for his astonishing, splendid, handsome first-born son. He was not a man who found it easy to be close to his children, and the resulting distance between them pained him. The girl of Yeremia's choice was from a solid, respectable family of modest fortune, but she had the invaluable dowry of superb good health and, best of all was her family's record of producing a brood of healthy, handsome children. Artin Boghos remembered his parents' grief at the loss of their many infants, and he thought that Negdar might bring a bride-gift which outweighed any concerns of money. He bred fine horses and strong, disease-free cattle, and he knew the value of a good bloodline.

He was sensible enough to keep this to himself. He astonished and delighted his firstborn by saying only that he would welcome Negdar Hovagimian into his family with the greatest of pleasure, and he had grown to understand and applaud his son's choice of this admirable girl.

Yeremia and Negdar had walked nearly as far as the river, and now they could see the trees bordering the riverbed and the swaying stands of rushes quite clearly in the bright light. A magical landscape spread all around them in shades of silver and grey.

There was a long squared stone lying on its side near the stepping-stones, and Yeremia paused there, pulling his wife down to sit beside him. She leaned into the curve of his arm and he pressed his cheek against her soft, sweet-scented hair.

"When I was quite a small boy, my father brought me here on a night just like this, with the moon bright enough to reap the second harvest. We stopped at this grove of trees, which were whispering in the breeze just as they are tonight, and we sat on this stone for a while, just as we are doing now." he told her, "He had hidden a farm cart in the grove, and when we got up to leave I didn't see it till I nearly walked into it. There was a pair of big strong mules in the traces, and a great pile of cushions and pillows inside it to save our rumps from bruises...."

"I'll wager he sent one of the men to clean the dirt from it first," Negdar smiled, "neither of you is that careless of your comfort!"

"Sssh, woman, you're interrupting the story! That night, he took me on a wild ride around the boundaries of our land, and it was wonderful, just wonderful. It's something I've never forgotten ... it was strange, you know, he's not usually an impulsive man and he never did anything like it before or since. It was one of the best gifts he could have given me, far better than any expensive bauble. When I saw the moon last night and knew that it was nearly full, I thought we could do it again, just the two of us."

She turned her head to see him smile, his teeth showing white against his dark skin. "Oh, yes, I'd like that very much," she said.

The cart was waiting, just where the first had been hidden all those years before. One of the farm dogs, a gangling white and tan pup, all legs and ears, had followed them at a distance, and he chose this moment to catch them up. He jumped up and down around the cart as Yeremia drove it carefully out from under the trees.

He gave Negdar a hand to climb in, and snapped his fingers at the dog to encourage him. "Good, he's just what we need. He'll chase some of the wildlife out from cover, but he's still too young to catch anything yet. Hold on, *here we go!*"

There was a good broad track all round the Eramian estates, and Yeremia gave the mules their heads. They were fresh and willing, and the cart leapt forward, rumbling and bounding along, racing its own moon-shadow, and gathering speed as the big animals leaned into the traces. To each side of them fields stretched away into the distance, strangely unfamiliar, with dusty rows of stubble etched sharply and edged with silver in the magic light. Low hedges rushed by and the occasional clump of trees loomed blue-black, leaned over them, and were gone. There was the familiar countryside scent of straw and dry grasses, hot earth and crushed herbs.

The cart hurtled on, bouncing and jolting, and throwing a great cloud of dust in their wake. Their speed was exhilarating, the wind of their passing was cool on their faces, and they laughed aloud, shouting and whooping encouragement to the mules.

Yeremia braced his strong legs against the boards of the cart, while Negdar held tightly on to the side and the young dog raced along with them, his tongue lolling out as he ran, making detours into the stubble when a movement or scent caught his interest. Suddenly a hare started from cover, leaping and racing across the fields, pale in the were-light.

Then there were seven or eight of them, their ears laid flat to their backs, their long hind legs giving them such speed that the dog was soon left far behind.

The ghostly white shape of an owl swooped low and drifted along in front of the galloping mules. He was beautiful, silent, and rare. He stayed ahead of them, his powerful wings lazily extended, cupping the air and easily keeping his distance.

"Oh look, Yeram. Oh, just look at him."

"What a beauty! We're very lucky tonight." He stood up in the cart and shouted with exhilaration.

The pup broke into frenzied yapping with the occasional adolescent drop into a deeper note, and cut sharply across the mules, narrowly missing an early death. In the middle of a field, a dog-fox was frozen in mid-step, one dark paw raised as he looked calmly at the oncoming hound, his mouth open in a mocking grin. In a moment, he flowed into a sinuous dash which left his clumsy pursuer looking foolish and panting helplessly, with his dusty sides desperately heaving. Abruptly, the dog gave up, sat down, and watched his quarry disappear into a distant hedge yet again.

They were driving along beside the river once more, still on Eramian land, and a light showed nearby as the mules began to slow. Their initial enthusiasm was waning now, and they were starting to blow heavily, so Yeremia brought them to a walk and turned their heads towards the welcoming glow. He drove carefully down a narrow, rutted track.

"Oh, I know! We're going to see our dear Sofia ... is she expecting us?"

"Of course. This is just about where the mules slowed down last time, so I thought we could sit under her vine, look at the stars for a while, and let the mules have a rest."

Sofia came to greet them at the gate, a thin, gaunt figure accompanied by an inquisitive old hound who touched noses and engaged in a bout of investigative sniffing with their friendly pup. Her face was beloved to Yeremia: her twisted smile and crooked nose, her hair scraped back into the too-tight bun which she had unconsciously copied from the Kyria, all reminded him of warmth and love given to him when he was just a scared little boy living with the fear that his mother might die. He leapt down from the cart, picked her up and hugged her, swinging her around while she laughed and scolded at the same time.

She returned his embrace briskly and kissed Negdar. "Still happy, my turtle-doves?" she asked.

Negdar blushed. "Oh, *yes*," she said, and she and Yeremia caught each other's glance, his knowing smile making her colour deepen even more.

Preceded by two officious cats and the elderly hound, they went to the yard at the back of her little house where they sat together on a long bench while she served them fruit juice chilled in the well, and a dish of salted nuts.

They sat close, looking at each other often as they talked, starting sentences at the same time, their hands touching unconsciously with a mutual movement as if they were confirming their closeness. The stars were bright above the mountains, and they could see lights twinkling far away, where distant villagers were also sitting in their yards to enjoy the cool of the night.

They told Sofia about the hares and the fox, and how the great white owl had flown along in front of them.

"Did he fly ahead of you for long?" Sofia asked.

"Yes, why?"

"No reason." She looked down at her hands. "Was it as much fun as the last time?"

"Yes, it was." Yeremia said, putting an arm round his wife and feeling utterly content. "It was wonderful."

Sofia walked to the gate with them to see them off, and waved as Yeremia whistled to the mules and set them to walk home at a more decorous pace. He lifted his whip in salute and Negdar blew her a kiss.

She saw Yeremia's arm slip around his wife's waist, and, smiling, she stayed at the gate to watch them till they turned the corner at the end of the lane.

Returning slowly to the courtyard to tidy up and blow out the lamp, she glanced up through the leaves of the vine, and saw that the moon was now riding high in the sky. She stood motionless, her hand still steadying the lamp. The benign harvest moon, that great silver disc, was gone, and in its place was a bloody red orb, streaked and mottled, ominous, sinister, somehow ... *threatening*. It was a witches' moon, a bloodmoon, brooding and dangerous, and while it was in the sky, curses, quarrels, angers and jealousies would be stronger and more bitter, and thoughts of resentment and hatred and revenge would surface in otherwise tranquil minds.

An owl flying under a harvest moon was a lucky sign, the villagers said, and the bird was a harbinger of a good fortune. The same bird flying under a witches' moon became a *syce* owl, a swift servant with a message of death, and it was considered one of the worst possible omens.

She was not superstitious, not even a little. She did not believe in luck and charms and incantations. So why did she feel as if an icy hand clutched at her heart?

Almost running, she snatched up a crock of olives from the store as an excuse for following them, and threw a blanket and saddle onto her bony mule. He turned his head, still chewing a large mouthful of hay, and looked at her, mildly surprised to be readied for a journey at this time of night, but he followed her out of his stable willingly enough. She left the cups uncleared and the lamps still lit, and hastened after them.

The two big lanterns in the courtyard of the farmhouse were burning brightly when she arrived. She felt rather silly to be visiting so late, but she still felt the dread which had taken her at first sight of the witches' moon, so she went to the kitchen door. Though she was always welcomed as a friend of the family rather than a servant, she did not take advantage of the Agha's kindness, and she never went to the front door. Also, she was really more comfortable in his kitchen than in his drawing-room. Besides this, she really had no idea why she had come, and she could not say she was here to see the lady Caterina, because she was now at sea on the first stage of one of her occasional visits to her family in Italy.

The Agha's cook opened the door and greeted her warmly. She was very happy to see Sofia; she would not go to her bed for at a long while yet, and she welcomed the chance to talk while she finished her work and set things ready for the morning.

Sofia felt that explanations were necessary. "Master Yeremia left without the olives," she said, setting the crock down on the white, scrubbed surface of the kitchen table. "They're my special *sarkistes*"

Cook wiped her hands on her apron and brought a plate of crisp, sweet, toasted almond biscuits and a pitcher of home-made lemonade. "Stay a while," she urged, and sent the kitchen boy to tell Yeremia he had a guest.

The Agha's old hound was privileged in his dotage and was allowed a place indoors now that his duties in field and yard were over. He was curled up in a basket near the empty fireplace and he woke, scenting Sofia's familiar presence. His nose was still good, though his eyesight was failing badly, and he got slowly to his feet. He came over to her, laid his grey muzzle on her knee, sighed loudly, and waited to have his ears scratched. Sofia obliged, ruffling his thinning fur and stroking him gently. There had been a time in her life when dogs and cats were the only trustworthy things in her life, and she was particularly fond of this one, who had been the Agha's companion for so many years.

Suddenly, he removed his head from her knee and hurried with his stiff-legged gait to the inner door, so that Sofia was unsurprised when Artin Boghos came into the room, followed by Yeremia and Negdar.

Her ears reddened guiltily as she told her little cover story, and she thought she noticed an understanding gleam in the Agha's dark eyes, but he merely said how very pleased he was to see her, and that he hoped she knew she did not need any reason whatsoever to visit this house, which had once been her home too.

Cook was a little flustered to have the Agha in her domain, and she bustled around with chairs and cushions and plates and biscuits, till Yeremia caught her about the waist, held her still while she protested, and made her sit with them while they had their second refreshments of the evening. Pink with delight, she brought a chair to the very edge of the group and sat down with them. Wait till she told her sister about this! Her sister's employer never did such a thing, dear me no, but then, the Agha was *real* nobility, and everyone knew she was not an encroaching person who might *presume*. Her cup was full when Yeremia waited on her himself, and with a flourish presented the plate and insisted that she have one of her own excellent biscuits. She sat happily in her little realm, eating her biscuit and unable to stop smiling with surprise and pleasure.

Sofia was just beginning to relax and feel reassured about her silly fears when there were urgent shouts outside. These quickly grew closer and louder, and all at once the great sheet of metal which hung beside the outer gate and served as dinner gong and fire-bell began to sound, its mighty brazen peal drowning out all the other noises. The two men leapt to their feet and threw open the kitchen door.

On the horizon towards the village there was a great mass of roiling orange flame and smoke, leaping high into the sky, and trailing ugly, glowing clouds filled with sparks and smuts, and the wind was blowing it towards the house. As they watched, a distant resin tree caught the flames and burst into crimson blossoms and streamers of yellow as its aromatic oils caught fire..

Artin Boghos ran towards the stables, but Sofia put a restraining hand on Yeremia's arm. "Be careful tonight," she warned. Surprised, he looked down at her with a quizzical expression. He patted her hand and nodded, then hurried after his father.

Women from the village began to arrive, and they helped to clear the kitchen table and lay out clean bandages prepared from old, well-washed and softened bed sheets which had been sewn ends-to-middle once too often and kept for this last use. Cook brought the pots of healing salves prepared by Sofia against just such an eventuality and which were kept with other remedies for farmyard injuries in a medicine box in the overseer's room.

There would be injured men brought in soon. This fire was huge and very dangerous, but at least the spring was nearby, and was still running well this year. The women told each other that their men would flood the irrigation canals and the flames would certainly be confined quite quickly, that the fields of standing corn would be saved, and that no one would be badly hurt. Then they waited.

After what seemed a very long while the men began to return one by one, and though there were many with singes and burns, one or two bad enough to scar, there were no seriously injured casualties. The worst harmed were the men who had inhaled fumes. They brought the smell of smoke and burning in with them, and apologised for dirtying everything they touched with soot and smuts, but for once Cook did not care. Her man was safe, the and the fire was out. It had burned half their barley in the outer fields before its extinction, and they were saying that it was no accident, but this they said quietly, and among themselves.

Once the worst injuries were cared for, Negdar and Sofia left the capable maids to deal with the minor wounds, closely supervised by Cook, and they went out into the yard to wait for Artin Boghos and Yeremia. Surely they should have been back by now?

The old hound stalked behind, but he did not stay with them. He broke into a staggering run, going to meet the four men who came into the lamplight in the outer yard. They carried a hurdle between them and on it was lying a man, tall enough for his feet to hang over the end, while another figure of equal stature followed in the darkness. Behind them were more men, leading horses and a mule.

Artin Boghos? Yeremia?

No one else had such height. Breath catching, hearts racing, they ran across the yard.

It was Yeremia. They brought him into the kitchen and laid him on the wooden table. The fire had not touched him. His face was peaceful, his eyes closed, and he seemed only to be sleeping. Artin Boghos went to Negdar, who was standing beside her husband's body. Her tears slowly welled up and dropped on to his face as she bent over him, and she was holding her arms tightly around herself as if she were ill.

"Negdar...." She looked at him, and the pain in her face struck him like a physical blow. "He was moving a great stone with some of the men. They were trying to block the main channel to make it overflow into the field ... he just looked surprised and fell down." Negdar made a strangled sound, and Artin Boghos went to her and took her into his arms. He closed his eyes tightly against this impossible, awful reality, but its truth was still there when he opened them.

Sofia could watch no more. She left them to their grief and went out into the darkness.

The old dog followed her and leaned, shivering, against her leg. She reached down and stroked his head, knowing that she could do nothing to help her dear ones. She had learned long ago that life was unfair and sometimes terrible, and that it would do no good to speak of the healing of time while grief was so raw and unbearable.

She took her mule from the stable and led him slowly home, so that the dog should not be left behind. He was trying to stay near her, sensing that something terrible had happened and not knowing what else to do. He wanted to be with her, with someone familiar whom he could trust.

At least she could look after this bewildered old animal, and see that he would not be alone on this ugly and terrible night, this night of a *syce* owl and a bloody moon.

There was nothing she could do for Negdar.

☞

Artin Boghos's spirited little wife Caterina brought two legacies to the family. In each subsequent generation there have been one or two most admirable, intrepid, and strong-minded female descendants. She also had an unusual diamond ring. The amazons appear with delightful regularity in all branches of our family, and the ring became the Melikian Legacy with the marriage of their daughter Hripsimé to Hairabed Agha.

Among Artin Boghos's male descendants there have been a fair share of libertines and philanderers, but he was a faithful husband and he was at one with his dear and well-loved wife. He missed her very much when she left on her occasional visits to her Italian cousins in Naples.

1859

Caterina's Voyage

THE *DONNA D'ASOLO* was not the fastest ship owned by the d'Asolo family, but she was the flagship, the finest in the fleet, and the most luxurious. Her cabins might be small, but they were clean, they smelled of beeswax and cedar, their brassworks gleamed, and their bunks were spacious. Her decks were spotless, her paintwork immaculate, and her guns and gear maintained to the highest standards. The *Donna's* crew were proud to belong to her, and their d'Asolo uniform of blue and white striped shirts and dark blue canvas pants was known and recognised instantly in all the great ports of the Mediterranean.

Artin Boghos had amicable business arrangements with Luigi d'Asolo, brother of the d'Asolo patriarch, and when he heard that Luigi was to sail to Italy aboard the *Donna*, he booked passage on her for Caterina. He reasoned that a vessel carrying Luigi would be more likely than others to provide a safe and comfortable journey for his cherished wife on her visit to her Carletti and Falangola cousins, and so Caterina duly sailed on the *Donna* when she left for Rhodes on her route to Brindisi.

She dined at the Captain's table and listened to Luigi's fulsome compliments with a tolerant smile, pleased with this pleasant break from routine and responsibility. Luigi was an elderly but perennially hopeful dandy with a fine, gallant turn of phrase and the most exquisite manners. Her young companion Eliana certainly seemed impressed, but she was a sensible village girl with a great deal of common sense and she was probably in no danger from him. Caterina thought, however, that charming Luigi must have been quite formidable when he was young.

The trim, well-run ship had made good time since leaving safe harbour, running fast before a strong and steady wind. She sailed in the company of two other merchant vessels for added security, and all three kept a constant watch, changing the lookout every two hours so that none should grow weary of it and relax their vigilance. The merchants had good reason for the watch they set: corsairs often had spies in the major ports, ready to leave in small, swift ships with details of a rich, heavy-laden merchantman and her ports of call. On receiving such news, the long low pirate vessels with their better manoeuvrability and superior fire power would leave their anchorage in the hidden bays and coves of the islands and fall on the ships like wolves raiding a flock of helpless sheep.

The voyage from Larnaca to Rhodes was uneventful, and it was this second part of the journey past the pirate lairs in the many convenient hiding places of the Peloponnese and the Ionian islands, which carried the most danger.

The *Donna* was the smallest and slowest of the three vessels travelling in the convoy and though she carried guns and fighting men as well as her cargo, the Captain frowned as he measured the gradual widening of the gap between his and the preceding two ships. Caterina watched him from her vantage point in the bows. She had made this voyage several times and knew the ship's routines, but this was her maid's first time at sea and Eliana was much enjoying it, with as yet no fear of any dangers to be encountered in this most exciting experience. She had long since recovered from her initial bout of seasickness, and she was on deck at every opportunity, determined to miss no part of the adventure. Caterina was amused, and envied her the enthusiasm and energy of youth.

She had last seen her Neapolitan cousins some years ago, and she had looked forward to this holiday with pleasure, but now, only halfway through the voyage, she found that she was already missing the luxuries of her town house and the peace, comfort, and familiar routines of Deftera. She decided that this would certainly be the last visit to Italy without her husband. She missed him far more than she had expected, and the necessary constraint of the narrow cabin and the constant movement of the ship irked her more than they ever had before.

She supposed she must be getting old.

On the second day out from Rhodes, the wind increased steadily, the waves grew higher, and the vessel began to pitch and roll more noticeably. Towering banks of heavy black clouds were overtaking them and it was becoming difficult to see the shapes of the other two ships ahead when Caterina decided to go below and try to rest.

"I will come too, *Jeera*," Eliana said, a little reluctantly.

Heavily accented Cypriot Greek made '*Kyria*' into '*Jeera*,' an idiosyncrasy which had not left Eliana's speech even after two years in the Eramian household. Caterina found it oddly reassuring. There was no need for Eliana to forgo her pleasure, so she told her companion that she might stay on deck if she wished, and went down to the cabin alone.

With a sigh of relief, she lay down on the folded blankets of her bunk. They were brought from Deftera, and they smelt of the lavender which grew in abundance at the farm and which was sewn into cloth bags to perfume the linen cupboard. She thought wistfully of Artin Boghos. They had been married for many years, but each night he would come to her bedroom to say goodnight to her, to hear about her day and to kiss her, no matter how late he came in from field or office, and she missed him very much. She was still thinking about him when she fell asleep.

A few hours later she was woken by the movement of the ship, the loud and urgent shouting of commands, acknowledging calls of sailors, and the sound of running feet on the deck above her head. Hastily, she put her shoes on and climbed the companionway. It was dark too early, with the unnatural dusk of lowering, heavy black clouds, and the lantern on the fore deck was already lit and swinging wildly with the ship's movement. She saw that the *Donna* had been made ready for a storm: everything was secured or cleared from the decks, while all but one of the sails were stowed safely away, and that one left half-furled only to give aid with the stability and steering of the vessel.

Soon the *Donna d'Asolo* wallowed in the depths of enormous waves, then climbed up and up, only to plunge terrifyingly from the towering crests with a mighty impact, sending huge black sheets of water high to each side as she hurtled into the oncoming seas. Spindrift was snatched by the wind from each peak and sprayed constantly across the deck, so that Caterina kept her feet with difficulty. She looked about for Eliana, and found her wedged into a niche between the cabin and the rail, wet through and exulting in the wildness of the storm. She called and waved to her, indicating that she could stay if she wanted to. She wished that she could view the scene with equal enjoyment and went back to the cabin, grateful for its warmth.

She dozed a little.

She woke once more as the wooden planks of the ship flexed and groaned, creaking alarmingly while the storm continued to increase, growing in ferocity beyond anything she had so far encountered. She jammed her elbows into the sides of the bunk and said a quick prayer to the Mother of God, kissing the gold crucifix which hung on its chain below the neckline of her dress.

In the gloom, she could just see that the opposite bunk was now occupied. "Courage, my Eliana," she called. The girl had finally understood the danger they were in. She had been thrown from her eyrie by the violent force of an extra large wave, but luckily a passing sailor had caught her arm and pushed her roughly through the cabin door to safety, saying something obviously very uncomplimentary in Italian. Now she held onto the sides of her bunk with white-knuckled fingers, but she clenched her teeth against a frightened whimper, and managed to give Caterina a brave smile. She was safer here. Assuming of course, that the ship did not founder.

The storm continued all through the night. Hour after hour, their beds fell sickeningly beneath them, then rose with frightening suddenness to hit them hard in the back and throw them upwards again, but at last, towards dawn the movement slowly began to decrease. The howling of the wind gradually diminished and Caterina felt a little less anxious. At last the ship rocked gently on the waves, but though they waited in the dark for some reassurance or news, no one came to find out how they were.

Both women were bruised and exhausted, but otherwise unharmed and they snatched a little sleep. When it grew light enough to see, they found that their baggage was scattered everywhere and that Caterina's precious perfume bottles were broken and scenting the mahogany boards of the floor. They cleared the glass away, repacked everything and stowed it all away. With some effort, they succeeded in pulling the cabin door open.

They came on deck to find a scene of destruction and wreckage.

Spars and rigging had been torn loose from above, and a huge boom still attached to its ripped and flapping sail had fallen from the mainmast on to the deck. The ship's rails were splintered in several places, and only the blocks of one of the great guns remained amidships, while the other was canted crazily against the base of the mainmast. Among all the chaos and damage and confusion, the Captain had still taken care to send a man aloft on the least damaged mast to keep watch.

Their two companion ships were nowhere to be seen.

The *Donna* was hove-to a short distance from land, and a sullen grey line of mountains rose on the horizon with the towering purple clouds of the storm still roiling above them. Lightning flashed in a great arc between the land and the clouds, and thunder boomed almost immediately across the water. Caterina shivered. The land was too close, and she understood the Captain's wariness in setting watch at once.

Some of the least injured men were beginning to clear the deck, while others were using axes to break up the wreckage of the fallen boom where it lay amidships. Caterina could see that a man was pinned beneath it, unmoving. Another groaned in pain nearby, and finding that no one was attending to him, she sent Eliana below for her medicine box and went to see what she could do.

It seemed as if fully half the crew were injured. The *Donna d'Asolo* was making no way, and she was effectively crippled until the wreckage could be cleared and her sails reset. A sudden loud splash was followed by an earsplitting metallic shriek and rattle as the ship's two huge anchors dropped into the sea and the chains were paid out to make the ship safe from drifting while repairs got underway.

There were indeed many casualties. To Caterina's surprise and a dawning respect, the elderly roué Luigi had taken charge of the worst injured men, and had organised a makeshift hospital on the after-deck, which had the least damage. He sported a magnificent black eye and an impressive swelling at the side of his jaw, but somehow he managed to retain an air of elegant insouciance, and to her further astonishment and admiration he was quite competently helping the ship's surgeon set a sailor's broken arm, when she brought her walking wounded to the deck.

"Put him over there, dear lady," he said in Italian, and he waved her towards a space by the rail.

Caterina and Eliana washed wounds with sea-water, stitched uncomplicated gashes with silk thread, splinted and bandaged breaks and strains, and helped the surgeon when required. Most of this was done in silence, and they were completely absorbed in their work.

They were startled by an urgent hail from the man on watch.

"What land is that?" Caterina asked as calmly as she could, tying a neat knot in a bandage torn from her spare petticoats. She had heard of this makeshift solution to a shortage of bandages in an account of the

Spanish Peninsular war, read to her by her eldest son by lamplight on a summer's night at the farm, but she had never expected to be finding herself actually required to use it.

"The captain doesn't recognise the shoreline," Luigi told her, "but I expect he seldom steers this far to the east. Probably it's an island. Let us hope it's a friendly one."

Three fair-sized boats were approaching fast under sail, long and low in the water and curved high at both ends. They looked like fishing boats, but as they came closer it could be seen that they were full of rough-looking men, and that the men were armed with pistols, daggers, and long knives.

She exchanged a look with Signor Luigi. Their forces were in no state to fight and the prospect looked bleak.

"Pirates?" she asked

"Opportunists, I would guess, but they're likely to be just as bad. They probably saw us while they were sheltering in the lee of that land and realised that we were in trouble and could not escape."

The few uninjured sailors rushed to take up defensive positions, but the Captain shook his head and gave orders for them to stand down. "We are outnumbered, and we have no cannon. We would have no chance in a fight," he said, "we should all be killed."

Signor Luigi jumped to his feet and remonstrated with him angrily. He pointed at the oncoming men. "They're just ruffians. It is not honourable to give up without a fight; they will probably kill us all anyway and it is better to die fighting than be butchered unresisting!" He pulled a pistol from under his coat and levelled it at the tall young man standing in the bows of the leading boat.

He was too slow. The man in the boat fired first, but he missed Signor Luigi as his craft shifted in the waves.

He hit Caterina.

Eliana did not scream, and she surprised herself even more by quickly catching her mistress as she fell. She lowered her gently to the deck. She heard the Captain swearing softly, and everyone else on board kept quite still as the men from the boats swarmed over the side. The raiders efficiently rounded up the able-bodied sailors and disarmed them, leaving them under guard while most of them went below to search the holds.

Having taken care of this, their leader approached the group waiting for him amongst the injured on the after-deck. He was a little older than Eliana had at first thought, and not quite as sinister. His loose, roughly woven linen shirt, sleeveless, patched waistcoat, baggy black trousers and heavy boots seemed the sort of clothes a villager would wear, rather than those of a corsair or pirate. She had imagined that the tastes of a corsair would run to bright colours and heavy gold earrings.

The man glanced at Caterina where she lay unmoving, with her head on Eliana's lap. He shrugged and turned to Signor Luigi and the Captain, who were regarding him with stony expressions.

"You can relax, Capitan, we are not interested in taking your ship. What is your cargo?"

"Oil, wine, cheeses, lace … nothing to interest you, I would think." he replied, coldly. He was watching Eliana examine Caterina's head wound. The ball had given her a glancing blow on the temple, knocking her unconscious but apparently not killing her outright. The wound was bleeding freely.

"You may regret harming that lady," he said, with some satisfaction.

"Oh? Who is she then, the valideh sultana?" The pirate grinned mockingly, showing very white teeth.

Eliana interrupted fiercely, fury making her reckless. "No, you butcher, she is *Jeera Katina,* the wife of Artin Boghos Agha! And if you have killed her he will hunt you down where you skulk in your filthy den! He will find you and he will eat your liver, wherever you hide. Oh, you will be sorry you ever harmed his lady!" She actually ground her teeth.

She had lost her city accent in her anger and her Greek reverted to the thick patois of the village, but he understood. His bold gaze assessed her appreciatively.

"Well said, *koritsi mou*, and bravely. But you forget. This dangerous Agha is far, far away and he does not know where we are now, or where we are from. And neither do you, my Capitan. Besides, we are not from this island and no one will find us easily."

Caterina moved slightly and made a small noise of distress.

"And who is the bravo who raised his pistol at me?" the pirate went on, ignoring her.

"He is Signor Luigi d'Asolo," the captain told him shortly, still distracted by his worry for Caterina.

Signor Luigi gave him an exasperated look, which was completely justified. The significance of his name and that of the ship would be obvious to their captor.

The pirate laughed. "That is well, at least I will have two golden ransoms to collect for the trouble of boarding you. You can keep your ship and your cargo – we'll be content with your valuables and your passengers." He pointed at Eliana, "And *you* will accompany your mistress to my 'filthy den'. I do not think she is much hurt but she will need your help."

With Eliana's arm around her, Caterina was able to sit up, and though somewhat confused, she rested with her back against a capstan and waited while her maid collected some necessary things from their cabin and put them into a bag, after which, still dazed, she docilely allowed herself to be transferred to the waiting boat.

The triangular sails were hoisted quickly, the high-prowed craft leapt away from the *Donna* and their captivity began. The women could not tell how long they sailed, but they did not land on the nearby island. Having passed it quite quickly, they continued north along the coast for some hours and at last Eliana had to accept that there was no chance that the Donna would ever find them. Her hopes of rescue faded and her spirits sank, but she did her best not to show it for her injured mistress's sake.

Caterina drifted in and out of consciousness. Sometimes she thought she spoke to her little son Bedros, but that was impossible, because he had died long ago, and sometimes it was her oldest son Yeremia, but that was impossible too. She knew she was confused, her head hurt badly, and at times she couldn't see properly or remember exactly what had happened. She gave Eliana a puzzled look. Surely the ship should be bigger than this?

Eliana drew her close and wrapped her warmly in the blankets she had taken from their bunks on the ship, and Caterina relaxed gratefully into the girl's arms, too tired and in too much pain to think any more. The scent of lavender was all around her as she closed her eyes.

By the time the boats were pulled up onto a small stony beach hidden behind a long projecting headland, she was once again unconscious. She was lifted with care and carried gently in a makeshift litter along a small and rather beautiful ravine to their abductor's village.

The pirate's lair was in reality a large, square and unadorned stone tower, in a village full of large, rough stone towers. Outside, it was stark and forbidding, a perfect complement to the barren grey rocks and the twisted and stunted trees which leaned away from the constant winds, but inside it was warm and comfortable. While it was certainly no filthy den, it contained nothing that was not functional, other than a smoke-blackened icon painted on wood depicting St.George spearing a rather puny dragon with a mighty lance. There were plenty of thick, brightly coloured, hand-woven rugs and cushions on the wide wooden divan which was built against all four of the massive walls, and the usual bundles of dried herbs and plaits of onions hung from the high, tarred rafters. Pans were racked neatly on shelves above a stone basin serving as the kitchen sink, there were several goatskins hanging from wooden pegs, and a huge scrubbed table bore a big woven basket of wrinkled apples and several rough red-brown pitchers with wax-sealed stoppers. There were sacks and some large pottery jars arranged round the huge central tree trunk which supported the floor above.

Wooden stairs in one corner led up to the sleeping quarters, and a fire of driftwood burned merrily, popping and crackling, and blue-flamed with salt, in a fireplace big enough to roast a whole goat. The stone slabs of the floor were strewn thickly with clean, sweet smelling straw, and dogs, chickens and livestock were kept firmly outside.

"*Ela, Athina mou*, my sister, see what I have brought you," their captor called cheerfully as they approached the tower.

The young woman waiting for them at the door wore the brightly coloured, striped skirt and embroidered blouse of an unmarried village woman, and her strong, classical face with its straight nose and level brows was proud enough for her warrior-goddess namesake. A long, curved knife with a chased silver hilt, topped with a round, roughly polished turquoise was thrust into the wide scarf tied around her sturdy waist below a black woollen waistcoat.

She greeted her brother sullenly and watched with some suspicion as the two women were brought in, but she hastened to help them up the two stone steps and did her best to make them comfortable when she saw how confused and hurt Caterina was, as she tried to sit up. When they were settled, she gave a bowl of hot soup to Eliana, and she sat with another beside Caterina where she lay propped up among several cushions on one of the fireside divans.

Gently, she encouraged her to eat a little. Caterina obediently tried to do as she was asked, but she could only manage a few mouthfuls. She felt horribly sick, as well as very, very tired.

"Poor lady," Athina murmured. "What happened?

Eliana glowered at the pirate captain. "*He* shot her."

Now that the raid was safely over and the immediate danger was past, he was inclined to be friendly. "My name is Alexandros, and I did not shoot at her. I was aiming at the skinny old *keratas* standing beside her. The boat moved." He shrugged. "It was chance."

Athina nodded. "That is so. Alexandros does not shoot women."

"He abducts them, though," Eliana insisted, stoutly. "He is a cowardly kidnapper and a pirate! He will surely hang one day. You will see."

"We do what we must," Alexandros said, scowling, "it is a hard life here. You too will see." He handed the bundle of their possessions to her and left them alone.

Outside, the wind howled around the tower. It rattled the unpainted wooden shutters and lifted the edges of a threadbare rug by the door, but Caterina felt safe and protected in the warmth of her blankets and the lavender-scent of Deftera. She was not afraid. She shut her eyes.

She did not waken for three days.

Eliana, however, was suddenly very frightened indeed. The days went by and the courage of her indignation vanished. She was aware that Alexandros watched her with a certain hunger, and she tended Caterina with a kind of desperate solicitude. She must not die!

Signor Luigi was lodged in another tower, and she had not seen him since they arrived. She did not want to be alone in this bleak and terrible place, which was surely the lair of bloodthirsty murderers and pirates. Also, if her dear mistress were to die, she was not certain that the Agha would still ransom her. Even so, she showed a haughty face to her abductors and looked down her nose at Alexandros.

Athina was much amused. She could see that the girl did not know that her brother would never harm a woman, and she applauded Eliana's refusal to show her fear. Spirited women were greatly admired in this wild part of Greece and Athina herself had the boldness of her freedom-loving ancestors. She liked the spirit of this too-slender maid.

"Don't worry, little sister," she laughed, as she watched Eliana turn an affronted shoulder to Alexandros' greeting, "I think he likes you. He isn't really a pirate, you know. This tower belongs to him, and he inherited my father's lands so that he is responsible for the entire wellbeing and prosperity of this village. What he said was true, it is not easy to live here and we do what we must to survive. Sometimes it is very hard. For us, and now for you."

Being sister to the village head man did not seem to have made Athina's life a privileged one. She worked constantly from first light till dusk.

There was always something to be done, and no one was exempt. Even Alexandros chopped wood, butchered their meat, and soaked, peeled, and wove thin, pliable branches into baskets for catching the lobsters he sometimes brought back when he took his boat out to fish. He mended nets with great care and neatness, and did the same for Eliana's torn shoe; he went out all night with the fishermen, came back tired and wet, and still took time to lift the heavy cauldrons over the fire for Athina and to bring the logs in for the day's use, before he wearily climbed the creaking wooden ladder to his bed on the floor above, where he fell into an exhausted sleep.

In the evenings, he and Athina often sang softly as he carved wooden spoons and plates, or blocks and pins for the boats. He repaired tackle and spliced ropes, his strong brown hands surprisingly deft at the more delicate work, and Eliana often found him surreptitiously watching her as he went about his duties. His sister, meanwhile, sewed and embroidered clothes, or combed and spun the wool which waited in tightly-packed bags stacked under the stair-ladder. She repaired the tear in Eliana's blouse and showed her how to embroider a traditional pattern, a row of stars and flowers, which would conceal the stitches, and the two women compared the regional patterns for lace which their mothers had taught them. Eliana helped Athina with pickling and drying vegetables and fruit, and preparing and cooking their meals, and though she was grateful that she had something to occupy her thoughts and stop her worrying about her possible fate, she would not allow herself to trust her captor's sister, or to forget that she was a prisoner.

Day by day, the sounds of their industry and their singing were woven into Caterina's drifting awareness as she moved from dream to dream. Sometimes she smiled at a familiar tune, and Eliana's heart leapt as she thought that she might wake, but her eyes remained closed, and the girl began to despair.

The *Donna d'Asolo* had sailed on with the news of their capture and the ransom demands which were to be delivered to the Eramian

Agha and the d'Asolo patriarch. Alexandros' man was already awaiting delivery of the money at the port of Rhodes, but who knew what might happen before he could arrange their release? It could be many weeks before Artin Boghos heard of his wife's fate, and Eliana feared that they did not have that much time.

Alexandros was not a happy man. He was experiencing an unfamiliar and unpleasant state of affairs. He was being spurned by a girl he very much liked, and whom he increasingly wished to please. He and his fellow villagers were not really pirates and this was the first time they had taken a ship, so that he was not hardened to a captive's pain or sorrow, and Eliana's loving care and concern for her injured mistress despite her own fear for herself had touched him, wakened a reluctant admiration, and began to weaken his resolve.

He brought Luigi from the neighbouring tower to visit the women, hoping to reassure Eliana.

The d'Asolo merchant had somehow managed to bring several changes of dress with him from the *Donna*, and he was as neat and gallant as ever. He sat beside Caterina, and took her hand. He was horrified at her changed appearance. "Che povera," he said, softly.

The words in her native tongue penetrated the mists of her dreams. "Che povera?" she repeated almost inaudibly, and her hand went to the crucifix around her neck. "Signor Luigi?" she whispered, opening her eyes and struggling to understand what had happened.

Her vision cleared and she could see him. She remembered at last. "Oh, have they taken you, too?" she asked, dismayed.

The elderly gallant kissed her thin hand. He held it gently, not showing his alarm at the feel of the fragile bones. "I'm afraid so, dear lady. But I'm sure that we shall soon be liberated by our families' generosity. See, they have looked after us well, and they mean us no harm. You must rest and get well, so that we shall all return safely together."

Even as he said it, he knew that it was not a likely outcome. Signora Caterina was very pale, much thinner, and very fragile, and he could see that the shot had caused far more injury than he had thought. She looked frail and very ill indeed. Concealing his reaction to her changed appearance, he smiled at her and said, "I will ask Alexandros to let me stay here for a while, and we will talk of better days and good times to come." He looked up as he said this, and Alexandros nodded.

At last, her captor had taken the measure of Caterina's decline and now he was experiencing another unfamiliar emotion. He was desperately sorry. He did not want her to die.

That evening, he and Athina talked to the other villagers about this dreadful outcome of their actions, and they resolved together that they should abandon their scheme and send Caterina back to her husband as soon as she was a little stronger. They would not wait for the ransom.

In the morning he told Eliana. "As soon as the Signora can travel, I will send her home and I will never do such a thing again. I am not hardened enough to be a corsair." He shook his head. "Whatever the others do in future, I will not take part in the theft of anyone's life, nor hold anyone captive again." He was a man unused to apologising to women for any action of his, but he hoped that if he must lose Eliana, at least she should take a better opinion of him with her.

She blinked back tears. "*Why* did you have to do it? The storm nearly sank our ship and we had many men terribly injured. You should have helped us, not robbed us!"

"We are poor. The ship was a fat merchantman, and we thought only that we might find money or something we could sell to make our lives easier. You know how hard it is here." He sighed and wished he could find some way to make her understand how their misfortune might seem a godsend to a poverty-stricken village.

Eliana bit her lip and fought the tears which came too readily now. She decided to tell him her greatest fear. "I think soon my lady will die. I think it is too late."

He reached out to her, aghast, but he took his hand back as she drew away. He could find nothing more to say.

The next morning Caterina regained consciousness once more, and he brought a priest to see her so that the rough, half-educated, rather pungent, but kindly man could sing the mass for her, and she was a little comforted. She thanked him with all her heart, though she had not understood a word of the archaic Greek Orthodox service. She wished she had a coin to give him for his trouble, but in truth it would have rather upset him for he took his ministry quite seriously: a gift to the church would be one thing, outright payment for the proper ministry of the sacrament would be quite another, and any money should tactfully change hands for some other suitable reason. He blessed Caterina and gave her the crucifix to kiss, remarking to Alexandros that he was right to have called him.

After he had gone, it occurred to her that Alexandros must believe that she was dying. Strangely, the thought did not trouble her. The mists were once more gathering at the edges of her mind, and it seemed that she again heard the voice of her little Bedros, her beloved Pietro. *"Mairig,"* he called, very softly.

She could see him now. He was proudly wearing the ornate Armenian costume which Artin Boghos had given him for his third birthday, and which he had put on at every opportunity. He held his hands out to her, smiling, asking to be lifted for an embrace. Filled with joy, she reached toward him but she could not quite touch him. The mists closed in, and she slipped once more into sleep.

Eliana tended her with the greatest care. She washed and turned her, massaging and oiling her elbows and feet, and watching closely for the darkened patches which heralded the beginning of the sores which had afflicted her grandfather in his last, bedridden days. In her dreaming, Caterina felt her gentle concern, and was reassured.

She could hear the deeper tone of men's voices among the whispered conversations which were taking place around her, but she could not see. She was very tired, and it was too much effort to turn her head. Far away, Bedros was calling to her.

She looked for him, her open eyes seeing beyond the room where she lay. In the cloudy, indistinct distance, Yeramia was walking slowly towards her, carrying the small boy on his shoulder. *"Mairig!* Why are you sleeping?" he said, smiling, and he set Bedros down so that he could run to her, but the child stopped just beyond her reach. Again he held his little hands out to her, and behind him Yeremia stood waiting. How very fine he was! All her children were beautiful, she thought, and she yearned towards these two with painful need.

She stretched her arms towards them, reaching for them with an almost unbearable love and delight, and suddenly she was free to embrace them, and to run with them towards a distant, welcoming light.

Eliana was watching Caterina with dread. Her eyes were open, fixed on something only she could see, and she was smiling. There was one last long sigh, and then nothing. Caterina's head fell a little to one side.

The girl started violently, as Alexandros touched her shoulder.

"The men are ready to row you across to the island as soon as you wish, so that you can take ship for home." he told her. He looked nervously at Caterina's still form.

Eliana closed Caterina's eyes and gently drew the blanket over her peaceful face. Strangely, she no longer feared for herself. She turned her head and spat at Alexandros' feet.

"She does not need you any more, you killer of women!" she said, contemptuously.

"My lady has already gone."

HERE BEGIN THE STORIES OF THE LIFETIME OF BOGHOS EFFENDI

Boghos Effendi was the seventh child of Artin Boghos and Caterina. He was a capable, immensely dignified and energetic man, which was fortunate because he became responsible for the future of the Eramian family after the deaths of the Heir and the Patriarch. He was titled Effendi and Bey, but not Agha, because the wide Eramian lands were now divided between several people, and the princely title of Agha requires the possession of great lands as well as great fortune.

Across the water the Terror grew under the rule of Sultan Abdul Hamid, and Boghos Effendi and his confreres in Nicosia quietly helped the Armenian resistance and aided those who managed to escape.

1884

Monkey and the Poet

ZAKAR AND GABIK were born in Turkey, in the years of the Terror before the real genocide began. The boys were milk-brothers, a tie as binding as that of twins, as strong as that of blood, and they were treated as true brothers. They were born on the same day, and when Zakar's mother found that she could not feed her little son, Gabik's mother happily suckled both of the babies, thereby prudently ensuring the future for her own child.

'Gabik' meant 'monkey.' He was baptised Andon Diran in the same ceremony as his brother, but he was a small, brown baby with a short body and long arms, and he had a comical, wizened little face with round, intelligent dark eyes. He was born with a full head of tight black curls and he resembled nothing so much as a curious baby monkey when he gazed at the world from his mother's arms. Everyone smiled when they saw him, and his nickname was given more from affection than mockery. He did not mind, he was used to the name by the time he found out what it meant, and he played up to it, becoming quick and light in his movements. He was a natural acrobat and clown who was never malicious or cruel in his practical jokes, and often these were made at his own expense to amuse others, because he preferred to find his pleasure in the laughter of his friends rather than in their discomfort.

Zakar was baptised Avedis Zakar, but while his mother accepted that it was proper for him to be given his grandfather's name, she liked to call him by his second name which had been her choice, and soon everyone followed suit. He was a sturdy, fair-skinned, healthy and intelligent child who shrugged off infant ailments and excelled at his lessons, and because he shared everything with Gabik, the deference and luxury which surrounded him did not make him unpleasantly proud. Of course, Gabik was educated with his brother, but he was easily bored in the classroom and learned only what pleased him, while Zakar delighted in knowledge for its own sake. He was intrigued by the subtleties of language and he particularly enjoyed books and other writings in Turkish, which has an almost unrivalled potential for sublime concepts and multiple meanings. It is a tongue which is often harsh when spoken but it is beautiful in verse.

Zakar began to compose poetry in both Turkish and Armenian, which is also capable of a beauty and subtlety which he found much harder to express using the too-exact structure of European tongues. By the time he was fifteen years old, he had published more than forty poems under his pen name 'Azad' and found himself acclaimed, and his poems eagerly awaited, discussed and complimented. He was rather shy about his work, and only his printer, his family and Gabik knew the identity of Azad the poet.

As he grew into young manhood Zakar became very devout, and two of his poems for Easter, *The Gardener of Souls* and *Shadow of Love*, brought a deluge of most gratifying praise from the literary critics. His family were therefore not greatly surprised when he announced on his twentieth birthday that he had found his vocation and wished to take vows of poverty, chastity and obedience in order to become a monk. There was now a younger brother to succeed to the family fortune, and there was no urgent reason for Zakar to marry and to produce an heir for his father, and so, having tried fruitlessly to shake his resolve, his parents reluctantly gave their consent.

While his foster-brother prepared to enter the monastery, Gabik

1884 Monkey and the Poet

examined his conscience and found his piety wanting. "I'm just not holy enough," he explained, "I'm sure you'll make a very good monk, most excellent of brothers, and that the life will make you happy and contented, but it's not for me. I'd be living a lie, and it really would be best if I stay outside the walls and look after my old mother, and thereby obey at least one of the Commandments."

It was hard to be parted from his dearest friend and childhood companion, but Zakar understood Gabik's decision, and though he was renouncing the world with joy, and he was glad to dedicate his life to prayer and service, he could not expect another to do the same without a true vocation. He asked his father to give Gabik a small farm which the family owned.

This prosperous little estate was in the mountains within sound of the monastery bell, so that at least the boys would be near each other, and it was to this peaceful place, four years later, that Gabik had brought Zakar after the night of the murders.

The monastery in which Zakar lived for those four years was under the protection of the local mosque, whose Imam was a friend of the Abbot, but even this pious and unworldly priest had many contacts outside the walls, and when he was told that the Sultan had turned his attention once again to the Armenians of the area, he feared for the safety of Zakar's father, who was another old friend. His wealth and social standing ensured that he would be in great danger, and he should be warned as soon as possible. The Abbot called Zakar to his office, explained his fears, gave him a dispensation to leave the monastery, provided a fast mount, and told him to ride to his family's town house to persuade them to leave as soon as they could.

Zakar rode with dangerous unconcern for himself or his mule, but he was still too late. The house was open and looted, the servants and survivors long gone, and only the dead were left.

The Abbot had also notified Gabik, who had been leading a quite different and far more dangerous life during the four years of their separation. He followed his brother to the town and arrived just a little afterwards. He found Zakar crouching outside his mother's bedroom, frozen with shock, shaking, and unable to move of his own volition, and so he brought him back to the little farmhouse at the foot of the mountains, and he left his brother's side only to return to the house with some men to give his foster family a decent burial at the end of the big garden, out of sight of the house. He had the mound disguised with rocks and boulders so that it looked as if it were part of the grounds, just in case anyone came there and wondered what had been buried.

It seemed that Zakar's mind had retreated from a world which held such evil. He could not eat, and he feared sleep. He was unable to swallow even one mouthful of food, and the sight and smell of any kind of meat brought on a violent fit of sickness.

At night he twisted and turned in his unfamiliar bed at Gabik's little house. He was deep in an exhausted sleep and he was dreaming, but he was horribly aware that he *was* asleep and he also knew that he was dreaming, and now he was terrified because he could not wake and he knew what awaited him. He had endured this torment every night since the murders, and it was slowly and inexorably killing him.

In the dream he stood on the broad sweep of the marble stairs which led up to the main entrance of his family's home, and he gazed up at the familiar front of the house. Moonlight poured from above the trees, a clear, bright light which showed stone benches, balconies, the delicate filigree of railings and the curves of lintel and columns, each sharply outlined in indigo and silver while the deep blue of shadows gathered behind ruined shutters and broken glass. In the stillness, there was movement only in the blank spaces of windows where torn curtains fluttered and swayed in the blackness behind the empty frames.

He went up the steps and walked past the huge and shattered doors which hung tilted on their broken hinges. The great chandelier was gone, there were no rugs on the black and white tiled floor, and no silver was displayed on the smashed slabs of the marble table in the hall where once his mother's morning callers had left cards and invitations.

1884 *Monkey and the Poet*

The polished oak panelled walls were splintered and bare of pictures. He moved across the chequered floor, and now he could hear a strange and unpleasant humming, low, but growing louder as he went towards the passageway at the far end of the hall where all was dim and shadowy. The nightmare moved implacably onwards, drawing him towards the plain wooden door which led to the kitchens and pantry.

This was his home, where he had lived and played as a child. He and Gabik and his little brother and sister were born in this house and he knew and loved every inch of it, but now it was terrifying, alien and horrible. It threatened some unbearable revelation, something which he could not endure to remember, a thing too awful to recall. He opened the kitchen door and hesitated. Some nights he almost managed to wake at this point, but tonight the memory was water in his hand, and the dream moved on without pause.

He went towards the louvered shutters at the tall windows and he threw them open, letting moonlight flood into the large, white-tiled kitchen. There was a stench of decay and corruption here, thick and sickening in the still, hot air of this summer evening. He breathed shallowly but could not avoid the suffocating smell.

Fearfully, he opened the pantry door.

The droning increased to a sullen crescendo, and a foul black cloud lifted from the shelves, boiling upwards and rushing past him. Thousands of flies flew into his hair and face, clustering at his eyes and lips and he put his head down, brushing the disgusting things away from his mouth and nose. He spat them out, revolted and sickened, until at last most of them were gone, then he opened his eyes and saw what was on the shelves. Strength left him and he sank to his knees.

He had found the men of his family.

Thick trails of blood had run from the bodies, and he was kneeling in a foul, sticky pool. The boys were lying on the stone shelves and the others were sitting on the floor, placed between the bottles and jars in the pantry. His father was closest to him, his broken spectacles placed neatly on his nose in a parody of normality, but normality was long past. Flies moved in his hair and his eyes were open, filmed and strange, staring blankly at his son through the starred glass in the bent frames.

Uncle Tomas was next, his mouth a bloody gash under his thick, black moustache, his teeth jagged and smashed and his tongue protruding from between blackened lips. Zakar wrenched his gaze away and found his little brother Aharon on the shelf above, the small, white, bloodless face still at last, his eyes half-closed and his mouth half-smiling. Beside the boy were his uncle's two sons, Etmon and Mateos, their dark curls matted and clotted with blood, their smooth young faces cut and bruised and their sweet voices silenced for ever, nevermore to sing in the choir or tease their solemn cousin into laughter, never again to cajole the gift of a coin to buy some wished-for treat.

Zakar groaned aloud in his anguish. He had arrived too late to warn them and to persuade them to leave, and he was too late even to die with them.

The nightmare had not yet finished with him and the dream moved on. He was compelled to rise from his knees and walk unsteadily through the kitchen to the back stairs by the servants' hall. He went slowly up two flights, looking in each of the ransacked, looted rooms, unable to halt his progress and dreading what he might find.

The thing he most feared was waiting in his mother's bedroom. No son should see his mother this way. Frantically, he dragged a curtain from the window and threw it over her body, pulling part of it across the maid who had died next to her mistress. Still there was more. Turning away, he glanced down beside the bed. There was a small, naked foot showing under the coverlet, but his mind at first refused to accept it, and he stood frozen in shock and denial.

No! Not Mariam. He would not look. *He would not!*

The dream was relentless. Slowly he knelt, reaching towards the child who was half-hidden under the bed. He touched her. She was real. With a final mighty effort he lifted his head away and screamed till his throat was raw.

Gabik ran into the room and shook him awake, lifting him from the pillows and holding him tightly till he ceased struggling.

"The same dream?" he asked, softly.

"Yes. But this time you woke me before I saw Mariam." Zakar slowly rubbed his hands over his face, and stretched his cramped limbs. "I'm going mad! This is happening to me every night, Gabik. I can't stop it until you wake me, and it's always the same. I can't change the way it goes and I can't wake up. It's unbearable to relive that night! I can feel my mind unravelling, slipping away, it's as if I'm thinking thoughts which aren't mine, and I can't bear to sleep any more, to know that I'm going back night after night to … that."

His brother could find no words of comfort for such a grief and terror. Their lives had been very different in the last four years. Zakar had no idea that Gabik was high in the councils of the Brotherhood and that in the course of his duties he had seen a great deal of the suffering of others and had done some bloody and unregretted deeds himself. This did not make it easier to deal with Zakar's tragedy and the horror of the bodies in the family house, and it did not make any of it easier to bear. It was too close to his heart.

Gabik had wished many times since that night that he had thought to delay his brother and he bitterly regretted that he had allowed him to go there first. Aware that Zakar was the true son of the family and that his arguments would therefore carry more weight, Gabik had let him go first, and had followed a little later, intending to add his own pleas for them to leave.

If only and *too late.* The most tragic of words in any language.

Zakar was pale and drawn and there was a yellowish hue to his skin. He had thrown off the coverlet, and his ribs stood out clearly. He was very weak. He could not eat even a plain crust of bread because of the constant nausea induced by these unbearable dreams, and so he was slowly dying of hunger.

Gabik knew what he would do if this were one of his men, but this was his brother, and he hesitated. Nevertheless, it was necessary. He had news to pass on today which he could not delay: Zakar would surely hear this information eventually, and it was better that he should be told by his brother. And it was part of his plan.

"Zakar."

Instinctively, Zakar knew that something very bad was to come. He groaned again, softly. Whatever it was, however, it must surely be nothing compared with the things he had already endured. "Tell me," he said, almost inaudibly, and turned his head into the coarse white pillow.

Steeling himself against pity, Gabik began. "I sent some men to the town to make the house secure and board up the windows, but when they arrived they found that everything had already been done and that it was even furnished and occupied. They also found that your house was the first one in the Armenian quarter to be attacked. It was a warning which people could not ignore, and it finally persuaded many of them that the threat was real and immediate. Some have already left, and there are more going every day. People in the town are saying that the new owner had your father and your family killed to secure it for himself before the Sultan's men arrive. They say that he did not want to take the chance of losing such a prize to a more influential Bey. He is a powerful man, and he knows that he will never be convicted of any crime against the Giavour...."

"What are you saying? *Who is he?*"

"It's Askeroglu. He doesn't know you're alive, of course."

"Askeroglu? He has no reason to hate us!" Incredulity and anger grew in Zakar as he understood what Gabik was telling him. With an effort, he sat up. "You mean, this vile thing was done just to steal a house for that gross, evil man? He set his monsters loose on children, and sent his murderers to kill women and servants, just to take our *house*? Dear God, he could have had it for the asking if he'd waited just one more week. We would have gone by then, he could have just walked in. He wouldn't have had to kill anyone, he could have just *walked in!*"

Gabik held his tongue while Zakar stared at him in disbelief. Then, knowing exactly what he was doing, Gabik poured oil on the flames. This would be the way to keep his brother alive, and he would do anything to that end.

"Maybe he did it for the pleasure of it."

Zakar stared at him. "For *pleasure?*"

"You know his reputation." Gabik watched as his words had the desired effect and the love and remorse which had caused his brother to feel such self-destructive guilt were consumed and destroyed by new emotions: a burning hatred and an overwhelming need for revenge. He had given Zakar a reason for living. Momentarily he wondered if he had started something far greater than he had intended, but he watched Zakar reach for the tray of food which he had pushed aside earlier, and he was satisfied.

Gabik waited at his little farmhouse while his brother's new reason for living began to take effect, giving Zakar this time to himself. Zakar ate, slept at last without the terrible dreams, and slowly regained his strength. He shut himself in his room, thinking, and though his initial blaze of hatred had banked to a more manageable level, he was unshakeably resolved to exact full revenge.

First he intended to blacken Askeroglu's reputation, then he would destroy his wealth, and finally he would kill him.

He wrote several letters in Armenian and English, and he sent some sheets of verse in Turkish to an Armenian printer in Izmir who owed his father several personal favours. Gabik's men followed up some interesting rumours which had been circulating about Askeroglu recently, and he wrote more letters after they reported their findings to him. He summoned some of his father's men who had been forcibly retired when Askeroglu replaced them with his own employees, and he sent them to an encampment in the forest at the foot of the nearby mountains. Here they were met by the Brotherhood who would hide them after Zakar's revenge, which would not be long in the planning.

In Constantinople and Izmir, and a little later in the town, verses by the well-known poet Azad appeared on printed sheets of paper which were pasted on hundreds of trees and posts, and which fluttered on doors and walls. They made fun of Askeroglu and his vulgar manners, and they discussed his allegedly extraordinary and revolting personal habits and his pretensions to gentility in the most hilarious and quotable way, and soon the poems were repeated everywhere and he was called 'nose-picker' and 'Eshekoglu' behind his back.

The discomforted Bey put up a reward for information leading to the capture of this troublesome poet Azad, and looked forward with pleasure to several interesting things he would like to do to him, but no one came forward to claim the very substantial amount of money he had offered.

The next set of verses implied that Askeroglu was addicted to unnatural practices and that he was seen behaving in some very unusual and inventive ways with a particularly alluring she-goat. The goat's name was the same as that of the Governor's wife. The Governor barely survived an attack of apoplexy when he read this scurrilous poem and he doubled Askeroglu's reward, but he could not stop the laughter. Relations between the Bey and the Governor deteriorated to frosty politeness and then to outright hositility.

The third poem was timed to coincide with a visit of the Sultan's auditors. It accurately detailed Askeroglu's embezzlement of government funds which were originally allocated for the building of new roads, and it provided evidence of the Governor's collusion in the crime. It went on to suggest several entertaining and physically impossible ways in which they may have spent their ill-gotten gains together. The poem was viciously funny, and easily memorised. Within hours of its appearance, it was being quoted, enjoyed and discussed in every salon and coffee-shop, and there was much speculation as to Askeroglu's probable fate and the identity of Azad.

The Sultan's auditors did not think it was particularly amusing, but they noted the interesting and useful information and the Bey found himself obliged to offer substantial bribes in every direction to head off a threatened inquiry, an impeachment, and his speedy removal to the capital for probable execution. This cost him far more money than he had readily available, and he was forced to sell much of his land and even some of his more prized possessions at a bargain price in order to raise the funds. He was consumed with anger and swore to kill Azad. He became even more enraged when threats and money were still unable to find the poet or even the printer, and he fantasized longingly about handing this man over to his retainers for their pleasure and his own amusement. He redoubled the efforts to find him.

Zakar was now ready for his next plan of action. He chose the night after the full moon, that same phase of the moon which had cast a clear light on the house when the murderers paid their visit.

A dozen of the Brotherhood and the same number of Zakar's men spread out in the garden, moving quietly around the outside of the house and keeping to the shadows, while Zakar and Gabik followed the wide driveway to the double sweep of steps which led up to the entrance of the house. The great doors had been hung once again on their hinges and their wood was fresh with paint. The broken glass on the paving stones was cleared away and the windows were glazed, new curtains were arranged in elegant swags and folds behind them, and lamps glowed in several of the upstairs rooms. Askeroglu had wasted no time in setting his new property to rights.

There was no one on guard. Why should anyone set a watch when they thought that all the family were dead and there was no one left to avenge them?

Gabik led his brother to the mound at the end of the garden where he had buried the dead, and they stood by the makeshift grave with heads bowed. Zakar knew the words which blessed the departed and committed them to God's care, but with his heart full of hatred and a cold anger, he could find nothing to say over the bodies of his family, and he added the loss of his faith and his vocation to Askeroglu's account.

He knelt and placed his hand flat against the earth, which still held some warmth from the heat of the day. He was remembering the small things, the little things which bring a whole person to instant memory, the touch of his father's moustache on his cheek when they embraced in greeting, the delicate scent of roses in his mother's perfume, and the insistent tug on his sleeve when his little brother asked to be lifted up and swung around. He solemnly vowed that their murderer would never enjoy his stolen home.

Abruptly, he stood. It was time for the next part of his plan. "Where are the servants?" he asked, "They should leave now...."

"None of our own people have stayed in his service to work for *him*," Gabik told him. "Not only the Giavour left, even the Turks went, too. Anyone now in the house is newly hired and well aware of what he has done."

"And so they condone it." Zakar walked through the ghostly, moonlit garden towards the house. He was tempted to let them take the consequences of their expediency, but even after the murder of his family he was as yet still constrained by his innate humanity, and he could not kill an innocent man for another's crime. After a moment of hesitation, he gave instructions to Gabik and his men to leave no one inside, and to bring everyone out.

At the north side was a small portico below a window, behind which was the second of two staircases leading to the first floor bedrooms. Gabik gave a low call to let the men know that he was going into the house, and Zakar gave him a shoulder up to the balcony. A few moments later he was through the window and the bars were lifted behind the front entrance. The armed men quietly moved inside. They worked quickly and silently, and fifteen minutes later they were gathered in the garden once again while Zakar counted them off and confirmed that all had completed their tasks. They had found six house-servants, and these were bound and gagged and set down on the upper lawn till they could be released later.

Zakar went back inside with Gabik to do the final tasks and check that the three other outside doors were secured, then he came out and closed the heavy double doors at the front, locking them with his own keys. He did not think that anyone would come to investigate, but he and Gabik waited just outside the porch with loaded pistols to prevent any attempt to interfere. Throughout the house flames suddenly blossomed, scarlet and yellow flowers of revenge.

Thick black smoke billowed through corridors and crept under closed doors, and the fire spread quickly, scented with cedar and oak and pine, and fed with wooden staircases and floors, shelves and panelling and beams. The crackle of its progress quickly increased to a roar, and at last there was the crash of falling timbers.

The brothers stepped back from the porch and stood shoulder to shoulder, looking up at the burning mansion, at the destruction of their home. They were turning to leave when a window on the first floor shattered and a chair crashed through it, going over the balcony and splintering to pieces on the stone walkway below.

Someone was at the opening. A man was trying to clamber on to the frame, but he was too fat to haul himself up and he hung there, outlined against the fire, his nightshirt in flames and his hair on fire. He was screaming in his agony, a dreadful high-pitched noise which cut through the sounds of the flames.

"That man should not have been in there," Zakar was shouting with horror. *"How did they miss him?"*

"No harm done. It's only Askeroglu." Gabik was completely calm. He did not take his gaze from the window. He watched the tortured man twisting and struggling while he burned, and he smiled a cold and satisfied smile.

Zakar stared at him in the bright moonlight. This stranger was his brother Gabik!

The Bey went on screaming.

Zakar could not let even his hated enemy continue in such torment, even though he was the loathsome murderer whom he had planned so carefully to destroy. He cocked his pistol and levelled it at the man he had vowed to kill, but before he could squeeze the trigger, his brother roughly pushed the gun aside and fired his own shot.

The burning man clutched his throat, fell backwards and was gone.

"Why did you do that?" Zakar yelled.

"I could not let you be a killer." Gabik still looked perfectly calm, and he was still smiling. He put his arm around Zakar and turned him away from the blazing mansion. "You have the right to burn your own house if you wish, but you should not let another man make you a murderer. I, on the other hand, am not a monk, and I have taken no vows."

An awful thought came to Zakar. Gabik had been in charge of clearing the house of its occupants. Had he known that the Bey was still inside? He stared at him as if he had never seen him before.

Gabik was his brother. He could not ask him such a dreadful thing, if he was wrong it would be unforgivable. But if he did not, he would always wonder if he was capable of deciding in cold blood to burn a man alive.

He could not ask him.

He carefully unloaded the pistol and went into the garden to oversee the freeing of their prisoners.

There was now a constraint between the brothers. It saddened them both, but Gabik offered no comment on the night's work, and Zakar still could not ask him.

Askeroglu was dead, and the hatred which had driven him on to vengeance was assuaged. In its place was an empty space, and he had nothing to left to do.

He was left with no ambitions, no aims, and nothing to live for. Worst of all was his loss of faith in the loving and merciful God who had been the heart of his life. He had seen too much and learned too much of evil, and he could never again return to the peaceful and contemplative routines of the monastery. Neither could he stay in Turkey: it would not be too long before the identity of Azad became known. He had no one but Gabik here and things could never be quite as before, now that there was a secret between them.

If his brother had deliberately left Askeroglu inside the house he had acted against Zakar's wishes. Although he intended to kill the Bey he would never have left him there to burn had he known that he was inside the house. The Bey would have died eventually, but not in such a way. Also, he was too aware of Gabik's overt pleasure in the act, seen clearly in the moonlight as he fired the pistol that night. Zakar had come to realise that he did not know him as well as he had thought. Their four years apart had changed them both, perhaps too much.

Reluctantly, he decided that it was best that he not only leave the city but also the country, and after some thought he chose to go to Cyprus. He sold the rest of his family's holdings and gave a handsome amount to Gabik so that he and his foster mother should never be in need.

At the harbour, the brothers embraced, and for a moment all was as it had been before, but Zakar left Turkey with no regrets, considerable relief, and the resolve that he would never set foot there again.

The funds he had raised from the sale of his family's lands were not enough to allow him to live as he had before he took his vows, but they provided a good enough income to live well, and Zakar bought a small vineyard in the mountains, where he grew very good grapes and built a small house. No one in Cyprus knew that he was once a monk, and the abbot and brothers of his monastery in Turkey were all gone when he made enquiries. The friendly imam had not been able to protect them from the Terror and they were either dead or deported in the atrocities which were still taking place there, so there was no real need to address this problem as yet, and he grew used to his quiet life alone.

The Armenian community welcomed him. He was obviously a gentleman and his reticence about his past served only to make him more interesting. They tried to bring him into the social life of Nicosia where he had taken a small town house for the winter, and though at first he used the excuse of his mourning period to avoid these, eventually he began to accept some of the invitations extended to him and he went to an occasional party or dinner.

At the house of Virab Effendi he met Nazli. She struck him at first as pleasant but unremarkable, and if anyone had to choose a word to describe her, it would have been 'sensible'. Her eyes were hazel, rather than dramatically dark and her hair was a pretty brown, not glossy and black like her sister's. She wore it loosely plaited into a thick braid at home, and arranged two braids like a crown around her head when she was formally dressed. Her clothes were neat and plain, and she had a soft voice and a reticent manner which led most people to underestimate her. This suited her very well.

As time went on, he began to see more of her. Her sister was the more beautiful of the two, but Nazli had no pretensions, no delicate sensibilities, and did not find it necessary to defer to his every opinion. She was a refreshing surprise, and he wanted to know her better.

This was quite easy, as he met her often here and there about the city, and at the concerts and parties which he had hitherto attended reluctantly, and which he suddenly found much more enticing. He liked her cheerful acceptance of things as they are, her pragmatic outlook and her enjoyment of the little, ordinary things of life. The great events of the years are naturally more dramatic, but they are rare occurrences, and the small pleasures of daily life are really what make it worth living. This insight led him to realise that he had not noticed such things since he had left the monastery.

He remembered that when he was a boy he had risen before first light to hear the wonderful song of awakening birds, and he did so again. He listened to the sound of rain on leaves and water, and walked with contentment among his vines under the bright blue sky. He breathed the unmistakeable, almost astringent scent of vine leaves, and the smell of water on the sun-baked earth as he walked in his sloping fields. He watched with satisfaction the results of his labour in the swelling of the grapes and he savoured the taste of his good wines. There was the peaceful sound of the wind in the branches of the pines on the mountainside above his house, the fierce beauty of an eagle circling lazily in the sky at midday, and the vast and majestic panorama of a million stars wheeling slowly above him on a moonless night. And there was Nazli.

For the first time since his family died, he wrote some poetry, and it was for her.

She read it and looked at him with sparkling eyes. "You're Azad, aren't you?" she asked.

He was astounded. "How did you know that?"

"Your poetry was sent here to Nicosia, and everyone read it and talked about it. I know your style, and now and then when we've been talking, you've sometimes used phrases I recognised. I remember that once you said that you dream in Armenian, but you have nightmares in Turkish, and I only thought that perhaps you had read Azad's work too and I meant to ask you about it. But now there's the beauty of this verse, and the fact that Azad has written nothing since you left Turkey. Dear Zakar, this poetry is wonderful – you put into words exactly how I feel about our mountains. I will treasure this for ever."

He was delighted with her intuition and was extraordinarily pleased by her praise, and now that the restraint on his creativity was gone, he found inspiration all around him, and especially in her.

Unused to the conventions of courtship because of his years spent shut away from the world in his monastery, he did not know how to proceed at first, but he found that she sought his company as often as he sought hers, and Nazli unselfconsciously let him see that she liked him very much. One day, he realised that he was contented, and that he had achieved a kind of happiness. At first he felt guilty that he could feel this way when it was such a short time since the murders, but on reflection, he did not think that his family would begrudge him some gladness in his life and he was thankful that he had chosen to come to Cyprus.

Then everything became complicated. One day, when they had gone to Zephyros beach for a picnic, Nazli's cousin gently teased him about the partiality he was showing for her. The cousin was smiling, but Zakar understood the purpose behind the remark and he realised that his fascination with this unusual and completely admirable girl had led him to seek her out a little too often, that this must surely have been noted by others also, and that he must now either declare his intentions or let her be. Unfortunately, he could do neither.

Boghos Effendi was Nazli's cousin. As the seventh child, and fourth son of Artin Boghos he had not expected that he would ever be required to shoulder the responsibilities of the Eramian patriarch, but his hero, his much loved oldest brother Yeremia died young, his second brother Virab was unable to continue in his duties while he fought the debilitating illness which it seemed may result in his death, and his next eldest brother Bedros had died in childhood.

Boghos was informed that the newcomer was becoming rather particular in his attentions to Nazli, and that someone must talk to him. His heart sank as he realised that it now fell to him to ask Zakar to declare his intentions towards his cousin.

Whether he wished it or not, Boghos was growing into his destiny. At forty-four years old, he was dignified and imposing at all times, never showing his chagrin at the duties which this unexpected honour required of him, and only confiding in his dear wife Yeghsabet that he rather regretted the loss of the freedoms enjoyed by a younger son. She was very surprised by this: she had always felt that he was by nature a little too reserved, but evidently he had been enjoying a full and colourful inner life of which she had been totally unaware. She suspected that the reality of these new responsibilities had put an end to the *possibility* of freedom, and that this was what he really missed.

1884 Monkey and the Poet

He summoned Zakar to spend an afternoon at Deftera in a week's time.

Zakar was no fool, and he realised that Boghos Effendi was about to stand in loco parentis for Nazli, and he did not know what to do or what to tell him.

He had taken vows and could not marry, but he found that he did want to marry, that he very much wanted to marry, and that Nazli was the one woman with whom he wanted to share his life. As he was forced to face these facts and to understand that he could not expect to find a happy conclusion to his problems, his new and fragile contentment was lost, and this second end of hope was almost too much to bear.

Meanwhile, Boghos had prudently made some enquiries before the meeting, so that he need not rely entirely on Zakar's replies, and he found that the young man was eminently eligible by family connection. He was also gratified to find that they shared a distant mutual ancestor, making him yet another cousin, and luckily too remote to be a forbidden suitor for Nazli.

As an added precaution, he went to Sourp Magar to interview some of the immigrants from Zakar's area of Turkey, and there he sat under an ancient plane tree at the monastery's farm and drank *zivania* with one of the Zeitouni farmers as he recounted the awful fate of Zakar's family and his tragic discovery of the murders. This explained the young man's somewhat straitened financial circumstances, but Boghos also heard that he was thought to be Azad, the poet who had destroyed Askeroglu's reputation before the Bey disappeared. He decided that Zakar had displayed admirable strength of character and ingenuity, and that these would be an asset to the family. Together with his acceptable ancestry, this would outweigh any reservations about his fortune, should Nazli's father decide to look favourably on his offer. The matter of his vows was another problem entirely.

Fortunately, he knew the Bishop well.

Unaware of Boghos Effendi's enquiries, Zakar was dreading the necessity of recounting the fate of his family. In the week before the meeting, he had a rare recurrence of the nightmare which had driven him to desperation before, and which once again made him too nauseated to eat. The nausea and hunger tormented him, he thought of Nazli as already lost to him, and he contemplated a future without her with despair. Since he could not listen to the birds or watch the stars without thinking of her, he did not listen or watch at all, and his days were a burden to him.

When he arrived for the meeting, Boghos greeted him affably and brought him out to Yeghsabet's rose arbour, her favourite place in the garden. Here, she had placed a rustic seat with a view of the pool and the distant mountains. He noted Zakar's pallor and sadness, and took pity on him, so he began by saying at once that he was prepared to help.

An hour later, Zakar's world was completely, astonishingly, and wonderfully changed. Boghos had even arranged for the Bishop to hear the renunciation of his vows and to release him from them if he truly wished. He had compassionately spared Zakar the necessity to go over the details of his family's murder by informing him immediately that he had already been told everything he needed to know, and that Zakar did not need to say anything more.

Zakar was overwhelmed by his reprieve, by the Effendi's kindness, and by the prospect of the new life that would now be possible for him. He could hardly speak his gratitude, but he tried to say that he owed a greater debt than he could ever repay.

Boghos waved his thanks away. As they walked from the garden to the courtyard where a groom waited with Zakar's horse, he felt that he could reasonably unbend a little. He nodded approvingly as Zakar took the reins. "That's a very nice, well-made beast," he said, "I'm glad to see you know your animals."

"Thank you, sir." Zakar was touched and surprised by this first purely conversational gambit from the rather stiff and forbidding man, who he suddenly realised would soon become his cousin by marriage. "My father loved horses, and he always took me with him to the sales when he intended to buy. Your own stables are famous, of course. I should like to see them one day, if I may."

Boghos surprised them both by patting Zakar on the back in a fatherly fashion. "Of course you may," he said, as they shook hands "and you should see the Bishop as soon as you can, after which you should go straight to Nazli's father to ask for her hand, my boy." He was vastly pleased with himself. Neither of them thought it was incongruous for him to call Zakar 'my boy', even though Boghos was not really old enough to belong to the previous generation, nor did it seem strange that Zakar called him 'sir'. He stood by the gate and watched the young man ride away.

There were some satisfactions in being the patriarch after all, he thought, as he returned to the house to tell Yesghsabet all about it.

In 1879, Cyprus was delivered from the jurisdiction of the Turks and it came under the protection of the British. It remained in name a Turkish province, but what the British once held, they would not easily let go.

At first the Greeks rejoiced, for they thought that at last they would have their freedom and union with their motherland, but this was premature. The British intended to stay. For the Greeks it was the end of hope for a very long time, but for the Eramian family this determination to remain in Cyprus was admirable, and they felt safer than at any time in the last hundred years.

Boghos Effendi became Head of the Treasury, which made him hugely powerful, and he entertained many eminent British visitors, and among these was Lord Kitchener, then Lieutenant Kitchener, who was sent to Cyprus to survey the island. The British liked to know exactly what they owned.

Young men of good family now had the opportunity to become commissioned officers in the British Army, and it was considered a commendable and character-forming career.

1885

The Hermit and the Hunter

MORNING COMES EARLY to the peaks of the Pentadaktylos, touching the tops of the trees with gold and creeping down the rough trunks of the tallest pines and the topmost slopes, to reach at last the foot hills of the mountains where it brightens a carpet of russet and yellow and brown.

There was a frost and a bitter wind in the night, but the hermit was snug and warm in his cave. He had narrowed the wide entrance with a wall of small tree trunks set deep in the soil, filled the gaps with closely woven boughs, and made a door from withies. He thatched these tightly with the harsh, tough grass which grew around the edges of the rills and seeps of clear, icy water which bubbled up her and there along the slopes. The tamped earth floor of his cave had coverings made of the cleaned and roughly tanned skins of *mouflon* and mountain goats, and his blanket was laid on a deep bed of sweet brackens.

He owned several thick pottery dishes and a wooden plate, cup and spoon which he kept on the rock shelf at the back of the cave, where he also had a small saw, a short-staved double-headed axe, and three long, narrow knives. The thin blades were deeply curved from years of honing with an oil stone.

His necessary stores were brought on his back from the nearest village, and were stacked on shelves in a home-made cupboard. A big jar of olive oil stood just inside it, beside two sacks of flour and one of beans, and a barrel of small sharp apples. On wooden pegs were hung bundles of dried peppers, herbs, roots, onions and dried fruit, and a good stock of dried and salted fish. He had two crocks of honey, a big pot of lard and a smaller barrel of olives, all of which he had prepared himself, and wrapped in sacking were several precious blocks of salt.

Once the snow set in he would be cut off for the winter, and he had prepared his home carefully for the cold, dark months. Beside the wall near the hearthstones at the front of the cave were stacked neat piles of kindling, short sticks, cut boughs and chopped logs, enough to last until spring. The summer had been a busy time, but now the weather was closing in and the days shortening, so that he went to sleep earlier and woke with the dawn.

Outside his cave was a pen and a sturdy chicken coop with a run to protect the silly fowl from predators, but his two cats and his dog slept with him in the cave during the winter. They were company, and they helped to keep him warm. They were safer inside, anyway. There were packs of wild dogs in the remoter parts of the mountains further to the north and they sometimes ranged nearer in the winter, hungry and dangerous, and hunting anything small enough or weak enough to be killed. The chickens would have to take their chances, though he did think that his handiwork would probably stand up to even the most determined assault.

When the sun's rays touched the front of his cave, he came out to say his morning prayers and to give praise for the new day. The big-boned clumsy red hound bounded out beside him and dashed off into the trees, while the cats followed more slowly, stiff-legged, placing their paws daintily, their rear views comical in their furry trousers and their tails curved inquisitively at the tips. They poked around in the leaves for a while, then disappeared after the hound.

1885   The Hermit and the Hunter

The hermit stood for a minute, watching them. He was old but hale, short and stocky, with big skilful hands and a shock of iron-grey hair. His eyes were a rich brown, surrounded by fine lines and set deep under their shaggy brows. He had a blade of a nose, which together with his usual cheerful expression gave him the look of a friendly eagle.

He folded his hands, knelt and bowed his head. Facing the splendour of the rising sun, he humbly gave thanks for the dawn, the sweet air, and the great bounty of God's creation, and he asked for a blessing on all the creatures of the mountain, and especially for the brothers at the monastery where he had spent much of his earlier life. During the day he would sometimes stop whatever he was doing and joyously praise his creator for something which had occurred to him while he was working, but he thought of his morning and evening devotions as the bracketing of his day.

He decided that he should take the opportunity of this sharp, clear morning to add a little more to his store of firewood. He gathered the tools he would need, wrapped them in a piece of rough cloth, which he would later use to carry the wood, and tied the bundle across his back, shifting it till it sat comfortably.

Whistling to the dog, which came noisily through the undergrowth to his side, he set off, eating an apple and a thick slice of pan bread as he went. The cats would look after themselves until his return, and the chickens had plenty of water and the freedom of the run, which he would move to a different location tomorrow. He began to sing one of King David's psalms in a strong, true baritone, and he did not at first notice the excited barking of his dog, ranging some distance ahead and off to the side of the track. He listened for a moment, then turned from the barely marked path into the patchy undergrowth between the trees.

"Bambo!" he called, "*Ela*, Bambo!"

The hound stopped yelping, and he could hear the big animal crashing about again, followed by the huffing noise that meant he was greeting someone with his usual affectionate enthusiasm. He was not a very clever dog, had proved completely useless for any purpose in farm or field, and the hermit had rescued him from a quick death by drowning. He was eminently suitable to be the owner of an inept dog which had been bred for killing, but which was more likely to lick any prey to death. The hermit was no good at killing things either, and so he no longer ate meat.

He could see Bambo's feathery tail waving enthusiastically above the bushes, and rounded the clump to find that his dog was happily washing the face of an unconscious or deeply sleeping boy. The lad had been able to cover himself with a great pile of leaves for the night, and only his head showed, where Bambo had cleared them away. He looked rather pale, but seemed to be breathing normally.

When he brushed off the rest of the leaves, he found that this was actually a young man, a little under middle height, dressed in a good woollen hunting jacket and cord breeches. Lying at his side was a very fine gun. He had a broad white brow below short-cropped dark hair, handsome, even features, and a soft young moustache. When he groaned and opened his eyes, the hermit saw that they were clear, dark, and rather mild. He did not look like a fearless hunter. The eyes were those of a mystic or poet, and his face was drawn with pain.

"Hello," the hermit said, smiling, "what happened to you?"

The young man tried to sit up, but fell back with a gasp of shock. "I think I've broken my ankle," he managed, through white lips, "and I can't begin to tell you how very glad I am to see you! I didn't expect to be found by anyone, this far from the nearest village."

"You're very lucky that my dog took your scent while you were underneath all those leaves. Bambo has a good nose, even if he is a useless hound and no asset at all to a hunter. God obviously has you in his care."

Bambo looked up when he heard his name, very pleased with himself. He licked the young man's face with a large pink tongue, and turned round once or twice in the leaves before lying down next to him with a gusty sigh.

The hermit knelt, pushed the dog gently away and took the injured youth's ankle in his big, work-roughened hands. He rolled back the thick woollen sock so that he could see the damage and he made a concerned noise as he saw the boy's leg. The ankle was very swollen, and was too constricted by the tightly- laced boot. There was ugly bruising at the top of the leather, which was cutting into the skin. "I think this boot should come off," he said.

He quickly untied the laces, drawing them out and carefully folding the leather away from the leg at both sides. He was as gentle as possible, but the lad stiffened and lay back in the leaves, biting his lip.

"This must hurt a great deal, but you're doing very well." the hermit told him encouragingly, as he gradually removed the boot. "You're very brave,"

"I wish I was," he said, and he clenched his hands and closed his eyes against the waves of pain.

Bambo pushed his wet nose under the nearest hand and gave a sympathetic whimper, which brought a gasping laugh and another attempt to sit up. He leaned back on his elbows and examined his rescuer. "What's your name?" he asked. "I can't just keep thinking of you as this mad animal's owner."

"My name is Yanni," said the hermit, "and the mad animal is Bambo." He put the sock and boot into his cloth roll with the tools. "Do you think you could hop on the other foot a short way? We're not too far from my home and I think you need some hot food and the warmth of a fire as soon as possible." The damaged foot had been icy to the touch, and he suspected that the rest of the lad was as badly chilled.

"My name is Ar ... er ... Ara, and I'm sure I'll manage with your help, but do you have anything to drink? I *am* very thirsty."

Yanni shook his head. "I'm glad to know you, Er ... Ara. And I'm very stupid, of course you must be thirsty, you've been here all night." He reached into his jacket pocket and brought out a small leather flask. "Only water, though."

"That's wonderful." Ara drank deeply. "Why does water always taste better up here?"

"Just one of God's mysteries," the hermit said, cheerfully. "Shall we go?"

Ara was astonished at the comfort of the cave, and the ingenuity of Yanni's arrangements. He sat by the open door, which folded back in two wings to let in the light and sunshine of the day. He had his back to the cave wall with his leg stretched out in front of him, while Yanni was frying eggs in a heavy black pan. He was feeling much better, though the pain still came in waves when he moved.

Bambo came in, too, circled him two or three times and again lay down next to him, giving another sigh of contentment.

"Shouldn't you really have a dog with you if you were out hunting?" Yanni enquired, mildly.

"Ah, well, I wasn't exactly hunting. It's just an excuse to be out on my own for a while." Ara's glance slid away from his host's measuring look, and he flushed visibly under his pale skin.

The old hermit thought that the boy must find it embarrassing to blush so obviously, particularly at his age, and he wondered what had caused it. Obviously all was not well with him.

He looked at the lad with the eyes of his intuition. He calmed his mind, recalled the events of the morning and let his subconscious supply him with the information ignored by his busier day-to-day thoughts. It was a talent which had at first served him well when he was still out in the world, but later it made him vulnerable to the grief and suffering of strangers, gave him the unwelcome reputation of a holy man, and overwhelmed him with the sorrows and mental anguish of those around him. Finally, together with his great sin, it made it impossible for him stay among his fellow men.

This time, he saw a boy in the well-grown body of a young man, a boy who was not strong enough to bear some heavy load, and who had gone hunting on his own, without food or drink, without a dog, and carrying a gun which had two cartridges in the breech and no extra ammunition. He looked at the gun. Ara had pushed it away from him and it lay among a drift of red and gold leaves which had blown in through the open door.

The boy followed his gaze and turned his face away.

Yanni took the eggs from the pan and put them on to his single wooden plate, adding a slab of pan-bread and a pinch of salt. He put these on his guest's lap and busied himself tidying and cleaning up, while Ara ate and recovered himself.

When he had finished, and cleaned his plate with the last of the bread, Yanni came and sat down next to him, beside the sleeping dog. Ara seemed better, with a little colour in his face, but the worrying, haunted look was still in his eyes.

"You couldn't do it, could you?" Yanni remarked, conversationally.

Ara started, but he could not move away, or escape Yanni's disturbing regard. He sighed, and realised there was no point in lying. "No," he said. "I couldn't. I suppose I'm just not brave enough."

The hermit shook his head "I don't think it's that. It doesn't mean you're a coward, just that a little part of you held on to the world." He paused, searching for the right words.

"No two people are the same," he went on, "Everyone is different: some people hear better than others, and some can see across to the far mountains. Others can bear physical pain which would make another want to die, and some people suffer too much pain of the spirit."

He paused, and looked directly into Ara's eyes. "And then it seems that everything is hopeless. The joy of life is gone, and only darkness lies ahead. Life is not worth living any more, and the only way out is to die."

Ara listened intently. "Yes," he said. "That is *exactly* how it is. You've felt this way, too, you must have, to know this. A great dark cloud swallows you up, and there's nothing good in life and absolutely no reason to go on with it. There's no way out, and it's unbearable."

Yanni's gift had given him an understanding and the ability to see another's spiritual distress, and though he had never experienced a despair the equal of Ara's, he did feel a deep sympathy with the desperate, unhappy lad. He had spent most of his life away from the world and this had limited his contact with others since then, but he knew he must try to help.

"I believe it *is* possible to live with it. You have to try to remember the important things, to try to hold on to them, even when they seem meaningless. Listen, *really* listen: everything passes. *Everything* passes! People who are suffering will either die, or they will recover. Pain will ease. Love will blossom or cool. Terror can give you courage if you take it and use it. Tears will dry and even the most painful of memories will one day begin to fade."

He took Ara's hand, and held his gaze. "If you dwell on your fears, you will endure twice the terror. If you worry about something you can't control, you suffer twice – once before it happens – and again afterwards ... and sometimes it doesn't happen at all! Everything in life will change you in some way or another, and you will only grow stronger if you can take whatever you are given and make it yours."

"It isn't an easy thing, though." he admitted honestly, thinking of his own great failure.

Ara was silent for a while, looking away from Yanni, out over the little clearing to the blue and silver depths of the far ranges.

"I'm the eldest son of my family," he said, eventually, "and my father expects more of me than my brothers. He has arranged a commission for me as an junior officer in the British Army, and he wants me to join the staff of his friend, Lord Kitchener." He clenched his fists. "It is the worst thing he could have chosen for me, but he won't listen. He's a strong and fearless man, and he can't see that I'm not like him. I wouldn't make a good soldier. I could never enjoy killing!"

"A man who enjoys killing would make a very bad soldier, I think," Yanni said, and he stood up, gently removing one of the cats, which had gone to sleep on his knees. "But it sounds to me as if you would make a very good officer, and an intelligent one. I will pray for you every day at dawn and dusk, here on the mountain, and hope that God will be kind to you and find a way for you to do your duty."

When he had made a rough bandage to help support Ara's ankle, which he believed was badly sprained but probably not broken, he and Bambo brought him slowly down the mountain to a *mandra* where he knew there should still be a villager with the goats. It was early autumn and the animals would not be brought in to the winter pens at the village for some while yet.

He handed the boy over to the men who came quickly to help, gave him his blessing, and went thoughtfully back to his cave, where he thanked God for allowing him to save a life. Perhaps He would set it against the record of his own sin, for which despite long prayer and meditation, he still could not repent.

Long ago he had helped someone he loved to escape great suffering because he could not resist her desperate pleas or bear to watch her long, slow death, and by his compassionate act he had damned his own immortal soul.

This was the teaching of the Church.

Every day Yanni knew the majesty of the mountains and sky, and the beauty of God's handiwork, and he saw too the smallest and humblest of His creatures, each of which was a unique and lovely miracle. He had come to believe that pain was a device to protect the body from further harm, not something to punish and torment it, and he could not think that the Creator of all this wonder was less compassionate than his humblest servant. He prayed that the Church was wrong.

He did not forget the young hunter. He hoped that he would grow strong and wise, and be spared such a choice as his.

As promised, he prayed for him at dawn and dusk every day until he died.

There were still places in Ottoman Turkey which were havens of good government under enlightened and humane Valis, and there were great cities where Giavour were present in very large numbers and in these, the oppressive and unfair laws were hardly ever enforced. The city of Boursa was one such place. There was a large Armenian community there, and they had their own churches and excellent schools, to which girls of good family were sent for their education. We do not know why Boghos Effendi's cousin Melikjan felt it necessary to become a judge when he was the Melikian Heir and he might have had a life of ease, but the family believes that he was a good man who did his best for his people.

1891

The Choosing of Elise

MELIKJAN WAS the eldest son of Hairabed Agha and his beautiful wife Hripsimé, the eldest daughter of Artin Boghos. He was one of the noble Melikians and a judge in Boursa, which was an exceedingly high position for an Armenian under the Ottoman Empire. He was Melikjan Melikian Agha, and he was a wise and gifted man whose judgements were recorded and cited in after days by teachers of law. Though he achieved his great office in Boursa, he was born in Cyprus, and he was the head of his family.

His brother Artin was born sixteen years after Melikjan, and he was most cherished and loved by his parents and his brother and sisters because he was an unexpected and late-born gift. They were very proud of the beautiful young child, and he was indeed an intelligent, talented and thoughtful boy, and he flourished in the love and attention that were lavished on him by his family, and now he was promising to be as eminent as his renowned elder brother.

Melikjan was living in Boursa when Artin was appointed Bey and was confirmed in his illustrious career, and there was only one important thing still remaining to be settled in his brother's life: at thirty-two years old, Artin was still unmarried. This was not because he was disinclined to take a wife, but it is forbidden in the Armenian church to marry within five degrees of relationship, and so he had the usual problem of young Armenians in Nicosia at that time: he could not choose among the several unmarried cousins of the right age, and his family would not approve a lesser connection among the artisan and immigrant families.

Melikjan was delighted with his brother's progress in Nicosia and he thought it was now time to find a suitable wife for him. There must surely be some eligible girls to choose from among the large Armenian community in Boursa, and he was considering this one day while returning on foot from the Court to his large and splendid house near the great mosque. His marriage to his own wife Vergine was arranged by his father, and she had come to him from an Armenian family who lived in Constantinople. She was a very striking woman, though rather wilful, and he was still much in love with her, even after some rather turbulent years of marriage. He was sorry that his dear brother Artin had not yet found someone with whom to share his life and start a family of his own, and he did not see why an arranged marriage should not work as well for Artin as it had for him.

His route to the Court took him past the school where many prominent Armenian families sent their children so that they could learn to speak and write the language of their distant motherland properly and as fluently as the Turkish they heard each day around them, and where they could learn the history of their ancestors and the practices of their religion. He enjoyed this pleasant walk each day along the broad and shady streets and he took his carriage only on days when it was raining, or when he was hurried.

He was passing below the high walls of this Armenian school, still

1891   The Choosing of Elise

thinking what to do about Artin, when the gates opened and a procession of uniformed schoolgirls filed out, two by two, to walk the short distance to the Orthodox church. They were quaintly demure in their grey, high-necked, long-sleeved dresses with plain white pinafore aprons, black knitted stockings and shiny button-boots, and he halted politely, pleased to watch them pass by. The smallest girls came first, carefully holding hands and vigilantly supervised by two teachers, and the older girls followed, carrying their gloves and bibles, keeping their eyes down and behaving like young ladies, as instructed.

All, that is, except for the last pair. They were perhaps fourteen or fifteen years old, their long, dark hair caught up with tortoiseshell combs and their heads together, sharing some confidence. As they passed him, the one nearest to him laughed, showing perfect, tiny teeth and a fetching dimple at the corner of her mouth. She saw him looking at her and her smile lingered a moment longer, as if she were sharing the joke with him.

He was astonished by her beauty. Her dark eyes were very fine, her skin was delicate and unblemished, and she carried herself like a queen. Her sweetly curved mouth with its suggestion of laughter was very appealing, while her determined chin gave an indication of a strength of character which made this otherwise too-perfect face more human. She was lovely. If her family were suitable and agreeable, she and Artin would make an extremely handsome couple.

Melikjan decided that he must find out who she was. As soon as he could, he visited the school and made an appointment to speak to the principal, a scholarly lady who was a little overwhelmed by this special guest. She had hoped that perhaps the judge was interested in the modern and ground-breaking curriculum which she had introduced, and which controversially included physics and chemistry, as well as the more traditional lessons for young ladies. She did not believe that a girl should be kept ignorant simply because she was female, and she sternly discouraged any instances of simpering, giggling and fluttering one's eyelashes. Only once in a while did she wonder that if perhaps she had been a little less learned she may not have discouraged her own suitors, but these heretical thoughts were firmly suppressed, and she often counted her blessings, which were many. Few women were as free as herself in this male-dominated region.

Melikjan explained that his family wished to find a suitable match for his brother, an eminent Armenian gentleman of Nicosia. He mentioned his brother's high post in the Government, and indicated that he was possessed of a respectable fortune. He described the girl he had seen, and asked for details of her family.

The principal concealed her disappointment and gave her full attention to the Judge's request. Of course she immediately understood the situation, and she knew at once whom he had seen. She looked at this impeccably dressed, imposing and courteous visitor and considered that Elise was very lucky to have attracted the great judge's attention if all his family were as well-bred and presentable. She knew Melikjan by reputation, and was delighted and flattered to find him not at all high-nosed and quite easy of address, and she willingly gave him all the information he needed.

She told him that the girl's name was Elise, that she was diligent, devout and intelligent, and that she did not put herself forward or behave in any unsuitable way. Her family was respectable, and they met the requirements for the ancestry of a girl who might marry a Melikian, but she had no experience of life in a great house or the management of the domestic affairs of an estate, and she was very young. Melikjan had slightly overestimated her age. She was only just thirteen years old.

He considered this no bar to making the arrangements. It was quite usual for a girl to marry and to live with her husband's parents until she was old enough to consummate the union, particularly if dynastic or financial liaisons were also involved, and his mother, Lady Hripsimé, would teach the young girl all she needed to know.

Next, he tactfully consulted other gentlemen regarding the family's position and reputation, and then he went to see Elise's father, a man he knew slightly and of whom he had heard nothing detrimental. All seemed very satisfactory. Pleased with the favourable information he had gathered, and the amenable reaction of the girl's father, he sent messengers to his mother and his brother to inform them that he had arranged a match for Artin.

He was sure that his brother would be delighted with the lovely Elise, and he was sure, too, that Elise would need to spend only a little time in the household to find out how kind and admirable his brother was. The wedding would take place as soon as his mother decided that the girl was old enough, and of course Artin would find it difficult to refuse an arrangement which his elder brother favoured, for as head of the family, Melikjan's decision was final.

No one consulted Elise.

Her father was delighted with Melikjan's proposal, and flattered to make a connection with such an influential family. He called Elise to his study and told her with the air of a man conferring a great favour, that she was to marry Artin Bey Melikian, a younger brother of the eminent judge Melikjan Agha, and that he was sending her far away to a foreign land to meet her prospective husband in the very near future. He passed her a photograph.

Numb with shock, she looked at the picture of Artin which Melikjan had given to her father, astonished that she had just been handed like a parcel to this slender, rather gentle-looking man, who seemed quite old to her. She was happy at the Armenian school and had many friends there, she loved her home and her life in Boursa and she did not want to leave. Elise was very innocent and still rather childish, and when she had thought about marriage at all, she assumed that she would marry someone from Boursa, and would be near her friends and her family. She had felt completely contented with her peaceful and predicable life, and this sudden, appalling news was too dreadful to contemplate.

She pleaded with him to let her stay a little longer, and not to send her away just yet. "Dearest papa," she began diffidently, twisting the silken folds of her pretty new dress between her hands, "could I not have a little more time?" The dress had been a surprise gift, and she would not have been so happy with it had she known that it was bought to assuage a little of her father's guilt at sending her away so young. "Please, papa? We have never met, he does not know me and I do not know him … and what if I do not quite like him? Or he does not like me?"

Her father thought of the advantages of this marriage and hardened his heart. "My dear Elise, how could he not be pleased with a pretty, dutiful and educated girl like you? And you will certainly respect and admire a young man of Artin Bey's fine address and intelligence." He avoided her eyes and fell back on his authority. "You must trust your father to know what is best for you. You will leave as agreed."

She was taken from school so that the arrangements for her splendid marriage could be made and she sadly said her farewells to her friends. She was measured for fashionable new clothes, and expensive little boots, gloves and hats. She had pretty new underwear of the finest cotton and silk, gored and smocked, and edged with delicate lace. She had dresses for daywear and evening, for walking, riding and attending the theatre. There were simpler chamber-gowns for wearing in her boudoir or at the family estate, together with fur-edged jackets and coats for the winter, and a magnificent ermine muff and matching hat. No one at her new home should say that she lacked anything.

She looked at the nightgowns with dread.

Elise knew very well that she had no redress and must obey her father, but she felt as if she were being cut loose from everything that gave her an identity and she feared that she could never again be sure of the future. She felt abandoned by those she had trusted and who had betrayed that trust, and she moved like some small pale ghost through all the activity. She had retreated from the events around her and was living in a kind of dream so that even the beloved old house where she had been born seemed suddenly strange to her, as if it were already fading into the past.

1891 The Choosing of Elise

Of necessity, Madame her mother had bitten back her immediate protest at losing her daughter so unexpectedly and so young and she had listened obediently to her husband's decision. He had complete power over the children she bore him, and there was nothing to be gained by futile resistance to the inevitable other than a great deal of unpleasantness. There were however, some things Elise should now know. The days flew by, and a week before the departure date, she went to her daughter's room.

She knocked softly on the bedroom door a little while after supper. Elise's maid had already left to go to her own hard bed in a small attic room in the servants' quarters, and her daughter came to the door herself. She looked very young and vulnerable with her long, soft brown hair loose around her shoulders, and her little bare feet showing at the hem of her white nightgown. She was mildly surprised to see her mother at this late hour, but in her present state of despair she had no curiosity.

She was taken into her mother's arms, and kissed and held lovingly. Her lack of response was not deliberate, but it hurt Madame sorely. She took her daughter's hands and drew her to the padded ottoman which was set at the foot of the curtained bed. They sat down side by side.

"Elise, I know how you are feeling." She felt the girl's slight withdrawal from her side, a negation more powerful than any protestation. "Oh, believe me, I do. I myself came to this house as a child, only a little older than you are now. My father was as pleased with my marriage as your father is with yours, and my parents sent me here, as deaf to my pleading as your Papa is to yours." She firmly put down a faint sense of disloyalty to her normally kind and indulgent husband, and went on resolutely.

"You never knew Papa's mother. She was a terrifying and autocratic lady. I do truly believe that if my dear parents had known what I was coming to, they would not have sent me quite as young as I was." She reached for a blanket from the bed and drew it around them both, holding Elise close with an arm around her shoulders.

"I was fourteen years old, and gently reared. I had never scrubbed a floor, nor even swept one, and I had no idea how to mend a stocking or what went into the making of a junket or the preparation of olives or preserves. I did not know that sunshine will fade a valuable carpet, or that salt poured on to spilt wine will help to prevent it from staining a lace tablecloth. The ordering of provisions for a household was a mystery to me, and I knew nothing of the prices of the things that were bought for the day to day running of the house. I could not keep accounts or arrange a large dinner party or ball, nor could I supervise a linen cupboard or manage the stores in a pantry. I knew how to order the servants to do things for me, but my ignorance of the actual performance of their duties was profound.

"When I arrived here, your grandmother told me to call her *Gesoor,* and made it quite clear that she considered me overindulged and spoilt, and that I was in need of considerable correction and schooling. Then she set about making sure that I got it. The first time she told me to sweep a floor, I held the broom awkwardly and wondered what to do with it. At length, I moved it around the floor a little and quickly returned it to the cupboard from which she had taken it. When *Gesoor* saw what I had done, she gave me a sharp rap on the shins with that same broom, and made me do it again properly. After this, she gave me a cloth and a bucket and told me to wash the floor.

"I waited till she had gone, and I threw the cloth down and stamped on it. Then I slipped secretly out of the house and I ran all the way home."

Elise was now completely absorbed in the story, and she had moved so that she could look at her very surprising mama. She couldn't help smiling at the account of her reaction to being made to swab a floor, but she was astonished that her competent, wonderful mother had ever been so ignorant, or so spoilt.

"Oh, *Mairig,* how unhappy you must have been!" she said, sympathetically.

Her mother hugged her again, glad that she was listening, and went on: "Our house was on the other side of town, but I was still crying with outrage and hurt pride when I got home, just before nightfall. I sat down and ordered my favourite dinner, which made me feel much better, and I waited for Papa to come home so that I could tell him that he had made a terrible mistake, that *Gesoor* was an ogre and a bully, and that I would not go back.

"My father was astonished and very angry at seeing me, and he asked me what had happened. When I told him, I could see that he was trying not to laugh, which made *me* very angry. He grasped me by the arm, marched me out of the house and took me all the way back to *Gesoor,* who received me with a look of deep satisfaction.

"There was no escape from my fate, and I am ashamed to tell you that I hated my dear Papa that night. However, I learned a great many things over the next year or two, until I knew what every servant does to make a house clean, warm, elegant and comfortable, and how to run it so smoothly that the master of the house is never bothered by anything concerning it, which is how it should be. Also, I was no longer capricious about meals, once I knew how much work went into preparing the delicacies I spurned. After this, *Gesoor* eased her iron grip, and we became friends.

"Dearest daughter, things will be very different for you! You must not be afraid of your *Gesoor*. The Lady Hripsimé could not be more kind and good-natured. She is called Dudu Kadin even by her servants, and she will be a wonderful *Gesoor* for you. She will welcome you with great affection, and I promise you that you will be happy there, and that one day you will be very glad to be her daughter.

"She is the chatelaine of a small palace in the city, and she must be sure that her daughter-in-law will be able to manage all of her responsibilities. We both know that you can do this, and that you would greatly enjoy it. *You* have not been indulged as I was, and the Lady Hripsimé will only have to show you the differences between the ordering of an establishment such as ours, and the more complex management of the palazzo and their house in the mountains."

Elise was a little comforted at this information, but there was still one thing about which she was completely ignorant. "Mairig, is it ... *frightening*, being married?"

She was so profoundly innocent that she did not even know how to ask about what she most feared.

Madame took her daughter's hands. "When I first came to this house, I was still a child, and I was married far too early to be a proper wife. Until I had my first sign that I was a woman, I slept in a small bed in *Gesoor's* room, and even after I would have been able to have a baby of my own, she kept me by her for a little longer until she was sure that I was old enough to bear a child without danger to both of us."

She paused and stroked her daughter's hair while she thought how best to reassure her. "As for the intimacy of marriage, your husband will not be a stranger to you, when the time comes for you to become his true wife and leave *Gesoor's* rooms to go to his bed. You will know him well by then, and he will be your dear companion, as your Papa is to me." She fervently wanted this to be true. Artin Bey seemed to be a gentle and kind man by all accounts of him, and she had every reason to believe that he would cherish and treasure her lovely Elise.

She put all the hope of her heart into this reassurance, so that her daughter should not be frightened of her new husband and lose the chance of having a loving partner. She wanted their marriage to be a delight to both of them. It would now be Lady Hripsimé's duty to enlighten Elise about the real intimacies of marriage.

She kissed her daughter and put her back to bed, smoothing the sheets and plumping the pillows with a little pat at each side, as she had done every night for each of her children after they moved from cot to bed. "My own dear girl, I will think of you every day, and send you this kiss, and when you look out at the moon and the stars, you will know that I see them too, and that I am thinking of you. I promise you, though, that a day *will* come when you will not need that comfort and then you will forget to do this, and will not think of me at all, caught up as you will surely be in your interesting new life."

She put her finger gently to her daughter's lips as she began an automatic denial, kissed her again, and left.

Elise closed her eyes. She was very tired. She had always known that one day she would have to leave her home and go to the house of her husband, but it had seemed so remote, so far in the future. She wondered if the Lady Hripsimé was as kind as everyone seemed to think.

She thought of her mother holding a broom, and moving it about because she did not know what to do with it. Smiling, she dozed a little, and finally she slipped into her first full night's sleep since she had been told of her great good fortune.

Artin Bey adored his lovely young wife. She was treated with love and respect, and she swiftly gained a reputation as a great beauty. Even today, so long after she died, if her name is mentioned people will say "Ah, yes, Elise was very beautiful, you know."

Having settled his brother's future, Melikjan returned his full attention to matters concerning the Armenian community in Boursa. At that time, relations between Turk and Giavour were cordial there, and his problems were mostly with his own people.

It is said that if two Armenians were to be marooned on a desert island, they would establish two different churches and three political parties. They are a disputatious, argumentative, intelligent, astute, but mostly good natured people, quite capable of being Devil's Advocate for the sheer pleasure of disagreeing creatively. A cousin of Boghos Effendi once memorably argued for both sides in a dispute about a business deal. He is reported to have won both times.

Possibly, even he might have held his tongue if he was brought before the wise Judge of Boursa.

1892

The Judge of Boursa

MELIKJAN HAD a distinguished career in Turkey before he returned to Cyprus to take up his duties as the Heir of his House. As well as his position as Judge for the Armenian community in Boursa, he was also the spokesman for his people in the courts and deliberations of their masters, and he had a reputation for honesty and wisdom in the execution of his high office.

One day, two men were brought before him with a dispute over a boundary, which had been going on for many years. The dispute had already been put before another judge of the court on one previous occasion and a decision had been given which awarded both of the men an equal amount of the land they claimed. Neither was satisfied, and after more arguments and bitter words, they brought the case to the Court once more, each hoping that he would gain more by a second hearing.

From his long experience, Melikjan felt that the judgement was probably fair since both men felt hard done by, but he carefully read the details of the case. After considering all the arguments presented to him, he found that he did indeed agree with his predecessor and he warned the two men that he believed the previous judgement to be correct.

Both of them protested loudly, and each still insisted that he was being deprived of land that was rightfully his and that the previous decision was in error, and that there was a miscarriage of justice, so our cousin told them that he would adjourn the case to give them time to take further thought. After this, he would ask them once more if they still wished him to try the matter again in the court.

Now, it was the custom in most parts of the Ottoman Empire to give discreet gifts to powerful officials and high officers of the government. These were not bribes, absolutely not – they were merely tokens of a great esteem and indicative of a deep and sincere respect for the person whom the donor wished to compliment. While it was known that Melikjan was not open to such persuasion, and that for many years he had regularly returned these presents, it was also known that he did not allow the fact that they *had* been sent to sway his true judgement either way. Each man felt that he might safely send at least a small token of his admiration to the great man.

The first plaintiff searched for the best and most delicious *loukoum* to be bought in the city and he packed the sweetmeats carefully in silver tissue and put them into a beautiful silver casket. The second man sent a large basket of the most perfect and ripest fruits of the season, the very finest he could find in all the bazaars and markets, and he sent with them a set of delicately engraved silver knives.

When the gifts arrived, each bearing the name of its donor – after all, the recipient must know who bears him such respect and admiration – Melikjan was exasperated.

The night before, he had attended a most agreeable soirée during which he had eaten rather too many rich pastries stuffed with cheese and spiced meats, and he had enjoyed several glasses of excellent red wine. He was normally quite abstemious, and today his stomach had rebelled against his breakfast rolls and coffee as a result, so that he was not in the best of humours. Consequently, he was more than usually displeased at this attempt to influence his judgement, and he began to wonder how he might prevent these bribes continuing, once and for all.

After thinking for some while, his glance fell on the unwelcome presents. He had left them on a small marble table beside his chair, and as he gazed at them, a solution came to mind. He smiled to himself and made certain arrangements.

The next day, he recalled the two men to the court.

He was dressed in his most splendid official uniform, with his sword and his fez, and as well as the usual court officers he was attended by four very large, very muscular guards, also in fine official uniforms thickly decorated with gold braid. They stood motionless behind his ornate chair with their muscular arms folded across their curved blades, and they were a stern and impressive statement of the court's power. The two men looked nervously at each other, and then at their gifts, each of which had been placed in front of the one who had sent it.

Melikjan watched them with an impassive face, and waited till they had begun to sweat a little.

Finally, he spoke. "I am most displeased that in all my years at this court I still have not been able to put a stop to the practice of sending gifts to me in the hope of swaying my judgement towards the donor's case. This custom is wrong, and it is bribery, no matter on how small a scale it is done. I have given this problem a great deal of thought, and I have remembered that there is in fact a very famous precedent regarding the return of unwelcome gifts." He frowned at them, and the two men shifted nervously. "I think this precedent might reasonably be applied to you. It is the case of Nasr ed Din Hodja and his birthday gift to the Vali."

The two men looked puzzled. "Nasr ed Din Hodja?" repeated the first man, blankly

"... and the Vali?" the second man asked.

The Agha's Children

The judge leaned back in his chair and said nothing, while the two men continued to look puzzled and worried.

One of the plaintiffs suddenly stared at his basket of fruit with an expression of horror.

"Have you remembered the example I mean?" Melkjan enquired, suppressing a smile.

"Lord, does it involve ... fruit?," the man asked, faintly.

"It does," confirmed the judge, still straight-faced.

In those days, everyone knew the Nasr ed Din Hodja stories. The man whispered hastily to his fellow.

"Do you think he would really do it?" the first man asked urgently, aghast at the information he had been given and looking uneasily at the four uniformed guards.

"Are you willing to take the risk?" the second man replied.

The two men stared at each other, then they turned as one to Melikjan and bowed very low. "We accept the first judgement," they said, and they left the court in great haste, with the laughter of the onlookers ringing in their ears.

"I thought you might," murmured our cousin, and he gave the fruit and the *loukoum* to the guards.

The citizens of a Vali's domain are well advised to keep on the right side of him. This is the story that persuaded the two men to drop their quarrel.

Nasr ed Din Hodja was a miser and a very wealthy man, but he claimed to be poor and did all he could to keep up this pretence. No one would steal from a man who had nothing, he reasoned, and no one would ask him for money, and so he wore old, patched clothes and rode an aged, bony donkey to maintain the image. Though he accepted the necessity of giving bribes to officials to ensure their promptness and co-operation, he resented the need to give away any of his precious gold and silver, and parting with even one coin pained him and made him miserable.

On the occasion of the Vali's birthday, all the notables of the city were expected to send a suitable gift to show their respect and their good wishes for the potentate's health, and these were to be presented at his palace on the morning of his special day. Nasr ed Din thought long and hard how he could give a suitable and acceptable gift without spending too much money, and after much deliberation he decided to take a basket and fill it with the biggest and sweetest figs from the trees in his garden. This of course, would cost him nothing, but he would certainly make sure that the Vali had the very best ones he could offer.

There was a queue outside the palace when the Hodja arrived, but he waited patiently and was soon the next in line to go in to pay his respects. All at once, even from his place outside the audience chamber, he could hear the Vali's voice raised in anger.

"What is this?" the Vali shouted *"Another* bowl of fruit? Is everyone under the impression that I am a donkey or a goat? Woe betide the next man who brings me *fruit*!" There was the crash of breaking crockery, followed by a yelp of pain, and the man who had gone in before him was hustled out, shaking and white with fear.

The Hodja began to tremble. It seemed that he had made a serious error of judgment but he could not turn back now because his name had been called. He gathered a little courage and went fearfully into the great hall, where the Vali was seated on his gilded throne on the marble dais, surrounded by his courtiers, and clad in silk and glittering jewels. Trying to control his terrified limbs, the Hodja bowed low and placed his basket of figs on the floor before the Vali.

There was a silence while the Hodja waited and the Governor stared at the figs. Gradually, he became red with anger and his neck swelled and his eyes bulged.

This time, however, he did not shout. He waved a couple of guards over to where Nasr ed Din was kneeling in deep humility, with his head still bowed. "Take this foolish man outside and return his figs to him, one at a time. Insert them into the place where they would normally leave ... and do the same to anyone else who brings me *fruit*!"

A few minutes later the Hodja walked with a little difficulty out of the palace, and as he left he noticed a good friend still waiting in the queue.

"I hope you haven't brought fruit," he warned, and then he began to laugh so hard that he had to lean on the wall.

"No, I haven't," his friend assured him, and noticing that Nasr ed Din was a little shaky on his feet, he asked him what had happened.

Wiping his eyes, the Hodja told him.

"But that's terrible!" the friend gasped, "I did not know you were so brave. You are a truly exceptional man to be able to laugh about it."

"It's not that," the Hodja said. "It's just that I saw my most detested neighbour about to go in after me. And he was carrying a *pineapple*!"

☞

In just a few years, oppression increased once more, this time involving even the largest cities. The humiliation and injustice became too much for some of the young Giavour to bear and in places there were rebellions and a refusal to submit to the worst of the abuses, but the response of the Ottomans was immediate and terrible, and the Terror was worse than before. The Ottoman government began to consider ways to rid their country completely of its troublesome and disturbingly large minorities.

Refugees began to arrive in Cyprus in ever-increasing numbers, and the Armenian community feared greatly for the safety of their friends and cousins on the mainland, and they tried to persuade them to leave. The monastery at Sourp Magar increased its accommodation for the new arrivals, employed as many as they could on the land, and cared for the women and children who arrived without families.

In Zeitoun, it was very bad.

1896

The Boy from Zeitoun

MIHRAN TROTTED carefully along the muddy track which wound around and down the flank of the mountain to the nearby town. It was just getting light and he kept his eyes on the ground ahead of him, avoiding the potholes and twisted roots that might trip him

He couldn't risk injury on this treacherous path, he had to stay fit and strong to look after his mother and little sister. They had only him to provide food and some money to get through the coming winter, and the winters were hard here, with long weeks of snow and bitter nights when water in the jug would freeze inside their small shack, and bedclothes would sometimes be stiff with frost in the morning.

He had placed a neat stack of chopped wood by the stone fireplace and brought fresh water from the nearby spring before he left, and he had set some of it to heat in their single iron pot so that his mother could make *zambucco* tea for Annik, when she woke. His little sister had a persistent cough, and drinking the tea and breathing the steam of the elder flower seemed to help her.

There was a whole loaf of bread in the cupboard, and a surprise for mama. Yesterday, the captain of soldiers had given him two pieces of *ekmek kataiffi*, and he had taken them home, carefully wrapped in a piece of newspaper. One for each of them. He smiled as he ran, thinking of their pleasure at finding the special treats waiting on the table for their breakfast.

Mihran's father had placed his mother and sister in his care when the world had gone mad and the soldiers had come to take him away. They had come for all the Armenian men and boys in the town, everyone over twelve years old, with no exceptions, but Mihran was only ten and they had left him with his mother. It was the beginning of the organised destruction of a nation.

He had seen his family's shop opened and looted by Turkish soldiers, all his father's stock stolen and their livelihood destroyed. Their neighbour's pretty daughter was kidnapped when the men took her father and his, and she had never returned. The next day some of the neighbours from their street forced their way in to his home to look for valuables, demanded his mother's jewellery and rings, and took anything else they wanted. Mihran had started to protest, but his mother wrapped him tightly in her arms, pinning his hands to his sides with a desperate strength so that the boy could not give them any reason to do him harm.

The world had suddenly become a dreadful, unpredictable, and terrifying place. They took the pots and pans from the kitchen, the pictures from the walls, the lace tablecloths and fine bed linen which had been his mother's trousseau, and the rugs and carpets from the floors. They took the chandelier with its lovely crystals, which his father had ordered specially from Italy, his mother's best clothes, and his sister's dolls, and they would have taken all of the furniture except that some of it was too heavy to move.

Some of them came back again the next day to look for more loot, pulling panels off the walls and tearing up floor boards in their search for treasures.

The Armenian families in this quarter of the town no longer had even the little protection which was previously afforded them by Turkish law, and it seemed that anyone could do whatever they pleased to them. When the news reached the nearby towns and villages that the men had gone and that only women and children were left, bands of young men began to come into the city to have a little fun. To begin with, they came at night, shamefaced, but later they grew bolder and could come at any time. Among the things they were looking for were girls.

There was now little left in their looted house to attract a thief, but his mother had hidden Annik anyway. She was only a child, but these men did not care about that. Soon they realised that it was now too dangerous to linger in their home any longer, and so they decided to follow Papa to the camp where he and the other men had been taken. Things were very bad there, and Mihran was sure that his clever father would have made his escape long ago if there had not been others who were too sick to leave with him. Some were ill and others injured, but the men of Zeitoun had kept together and put differences aside once they reached their destination, and so most had survived.

It had been a hard journey for Mihran, but even more so for his mother and his little sister. At first, they camped under the trees near the compound, but soon he began searching among the thick woods for a better place, knowing that they would need somewhere warmer when the summer had gone and the days grew shorter and colder.

He found an old and derelict cottage hidden in the denser woods on the opposite side of the mountain, high above the town where the soldiers had their barracks. The place was abandoned long ago and was nearly a ruin, with only one of the two rooms still standing complete with all its walls. The thatch which still covered the roof was mouldy and patchy, but the mud brick walls were thick and sturdy, and Mihran repaired the broken shutters as best he could so that the cold winds could not blow in.

He carefully fitted stones into the holes in the walls, and he cut and trimmed reeds from the river that flowed through the town at the foot of the mountain, and inexpertly but successfully repaired the thatch. Admittedly, there was still a small place in one corner where he had not been able to patch it well enough to stop a little water coming in, but the old box-bed was dry, and it was built above the floor level so that no draughts reached them while they slept.

Nearby, he found three round tree stumps which had been sawn, left to weather, and forgotten. He rolled them the little way to the house and set them by the fireplace, where they served perfectly as stools. He scraped and cleaned the old fire-dogs which he found hidden in the rubbish and leaves when he first cleared the cottage floor, and he proudly replaced them on the hearth. There was an old *fourno* oven in the overgrown garden, and he cleared out the rubbish which had blown inside it and searched in the tall grass to find the rusty iron door. He brought piles of fresh, ferny bracken for the bed and hung bunches of sweet herbs from the rafters. When he had finished and the fire was lit, it was cosy inside.

Mihran's mother was astounded at her clever son's ingenuity, and she was very very proud of him as the three of them stood outside this new home which he had made for them. She went inside, exclaiming over the fire-dogs and the raised box-bed, and she said that they would be snug and comfortable here. "You have thought of everything! Your father would be so proud of you, best of sons," she said, simply, and Mihran thought that his heart would break. He remembered the comfort and beauty of their home in Zeitun, and how his mother had cherished the lovely things it contained. Now she had one room in a ruined cottage, and only him to take care of her, and she was happy even with this.

A small patch of cleared ground behind the house still had mulberry bushes and fruit trees growing wild, and later Mihran begged cuttings and seed from houses in the town so that they had some beans and root vegetables to eat and to store. There were walnut and hazelnut trees further down the mountain, and the twisted old apple tree beside the shack bore so heavily that year that its branches touched the ground. His mother peeled, sliced and dried the fruit, hanging the rings in great strings from the rafters for the winter to come. There were mushrooms, blackberries, wild raspberries, rosehips and hawthorn. Mihran's mother used the leaves of the hawthorn in salads, and she made a cordial from the berries and the rosehips against winter coughs. Garlic and wild celery grew on the sheltered banks of the river and water cress grew in its shallows. They worked hard to find and preserve this bounty of the woods, and with a little care, they would manage nicely.

Their safety depended on secrecy, on keeping their makeshift home hidden from danger, and Mihran was careful to vary his approaches to the track which led to the village so that he trod no obvious pathway which might lead someone to their refuge.

On Friday each week, when he had no work, he would make the long trip over the mountain to the concentration camp, where the guards turned a blind eye to the thin, ragged child who stood pressed against the wire to have a few words with his father. All week, Mihran looked forward to seeing him. He clasped his father's fingers through the mesh, and he memorised exactly every word he said and how his father looked, so that he could tell his mother everything on his return and reassure her that he was well. When the guards waved him away, he would stay in the shelter of the trees to watch him just a little longer before turning to make the long journey back.

Meanwhile, he had to earn what money he could, and to see that his little family were cared for.

The townspeople and the Turkish army captain for whom he now worked saw only a skinny, smiling boy wearing old, patched and very clean clothes, always cheerful and eager to please, and they pitied him and were charitable, as the Prophet had commanded. They thought he was a Muslim, and a Turk, and they found him jobs to do, for which they occasionally gave him a coin, but more usually he came home with food or much appreciated cast-off clothing. With this and the produce from the garden which his mother tended, the little family fared very well.

The Agha's Children

Today, the sun had begun to cast long golden beams through the trees, and morning mist had gathered in the hollows by the time Mihran reached the Army camp. He stopped at the gate and solemnly saluted the soldier on guard.

The man returned his salute and smiled at him. "No hurry, *askerh*. The Captain isn't here yet. You've plenty of time to make the coffee!"

Mihran passed through the gate and quick-marched across the parade ground. He called in at the cookhouse and got some glowing charcoal which he carried to the office in a tin pail, and he set the thick, sweet Turkish coffee to brew so that it would be ready when the Captain arrived. He used a little of the coals to burn some fragrant, dried olive leaves to sweeten the air, then he swept the floor, emptied the ashtrays, and tidied the desk.

The boy had quickly made himself indispensable to the captain, who was a troubled man. He was not cruel by nature, and he was sometimes deeply disturbed by the things he had to do. He had not joined the army to be a hero, but certainly he had not joined to be an executioner either, and more and more frequently he had trouble sleeping. When he did sleep, bad dreams often woke him too soon.

It was pleasant to have a smiling face around the barracks, someone who anticipated his needs and cheerfully ran to get cigarettes or brought a *nargileh* from the officers' mess when he worked late, and who kept his papers tidy and his office clean. In fact, the captain had come to take his young servant's presence very much for granted, and he no longer bothered to lower his voice or make sure the door was closed when he had to deal with a sensitive matter.

And of course, Mihran tidied his official papers. Like most Armenian boys, he spoke Turkish fluently, with no accent, so that he could easily pass for a Turkish urchin down on his luck. At home he had first learned the thirty-eight letters of his own language, but he had also been taught the exquisite flowing lines of the old Turkish script which was still in use at that time. Naturally, the captain had no reason to think that a little beggar boy could read. In this way he sometimes gained important information, which he passed to his father on his weekly visits. It was surprising how much a man could do while locked in a prison camp.

Later that afternoon, Mihran was sitting on the ground outside the captain's office ostensibly repairing a broken bridle, but in fact he was watching everything that went on in the barracks.

An unfamiliar officer headed his way, a hard-faced man wearing a uniform with the insignia of a colonel. Mihran dropped the bridle and jumped to his feet, ducking his head and assuming an expression of awe. Quickly, he knocked on the captain's door and ushered the officer inside, bowing low. The door clicked as he pulled it to, but the lock did not engage properly, due to a little tinkering he had done quite early on in his employment. He sat down again, slightly closer to the door than before, and appeared to have fallen asleep in the sun.

The officer was talking about work details and plans to make new roads. Mihran went on listening, and what he overheard next made him want to leap to his feet and run. He should get up and go from here as fast as he could, he should race like the wind, and not stop till he reached his father.

But he must not. He *must* not. He must do nothing unusual.

His heart beat fast and sweat broke out on his forehead, but he bit his lip and forced himself to keep still, to breathe slowly and evenly like a child asleep.

When the officer had gone, he went to the cookhouse and prepared a glass of hot, sweet tea. He placed it on a round brass tray, laid a small spray of jasmine beside it, brought it to his captain and put it quietly on his table. He noticed that the ashtray was overflowing onto the desk, so he replaced it with a clean one. Then he left, taking the dirty ashtray with him. At no time did he give any indication that he knew of the terrible orders the captain had been given that day by the colonel.

It was hard, the hardest thing he had yet had to do, but he waited till the usual time before leaving, which he did with a smile and a wave to the guard. He sauntered along till he reached the cover of the trees.

Then he broke into a run, rushing headlong up the path, not looking where he was going. Branches whipped his face and scratched his legs, and he sobbed for breath with tears running down his cheeks, but he did not slow down, and when he reached his home he was unable to speak for a few minutes.

His mother made him sit and drink some water, and his little sister brought him a small piece of her sweet, which she had saved specially for him. It had been hard for her to keep some for him and not to eat it all, but she had managed it and now she wanted to see him enjoy it. She sat on the floor by his knee, put the little slice of *kataiffi* into his hand, and looked at him expectantly. She was only five years old, and she did not understand what was going on.

Still breathing hard, Mihran looked at the sweetmeat. It was just a sticky little piece of cake. He stared at it as it lay in the hollow of his grubby palm, and the treasure of his sister's loving sacrifice was suddenly too much for him.

He thought of all the little girls whose sweetness had died at Zeitoun and at Marash and Moush and Aintab, and he could not bear the grief. He was overcome with a sudden burning hatred and contempt for the weak and cowardly man who was going to take all this great mountain of evil and add his own contribution tomorrow.

Unless he could prevent it.

Annik was still watching him anxiously. He thanked her for her little gift and ate the sweet with very small bites so that she could see that he thought it was delicious. She watched till the last bite and then she went happily away to play with her straw doll.

He put his head in his hands.

All at once he realised that there could be a way to get to his father. In fact there *was* a way, but it was a very, very dangerous way. He could prevent it if he could get there in time, and if the captain delayed because of his reluctance to do this horrible thing, and if that delay was just long enough for Mihran to reach the camp before him.

1896 The Boy from Zeitoun

He needed his good boots.

Quickly, he explained to his mother. She paled, but said nothing and brought him the only pair of shoes he had. She had put them safely in the roof space, away from rats and mice. After months without shoes his feet were toughened and hard, and the soles were thickened, but he could not go barefoot tonight. He would need the protection of these stout leather boots, which had been a little too large when they were given to him with his other presents on his tenth birthday.

His heart constricted painfully. On his tenth birthday the world had still been a safe and wonderful place, and his family had been free and happy together.

"Every year you've grown so tall. Next year we'll buy you a horse of your own," his father had said, and Mihran had been very proud. He had thought it would be wonderful to be a man as tall and strong as his father.

On the day when the soldiers took him away, his father kissed him, hugged him, and told him that now he would be the man of the family, but he did not feel like a man yet, and if he could not run fast enough tonight he would not have a father.

He took the boots from his mother's hands and laced them on. He unhooked a skin of water from behind the door, and took a piece of the bread he had been so proud to bring home, then he kissed his mother and sister, and left.

His usual route over the mountain would not do; it did not go directly over the peak, and he would arrive at the camp long after dawn. That would be too late. He would have to go by *gehennem yol*, hell's path. He looked up at the sky, where there was still a little light to the west. The moon would not rise for another two hours, and he would have to make the best of it.

He paced himself, counting a hundred steps running, then a hundred steps at a fast walk, and he ate the bread as he went. It was good hard brown bread, full of tasty seeds and studded with pine kernels, and it had been given to him by a kind young wife of the town whose mischievous three year old twins were always escaping. Mihran had brought the two little boys safely back to their mother when he found them by the river trying to catch fish with her best colander, and in gratitude and relief after the hours of fear for them she baked an extra loaf for him each week. He collected it every Saturday.

On Mondays he would take his brown pottery dish to the dairy, where it would be heaped full with a wonderfully thick and creamy yoghurt, and he earned this by carrying milk to the barracks three times a week. On any day of the week he might be given some left-over pastries or fruit if he went by the market on his way home. As he ran, he wondered how it was that people could be so kind to him while they thought him one of themselves, while they would curse him and not raise a finger to help him if they knew who he really was. Just a few careless words would mean starvation for his family and turn him into an outcast.

The light faded. For another hour he ran a little slower, taking care to put his heel down first so that he would not trip, and rolling his weight to the outside of his foot to prevent turning his ankle. At last, the moon began to rise and he increased his pace again, glad that he would not have to cross the shale in full dark. The shale gave *gehennem yol* its name.

Gehennem yol, hell's path, deserved its reputation.

There was a great slope of razor-sharp shards just below the peak of the mountain. The path before it and after it was good, but the unstable silver shale claimed the lives of unwary travellers. It was almost impossible to cross without local knowledge, and even those who were lucky and survived bore white criss-crossed scars and the wider marks of deeper cuts.

He had been told that if he could get across the first quarter of the shale, he could angle sharply up towards the peak, where there was an outcrop of solid rock just below the treacherous shards, running in a diagonal line across the rest of the slope. As long as he could see to keep to the proper angle, he should be able to get to the far side. Of course, the people who told him this had never attempted the crossing themselves, but they had told him that some relative or friend, or someone who knew someone else had done it and survived unscathed.

He wouldn't mind the scars or the pain, he told himself staunchly, if they were rewarded with his father's life.

Mihran was strong and wiry and his legs were used to the climb from the town to his home every day, but this run was far, far longer, and he wished that he could rest, just for a little while. He carried on. He walked, then ran, walked, then ran, over and over, mile after mile, and his breath clouded in the colder air at this altitude. It felt like knives in his throat.

At last, he reached the shale. It stretched before him, innocent and smooth and silvered by the moonlight, a gentle slope, deceptively easy-looking. Cautiously he started across it, hoping that he was far enough up to find the ridge of rock. The shale hissed and slid under his boots, and he put out a hand to the incline to steady himself as, to his horror, it began to move. Sharp pain lanced through his palm as he leaned on the knife-like slivers, and he staggered a little, barely managing to regain his balance as part of the slope fell away below him, gathering speed and roaring like a wave as it went.

Panting, he stood still. The noise gradually lessened, the roar slowly diminished to a hiss, with the occasional rattle of a dislodged stone, and at last all became still. Blood dripped from his palm, almost black in the moonlight, making dark spots on the lighter stone, and he closed his hand tightly on the cuts till it eased, trying to remember what else he had been told about *gehennem yol*.

Don't try to walk in the way you normally would, they had told him. You make sure that the foot you stand on is firm, then you slide it forward, feeling for movement underneath. You let the mountain tell you where to stop. This was better than no advice at all, and he *had* nearly gone down in that roaring rush, when he tried to walk normally. He took a deep breath and started off again.

Slowly, he inched towards the ridge. The night was now very cold and he was high on the mountain, so that the sweat which ran from him cooled at once on his icy skin. The shale seemed endless and he had to resist the need to go a little faster, but gradually he could see that he had made progress. Slide, stop, feel for any movement. Slide and stop, again and again, until at last he thought the footing was a little firmer, a little shallower, a little less likely to shift, and then he was sure he had found the ridge.

He took a precious moment to look for the angle he must take, and in the bright moonlight he found it easily. He moved his foot, and chanced to look down. His strong brown boots were cut all about, and deeply scarred and gouged by the knife-like pieces of rock, but they had protected him well. He was grateful for his father's loving care in choosing the best. Tonight it might save both their lives.

Now he could move faster, and he began to make up time. In another hour he was off the shale and back on to the good path. The cold mountain air still hurt his throat and lungs and he felt that his legs were heavier and harder to move, but still he went on. Too much was at stake to falter now. It could not be much further.

He was so tired that he nearly ran into the wire shortly after he joined his usual route. He stood in the shadow of the trees, breathing hard and wondering if he had enough wind left to call to whoever was nearest the fence.

The sun was beginning to rise and he could see into the prison. He had run all night, and the camp was stirring, but there was still time. One of the prisoners came a little nearer the wire, stretching his back and scratching under his shirt. He relieved himself against one of the fence posts, giving Mihran time to drop down on his side of the fence and slide through the grass towards him. He whistled a soft warble, and repeated it to catch his attention.

"Don't look this way!" he warned as the man turned his head to see

1896   The Boy from Zeitoun

who was there. "I'm Mihran from Zeitoun. I have to talk to my father before anyone comes to the camp from the barracks today. It's a matter of life and death!"

"Wait," the man said at once, and he wandered back towards the flimsy sheds where the prisoners slept. A few minutes later, Mihran's father ambled unconcernedly towards the fence, apparently on the same errand as the first man.

"Mihran?" he called, softly.

The boy felt tears spring to his eyes. "Father!" he whispered, and for a moment he could not go on.

"Listen," he managed hoarsely, "the soldiers from the barracks will be coming here early this morning. They are visiting the camps in turn, and they will ask for the men of Zeitoun for a work detail. They will offer extra food and *raki*, saying there are roads to build and ditches to be dug near the town. But the last ones won't be ditches, father! They'll be graves."

"When they ask each man which town or village he is from, you must say anything *except* Zeitoun. Try to warn everyone...."

The guard, who was lazily smoking a cigarette in the tower a little way beyond them turned their way, tossed the butt over the edge and leaned on the rail.

Mihran melted back into the grass, and his father moved away to the sheds. From the concealment of the forest the boy watched every step with hungry eyes until he went inside.

He had done it!

And now he must get back to his home, to let his mother know his father was safe, and to ready himself for another day at the barracks. He turned away from the camp and trotted homeward.

His weariness seemed less, and his spirits lifted as he thought of his mother and Annik. He still had his little family.

Best of all, there was always the chance that they would be together again one day. And it was all because of his father's gift of that good pair of boots.

In the safety of their bright island of refuge, the Eramian family was prospering. Boghos Effendi was now in charge of the family, the Deftera farms and the estate, and his management was excellent. Though he did not have the rank of Agha, in those days 'effendi' meant 'lord' and it was a noble title. Nowadays, however, anyone in the middle East may be flattered by this address, and it has no more meaning than 'Mr.'

Boghos Effendi felt that he must at all times maintain an image of authority, dignity and prudence, and in some ways it cost him dear.

1897

Carpe Diem

ALEKSAN HAD been banned from Nicosia and rusticated to the farm by his father. He was to stay at Deftera and keep out of Boghos Effendi's way until his latest regrettable exploit was forgotten. He listened contritely to the angry lecture and complied with his father's instructions in a suspiciously docile manner. Boghos Effendi rightly suspected that his son might be looking on his banishment from the city as a fortuitous way to avoid his creditors and he determined that Aleksan should have a short leash at Deftera. He was a stern parent with firm, old-fashioned Victorian ideas about the duties of children and an equally firm hold on their purse-strings, and Aleksan had just about run out of credit in both respects.

There was much to do on the farm at all times of the year, but Aleksan preferred hunting, riding, and relaxing and drinking in the local tavernas to working up a sweat in the heat of the day. After all, what were all the servants employed for?

Carpe Diem, seize the day, that was his motto!

Of course, when he did put his mind to it, he could easily do the work of two men. He was not tall, but he had the athletic build and heavy musculature of his father, and he could lift a great sack of grain in each hand without difficulty and load them onto the wagons by himself.

He was famous for his strength, and the previous Easter he had fought five men at once when they attacked him in a Deftera taverna, and won too, and he could drink and sing and boast as well as any man in the village.

He had smooth pale skin, a particularly sweet smile, mild brown eyes, and thick, wavy hair, and he knew he looked very well in his crisp white shirt with its wide sleeves under his favourite embroidered cross-over waistcoat, and with his black, tight-fitting riding breeches tucked into highly polished boots. He had thick, curly hair, fine white teeth, and a luxurious, soft moustache. All in all, he was a very fine fellow.

Under the careful management of his grandfather and father, the farm to which he had just been banished continued to thrive and it was a gracious place to live The elegant and carpeted reception rooms led on to shady balconies, and with a paradise garden as well as the cold, spring-fed pool with its lilies and fish, there were places for ladies to take gentle exercise without leaving the grounds. There were stables, still rooms, bakeries, kitchens, store rooms, guest quarters and servants' rooms, and the old water mill still turned beside the outbuildings for the chickens and cattle. There were rooms for the racks of silk moth cocoons, and others for spinning and weaving, and there were cool rooms above the stream for the buttery and for laying out the great pans of milk to settle.

On one side of the yard, away from the house and the risk of sparks, were the great white humps of the *fournos,* set on their stone stands and ranging in size from the smallest ones for baking one or two dishes, to huge bread ovens which could take twenty loaves at one firing. Their high stacks of wood and their paddles and doors were laid ready beside them, and their yard was paved with good, dressed stone and kept free of weeds.

The red-tiled main house was fine enough for the honoured patriarch of the family, and as well as the horses and mules for work and riding, there were now two camels in the paddocks. There was even a set of secluded rooms for the wives of visiting Turkish dignitaries and the house lacked nothing for the comfort and contentment of its occupants.

Aleksan had initially envied the Turks their four wives but after some thought he decided that there was too much effort and expense involved in keeping them all happy. No, he was better off being fancy-free. He would have to marry one day, he supposed, but for now he was very satisfied. He was well aware of his father's views on his carefree way of life, and he suspected that his more obedient and reliable brother Stepan would inherit most of his share of his father's estate. It was probably for the best, he reflected; farming was too much like hard work.

Stepan was a careful man who knew the value of everything, and, moreover, he had sensibly decided to marry their cousin, Shenorik. She would share her Guvezian father's lands with her sister, bringing a very good dowry to the man she chose for her husband, and Stepan had already asked for her hand twice. Astonishingly, and to Aleksan's amusement and the chagrin of Boghos Effendi, who favoured the match, the high-spirited and independent girl refused him on both occasions.

Aleksan secretly enjoyed his pedantic and worthy brother's discomfort, but he pitied Shenorik, who would undoubtedly be forced in some way to marry him in the end. Actually, he was quite sorry for Stepan too, which was an unusual emotion for him to feel about this somewhat annoying brother, but he was sure that slender, vibrant, flashing-eyed Shenorik would not be a complaisant or easy wife. No indeed, this was not a girl to be commanded, even by Stepan.

Enough of life's little problems. Today was another beautiful morning in a string of beautiful mornings. Aleksan whistled cheerfully as he saddled Janavar, his new gelding. Janavar was a fine high-spirited grey, with a kind eye and no viciousness about him, and he was certainly misnamed. The care of his horses was one of the few things he took very seriously, and he could talk knowledgeably on breeding, ailments, training and bloodlines when he cared to do so. The sun was just rising as he led the big horse from the stables, and he nodded to various servants going to dairy and bakery to start the day's work. Soon the place would be bustling with folk about their business and he intended to be gone by then.

A pretty young maid passed him, carrying two chamber-pots from the bedrooms to the privies. Aleksan smiled at her, and made a sympathetic face when he saw her wrinkling her nose over her unpleasant duty.

"Many a lovely flower blooms above, er, fertiliser," he told her gallantly, with an eye to future, more private meetings.

She averted her gaze and hurried on past. He sighed. Perhaps his reputation was getting a little too well-known. But then, some women found that a challenge, didn't they?

He fell into a pleasant daydream about the lovely Eugenie who lived in the village and who had made it quite clear that *she* found him attractive. She was buxom and bonny, with masses of dark, silky hair which she wore piled up in a loose knot, and she had a milkmaid's creamy skin, a sly smile, and a rather knowing air about her. She lowered her eyes demurely when he greeted her, but she would steal admiring looks at him while pretending confusion at his gallantry and complimentary remarks. He expected that she would probably be fat when she was older, like her mother and sisters, but now in the first sweet softness of maturity, she was very enticing.

He had sung a poem 'extempore' in the square last Sunday evening when the village girls paraded with their families in the welcome coolness, and Eugenie blushed and walked past him as closely as she dared. The poem had been a great success, and he basked happily in the compliments and encouragement of his friends, who cheered him, and clapped him on the back and told him he was a fine fellow and a natural poet. Of course, he then had to stand his round.

Several rounds, as it happened.

It was very pleasing when the villagers saluted him with respect and called him '*affendigo*' just as they did when they greeted his father. His family owned the abundant spring of sweet water which rose on their land, and this supplied all the household and irrigation needs of the villagers, so of course it was only prudent of them to be respectful, but Aleksan liked to think that they admired him for his own sake. As they all agreed, he *was* a very fine fellow, after all.

He took a deep breath of the fresh morning air, full of the scents of the earth and the oregano that grew in dusty grey clumps along the path, crushed by Janavar's great hooves. The whiskery barley, turning gold now, rustled and swayed waist-high in the breeze, and still thinking of Eugenie, he unconsciously turned his horse towards the near borders of their land, where her family had their little mud-brick farmhouse and single cow. Here, his father's land ran with the borders of HajiGeorgiou's farm.

Young Taki HajiGeorgiou was in love with Eugenie, and would surely ask for her hand soon, but Aleksan meant to woo her first. Not, of course, that he could marry her. Though there were few suitable Armenian girls of the right age in Nicosia, certainly he could never face the wrath of his father if he foolishly proposed marriage to a villager. No, his proposal would be most pleasurable, but considerably less respectable.

The sun rose higher and he took off his jacket as the morning warmed. Life was good. He began to sing the song which had been such a success last Sunday. His voice rose, true and clear. It was a very fine thing to be young and strong, and to be the son of Boghos Effendi!

Two fields away, young HadjiGeorgiou was weeding one of his father's bean fields, and deepening the irrigation channels. The rich red-brown soil was too dry, really, and he would have to talk to his father to arrange extra irrigation with Boghos Effendi's overseer. He frowned, his old resentment coming to mind. Water should be free to all – it was as necessary as air. The sound of Aleksan's song came to him just then, borne softly on the breeze. He listened with pleasure for a moment or two, his black mood lessening. Whoever it was had a good voice. He opened his mouth to join in, and then all at once he realised who the singer must be.

His anger came back to him, stronger because of his inadvertent admiration for the voice of a man he despised. He threw the hoe on the ground and clenched his fists impotently, knowing that it would be pointless to tackle him. He was outclassed physically – he knew well the strength of Aleksan, he had been in the taverna when the five men had attacked him.

His resentment and jealousy increased as the singer approached. Driven to recklessness with the knowledge that he could do nothing to this man who was fast supplanting his place in the affections of the girl he wanted for his wife, and whose casual attention might ruin her, he ran to where had left his shotgun. As Aleksan came along the path, still on his own land, Taki leapt out and confronted him. He raised the shotgun and pointed it at his rival.

He would see how brave Aleksan was now! It would be good to watch that arrogant, smiling face become white with fear. Maybe he would even beg for his life, and that would be something to tell the other young men of the village.

Taki had seriously underestimated his rival. Aleksan was brave and impetuous, and he was not a thinker. He reacted instantly, completely without premeditation, and so without warning. He kicked the startled horse so that it sprang forward violently, and he threw himself from the saddle down onto Taki, bringing them both to the ground. The shotgun flew from Taki's grasp without firing, and he found himself underneath the considerable weight of his erstwhile victim, having his face ground into the dirt. With a strength born of mortal fear, he managed to scramble to his feet with his opponent still on his back, and jerked his head back hard, breaking Aleksan's nose. This made him let go momentarily, and the fight deteriorated into an undignified scramble.

Just then a neighbouring smallholder came along the path. He had been following Aleksan, having spotted him riding past from the roof of his house, and he wanted to invite him to come for a few drinks that evening. He saw his friend seemingly getting the worst of the fight because at that moment Taki had rolled over on top of him, so he ran to them and pulled Taki away, pushing the two of them apart.

"Hey, don't fight, *regumbaré*," he grinned, thinking he might mollify them both with a drink, "Let's go down to the taverna!".

Aleksan goodnaturedly got to his feet, wiped a smear of blood from his face and felt his rapidly swelling nose with some care. It hadn't been a bad fight, if a little short. He would have won it of course, if Marios hadn't come along.

His well-trained horse stood quietly nearby. He turned away to catch Janavar's rein and then, too late, he saw that his enraged assailant had recovered his gun.

Quickly, he jumped to the side of the path, but this time he hesitated, realising that there was no cover near enough for him to reach before he could be shot.

Shaking with hatred, Taki aimed his gun at the part of Aleksan most responsible for his gallantry.

There was a moment when everyone kept quite still, and Taki had the immense, if short-lived, pleasure of seeing a momentary flicker of fear in Aleksan's steady gaze.

Aleksan at once resolved not to beg for mercy. All he needed was one instant of inattention. He always got out of trouble, always had, always would. This villager wouldn't dare to shoot him. He was Boghos Effendi's son. He was right. After a long moment, Taki lowered the gun. The trigger, which had moved a little when he dropped the gun earlier, clicked back as he did so and the roar of the gun was shocking.

Aleksan gave a great shout of pain and fell.

Taki didn't wait to see what he had done. He grabbed the weapon, which he had dropped in surprise when it fired, and disappeared through the bean sticks at a headlong run.

The shot had fortunately missed the spot at which Taki had originally been aiming, but the wound was bad enough. There was a ragged hole in Aleksan's thigh and he was bleeding profusely. Hoping desperately that he wouldn't be held to blame for his ill-timed intervention, the hapless neighbour tore a strip from his shirt and stopped the bleeding as best he could, but Aleksan was white with pain by the time Janavar could be caught a second time and Marios managed to pull his friend across the big grey's saddle to take him back to the farm. It was a long, agonising journey for the injured young man, and blessedly punctuated by moments of unconsciousness.

Janavar's glossy flanks were soon soaked with blood, and the dramatic arrival of the neighbour leading a blood-soaked steed which bore the seemingly lifeless body of the young master caused immediate panic.

Servants rushed to take him gently down, a man was sent to Nicosia for the doctor, and another was sent to bring Boghos Effendi. Old Marta, who had dosed all the many Eramian children through their infant illnesses, competently bandaged master Aleksan's thigh and put him to bed. She muttered darkly about chickens coming home to roost throughout, and for some reason she made him drink plenty of water.

"He'll live," she said, shortly, pushing her way through the crowd outside his room when she had finished. "and he'll have a wonderful scar to show the ladies if that fancy town doctor doesn't bleed him to death."

A little later that day, Aleksan had to face his father. He would almost rather have faced the shotgun again.

Boghos Effendi had strictly guided his sons, even in their infancy. Having been brought up by a father who was taught that sparing the rod would spoil the child, and believing his own character to have benefited from this, he in turn applied the same precepts to his children. He would not have dreamed of letting them know how much he loved and worried about them, and he did love them very much indeed, every one of them. He believed that a show of weakness would only encourage familiarity and undermine his absolute authority, and none of them knew how hard it was for him to smack an infant hand or turn his coldest gaze on childhood misdemeanours.

Unfortunately, today he had left an important and potentially immensely profitable meeting with a grain buyer in order to deal with the latest exploit of this most troublesome son, and he was not disposed to be lenient with him.

Aleksan had been moved to a bed in one of the guest suites, where his mother sent the plainest servant girl she could find to attend him, but he was in too much pain for gallantry, anyway. The fairer sex would be safe from him for quite some time to come.

He had lost a lot of blood, and the doctor took some more, something he could not understand – surely he had bled enough when he was shot? He suspected that when there was little for them to do, the medical profession bled their patients in order to have something to put on the bill.

At last the door opened, and his father came in. There was a chilly look in his pale eyes and his face was grim. Without speaking, he seated himself in a chair by the window and regarded Aleksan impassively, smoothing his luxuriant white moustache with one blunt finger, a bad sign. He was quite obviously pondering a suitable punishment, and Aleksan endeavoured to look contrite, but really, what had he done? He was riding on his own horse on his own land when he had been attacked. He decided on a humorous approach.

"My singing really wasn't *that* dreadful, Father." he joked weakly, giving his father his most winning smile.

Boghos Effendi continued to look at him without expression.

"What is to be done with you?" he mused aloud. "A son totally without talent, and with no aptitude for any kind of work."

Aleksan tried to seem contrite. "Surely I'm not that bad, sir?. I'll keep out of HadjiGeorgiou's way in future. He won't get another shot at me."

He brightened, as an excellent idea came to him. "Maybe you should send me away for a while. For my own good, naturally. Perhaps to Paris?"

"Don't be ridiculous. Is your own pleasure all you can think of?" Boghos Effendi snapped, regarding Aleksan with immense irritation. "I have left a meeting in which I was negotiating the sale of half our crop of barley to a factor from Lebanon, merely to find that you have disappointed both myself and my good neighbour HadjiGeorgiou by not dying an early death. One which has often been predicted, I might add."

He paused, suddenly recalling the shrewd bargaining and steely eye of the Lebanese factor. Hmmm. Perhaps it was not such a bad idea. He paced to the window and back, thinking, while Aleksan awaited his fate with commendable stoicism.

The Lebanese factor would be an excellent teacher for Aleksan. His quiet and polite sons were fully as competent as their admirable father, and the family was rapidly becoming influential in Beirut. Perhaps he could do something with the boy. It was worth a try.

"I have decided to place you in the care of a man who expects nothing of your family and has absolutely no concern for your position or wealth. You will go to Lebanon as soon as you are well enough to travel, and you will not return until a certain grain factor says that you are fit to bargain as hard as he. Young Hadjigeorgiou can wait for his chance to take another shot at you, after that."

Expecting no argument, Boghos Effendi turned on his heel and left, closing the door gently behind him.

Aleksan lay back on his pillows. Not so bad after all. And the old man did care for him, or he wouldn't have made that crack about Taki. All this was arranged for his protection, no doubt about it!

Lebanon, hey? He'd heard about the nightlife in Beirut. This was going to be fun. Everything always was, eventually.

1897 Carpe Diem

Twenty years later, Aleksan applied for British Nationality. His certificate describes him as being five feet 9 inches tall, having a broad forehead and round chin. His complexion was white, his eyes were brown and his hair was black. Under the category of 'any special peculiarities' the recording officer had written: Right eye artificial, three scars on side of face. It seems that Aleksan went on in his own merry way, despite all Boghos Effendi's efforts.

Some of the Eramian descendants left Cyprus for other countries and they married and established families there. Remembering their terrible history, they mostly chose lands which were under stable British control, but not in any case a country governed by Shariya law. A few of them took on the culture and language of their new homes and forgot their ancient homeland, but most of them remembered their ancestors with pride and respect while entering fully into the life and customs of their adopted lands, and this story tells of one of these cousins.

1899

The Diplomat and the Hodja

O NE OF OUR COUSINS left this beautiful island, and by his hard work and quick wits advanced to hold a very high post in a foreign land. He was a tall, impressive and dignified man, and by degrees he progressed till he was second only to the chief minister of the King's government. He spoke many languages and he knew the customs of many nations, and so he was at ease in any company.

Though his birth was modest, he was proud of his ancestry and cherished his Armenian heritage, and he and his children learned the language of their ancestors, and they read the legends and history of their people so that they would remember their motherland far away in the mountains, at the crossroads of Europe and Asia. He told them the stories of their heroic forebears, of the band of brave young men who chased on horseback after the entire Persian army and stole back the bones of their kings and hid them so that they would never again leave their native land, of the intrigues, decadence, luxury and murders at the Cilician courts of the Armenian princes, and of the beautiful princess whose father built her a lovely little castle in the sea, a jewel in the waves, so that she should be safe and protected while he fought his enemies. It was still there in the sea off the coast of Turkey, he told them, and one day he would take them to see it.

As his power and influence grew, he was often flattered and courted by all kinds of people, but he was not changed by his fame and success and treated all men with the same courtesy. He did not place a staff of eunuchs and greedy underlings between himself and petitioners and he was accessible as easily to the poorest citizen as to the King's chamberlain, so that no one was barred from justice or redress.

The court was full of intrigue and alliances and plotting, a veritable labyrinth of Byzantine diplomacy, and after some years there he attracted the envy and ill will of some high-ranking and corrupt courtiers, who would have liked his office for themselves or their protegés. Our cousin had tried to carry out his duties without recourse to sharp dealing of any kind, but it was difficult to do so in the complex and shifting political currents of the times. His own partisans worked on his behalf, but eventually those jealous men who disliked him gathered together and planned his downfall, finding ways to undermine his authority, and to diminish his reputation with the king.

Gradually, the money the treasury allocated to him for the discharge of his duties reduced to the point where he could not go on doing his work as he would wish. At last, he was forced to ask for a meeting with the highest and most powerful men of the government to explain his difficulties, as they had begun to doubt that he was using his funds with proper care, and they listened to the rumours spread by his enemies that he was becoming dishonest. These enemies most often said that he did not run his affairs efficiently enough, and that he was careless of the great king's money.

On the day appointed for his hearing, he watched his peers and judges gather in the great hall of the palace, together with spectators and representatives of the people, and he saw that there were several

Turks among them. Their presence reminded him of that Solomon of their people, the Judge of Boursa, and all at once, he knew what to say. When the King called on him to speak, he stood up confidently.

"I am an Armenian," he said, "and my people have learned many things from our masters in Turkey."

The Turks frowned and looked uneasy. They feared that he might mention the oppression and injustice that his people were enduring at that time and this would embarrass them in this great court and among these people of influence and standing.

"The Turks tell many stories about a cunning but very mean old man named Nasr-ed-din Hodja." he began. "At one time this man owned a donkey. The donkey was a good animal and he worked hard for his master every day, but the Hodja had heard that there was a way he could get even more work from him. It was called 'efficiency'. To achieve efficiency, all that was needed was to give the donkey only three quarters of the normal amount of food.

The Hodja thought it was worth a try and the next day he kept back a quarter of the feed. His donkey was an obedient, good-natured and sturdy animal, and he went on working just as hard.

The Hodja thought, "How I wish I'd heard of this before, I could have saved myself a lot of money! This 'efficiency' idea is a really marvellous thing."

After a little while, he wondered if perhaps it would be possible for the donkey to be even more efficient, and he decided to reduce the poor beast's feed to half of the original amount. The donkey became rather thin, but he was still a strong and willing animal, and he went on working.

The Hodja was delighted. "Well, well!" he said to himself, "This is even better, but maybe the donkey could be yet more efficient." And he reduced the feed to one quarter. The donkey hung his head and went on working.

The Hodja was amazed. He couldn't think why this 'efficiency' was not more widely practised, and, being a miserly and crafty old man, he decided to stop feeding the donkey anything at all.

Even this good-natured donkey could not work without any food, and at last he died in the night. When the Hodja saw him lying dead in the stable, he took off his fez, hurled it to the ground, and then he jumped on it.

"How can you do this to me?" he shouted at the poor, faithful donkey, "Just as I reach *perfect efficiency*, you die!" And he jumped on his hat again.

Our cousin looked at his audience. They waited.

"I feel like that donkey," he told them.

Everyone laughed, and the King gave our cousin the gold that he asked for.

☞

The political situation in Europe at this time was now dangerously volatile while the great powers were competing for pre-eminence everywhere, but in the normality of Nicosia the family was concerned with day to day events, and the machinations of Kings and Emperors hardly touched them. They worried about their businesses, their loves and hates, and their families' futures. They did what they could for the poor souls fleeing to them for refuge, and then they enjoyed the celebrations and entertainments which lightened their lives. Life was uncertain after all, and a man might die of something as small and insignificant as a scratch or an insect bite in the days before antibiotics.

1910

A Man's World

SHENORIK WAS a spirited little girl, cheerful, pretty, and a little spoilt. She was also intelligent and courageous, and she had a lively curiosity which often got her into trouble.

She was usually unrepentant for her misdeeds, even when seeming most chastened, but she knew very well that she had better apologise meekly and *seem* sorry. She did this convincingly.

She was tiny and fine-boned like her mother, but she was also fierce and fearless. It was not surprising that her more docile, biddable, and obedient sister Araxi, who never caused her parents a moment's worry, was her father's favourite. To his credit, Apgar did his best to be even-handed with his pretty daughters, but as children often do, Shenorik knew that he loved little Araxi the best and that even her brother Hagop was more important than she, because he was a boy. She did not mind. She had an excellent opinion of herself and that was sufficient. She was never bored, never frightened, never overawed by the wealth, importance or dignity of the great men who visited her father, and she would greet them with a charming composure when she was old enough to leave the nursery and make her first appearance at the adults' dining table.

Later in her life she would remember these days of gracious living with nostalgia, as the farm which had been her childhood home slowly deteriorated under the less expert management of its new owners. When she was a child, though, it was still a wonderful place.

Her lack of size never held her back when she felt the need for action. When she was just a little girl she once attacked her older and much larger cousin Stepan because he had teased her favourite puppy a little too boisterously. The little animal gave a sudden yelp and slunk away whimpering, with its tail between its legs, glancing back at him in reproach. She temporarily had the advantage of height as he knelt in the stable-yard to call the puppy back to him, so she seized the moment and jumped on his back, pulling his hair so hard that tears came to his eyes.

"How do you like it yourself?" she demanded, eyes blazing, and she advanced on him again, intent on further retribution.

Astonished, he got to his feet and backed away, laughing. "It was an accident – I wouldn't hurt him on purpose," he protested, fending her off with both hands. "And anyway, it's only a dog!"

"Yes," she said, "but it's *my* dog," and she tried her best to kick him.

Stepan felt a reluctant admiration. He was five years older and nearly twice her weight, but she went on trying to hit him until her mother came out of the house and pulled her away, apologising to Stepan for her daughter's unladylike action and scolding her for such rough and hoydenish behaviour.

'She should have been a boy," Apgar sighed, as his wife told him later about their daughter's efforts to kick her cousin. "She would have been much happier."

He was right, and she would have been a wonderful farmer too, but she did not waste her time wishing for something she could not have.

She was always one for action. As she grew older and realised that her brother would never be coaxed or coerced into following their father at Deftera, she began to take more interest in the working of the land and the many tasks necessary for the day to day well-being of its workers and their masters.

She watched the silk-moth caterpillars spin their cocoons and saw how they were harvested from the mulberry trees. She helped to store them and to unwind the cocoons after their softening in the great wooden tubs of hot water. She knew how to spin the silk and how to weave, and one day her grandson's wife would marvel at the little lace jacket she had made for herself with its tiny waist and handmade buttons.

She learned how to brew beer, how to make wine from the farm's own grapes, and how to make a tasty wine vinegar to go with the olive oil which was pressed from their home grown olives to dress the salads grown in their gardens. She distilled rosewater from the petals of roses she herself had picked, and she embroidered the flowers she saw in the garden into a colourful circlet of her own design around an ornate letter G for her family name. Her mother had it framed and it hangs in her grandson's house.

She watched the wide, shallow pans of milk being set for the cream to rise, and she helped to turn the great churns to make butter. She added rennet to fresh milk to start the making of junkets and yoghurt and the curds for cheese, hanging the dripping muslin bags in the dairy to solidify, and remembering how often they should be turned to drain evenly. She bottled and dried many *okes* of fruit from the farm's orchards, and roasted and salted the nuts which her father so enjoyed. She counted and labelled rack after rack of jars and bottles in the storerooms and she enjoyed the work and the sense of achievement it gave her.

The *fournos* in the yard were fired every morning and she helped to stack and light the fires inside the big round mud-brick ovens, and to rake out the charcoal. The trays of meat and vegetables were placed in one of them, and the big round loaves of bread, made with the farm's own flour from corn grown in their fields, were racked in others. The ovens were closed with round metal doors wedged firmly into the openings. These were plastered carefully around with more mud to make a tight seal, and the food was left to bake. Hours later, the meat and the loaves would be taken out, fragrant and hot, and cooked to perfection. The bread had to be baked very early so that it could be used for daytime meals, while dishes for dinner could be set to cook later. Shenorik crept out of her bed before dawn to watch the cooks and bakers so that she knew how to calculate the heat of the ovens, and how long each item would take to bake.

One day, she would supervise the feeding and care of her own workers, and sometimes there would be more than fifty extra men at harvest time. She would be able to supervise all aspects of farm life, ensuring the smooth running of every activity while planning for winter shortages and seeing that everything necessary was made, stored and ready when called for. All this was far in the future, and she did these things now because she was interested, and because she enjoyed it.

While her free time was spent at the farm, she also acquired the accomplishments of a young lady of good family. Among other things, she learned to speak French, as well as Armenian, Turkish and Greek, and she had piano lessons. Shenorik did not enjoy these, but she persisted doggedly, and could play well by the time she was called on to perform at the parties and dances given by the other Armenian families in the city.

She loved to go on long walks and she went on expeditions to the mountains and to every picnic she could manage. She wrote in her diary every day of her life, and these she kept carefully until she died. By the time she reached marriageable age, she was thoroughly happy with her life, and she took pleasure in helping her mother around the farm, gardening, brewing, baking and distilling her famous rose water, and helping to stem the decline of the old place.

Meanwhile, her younger sister Araxi, who had no aptitude for farm management, fell desperately in love with their cousin Aram. The two of them spent a lot of time behaving in what the unsentimental Shenorik considered to be an unnecessarily foolish and undignified manner, and she decided she'd be very happy to see them married and established in their own house, where they could be as silly as they liked.

She herself was resolved not to marry. She didn't see why she should settle for someone she hadn't chosen, and there were precious few eligible Armenian youths in Cyprus. She did not wish to marry any of *them*. She was sure that her capable mother Huliané could manage the farm on her own if necessary, and she did not see why she should not do so, too.

It was at this point that Stepan decided to propose.

He had thought about it very carefully. Although his first duty was to please his parents, he had not developed strong feelings for any of the eligible Armenian maidens suggested by them. He was a practical young man and he admired Shenorik's capable management of her tasks around the farm. Also, he thought she was pretty as well as eligible and would be an excellent choice for a wife. So it was logical that he should propose.

First, as was proper, he asked her father's permission to pay court to her.

Apgar was delighted. It was the perfect match. Stepan was steady and reliable, and best of all, he was the son of Boghos Effendi. Shenorik would bring land to the match, and Stepan would bring land *and* money. He would have no hesitation in leaving the larger part of the estate to his daughter if she married Stepan. With relief that both Shenorik and his land should be so well provided for, he shook the young man's hand enthusiastically and gave his blessing.

Shenorik heard his confident proposal with some exasperation. She refused him. In fact, to his horror, she told him not to be so ridiculous.

It was not because she disliked Stepan so much. No, it was because a wife must *obey* her husband, and she was in no hurry to acquire a master. Why couldn't she manage a farm on her own?

Her cousin was somewhat surprised and discomforted and also a little put out, but he was not disheartened. He had an equally good opinion of himself, and he was certain that she would accept him eventually. After all, who could offer more than he, in respect of either family or fortune?

He was rather more taken aback when she refused him a second time.

Apgar was not only surprised, he was also extremely annoyed. He called his awkward daughter to him and asked why she had refused this flattering and most suitable offer. She stood very straight and told him firmly that she did not love Stepan, that she did not wish to be married, and that she would be very happy to remain a spinster all her life and manage the farm on her own. "I can do anything, you know I can, the dairy, the still room, the bakery or the store rooms." she said, with pride. "Everything Mother can do, I can do too."

Apgar prayed for patience. "Can you do everything that *I* do?" he asked. "Can you handle workers who prefer to shirk, stockmen who neglect the herd, hired hands who steal from you? Can you face down a drunken villager with a grudge, or give orders to a shepherd who knows more about his sheep than you will ever learn? What will you do with a dishonest tax collector, and how will you fix prices with the factor who buys your corn? However much you know, there will always be things you cannot do because you are a woman. You will need a strong husband, and later on, a strong son."

She would not believe it. She did not wish to believe it. It was not fair and it was not just that men should have all the rights and privileges and that women should obey and be subservient, just *because* they were women. They glared at each other with mutual misunderstanding and frustration.

Shrugging, Shenorik repeated that she did not love Stepan, that she would not marry him, and she left the room.

Apgar threw up his hands and told his wife that she must talk to her daughter.

Huliané noticed that Shenorik had all at once become *her* daughter and not *their* daughter, and she understood how frustrated and angry he must be. She put out a hand and gently stroked his cheek. He looked weary. He seemed so much older these days, or was it just that she did not notice the changes now unless something happened to make her look at him properly? Whatever it was, Apgar was tired and grey, and showing the signs of age. She felt a sudden fear, realising fully for the first time that he might die before herself, and she could not bear the thought of life without him.

She told him not to worry, she would think of something.

Later, she tried to explain to Shenorik that her father was right. The only way her headstrong daughter could be happy would be to accept the best compromise she could get. She was not the first young girl to resent the male-dominated world they all inhabited, but there was nothing they could do to change things. At least, not at a stroke. If change came at all, it would be gradual, and not in their lifetimes.

Shenorik would not listen.

When cousin Stepan was refused for a third time, Huliané went secretly to see him. She told him that she had a plan, instructed him in what he should do, and explained exactly what she had in mind to help his suit. The scheme was a little hard on Shenorik, but marriage to Stepan would eventually give her everything she wanted, if only she could be made to see it.

Apgar was also primed by Huliané, and he reluctantly called their daughter Araxi to his office to tell her that she could not marry her fiancé because the eldest daughter in a family must be married first. He remembered Huliané's strict instructions, hardened his heart, and was adamant about this: it was against all propriety for the younger daughter to marry before the elder, and she would just have to wait.

Araxi pleaded with him desperately, then she burst into tears. Horribly discomforted, Apgar left the room in great haste. He could not bear to watch his favourite daughter cry but he dared not weaken and perhaps ruin his wife's plans. He decided to spend all his time during the next few weeks at the farm, being extremely busy and hopefully unable to be found either by wife or daughter.

Araxi was distraught. She confronted her sister and accused her of selfishness. She said that it would be Shenorik's fault if she and Aram never married and she died a shrivelled old maid. She said that it would also be her uncaring and heartless sister's fault if she never had children, adding darkly that she would be sorry for the rest of her life if anything happened to her. She cried herself into a stupor. Next, she said that she would never talk to anyone ever again, and then she locked herself in her room.

Shenorik said airily that she didn't care, but she soon began to feel isolated and miserable. Her mother was always too busy to spend time with her, her father hardly spoke to anyone and left the house whenever possible, and Araxi's unhappy presence was a constant reproach.

Obediently, Stepan waited another three weeks before he called at the town house, ostensibly to see Apgar. Shenorik was in the drawing room when he was shown in, and of course she was obliged to be polite. Initially wary, she found it rather pleasant to talk to someone who did not seem to think she was a selfish ogre, and she agreed to walk with him in the Municipal Gardens and listen to the band.

He was cheerful and attentive and did not mention his proposal at all. He told her all about the new ploughing and planting machinery that he'd seen in Athienou when he visited his Melikian cousins, and about the high milk-yield cattle they had bought from Europe. She found herself feeling inordinately pleased by his assumption that she would know exactly what he was talking about, and that he did not explain anything unless she asked.

He asked her advice on some small problems they were having around the farm, and he made her laugh once or twice. He bought her a plate of creamy *mahallebi* with rose water from the push-cart in the park, and had one himself, and she was rather sorry to see him walk away after he returned her to her home. Sighing, and feeling very hard done by, she went indoors to face the accusing silence of her sister, and the distant politeness of her parents.

The next week, Stepan called again and asked rather diffidently if he might take her to the theatre. He told her that he had no one to go with, and she would do him a favour if she would accompany him. It was a very funny play, and afterwards, still thinking about it, she absentmindedly took his arm. He said nothing, took no advantage of the small gesture, and left her at her door with a smile and a tip of his hat. Again, her heart sank as she went in to her unfriendly welcome.

Araxi was a folorn and lonely presence around the house, her pale, unhappy face and quiet misery a constant reproach at breakfast and dinner, of which she ate little. Her father greeted Shenorik briefly at breakfast and left the house as soon as possible each day, and her mother always found some excuse to keep busy and out of her way.

Her cousin slowly became a friendly and reliable fixture in her life, and she began to look forward to his visits. Summer gave way to autumn, and as he placed a soft blanket over her knees one late afternoon, so that they could sit on a bench and admire the autumn beauty of the trees, she suddenly found herself telling him about the atmosphere at home. He listened sympathetically, and gave her a clean white handkerchief to blow her nose. She was not crying, she *never* cried. It was just that the cold had made her eyes run.

He was understanding and apologetic, saying that it must be all his fault. "I really am sorry. I don't know what I can do to help." Somehow, his arm was around her, but he took it away guiltily as she indignantly sat up straight.

"It's *not* your fault, well, not entirely," she amended honestly. "And I'm not stupid, I can see what they're trying to do. They think I'll get married to escape things at home."

Stepan looked pensive. "Well, I suppose we *could* give it a try, you know. I mean, we could show them all how well we could manage things between us. No one could run a farm like you! You would have the biggest, best-run estate in Cyprus. I've always wanted to build my own house, and I could do it, I could build one just for you, here in Nicosia so that you'd have a home of your own to run just as you pleased, with no one to give you orders or make you do something you didn't want to."

"But then they'd think they *made* me marry you! They'd think they'd won," Shenorik said, torn between misery and anger. "And they would have!"

"No, no, they wouldn't." Stepan was upset by her tears. He'd never seen Shenorik cry. It unnerved him, and he hastened to reassure her. "Listen, really *we* would be the winners. You don't dislike me too much, do you? I wouldn't want you to marry me if you didn't think we could be friends, but it would be very sad if we missed the chance to be happy with each other." Then he said the most romantic thing he'd managed in his entire life. "I'm not much good with words, but there's absolutely nobody in the world I'd rather come home to every night than you! If *you* were in any house, it really would be coming home."

Shenorik could tell he was speaking the truth. She crossly brushed her tears away, and took a deep breath. "As a declaration, that's so very much like you, Stepan. Of course I don't dislike you, but I'm glad that you haven't mentioned undying love. I wouldn't have believed *that*. But friendship, now. I suppose that's not a bad start, is it?"

It was definitely not a bad start, and their marriage and their life together was built on it.

Stepan built the house he had promised Shenorik, but many years later, when she was an old lady, she was forced to leave it as the Turks partitioned Nicosia

She was on her own in the house, and at first she locked the doors and refused to leave. When a curfew was imposed to keep public order, her friendly and worried Turkish neighbours in Mahmut Pasha Street conspired to help her as she stubbornly remained, with the fighting drawing ever nearer. These good neighbours told her to let down a basket each day from the balcony over the street, and they put the things she needed into it, so that she could haul it up and have enough to eat.

Eventually, the partition of the capital became a fact and the looting and destruction began as Greeks and Turks fought each other. Fearing for her life, Shenorik's son Boghos, and her son-in-law Kaloust went into the Turkish Sector with a Red Cross escort and insisted that she leave, taking only what they could carry with them.

Her possessions, little treasures, books and furniture, everything she had was stolen, and she never saw her house in the old Armenian quarter again, but she had her son and daughter, and her great family of cousins, and she went to live once again at Deftera, where she created beauty in the gardens and order and comfort in the old farmhouse.

Refugees were still arriving at the Cypriot ports of Larnaca and Famagusta, but now they came from Syria and Egypt and Lebanon too, as some of those middle Eastern countries under Ottoman rule or influence also became caught up in the madness. Most of these were not destitute, however, and they came with their possessions and their families.

Many of them spoke only Turkish or Arabic, or a little thickly and incomprehensibly-accented Armenian. The wealthier 'old' Armenian families, including the Eramians, took their children away from the Armenian schools and sent them to the American Academy or to Catholic convent schools, so that their speech and manners would not be affected by the ignorance of the newcomers. The newcomers did not care. They got on with making a life for themselves and their children.

1914

The Constant Lover

AT THE TIME when the genocide was at its height, Rafael's family came to Cyprus from Alexandretta, which was under Turkish control. This meant that the family could live without fear, but it also meant leaving much of what they had. Having escaped Ottoman domination, Rafael discarded the legacy of Turkey from every aspect of his life, and he changed his name from Keukjian with its Turkish origins, to Armadouni, which is the equivalent in Armenian. It means '*he has roots*,' and because he was allowed to take pride in his ancestry in this new country, he found it singularly appropriate.

His family was large and not wealthy, but they were respectable and solvent, and their sons were intelligent and literate. Rafael had qualified and worked as a teacher in Syria, and he soon found employment teaching at the Armenian School in Nicosia. He liked the children, enjoyed his work, and he was a pleasant, handsome young man from a respectable family. He could reasonably have expected to marry a nice Armenian girl and look forward to a happy and relatively uneventful life. Unfortunately, this was not to be.

He fell in love with Elbisse, the youngest daughter of Boghos Effendi.

Elbisse was in no way an average girl. She was small and rounded and pretty, with a ready smile and amused dark eyes, and under her demure and obedient exterior she was one of the handsome, strong-willed women that are found among the descendants of Caterina Carletti. At twenty-eight years old she was still single, having steadfastly refused to marry any of the hopeful young men chosen for her by her formidable father. She was perfectly happy with her situation, and in no hurry as yet to put herself or her fortune into other hands than her own.

Unluckily for Rafael, Elbisse was a daughter of the Eramians. She was therefore descended from one of the 'old' families, and the Effendi was a man of wealth and he held high office. He had a keen eye for his own position in society and a heavy hand where his offspring were concerned. He loved all his children, without of course, indulging them too much, but little Elbisse was his youngest, and she was also his secret favourite.

It was odd, therefore, that she was the only one of his children who regularly defied him. Her infant will had been the match for his from the moment she had given him her first baby smile, and she happily did as she pleased thereafter, uncaring of his disapproval and conducting herself with a blithe disregard for his anger, and this won her the astonished and envious admiration of her siblings.

Rafael knew from the beginning that winning her would be a difficult, if not impossible task, but he could not stop thinking about her, the way she placed her hands neatly on her lap when she sat down, the sweet curve of her neck as she turned to listen to someone beside her, the way she gave a little skip to keep up with a taller companion, and he could no more keep away from her than stop breathing. He began to go to all the places where he was likely to meet her. He went to picnics and dances, and he rode a stubborn and bad-tempered hired donkey on expeditions to the mountain monastery of Sourp Magar for the feast day of the Saint. He never missed church on Sundays. He hiked in the high ranges and made polite conversation at receptions where he could watch Elbisse with her family, from a distance. He dressed as a corsair and twirled his moustaches (specially waxed for the occasion) at fancy dress parties, and he flattered Armenian mamas till his smile ached.

He went hunting for moufflon and slept out in the mountains, building campfires among the tall pines in Troodos in the warm summer nights and roasting lamb on the spit with the other young bloods, among whom was the somewhat older Aleksan, one of Elbisse's older brothers. He rode his horse a little too fast, spent a little more money than he should, and he learned to hold his brandy like a gentleman.

It was several months before these admittedly enjoyable efforts finally brought their reward.

To his happy surprise, Aleksan invited him to spend a few days at the family farm with some other guests to celebrate his sister's birthday. He was torn between a keen anticipation at this chance to spend some time with Elbisse, and the fear that he could ruin everything and might not make a good impression. He worried over the choice of a gift, and settled eventually on a little book of poems, bound in softest leather, the edges of the pages gilded, and the title inscribed in gold. This cost him a large part of his wages, but he did not care, as long as Elbisse gave him a smile. He had a few sleepless nights when he lay awake rehearsing various scenarios of success and failure until light crept through the shutters, but at last the great day arrived and he rode out to Deftera.

He found a large and well-run estate with an impressive country house. The three original arches of the oldest part of the house still looked out over the pool, and the stream still rushed chuckling underneath the house to turn the mill, purling on down to join the Pedios a little further on. Smooth stone flags had replaced the round brown pebbles which lined the covered walkway bordering three sides of the pool, but the guest rooms and public rooms still surrounded it, their whitewashed walls turning a mellow gold in the last of the sunset.

The soft and soothing sounds of night-time *zizziros,* the Cypriot cicadas, were just beginning to take over from their more strident daytime cousins, and birds dipped and swooped over the darkening fields as a cooling breeze from the nearby peaks began to reduce the stifling August heat. Servants moved quietly about, lighting lamps and preparing the rooms for the evening's entertainment, and an appetising aroma of roasting lamb drifted from the stone-lined charcoal pits behind the kitchens.

Rafael leaned on the wooden rail, pretending to admire the unusual blue water lilies while watching Elbisse from the corner of his eye. She sat a short distance away, talking to her sisters Hanemie and Zabelle, while Aleksan lounged nearby in a wicker chair with his feet up on the balustrade and his hands tucked into his fancy waistcoat.

Elbisse caught his glance and turned her head towards him, smiling.

As their eyes met, Rafael felt as if he had been struck, and he was suspended between one breath and the next while she looked at him. He thought she must surely know how fast his heart was beating and that his feelings must be plain on his face for everyone to see.

A loud shrieking suddenly broke out in the trees, and his timeless moment fled. To his surprise, two little grey monkeys appeared and leapt from branch to branch, pelting each other with the walnuts they were tearing from the trees. Laughing, Hanemie called them down and clipped leads to their red leather collars. They sat quietly on their own special little chairs, accepting treats from the three sisters while the guests gathered round to admire them. Rafael moved closer and began a conversation with Aleksan, all the time completely and excitingly aware of Elbisse, a few feet away.

A clock chimed melodiously in one of the rooms behind them, and Boghos Effendi and his wife Yeghsabet came through an archway to join them. Aleksan hastily jumped to his feet, took his hands out of his pockets and smoothed his moustache in unconscious mimicry of his father. He greeted him respectfully and brought him to meet his guests.

The Effendi had made no concession to informality and was wearing his usual stiff-collared shirt and tailored broadcloth suit. He moved among the young people, greeting those he knew and awaiting an introduction when he did not. He smiled kindly as he took Rafael's hand.

"Ah, yes, the schoolteacher. Armadouni, now, is it not?"

Rafael nodded. "I thought it was time to lose the Turkish flavour of our old name now that we've settled here. Armadouni sounds better, too."

"Indeed it does," agreed Boghos Effendi, "and though we would not wish to offend our kindlier Turkish neighbours here in Cyprus, it's quite proper to keep one's heritage alive." He patted Rafael's shoulder and moved on to greet the others.

So far so good.

Dinner had been set at a long table outside under the trees, and Rafael found he was seated opposite Elbisse a few chairs down from the head of the table, which of course was her father's place. While this meant that he was in the perfect position to watch her, etiquette required that one never spoke across the table and conversed only to one's immediate neighbours at each side. He could only look at her. Nevertheless, it was enough, and in such delight the stars were brighter, the food more delicious, the wine more intoxicating, and the company wonderfully pleasant and witty.

To his left, Elbisse's sister Zabelle tried to have a conversation with him, asking about his work and his family and how he met Aleksan. Somehow, Rafael managed to make coherent replies, murmured the right encouragement at suitable moments, and meanwhile he continued to admire Elbisse, who was looking particularly wonderful in the lamplight.

After a few minutes, Zabelle gave him an amused look, naughtily winked at her sister across the table, and devoted her attention to her plate.

On Rafael's other side, Yeghsabet enquired politely after his parents' health, and that of each of his brothers and sisters. She went on to ask how he was getting on the at the school, while noting how the colour rose in her daughter's cheeks when she glanced at him from across the table and found him looking back at her.

Well, well, she thought, so that was how the wind blew.

Her daughter had taken a long time to make her choice, and she could have made a worse one. The young man was pleasant, well spoken and presentable, but to be quite frank, on a teacher's pay he could not keep Elbisse in the manner to which she was accustomed. People would inevitably call him a fortune hunter, and she feared that one of them would be her husband. Boghos Effendi's favourite child would have a comfortable inheritance one day, and he was unlikely to look favourably on Rafael's suit. The young people would have a difficult time ahead of them if Rafael's obvious feelings were truly shared by her wilful and headstrong daughter.

After dinner, the evening passed pleasantly in conversation, charades, music and dancing. Elbisse was an excellent pianist, and Rafael knew that he had a very good singing voice. He had practised frequently for just this possibility since he first received his invitation, and he was quite confident that he would not disgrace himself. Aleksan sang well too, so the three of them made music together beautifully and this part of the entertainment went on for longer than usual by demand of the other guests. They sang many of the popular tunes of the time and he and Aleksan made everyone laugh with their version of a punning song. They won prolonged and genuine applause, and many requests for encores.

Boghos Effendi smiled approvingly at the musical group, and startled his son by complimenting his voice. Aleksan seldom won his father's approbation. He was far more used to being lectured for his misdeeds as the black sheep of the family, and the unaccustomed warmth of his father's regard made him nervous. He put a finger inside his collar to loosen it, but he was secretly very pleased.

When the two men finished singing Elbisse continued to play so that people could dance, and Rafael managed to stay by her side on the pretext of turning the pages of the music for her. After another half an hour or so she called for one of her sisters to take a turn, and she gathered the pages of the music together neatly before rising to join the others.

Rafael put a hand under her elbow to aid her, as a gentleman should, and he felt her hesitate and lean a little against him. Hardly daring to believe that he had received this delicate hint, he took the chance she offered. "Elbisse," he said, softly, "will you walk in the garden with me?"

She looked up at him, laying her hand on his proffered arm. "It's a beautiful evening, isn't it?" she smiled. "My mother has planted part of our garden with night-scented flowers, and they'll be perfect tonight. Shall we go and see?"

For a moment they were unable to look away from each other, and again Rafael's heart beat so hard that he thought it must be audible. In fact, their attraction for each other was becoming rather obvious. They had made the mistake of looking at each other a little too long, and they were paying too little attention to the other guests.

Boghos Effendi gave them a long look of his own as he passed in a stately measure with Yeghsabet. He frowned. "I do not like that connection," he told his wife, noticing her indulgent smile, "Do not encourage it. Young Armadouni is well enough, but Elbisse must marry a man of substance. Perhaps I'd better make that clear."

Yeghsabet bit back her first response, and lowered her eyes. She knew the futility of direct argument with her husband and she had her own ways of managing him. She was the daughter of Stepan Agha, the Stepanian patriarch, and though her birth was every bit as good as her husband's, she had none of his lofty attitude regarding immigrant families. Everyone's ancestors were immigrants at some stage, after all, and if Elbisse wanted the Armadouni boy, there really was no good reason why she should not have him. She had shown no partiality for any of her father's choices and quite frankly, neither had Yeghsabet and she did not wish her daughter to be forced to take some wealthy dilettante against her will.

Admittedly, Yeghsabet's own marriage had been arranged for her by her father, but then, she had not had any other choice in mind, and quite cheerfully obeyed his wishes. She had come to love and respect this difficult, powerful and intelligent man, appreciating his essential kindness and decency, and she was well aware that he tried to do the best thing for his family according to his narrow upbringing. She wondered with exasperation which of her husband's ancestors had started this silly idea that a father should not show too much affection to his children. Sighing inwardly, she took steps to prevent a confrontation, and tried a diversionary tack.

"One of Yessayi's family might serve," she mused aloud, "or perhaps a Guvezian. Did you have someone in mind?"

Boghos did not miss a step, but he gave her another of his terrifying frowns.

"Much too old for her," he said gruffly, "She's not on the shelf just yet."

"Well, you're probably right, my dear. I suppose it is a little soon after the last attempt to choose a husband for her. Perhaps it *is* best to wait." She looked up at him guilelessly, and hoped she hadn't overdone it.

He smiled down at her, mollified. "She'll be lucky if she has a marriage like ours, most admirable of wives," he told her, "but don't think I'll change my mind because I do not choose to insist on my plans for her!"

Rafael returned to Nicosia elated and depressed by turns.

He had been alone with Elbisse!

He replayed their time in the scented garden over and over again in his mind, remembering every word, every glance she gave him, wishing he had been more eloquent, more witty, more ... impressive.

During their conversation she had told him that she often took a book or some embroidery down to a certain glade of trees on the banks of the Pedios, where she could enjoy the shade and listen to the water and the wind in the branches. Of course she had all these things at the farm, but there she was always overlooked by someone or other, and the house had many servants or maids. Sometimes she liked to be alone. He thought he knew the place she meant, he had taken a picnic there once with friends. There was usually more mud than water in the bed of the river at this time of year, but it was still a pleasant place, murmurous with the sound of breezes in the leaves and the soft calling of doves.

They contrived to meet at this grove as if by accident, and occasionally they were able to talk together at gatherings of their friends. When they could not see each other, they left messages in the hollow of one of the trees at their glade. They tried to be content with the little time they had together and they wrote loving letters and sent each other long messages and lines of poetry. Some of these were occasionally carried by Aleksan, who sympathised with his sister and her beau and blithely ignored his father's disapproval. They promised faithfully that they would never ever be persuaded to marry anyone else.

Elbisse told Rafael about her father's previous attempts at matchmaking, and warned him that they would not be the last. She feared that her father would never look kindly on him as a suitor, even though neither of the pair was in the first flush of youth, and they surely should be old enough by now to have reached years of discretion and make their own selection of a partner. Boghos Effendi did not easily change his mind.

It seemed they had no hope.

After some despairing thought, Rafael realised that in fact he had no choice but to approach Elbisse's father. An elopement was unthinkable, and this did not even enter into the possibilities they considered. There were really only two alternatives: either he could face Boghos Effendi now, or he would have to face him later. Rafael went to the meeting with considerable trepidation.

The Eramian family's home in the walled part of the city was near to the Melikian mansion behind the Armenian Church, a large traditional

Cypriot town house with balconies, tiled roofs, and a courtyard garden. He arrived punctually on time and was shown to the drawing room, where he was left for half an hour to cool his heels. He used this time to compose himself, rehearse his speech, and to admire his surroundings.

These were eloquent of the family's status: thick carpets, crystal from Bavaria, a Murano chandelier, and elegant, polished furniture copied locally from the styles of Europe. His heart sank. He looked at the floor and twisted his fashionable straw boater in his hands. Suddenly, the hat didn't seem quite as modish as it had a little while ago.

He was back in the street in very short order. The interview had gone just as badly as he had feared. He was told frostily that he certainly would not be allowed to marry Elbisse, and that he would be well advised to put any further proposal from his mind. Boghos Effendi, very much the patriarch at his most forbidding, went on to say that any further attempt to see his daughter would result in her confinement to the house, where he would be completely unable to communicate with her.

He did not take into account the excellent postal service Cyprus enjoyed under the British administration.

They did not completely despair. As yet, none of the servants had betrayed their meetings at the glade, thought they must have known about it by now, and they both hoped this would not change. It was their lifeline. At least they could still see each other now and then, even if it was only from a distance, and this was their only consolation as month followed month. Elbisse's stubborn nature matched her father's, and soon it was a year. Neither side relented.

The couple were made of sterner stuff than Boghos had thought. Elbisse was paler and rather thinner, but still stubborn. She refused to meet any of the young men he entertained at his house and at the farm, and she kept to her room except at mealtimes, when she could not avoid a house guest, but she remained quietly and adamantly opposed to her father's will throughout.

Rafael greeted Elbisse's father respectfully whenever they chanced to meet, and had to be content with a chilly sketch of a bow in return. Boghos Effendi was far too well bred to ignore the greeting of a respectable man in public, even if that man had presumptuously stolen the affection of his favourite daughter, but he returned only the minimum of recognition and gave the young man no encouragement.

Rafael tried his best to stay hopeful, worked hard, and did a great deal of thinking. If a teacher's job was too lowly, and too badly paid to please his prospective father-in-law, what else could he do? What would change the mind of a man like Boghos Effendi? He could think of several eminently respectable professions, but all of them demanded considerable financial outlay and a long period of study abroad.

He could see no alternative, however, and he resolved to show his faithfulness and determination. He borrowed the money he needed from Elbisse's brother Stepan, bade a miserable farewell to his beloved, and went to France to study dentistry in Paris, at one of the best Universities in Europe. It was an exciting and fascinating place, and he could have been completely happy there had not the absence of Elbisse made him feel so wretched. Meanwhile the two of them grew older and still their love proved constant and was unchanged by their years apart.

Two years passed, and then another.

It was difficult not to lose hope, but Elbisse and her father had the same unswerving, stubborn nature, and neither would give way. They were equally implacable and unyielding. Yeghsabet watched them with great sadness, and pitied them both. Neither Elbisse nor Raphael had been young when they met, and she thought it was tragic that they were denied this best time of their life together. She instructed her maid to intercept any letters which arrived from France and to pass them to her before the post was taken in to her husband. She slipped these under her daughter's pillow and told herself that she had not exactly *given* them to Elbisse.

It was four years before the lovers were reunited, and this was only because Boghos Effendi suddenly died. Elbisse had loved her father very much indeed, despite their differences and she found it hard that her happiness should only be gained by his death. He had loved her too, and was good to her in his own way. She missed him very much but she put her grief aside to help Yeghsabet, who seemed to have become old and shrunken almost overnight. She saw that there was a terrible fee to pay for love, a price which was to be paid by the survivor.

However, at last the steadfast devotion of patient, faithful Rafael and his beloved Elbisse could be rewarded. Rafael qualified in his chosen profession and set up his surgery, their marriage took place, and their life together was long and rewarding, and blessed with much contentment and two fine sons.

Miss Elbisse Eramian

☞

Now the final, dreadful stage of the genocide began. The Ottomans decided that all the cities, towns and villages should be cleansed of this troublesome minority and that all the Armenian people should die, and this part of the slaughter was very well planned.

Some of the Armenian intelligentsia and meritocracy thought themselves safe from the atrocities because they were an integrated, respected and influential part of the Ottoman empire, and they were astonished to find that they, members of the government, doctors, professors, scientists, lawyers, and merchant princes, were as easy to kill as the most illiterate and humble peasant. Armenian soldiers serving in the army were separated from their Turkish fellows and had their weapons confiscated on various pretexts, after which they were marched to their deaths. When it was over, one million and five hundred thousand men, women and children had died, many in the most horrible and agonising of ways, and their lands and possessions were stolen.

1915
Hasmik and the Death March Major

THE LINES OF WOMEN and children wound slowly across the parched and stony landscape. They shuffled along in their hundreds, and they would have moved faster if they could, but their tired bodies were starved, they had endured hunger, thirst, beatings and casual rapes for days and weeks and months, and they knew it would not be long before the next band of men came to have some fun with the defenceless *Giavour*.

The little they had been able to take with them when the soldiers forced them from their homes had been sold or stolen early on, and they ate what they could find along the way or they died.

For some, death was preferable because their lives were a kind of hell. They were not the first to flee along this barren desert road; it stank with the smell of death, of corpses fresh and old, and it was rank with human waste and urine. It was not wise to leave the ragged, suffering crowds for any purpose, not even to answer the call of nature or to bury a loved one in a shallow grave. There seemed always to be someone watching, some man, single or in company, who would be quick to take the opportunity to abuse a lone woman or child.

There was no one to protect them. Most of their husbands, fathers and sons had been taken away months before, even before they were turned out of their homes to suffer and die on this road. Those men who had been with them when they set off so long ago had died under the swords, or knives, or feet and fists of the predatory gangs of soldiers and villagers along the way, those ordinary men with families of their own who had been given the permission of their religion and their state to regard these pitiful, helpless people as less than human, as *things* to be used or killed or sold into slavery as the fancy took them.

The murder of a nation was taking place.

It brought out the very worst in them: it turned men and boys into monsters, laughing as they urged each other on to even more dreadful acts, each unwilling to seem less zealous in his punishment of these people for the crime of daring to exist, of daring to plead for mercy, of daring to be helpless. It was as if the prisons had been emptied of murderers, perverts, sadists and paedophiles, and all of them had gathered at this road.

They learned not to hope for compassion or pity, and that it was best to endure silently. Except of course for the children. They still wept when they were hungry, a thin, hopeless wailing, and the little ones cried and struggled and called for their mothers when they were taken away from their families to be sold into slavery or to provide some moment's pleasure.

Cruelty was commonplace and death a daily event.

Thousands more followed behind Hasmik's group, and thousands more would follow after those, until hundreds of thousands of women and children had walked and suffered and lived and died on this terrible, hellish road. The route through Turkey to Aleppo was littered with the bones and bodies of those who had gone before.

Hasmik had been a boy for the last two months, ever since her brother was beheaded for trying to stop Luisine from being dragged away by a platoon of soldiers. The Turks had swords, and they held Mikail still, with his arms dragged behind his back and his neck pressed against a flat stone. Their officer hacked at him inexpertly and his life bled away into the thirsty soil while the soldiers counted aloud the blows that killed him. Hasmik tried to support her half-fainting mother. She did not want to watch but she could not tear her gaze away, and she stared in horror as her beloved brother strained against their hands, pleaded uselessly for his life, and died. His wide, dark eyes were still open and they became caked with dust as his head rolled away, a sight which would haunt the days and nights of his mother and sisters till the end of their days. Now he was just one more corpse to rot in that wasteland of stones and terror. He was eleven years old.

They took Luisine anyway, and she died of their attentions somewhere in the hills.

Hasmik was wearing Mikail's dirty ragged shirt, still stained with his blood, rusty against the deeper red. There was no water here for washing clothes or bodies, it was far too precious to waste in such a way. His old, patched breeches fitted her now she was half-starved, and with her hair cut roughly short and her face unrecognisable under its covering of grime, she made a believable boy. She smelt dreadful, and she had lice and fleas. Altogether she was most unpalatable, even to those who enjoyed boys.

It saved her almost till they reached Aleppo.

The Turkish officer rode slowly along the road, casually inspecting the women as he went. Actually, he was supposed to be estimating how many refugees would be likely to reach Aleppo in the next few days, but there was always the chance there might be something special among the new arrivals.

Hasmik was carrying her little sister on her back as she walked. There were only three of her family left alive now. Krikor had died in the middle of the night from dysentery and fever a few days ago, quietly and with no fuss, so that they thought in the morning that he was only asleep. Her remaining little sister was listless and weak with hunger, and her weight was so slight that she was no burden. The child's body was too wasted, her skin stretched too tightly across her cheekbones and her eyes were huge and bruised in the pinched little face, but she made no complaint and she slept most of the time. She desperately needed food, and Hasmik was distracted enough to lift her head and look up as the officer passed by, hoping that it might be one of the relief groups which rumour said were helping the refugees in Aleppo.

She met his eyes and knew at once that it was a terrible mistake. She looked down and concentrated on the road in front of her feet, and the cracked, dusty heels of the woman ahead.

"Let him not notice me." she prayed, desperately, "Please God, please let him not notice me."

The Major reined in his horse and gave her a long, thoughtful stare. There was something strange about this dirty boy carrying a child on his back. Those eyes had been extraordinary, very dark and slightly slanted, and with lashes like a girl's. The mouth which tightened as their gazes met had been a soft rose-pink. He nudged his horse into a walk and kept pace a little ahead of her.

Beside her, Hasmik's mother began to pray too.

The Major was still puzzled. Sometimes these people made their girls into boys in an attempt to keep them safe. He looked at her more carefully. Yes, there it was, the difference. She did not walk quite like a boy. There was a slight softness about her as well, if you looked for it, and he was experienced in assessing a woman. She was a girl, maybe thirteen or fourteen years old. Probably untouched, and that in itself was desirable.

He pointed her out to two of his soldiers and told them to bring her out of the line. Seeing the girl's mother weeping as she took her last little daughter into her arms when the men took the child from Hasmik's back and dragged her away, he decided to be generous. He could afford a gesture. "Give the old woman some food," he said. "Enough for a few days."

Hasmik's mother was not in fact old, but hardship and starvation had made it seem so. She had learned how to stay alive in the months of travel, and she would later share the bread and meat with two bigger, stronger women who could prevent the rest being stolen, so that she and her only remaining child would have a chance to survive. An amount sufficient to feed healthy soldiers for a few days would feed starving women for much longer, so the bundle of food lasted long enough to get them to Aleppo, and the Major's afterthought saved four lives.

Months ago, she had told her girls what to do if they were to be taken by soldiers.

"It is something no mother should have to tell her daughters," she said, bitterly, "but you may live if you do not struggle. Do not look at them. Do not beg, it will do no good. Do not call attention to yourself in any way." She knew that they might die nonetheless, but if they did not anger their kidnappers, there was at least a small chance that they might be allowed to live.

She had survived one such attack herself, and she buried her pain and shame and utter humiliation deep in her heart in order to go on, to keep her little family together. They would have had no chance without her.

She had hoped that Luisine might return too. At that time they had been near the front of their group and they waited as long as they could by the road while the procession walked past, but her daughter did not come back to them. The rest of her children could not survive without the band of other women, and so at last she was forced to make the terrible and bitter decision to follow them and to abandon all hope for her eldest girl.

Hasmik remembered that her mother's advice had been no use to Luisine and she did not go quietly. She struggled and bit and screamed. She lashed out with feet and fists, and tried to throw herself from the horse when they lifted her up in front of the Major. He took one look at her lousy, flea-ridden hair and dropped her back into the dust.

"Dear me," he remarked, mildly, "how unladylike," and he had her feet and hands tied, so that she could be thrown across the back of a mule for the journey back to barracks.

On arrival at the compound, she was carried, still kicking, biting and cursing, to the officers' bath house, and here she was treated with the first kindness she had encountered for a long, long time.

Hasmik was born in Turkey and she spoke the language naturally and elegantly, with an educated accent, so that the curses she had learned from the angry, desperate women on the death march sounded extremely odd. The bath house attendant, a thin, stooped, and elderly man, tutted at the two soldiers who pushed her through the door so roughly that she fell, and he raised an eyebrow at her language as he helped her to her feet.

"If I may offer some advice, *hanumefendi?*" he asked softly, as he took her bound hands in his and began to pick at the knots.

Startled to hear a kind voice, she hiccupped, and stopped cursing. "I may not take it," she said, eventually, fully intending to make a break for freedom as soon as her bonds were loosed.

"No matter. But I would most strongly advise you not to run from here. The soldiers would certainly catch you, and if they did not know you were the Major's lady they might ... harm you."

"I'm *not* the Major's lady!" she protested indignantly.

"But you must see that if you are not his, then you may belong to anyone, or worse, to many." He waited to be sure that she understood him, and then he placed a cup of chilled fruit juice, beaded with moisture, on a small table near to her hand.

She was silent as she considered the implications of his remark. She drank the fruit juice quickly, while she thought he was not looking. She had never tasted anything so wonderful.

Meanwhile, he quietly pottered about, bringing soap of two kinds for hair and skin, soft thick towels, sponges and loofahs, and a fine-toothed comb to tease out nits and fleas. He opened the taps to the sunken marble bath and dropped a little precious, scented oil into the hot water. A lovely fragrance filled the room as the water steamed gently.

At last he came and stood before her. She was sitting perfectly still, beginning to feel utter despair, her body sore from the jolting she had endured while she was tied across the bony back of the mule, and her heart breaking at the thought of her grieving mother, alone now with her little sister on that terrible road, and terrified for herself at the thought of what lay ahead. She had resolved to show no weakness and she kept her face impassive, but a tear slowly tracked a cleaner line down her grimy cheek.

The gentle old man looked at her with pity. He wished he could save the poor child, but since this was impossible, at least he would try to make her as comfortable as he could. "If the *hanumefendi* will allow me to help her," he said, bowing, "let us see if this good hot bath will take a little of the pain away."

"Nothing can do that," she told him, shortly, and stayed where she was.

"Your pardon, but I meant the pain of the body, not the pain of the heart." He looked at her and thought for a moment, and then he understood the reason for her reserve. She had probably never met anyone like him.

"My lady should not feel awkward with me," he went on, "My name is Nasr. I am not a man such as you have known. His Excellency would not allow a proper man to attend his lady, and I am a eunuch. I was cut when I was a child, younger than you are now, so I never grew to manhood and the bodies of young women seem only wondrous works of God to me. My presence at your bath is no more threat to you than the company of another woman, and besides this, I am old. I have been an attendant at the bath for many, many years and you need not notice me or even speak to me if you do not wish to. I promise you that the bath will feel wonderful, and you will have some good food afterwards."

Hasmik's stomach disobligingly growled at that moment. The old man's understanding smile and sympathetic eyes touched her, and made the first tiny crack in her resolve.

"Come," he coaxed, "let's see if the bath is as good as I think it is,"

The Agha's Children

Hasmik was only twelve years old, and she had suffered hunger, pain, terrible grief, terror, and humiliation. She had lost her home, her possessions, her family, and her youth, and she found it difficult to resist this gentle, harmless old man who showed her such thoughtful kindness and compassion.

Further, she had fully understood Nasr's tactful warning, and she knew that even the repulsive attentions of the Major would be infinitely preferable to the brutality of a platoon of soldiers.

She submitted to the bath, and later to the inch by inch delousing of her hair, and the soaping and cleansing of her body. He tended to her gently, and did everything with the utmost care for her youth and modesty, explaining everything he would do, and telling her often how pleasant it would feel to be clean and comfortable. She allowed him to dry her and to examine her with careful delicacy for any remaining fleas or other vermin, and finally to smooth a wonderfully soothing cream into her dry and thirsty skin.

He brought underclothes, a satin evening gown and matching slippers, and he helped her to dress.

At last, he presented several perfumes for her approval, and he praised her final choice. "My lady has known these things in the past, I think," he said, as he put the crystal bottles back into their polished, satin-lined cedar wood case.

She put her head in her hands and fought the tears. Her lost and beloved mother bought a similar perfume for her two oldest girls last Christmas. It seemed so very long ago.

Nasr busied himself with tidying up and putting things to rights so that she could regain her self-control before he spoke again.

"Someone will come soon to take you to His Excellency. He is an experienced man, a cultured man. Do not be afraid that he will beat you or harm you."

"I am *not* afraid," she said, but she was lying.

1915   Hasmik and the Death March Major

The Major was very pleasantly surprised when Hasmik was escorted to his quarters half an hour later. Her short dark curls shone, and apart from one large bruise, which would fade, the smooth golden skin of her shoulders was unmarked above the fashionable dark green satin of her gown. Her eyelids were subtly darkened, her lips softly rouged, and a sophisticated perfume surrounded her. Her response to his polite greeting was framed in cultured accents, and there was no trace of the dirty, foul-mouthed, flea-bitten urchin who had been taken from the line of haggard and starving women earlier in the day.

He asked her name, decided that he did not like it, and told her that he would call her Yasmin, which he found less outlandish.

All she had left was the name her mother gave her, and she refused to let him take her identity away. She would not answer to his choice and she corrected him quietly each time he called her by the new name.

He frowned, but he let it pass, and he set about charming her. This was a fruitless task and eventually, faced with her unswerving but courteous resistance he gave up the attempt and resorted to getting her drunk before the evening's end. He detested violence, at least in the bedroom.

In the morning, her dark eyes glared angrily at him above the sheets, which she held tightly under her chin. She would not speak to him.

He was amused by this pretty, defiant child and her air of stubborn superiority. He decided to keep her.

Hasmik decided to die.

On the second day of her fast, the Major had an excellent idea. He sent for Nasr and appointed him Hasmik's personal attendant, with the express duty of making sure that she ate and was healthy.

When she opened her eyes on the third morning she was feeling very weak. She could not stop thinking about her mother and sister, their loss was a constant pain in her heart, and she wished she had not woken at all. She had already been half starved when she arrived, and though she had eaten a little at the Major's table, another two days without food had sent her well on the way to her goal. She could hear someone in the room and looked cautiously over the covers to see who it was. Nasr was moving quietly about the room, sweeping up the crockery she had thrown to the floor the previous evening, and arranging roses in a crystal vase which she had not seen before. There was the tempting aroma of fresh coffee.

She watched him for some time without moving.

After a while, he noticed that she was awake and brought her a cup of the coffee and a plate of tiny cakes on a breakfast tray.

He put the tray on the bed next to her, brushed a tendril of hair away from her eyes, and smiled. "Good morning, *hanumefendi*," he murmured, "I am so very happy to see you again, and to see also that my brave lady is well."

Had it been anyone else, Hasmik would have thrown the tray to the floor but she felt a bond to Nasr, who had shown her kindness and respect, and she regarded him gravely but did not move or speak.

He brought the little branch of roses and showed them to her. "I picked these for you on my way here. They are red, for your valiant heart, and see, there is still a precious jewel of dew in the heart of this flower." He sat cross-legged on the floor beside the bed, and he went on talking softly, coaxing her to listen. "Life is the great gift of Allah, *hanumefendi*. He has given you a greater trial than most, and a greater courage, and if you look into your own heart, you will find a precious jewel there, too. In you lives the memory of your dear ones, and the future of your father's House. These are your legacy for the years to come."

Hasmik listened. Nasr was a man with true courage, and he was the only one who could have reached her on this day. He knew her intention, he had not only lost his family, but he had lost his manhood and his freedom too, in a violation quite as dreadful as hers. He had the courage to resist the temptation to end his life in the only choice a slave has the freedom to make: the decision whether to live or die. With an

1915 Hasmik and the Death March Major

extraordinary compassion and understanding he was trying to comfort her in her present misery, and to give her hope.

Nasr saw that she was paying attention to his words. He smiled. "And now I have you to thank for my present good fortune, because the Major has chosen me to look after you and I am to be your personal servant, responsible only to you! It is against all custom for a lady to have a man to wait on her, but you know my condition, and so it is my great pleasure to serve you and to leave the hard work of the bath house to someone else." He offered her the plate of cakes for a second time.

She was very hungry. The coffee smelled so very good, and the little almond-flavoured cakes were her favourites, just like the ones they had at home.

Home. The thought stabbed at her.

Flinching, she waited for the pain of loss to overwhelm her again, but her hungry young body insisted on smelling the coffee and her mouth watered. There was a long moment when her future hung between life and death.

Her body chose life.

Hasmik became the Major's official consort and hostess. She was well bred and well educated, and her only fault in his eyes was to have been born to the wrong race and the wrong religion. She refused to convert to Islam, against his express wishes and the threat of abandonment, but still he kept her.

She managed his household. She received his guests graciously and entertained them faultlessly; the dinners were arranged to perfection, the flowers, the music, the service all beyond reproach. The Major's staff began to take pride in their work and his soldiers stopped making jokes about his fancy Armenian whore, but they were greatly astonished when he took no other women for his pleasure. He was intrigued by her. Always she kept something of herself back, a little aloof, unreachable, unpredictable.

She would smile at him distantly with her mind elsewhere when he was at his most complimentary and romantic, and instead of annoyance he felt amusement.

She would ignore his expensive gifts and cherish a flower which Nasr had given her, and he would be a little chagrined, but forgive her.

He gave her a pretty, pampered lapdog which she immediately passed to her servant, and instead she adopted a scrawny, flea-bitten little yellow cur with big anxious eyes and a bad habit of watering the carpet. He did not understand that the starving little beast reminded her of herself.

He found that she had been with him six months, and then a year, and he was surprised at his own surprise. His life was certainly more comfortable and he was more contented than he had ever been, and when he was posted to Cyprus as escort to the Turkish envoy, he decided to take her with him. Hasmik heard his decision with apparent calmness and gave no sign of her inner turmoil. She had not told the Major that she was pregnant, and she dreamed that now perhaps her child would not be born in the land of her slavery. It was an easy captivity perhaps and she was a great deal more fortunate than many of the women of her race who had been taken into bondage, but it was slavery nonetheless and an insult to the soul.

She would go to this island, this green and lovely place where people were free. Cyprus ... Kibris ... Kypros. It was beautiful in any tongue. To leave this terrible, satanic land, and perhaps to be among some of her own people. To have a little respect, and maybe to hear her own beloved language spoken once again. She began to make plans, and a little hope crept into her heart.

Nasr was to stay behind at his own request, and his company was the only thing she would regret leaving behind. He had saved her when she could find no reason to live and he was her friend in this evil and dangerous land. Once, and it seemed so very long ago, she had felt secure and happy in Turkey; it was her home and she had been proud of the country of her birth. Now she knew only that it had become a terrifying and barbarous place, inhabited by madmen, perverts and murderers. Her beloved dead were not even buried in its soil: their bones would have been scattered by animals and reduced to dust by weather and time. There was nothing to hold her there.

With every mile the ship sailed, she felt the terror of Turkey receding, as if the vessel were racing across the waves away from some great darkness, some sinister cloud. She could not wait for her first sight of the shores of the island she already thought of as a kind of Eden, a place of light and freedom, and she stood at the bow of the ship, smiling as she had not done for years. The Major went to her side, pleased to see her delight, and very glad that he had brought her with him. "Are you happy, Yasmin?" he asked, tucking her hand affectionately under his arm.

"Hasmik," she corrected him, automatically. But she smiled and nodded.

The Major had been provided with spacious quarters in the capital, and Hasmik waited until he was properly settled in, and occupied with nargileh and newspaper. Then, quietly, she left. She went to the only man whose name she knew in this city, and she asked for his help.

Boghos Effendi left his work and saw her at once when she sent in her father's name, that of an old friend and business associate in Turkey for whose safety he harboured the gravest fears. His man said that the young lady had called unattended, and that he had left her to wait in the salon. Boghos would be very glad to see his friend's daughter and to have news of their family, but he was surprised that such a young girl was allowed to walk in the streets unaccompanied by maid or servant.

His first glance showed him her expensive and fashionable clothes and her self-possessed air, and he halted his steps. He had known her father since this girl was a baby, and this poised, cosmopolitan young lady was not what he had expected.

He looked at her again, and he saw tears in her eyes as she began to take the steps which he had halted. She kissed his cheek and embraced him, calling him Uncle, and this was the first time that she had voluntarily shown affection to a man since her abduction. They sat down together, and she told him what had happened to her.

As she spoke, he regretted his initial hesitation. He had heard many stories of cruelty and brutality to his people in his lifetime and he had heard many times of the Death March. He had tried to help those who fled to Cyprus for refuge, but Hasmik was the daughter of his good friend and he was overcome with pity and anger. He offered her his protection and full support in whatever she chose to do, and he sent a servant to bring his wife to them. Hasmik would need the resourceful and irreproachably respectable Yeghsabet to help her to regain the honour and reputation which had been taken from her so brutally. The three of them talked until the afternoon was gone and they were ready to start a plan of action.

When Hasmik eventually returned to the Major's quarters, she was accompanied by two of Boghos Effendi's men and a haughty maid lent to her by his wife.

The Major was surprised to be told that the lady Yasmin was awaiting him in the reception room, and even more surprised when he saw her companions. His surprise became outright shock when she told him bluntly that from the moment that her foot had touched the soil of Cyprus, she was no longer his slave. This island was now under the control of the British and the practice of slavery had been abolished in the last century in the lands under their governance. He had lost his power over her.

Furthermore, she had come to tell him that if he wished to keep the child she was expecting, which may well be a son, he would have to marry her, and in order to do that, he must convert to Orthodox Christianity and take an Armenian Christian name and surname.

He recoiled. He could not have been more astonished if his horse had suddenly spoken to him and announced its independence. She could not possibly know what she was asking of him!

He would never be able to return to his homeland. He would have to pay lip service to a religion which was repugnant to him. He would have to answer to a name which was not his own. And if he did not do as she asked he would lose his Yasmin, his wife in all but name, and perhaps his son. A son! He stared at her, speechlessly.

He abruptly understood a little of what he had done to her.

While he remained dumbfounded, she turned on her heel and departed, leaving Boghos Effendi's card on his desk, in case he should wish to contact her.

The sudden conversion and marriage of the Major created less of a stir in Cypriot society than it would if his bride been born on the island. The Armenian mamas, while professing to be shocked at her decision to marry a Turk, no matter how well-born, wealthy or willing to convert, were nevertheless prepared to admit Hasmik to their society, particularly as Yeghsabet and her daughters went about with her. Soon no one thought any more about it.

Hasmik forgot nothing.

She often dreamed of her suffering, and the terror, death and grief which had come to her family on that hellish road to Syria and she woke crying, trembling and afraid. Though she heard no news of her mother and sister, they still lived on in her heart and she yearned for them, and prayed for their safety every night. Even when she was an old lady she would hasten to see any Armenian who arrived from Aleppo, but no one had heard of them or seen them, and at last she had to believe that they must have been among the many hundreds of thousands who died of disease, starvation or abuse in the refugee camps around the city.

She never loved the Major and she could not forget his actions nor forgive him for his casual cruelty and sadistic treatment of her people, but she hid her contempt and disgust for the sake of her children. She was his dutiful and treasured wife and so her sons were legitimate, and his heirs, and they grew up safely in freedom and the knowledge of their language, heritage, religion and ancestry.

Each Sunday, Hasmik went to the old Armenian church and knelt before the altar, where she spoke the names of her mother, her father, her sisters and her brothers so that they would not be forgotten, and she prayed for the peace of their souls before lighting a candle for each of them.

As Nasr had predicted, she had preserved her family's memory and she had secured the future of her father's House.

☞

HERE BEGIN THE STORIES OF THE LIFETIME OF BOGHOS ERAMIAN (UNCLE BOGHOS)

These are the years of the post-genocide generations, the children of the 'old families', and of the refugees. None of the family's history of this time is as tragic as the earlier years, and some of the refugees had nothing but good fortune and a gentle life.

Uncle Boghos was the grandson of Boghos Effendi, and he was only three years old when Diggin Zabelle came to Cyprus. They have known each other nearly all their lives.

1918

A Place of Refuge

The Meutemedian Family. Zabelle is at the back, between her brother and Hairabed.

DIGGIN ZABELLE Melikian is tiny, a little bent now, but always beautifully groomed. She is also blind. She has found this a disadvantage in more ways than one, as although she is 97 years old and growing very fragile, she loves to have visitors and people often feel awkward when they visit the blind, so that few of them now call on her. And of course she has outlived all her friends.

At one time, when she resided with her husband and his extended family in their enormous and lovely old mediaeval stone house in the Armenian Quarter of the walled city of Nicosia, she was surrounded by relations and servants, and was a famous hostess. When the Turks invaded Cyprus, they destroyed this wonderful and historic building and looted its treasures, selling many of them in foreign countries so that some precious items appeared later at auction in America. They even sold the banisters, which were beautifully carved, as well as the furniture and the carpets. What they could not take, they smashed, and it is perhaps one very small mercy that she has been spared the sight of the total ruin and dereliction of their little palace.

Diggin Zabelle speaks French, Armenian, English, Greek and Arabic, but she is also just a little deaf now, so when we visit her a sudden switch from one to the other can disconcert her while she is thinking in one language, and listening in another. She regrets most of all that she can no longer see to play cards because this was one of her most enjoyable pastimes, but she listens to the radio in whichever language takes her fancy, and so she keeps up with the news and current affairs.

All in all, she has come to terms with her present life though she is impatient with her increasing frailty. "I am not good," she will always tell us gravely, when we enquire after her health, "no, not at all." Then she will sit between us and take one of our hands in each of her soft hands and say, "But when you telephoned that you would come, I went at once and made the *pilavouna* for you. And you must have some of my ice cream. I have made it specially for you too, and I know that you will like it!"

So, even if we are trying not to get fat by eating too much of the wonderful food of Cyprus while we are there, we always have some. And we definitely do like it.

Every Armenian lady of a certain age has her own speciality, a dish which is hers alone and at which she excels, and *pilavouna* or 'flaouna' as it is more generally known, is Diggin Zabelle's. It is a delicious cheese pastry, made with sesame seeds and eggs. Her particular recipe involves cheese of Paphos, which we have never been able to find, but whatever it is, it gives her *pilavouna* a most enticing taste. The small ones take exactly four bites.

To make this special treat, she goes into the kitchen with her Sri Lankan maid and they work together to bake fresh pastries for the visitors. Diggin Zabelle recalls where everything is, and tells her maid from

1918   A Place of Refuge

memory exactly how much flour, eggs, cheese, etc. they will need, and the maid does the work while her mistress remembers how long this or that should be mixed, or baked, or left to stand, and what temperature the oven should be, so that everything will be perfect. This gentle and rather shy maid told us when we were leaving, that she writes everything down so that when she goes back to Sri Lanka she will give her own family the taste of delicacies from 'my lady's kitchen.' It's nice to think that Diggin Zabelle will be remembered in this way so far from her home.

When her guests have eaten, she will recall old times for us, and although she can no longer see them, she will bring out her photograph album and tell us about the people in the sepia pictures. One picture stands out especially: a portrait of her as a sixteen-year old girl, just engaged to be married. She still has the sweet roundness of childhood, and has unselfconsciously put both hands into those of her fiancé. She looks blissfully happy, and is delightfully unaware of her lack of sophistication in showing such happiness; and this is probably one of the things that entranced this very much more experienced son of a wealthy and reserved family. She was a charmingly natural girl, and she grew into a soignée and poised lady. This is the story she told us:

I was born in in 1908, in a town called Zagazig in Egypt.

We lived happily there without fear, though we had heard the stories of refugees from the oppression and murder of the Armenians in Turkey, and we knew that hundreds of thousands of our people had been killed there. We grieved for them, and helped the refugees when we could, but we did not think that such a thing could happen in our own land.

I was ten years old, and my sister was nineteen when something happened in Cairo that changed our lives and our future, and made us fear that we too were suddenly in mortal danger. We heard that a riot had broken out in the capital and that it had quickly spread through the streets. Some Germans who had been caught up in it and could not get away threw things at the crowd which was pushing them this way and that, and the people panicked, thinking that these things might be explosive or dangerous. They ran about shouting *'Alemani, Alemani'*, but some of them heard it wrongly and thought that they were shouting *'Armeni, Armeni'* and they rushed to the Armenian quarter and began attacking the people in their houses and starting fires.

My father became very grave and worried when he heard about this, and he and my mother talked together for a long time and they reluctantly decided that they could not risk the lives of their young family if things were to get worse. They told me that we were leaving the house where I was born and which was all I knew, and that we were going by sea to an island, a place completely surrounded by water. There, we would be safe from harm, but we must leave behind our friends and our home for ever and I would never see it again.

I knew that I had no choice and must obey my father, but I did not sleep at night because I had never been on an island, and I was frightened that it was a dangerous place to be. What if the water one day rose high enough to cover the whole of the land? We should all drown. I could not sleep well for a very long time. I worried about it every time I laid my head on my pillow, and it was an even longer time before I truly believed that my fears were unfounded and that the water would never cover such mountains as we have in this beautiful land.

We landed at Famagusta on the first of April 1919, and we stayed in an hotel there. Everything was different and strange, and we were very sorry to find that there were only a few Armenians in the town. My parents decided that with so many dreadful things happening everywhere to our people, they would feel happier if we could live where there were more of us, so we took a train from the coast to Nicosia to look about. In the capital city there was a thriving Armenian community and so we felt more comfortable there, and we rented the top floor of the house belonging to Sara Hatchadurian, to stay awhile and see how things were.

1918 A Place of Refuge

After a while, my father and mother began to feel that it had been a good decision, and they looked less sad and worried. There were families who had been there for a hundred and fifty years and they were respected among both the Turkish and Greek populations, having the titles of Agha, Bey, and Effendi, and they ran businesses and held important government posts.

Some had wealth and position, but there were also plenty of artisans, merchants and traders, and there were many shops and businesses with Armenian names. Also, there was a good congregation at the church. Best of all, the island was under the jurisdiction of the British Crown, and so it seemed to us that there was a reliable rule of law here and that we could live safely and without fear.

On the first Sunday of our stay in the city, we naturally went to church.

It was a lovely day, the sun was shining, and we went early so that we could be there at the beginning of the service. It was a very fine stone church, and very old, and it was overlooked by the little palace of the Melikian family, whose patriarch had been Hairabed Agha, and was now his son Artin Bey.

Artin Bey Melikian had left his marriage late, and though he was at this time 61 years old, his eldest son and heir Dikran was only 23 and still a bachelor. He was a handsome young man, well mannered and with a good nature that was very appealing, but he had not yet found the girl he would like to marry.

Dikran was standing at a window overlooking the church and idly watching the worshippers arrive for morning service, and so on this first Sunday of our first week in Nicosia, he saw my sister Alice standing in the sunshine with my parents.

He looked long at her, and wondered who she was, and then he hastily got ready and rushed downstairs to join the congregation. He was a little in love from her very first sight of her and he could not wait for a chance to meet her, and so after the service he introduced himself to my father and welcomed him to Nicosia. He looked at Alice with admiration, and he told her that he had not been able to wait to speak to her. She found this very romantic and she was inclined to like him from the beginning too, and so eventually they married and were very happy and contented together.

Dikran's younger brother was named Hairabed, after his famous grandfather the Agha, and he was just sixteen years old at this time. I was only ten years old myself, but I liked him because he was polite and he did not mind talking to a little girl who was on her own. I thought it was very pleasant to spend time with him and to hear about the island and his life, and we often found ourselves sitting together while his brother and my sister were looking into each other's eyes. He was very considerate to an awkward child and he was never unkind, and he was handsome and popular besides, and very soon I fell in love with him, but of course I did not say anything about it. We saw each other frequently, and I loved to dance with him or just to be in his company, but I *was* only a little girl and his attention to me was only that of a well bred young man with his sister-in-law's relations. It was some years later, when he noticed at last that I had grown into a young woman, that his interest changed.

One lovely spring evening, we were sitting outside on a balcony of their house, at ease with each other and feeling pleased to be alone together, when he unexpectedly asked me to marry him.

Oh, I was so surprised and happy! Of course, I said I would love to marry him, but suddenly I realised that perhaps it could not be – in Egypt, our church would never allow the marriage of a couple whose brother and sister had already married each other. I was sure it was the same here, and my heart sank. Sadly, I told him my fears, but I had not taken into account the Melikian wealth and influence. Hairabed would not say such things to me of course, but he was sure that the Bishop in Nicosia would have no objections once his father had a little talk with him, and he thought that after this small delay we could marry soon.

The Bishop was indeed very kind, and any objections were overlooked. After all, there was no blood connection between the two of us.

Then Hairabed asked my father for my hand, but to my horror, he said he was unable to give his consent to our marriage because he was the younger son of my grandfather and his elder brother made all such decisions for the family. We had to wait again, and I began to wonder if we should ever be together.

However, my father wrote at once to request my eldest uncle's permission and to tell him about Hairabed, and I waited anxiously for his reply. Things were so in those days. It was very trying.

To my relief my uncle sent his permission at last, and we were married in the very church where Dikran had first seen my sister. Hairabed was my only love and we were very happy together. I have been fortunate, and I have had a good life, though I wish my dear husband had lived longer, and I am only sad to have outlived all my friends.

Diggin Zabelle turned her face towards us and reached out her hands. She has this polite habit of facing someone when she speaks to them, even though she can no longer see her guests.

"It was kind of you to listen to me, I have enjoyed telling you my story."

"No, no," we hastened to assure her, "we are grateful to you for spending time with us."

"You will come again soon?" she asked us, as her smiling little maid showed us to the door, "I shall try to be here for you but as you know, my health is not good. Do not leave it too long."

Mustafa came into the lives of the Eramian family only briefly, but he made a lasting impression on them. He was a man to frighten the children with, so that they will stay safely in bed at night.

Uncle Boghos was a nine-year old boy then, but like so many of his ancestors he has always loved horses, and his memory of the beautiful stallions brought to Deftera by the King of the Hejaz is very clear. He also remembers very well the dignified guardian eunuchs and the aristocratic, supercilious racing camels.

Later, when he inherited the farm, he bred his own fine, swift horses at Deftera and he had many notable successes at the Nicosia race track.

1924
Mustafa the Assassin

WHEN UNCLE BOGHOS's grandparents Huliané Eramian and her husband Apgar Guvezian inherited the farmhouse which had been built by their ancestor in the eighteenth century, it was very different from its modest beginnings. The original three arches still looked out over the pool with its cool and swift-running water, but there were a great many newer rooms. Even though some of the original lands had been left to other descendants, the two young people inherited a sizeable estate, and they were related to all of the six Armenian 'old families' by birth or marriage. These families were among the first of their race to settle around Nicosia and they were then great landowners, but at this time, not one of their descendants still qualified for the high title of Agha.

Huliané and Apgar welcomed any of their family who needed to escape from the heat and dirt of the city, and they enjoyed the company of their cousins and took pleasure in arranging musical evenings, entertainments, dinners, picnics and parties for them. They were also hosts to titled and powerful people of many nationalities, and they entertained them well. Once in a while they would be requested to accommodate a guest of the state, and sometimes they were asked to take one who could not officially be welcomed.

The Agha's Children

In 1924 when the King of the Hejaz was forced to flee by his angry people and they put his son in his place, he fled to Cyprus. By this time, Apgar had died, and the competent and resolute Huliané was solely in charge. She missed Apgar terribly, but she was trying to manage the farm with the help of her daughter Shenorik and her reliable son-in-law Stepan, who were living close by at the newer farmhouse. This had been built at the second spot their great-grandfather had considered when he first rode over his land, the site which was away from the river and nearer to the village of Deftera and the Nicosia road.

With the loss of Apgar's steadying hand, the older Three Arches farmhouse began to show its age, and it had begun a gradual and sad decline. Huliané's only son Hagop had no love for farming nor any real interest in his heritage, and her daughter Araxi married a man without experience in agriculture. Though the estate had been split again by the daughters' inheritance, it was still too large a concern to prosper with an inexpertly supervised workforce. At the time the King came to Cyprus, however, Apgar had been gone for only two years and the farm was still basking in the last of its summer.

The government was now wholly British and the Turks had lost even the illusion that it might be returned to them one day.

The King had been a good friend to the British and so he turned to them for refuge when he was deposed. The administration was unsure what the ex-King intended to do, or how much support he might muster if he tried to regain the throne he had been forced to leave against his will. He was welcome to stay in Cyprus but they did not want him to make any trouble and of course they would also like to have good relations with his successor, so it was arranged that he would lodge at Deftera when he first arrived. From there he could make arrangements for his future and for his life on the island without involving them.

He was an elderly and dignified man with an autocratic manner and an impressive, bushy white beard. His uniforms were heavy with bullion and the orders he wore glittered with diamonds and jewels. Even when dressed in the flowing, comfortable costumes of his Arab ancestry, his robes often bore a narrow border of embroidery in gold and silver, and everything he had was of the finest. He brought with him his wives, some black African eunuchs to guard them, three beautiful Arab horses, two camels, an ostrich and a large retinue of servants and bodyguards.

The King also brought with him the hatred of his enemies and the unwelcome responsibility of guarding him against an assassin's knife.

Huliané's son-in-law at the neighbouring farm was a careful and sensible man, who could always be relied upon to do his duty. Stepan was also rather stolid and unimaginative, and a man to inspire respect rather than admiration, but he had a very strong sense of family responsibility. His energetic mother-in-law seldom needed his help as yet, but it was reassuring to know that he was there, and at her request, in this emergency he agreed to help with the security of their somewhat alarming guest.

Stepan knew that he could not expect aid from the Government, and he decided to supplement the King's own guards with a dozen reliable men from the village. This would severely deplete his own permanent labour pool, but it was a family matter and therefore a necessary inconvenience, and he did not hesitate to offer them.

Accordingly, when the assassin hired to kill the King arrived in the village of Deftera, he found it impossible to get closer to his victim than the stables, where he had taken a job as a groom. His name was Mustafa and he was a Turk who had once been a farrier. He was tall and bearded, and because of his previous profession he was strong and muscular, and he had a knowledge of horses which enabled him to do his new duties well enough to avoid suspicion. Once established at the farm, he tried everything he could think of to get into the inner rooms where the guest quarters were, but he was thwarted at every turn. The lads from the village and the King's men were everywhere and a groom had no business in the house or the kitchen, so at last he had to accept that he would not be able to kill the King.

Mustafa had been paid a great deal of money to do his evil work, and he knew he had better prove to his masters that at least he had made the attempt. Besides, he enjoyed killing for its own sake, so seeing at last that he would not get near his real target, he crept at night into the stables where the King's magnificent horses were kept.

He went into the nearest stall and ran his hand along the glossy white neck of one of the big stallions. The beautiful animal turned his head and regarded him enquiringly with mild dark eyes, nuzzling his hand in the hope that he might have brought a morsel of carrot or some other treat. Mustafa stroked and patted his neck in a friendly way, savouring the moment, then, feeling for the jugular vein, he pressed the point of his long, razor-sharp knife against the soft skin and quickly cut deep into it, drawing the blade right across to the opposite side.

With his windpipe severed, the poor beast could make no noise, and he fell down, kicking helplessly and pumping his lifeblood into the straw on the stable floor.

In the next stall, the second stallion smelt the blood and he was alarmed and angry. He began to rear up and lash out with his hooves, shaking the boards which divided the stalls with the force of his powerful blows and neighing loudly. When Mustafa approached him, the big horse rolled his eyes and bared his teeth, kicking out at him and making it impossible for him to get close enough to do a good job. Mustafa slashed at him again and again with his wicked knife, but the stallion would not give in, and he fought and screamed and tried to kill his attacker until the assassin began to worry that someone might hear the noise and discover him, so he quickly made his escape, leaving the third horse untouched.

The injured horse was in a sorry state, but there were skilful men at the farm who knew how to treat the wounds so that they would heal cleanly. The great stallion's body was badly scarred but he lived, and he recovered very well, and because he was left to convalesce with the mares at Deftera when the king went to live in the Troodos mountains, the next generation of foals grew wonderfully fleet and their noses arched in a wonderfully patrician way.

Mustafa left the village and fled to Nicosia where he went to ground inside the walled city, and he hired rooms in some old arches beside the Paphos gate. He left his long, sharp knife in his lodgings when he went out, tied securely into its fancy tooled-leather scabbard. It would be noticeably out of place on the person of the man he intended to become. He shaved off his thick black beard, leaving only a fine moustache, and he cut his long black hair to a European length. He took to wearing proper trousers with a clean white shirt and a thigh-length jacket and a fez like a respectable man, and he threw away his baggy *vraga* and his long, heavy boots.

He was a clever and resourceful man, and when he wished, he could be charming and very plausible. He abandoned his rough speech and fierce manners, speaking softly, and smiling, and showing only a pleasant face. However, as the saying goes, a sow's ear cannot be made into a silk purse, and beneath the fine new clothes and pleasant manner, Mustafa the Assassin still lurked.

He made some new friends too, men who recognised the sort of person he really was, but who saw that he had plenty of money and thought that he might be useful, and he began to feel secure and relax his guard. These new friends took him about the town and particularly to the dim and smoky cabarets of the red-light district where he might evade the rules of Islam regarding strong drink, and where he could meet pretty, complaisant ladies of the night. They introduced him to men who could find him anything he wanted, and who let him know that they regarded him with great respect. He had plenty of money and no need to work, and he began to enjoy himself immensely.

One night, he was returning a little drunk to his lodgings just before sunrise after concluding a most satisfying assignation, when he looked up and saw a lovely girl sitting at the screened window of a first floor balcony.

Most houses in the city had these projecting balconies built above street level, and they were closed in with fretted shutters so that the smallest of cooling breezes could be enjoyed. Also, anyone inside could see out without being in view themselves. This beguiling maiden was brushing her long, blue-black hair in the lamplight, and she had opened the screen-windows in the cool early morning air, not expecting anyone to be about at that hour. Mustafa stood in the road beneath, gazing up at her, and in a moment or two, she noticed him. She closed the screen, waving a smiling farewell.

He went home and slept well, but he could not get her out of his mind and next day he took one of his friends to the street and asked him who lived in the rooms above.

"Oh *kardeshim*," said his friend, "you aspire too high. That maiden's name is Sureiya. She is justly famous for her beauty and her sweet nature, and although she is a courtesan, she is not a one-shilling or even a two-shilling woman, and she chooses for herself the fortunate man she wishes to honour with her favours. Her present protector is a very bad and very dangerous man, and you would be well advised to forget her."

However, Mustafa could not forget her, and his wish for her only increased when he was told that he could not have her. After all, he thought, I am as good as the next man, and my money is as good as anyone else's, and besides, she is only a courtesan, so why should she refuse me? He hired musicians to sing under her window and he sent gifts of flowers and jewels and perfume, but always she refused him, and she returned the gifts at once, politely and quite firmly. She wisely gave him no hope of gaining her favours, but Mustafa would not accept that any woman could really resist a big, bold man like himself. He could not believe that she really meant it, and, ignoring her refusals, he still hoped to succeed in his suit and win her for himself.

One night he had been drinking with his friends and he had reached the stage where he was ready to take insult from any small thing. He began to think about Sureiya's gentle rejection of him, and he staggered to his feet, his face reddening with injured pride. He made his unsteady way to her house, where he made an exhibition of himself and shouted in the street and knocked loudly and he refused to go away until she came to the door. After a while, for the sake of her neighbours Sureiya came down, and Mustafa roughly pushed past her into the house.

No one saw her alive again.

When she was found the next day the unfortunate young girl had been beaten and strangled, and her jewellery box was missing. After talking to the neighbours, who had seen a man they thought was Mustafa making a scandalous row, the police made out a warrant for his arrest. He went to ground once more and stayed in his lodgings, and did not go out.

Sureiya's protector was just as dangerous a man as his reputation had claimed, and moreover, he was very fond of the lovely young courtesan, and he missed her very much. He wanted her killer brought to justice and he let it be known about the city that he would be most pleased with anyone whose information led to Mustafa's arrest, and that his gratitude for their help would be generous and immediate.

Mustafa's new friends weighed their loyalty to him against the reward and the future good opinion of Sureiya's patron. This took very little time and there was really no debate, so very shortly thereafter, the erstwhile assassin was removed from his hiding place and sent to one of the government's prison farms in the mountains to do some productive work while awaiting trial.

The work was hard, but the prisoners were not ill treated and the food was good and plentiful so that they would be strong and could do their work well. Soon Mustafa lost the prosperous little round belly he had grown while he was a man about town, and his body became fit and hard once again. He behaved well and modestly, always humbly denying his guilt and claiming that he was the unfortunate victim of mistaken identity. He addressed his jailors respectfully and did his work without complaint, and eventually he ingratiated himself with the prison governor who made him a Trusty and gave him privileges.

One of the governor's house servants was a girl from Deftera, and her name was Eleni. Without his beard, she did not recognise Mustafa as the man who was lurking around her village just before the notorious assassination attempt on the King of Hejaz, but he did seem familiar and she felt rather sorry for him. He noticed this, and he took advantage of her sympathy. She believed him when he told her that he was not guilty, that he had only argued with Sureiya and then gone on his way, and that if he were to be executed for the crime of another man, it would be a very great injustice.

He seemed rather shy and diffident, and he craftily let Eleni see that he admired her very much and that he would be more than a friend if only things were different, but that he did not feel that it would be proper to court her while he was under such a cloud. Eleni was a sturdy country lass and she had never before been told that she was as graceful as a lily, that her eyes were like deep and mysterious pools, and that her smile was a sweet as a summer dawn, so she had no defence against clever Mustafa's beguilement. Her heart beat faster when she saw his tall, strong form among the other prisoners, and she dreamed of his slow, caressing smile and burning glances. She mentioned him in her prayers every night. She had fallen in love.

The prison governor was fond of his good servant Eleni, and over the months, he too had come to believe that there was at least a chance that Mustafa might be innocent. Eleni went to him and cried bitterly, and told him that she and Mustafa wished to marry, and she pleaded with him to help them. Her fiancé had accepted Christianity, she said, and he would take instruction and be baptised into the Church and live peacefully with her in her home village, where they would have many children and grow old together.

The governor pitied Eleni when she said that they deserved a chance, and after some more persuasion, he agreed to help. He falsely swore a statement that he had been playing cards with Mustafa all evening on the day of Sureiya's death, and that it could not have been his good friend who paid the early morning visit to the unlucky courtesan in the red light district.

The police knew very well that this was untrue, particularly as this statement was sworn so long after the event. They were deeply angered by this unexpected turn of events but they could not possibly call the prison governor a liar, because he was an Englishman and one of their masters, so they were forced to release the assassin.

Eleni and her fiancé went back to Deftera, where, as promised, he took instruction in the Orthodox religion and was solemnly baptised with the full ceremony in the church in the village, and he took the new name of Evagoras. Now he would never be able to return to a Muslim country on pain of death, and Eleni was satisfied that he really meant to be a good and faithful husband. They were married in the church where he had been baptised, with the prison governor in attendance, and with all the splendour and ritual of a traditional Greek wedding, after which Mustafa set up house with his bride and they seemed to be living happily as man and wife.

Mustafa bargained with himself that the new life he had gained was better than a much shorter one terminated by the hangman's noose, but again, underneath the smiles and piety, the old Mustafa still lurked. As time went by, he began to feel a little uneasy in Deftera, and he was worried that even with his changed appearance, someone might eventually recognise him. He persuaded his new wife that he would be happier working at his old job as a farrier, and that they should go to live in the village of Athienou, near to the Pentadaktylos mountains and far from Deftera. At this place there were great fields of corn and many mills to grind it, and therefore there would be plenty of mules needing his skills, and he could easily make a good living for them both by returning to his first profession.

For a while, all was well, but Mustafa was still pretending to be something he was not, and secretly he started drinking again. He began to go into Nicosia now and then, the better to gamble and to buy alcohol, and soon he was staying away for several days at a time, getting wonderfully drunk, basking in the flattery of those who ran the cabarets and bars, and spending some more of his assassin's fee which he had sensibly hidden, together with Sureiya's jewellery, before he was arrested.

During one of these visits he went to a night club and once again he drank too much brandy so that his first pleasant glow slowly changed to a sullen introspection. He began feeling angry and resentful and looked about for someone to blame. Scowling at a Greek youth sitting on his own at another table, Mustafa loudly asked if he was looking for a fight, but the lad merely looked surprised, said no, and prudently left. Mustafa stood up rather unsteadily and followed him from the red light district to the road which runs next to the top of the city walls, and there he caught up with the boy and started pushing him and calling him a coward.

The young Greek had done his best to avoid trouble, but he was just drunk enough that he could not continue to ignore the insults, and the two of them began to fight. Luckily Mustafa had not yet taken to wearing his long knife again, and their drunken, inaccurate blows mostly swung wide, half of them missing each other completely, and the other half having little effect other than to amuse the crowd which had quickly gathered to watch the fun.

Their fight moved across the road to the edge of the great walls which still girdle the old city, and under the light of the moon they moved closer and closer to the unfenced drop. When Mustafa saw this, he took his chance and he deliberately gave the boy a sudden strong push so that he fell with a despairing cry over the edge of the wall and broke his neck. The assassin looked around belligerently. Strangely, everyone had gone, so he went quietly back to Athienou and carried on as if nothing had happened, assuming that he had got away with a dreadful crime yet again.

This time he was wrong. Though the night-time inhabitants of the red light district had melted quickly into the shadows, a friend of the young man whom Mustafa had killed was emptying his uncomfortably full bladder behind some bushes. He was a horrified witness to everything, and with great good sense he remained hidden in the thick bushes till Mustafa left, so that he stayed alive to tell the tale.

He went to the victim's village and he told the boy's neighbours, friends and family what had happened. The women wept and screamed and tore their hair, and the men of the village went angrily to the house of the boy's father, to decide on a course of action.

They determined to take revenge themselves. It was well known that Mustafa had escaped justice in the past for the murder of the lovely courtesan Sureiya, and they resolved that he should not escape a second time. As it seemed that they could not rely on the forces of law they would conclude the matter without recourse to the police, and this way they could be certain that the victim's blood would not cry out for vengeance and he could rest in peace. At this point their own police officer, who was the boy's uncle, took off his uniform and put on *vraga* and boots, so that he might go with them.

They went to Athienou and waited in the fields outside the village till after the short Cypriot dusk. When the birds had all gone to roost and the last of the sunset had faded, they went stealthily through the village to Mustafa's two-storey house. If anyone saw the men walking past, silent and armed and grim of face, they closed their doors and windows and told themselves that nothing was there.

Mustafa was at home, pretending to be a good citizen, and quite early he went into the upper room. After a minute or two, the lamp went out and all was dark and still.

Quietly, they slipped the wooden latch on his door and went up the ladder to his bedroom, where the murdered boy's father ordered Eleni out of the room. She clung to Mustafa, screaming and pleading, and two of the men were forced to tear her hands from his nightshirt. With difficulty because she was still fighting and crying they carried her down the unsteady ladder to the kitchen, where they tied her to a chair, after which they went back upstairs to do their part in exacting justice for Mustafa's crime.

Ignoring his frantic declarations of innocence and another mistaken identity, and his pleas for mercy, each man shot Mustafa at least once so that no one could be sure who had killed him and only God could judge them.

When Uncle Boghos was a youth, many of the mountain villages had no outside interference in their affairs for many months at a time, other than the visits of tax collectors, and in the remoter areas it could take several days' travel to reach the nearest big town. Consequently, the local landholders and wealthy farmers were great men, and they had power over the landless and those who depended on them for work or water. Though Deftera was near to the capital, the Eramians had great influence in the village for many years, because of their control of the year-round springs.

Irini's village is in a wild and beautiful part of the island, an appropriate background for these dark and dramatic events.

1930

Irini's Revenge

IN THE SOUTHWEST of the island there is a small village which is a little way up a mountainside and overlooks the sea. Though our cousin Kapriel's house is in the middle of the village, it has a courtyard with a splendid view, looking over a pretty valley and a small ravine across to the next range of the foothills. Every morning, the olive trees slowly appear in the mist which hangs low over the fields, and their dark and ancient shapes are beautiful in the golden haze. In the evenings they cast long black shadows as the last rays of the sun slant low and red across from the sea. Kapriel has lived in his old stone house a long time and is part of the village, and he is contented there.

He is so contented that it is difficult to prise him away, even to go with us the short way down the twisting road to a taverna near the harbour for a fish dinner and a cold beer at the weekend.

Once, when we had managed to winkle him out of his beloved workshop to come with us to the sea, we took him to our favourite restaurant near the small harbour, where we relaxed, enjoyed our drinks and waited for the owner's boat to come in. When the fishermen arrived and they pulled it up from the water, we went to look at the fish they had caught. It was a huge *xifias,* its eye still bright and its rough skin silver and green and grey. It was a magnificent catch and so large that the sword of its nose thrust aggressively over the side of the little boat.

Half an hour later, we were presented with thick, succulent steaks cut from the middle of the fish, grilled on charcoal and dressed with a little dark green olive oil and lemon juice squeezed from fruit grown in their garden. As is the custom, a cold, crisp salad and chunks of fresh, fragrant *daktyla* bread had been served to us first in order to occupy us and to ease a little of our hunger, and the fish followed, accompanied only by smoking-hot, golden, crisp edged chips.

There is a wonderful flavour to these chips, made from the odd-shaped Cypriot potatoes grown locally in rich red soil. These potatoes are shaped as nature makes them, and are not specially tailored to European rules and petty decrees to be exactly the same size, or without their natural bumps and lumps, or smoothly curved to please the European eye, and they are not treated with preservatives to stop them sprouting inconveniently. In this part of the island, even potatoes are food of the Gods, and chips have never tasted as wonderful anywhere else in the world.

Sima is Kapriel's wife, or as she might say: Kapriel is Sima's husband. She has lectured at Harvard, and has a University degree and an intelligent and inquisitive mind, but she can also prune vines so that they bear a bounteous harvest, and she has picked and bottled her own olives, and knows how to roast and salt almonds from local trees so that they are crisp and mouth-watering. A neighbour taught her how to make *halloumi,* the unique and subtle sheep's-milk cheese that is the speciality of Cyprus, and she cooks delicious dinners with tender lamb and herbs, which she serves outside by candlelight in the velvet evenings. A dinner with the two of them is a precious gift, a warming memory of laughter and pleasure to savour in the cold, dull, grey and miserable winters of London. Sima leaves a shallow pan of water in the courtyard for the resident frog, and she doesn't lock her door.

They have a workshop in an old village house a little way down the

1930 Irini's Revenge

road to the sea, with a *fourno* in the garden and a huge old fig tree leaning across it. The figs are plump and luscious and black, with honey-sweet juice and sensuous velvety skin. Kapriel has set a long wooden table under his venerable and shady vine, with some straw-seated taverna chairs placed around it. Pieces of old pottery, a stone axe, a lamp, bits of shell or fossils, pebbles polished and shaped by the sea, and one or two flowers in dishes or small jugs are scattered along it, whatever he has found which is lovely or unusual or both. Against the rough stone walls of the old house he has placed bits of discarded machinery of many purposes and sizes, which he saved from being sent to the scrap yard, and these have the beautiful shapes of things that are perfectly made for their purposes and, moreover, were made by the careful hand of a craftsman.

In the summer, passing tourists see the sign which Sima has painted and put outside the workshop, and visitors often call into to see Kapriel and perhaps choose some of his work to take home. He enjoys talking to them, and as with so many of his countrymen, he can discuss his work in several languages. If he particularly likes a customer, he will leave his bench and offer tea and a chair at the long table in the courtyard, where he will have a longer conversation. Those visitors who assume that he is a stereotype, a unlettered villager who can neither understand their language nor take offence at their rude or ignorant remarks, will receive extreme politeness and considerable pity, but no tea.

We were sitting on a wall near his workshop, swinging our feet and waiting for Sima, when we first saw Irini. She was very old and bent, and very small; a tiny figure dressed in a rusty black skirt and a knitted black jacket with holes at the elbows, her feet thrust into cracked and dusty old shoes and a black headscarf tied uncomfortably tight around her thin white hair. She walked with a strange gait, leaning on a knotty stick which still had its bark. Progress was made by moving her weight from one side to the other and bringing each leg stiffly forwards, so that her thin little body swayed from left to right with each step.

"That is Irini," Kapriel told us, as she approached. "You wouldn't think, would you, that she was once the loveliest girl in the village, and that she is also the richest. My neighbour told me that if you took a good horse and rode him all day over the mountain and down towards the sea in that direction" and he pointed up the mountainside to where the fire-watch was kept, "you would still be on her land."

"Why doesn't she buy herself new shoes," I asked, "and maybe some new clothes?"

"Land is for keeping, *couzenes*, not for selling," Kapriel replied, and he jumped down from the wall politely as Irini slowly came towards us.

"*Yassou, Irini, eiste gala?*" he called to the old lady. "Are you well?"

"*Eimai gala, paidi mou,*" she replied, gravely. "I am well, my son." She gave us a radiant smile, black eyes twinkling among a hundred creases, her little face angled up towards us to compensate for her bent back. She paused for a moment to catch her breath, bestowed on each of us another smile and a sprig of mint from the bunch she had picked on her walk, and continued on her painful way.

Kapriel seated himself on the wall again. "I told you that Irini was once the most beautiful girl in the village, but she was also the most tragic," he said, chewing a bit of the mint, and he told us her story while we waited for Sima.

Irini's parents were the village midwife and the carpenter. She had no brothers or sisters, and by the time she was fourteen, she had grown to be graceful and slender and beautiful, and to her wondering parents she seemed like an angel which had flown down to earth to bring delight to ordinary mortals. Indeed, there was a painting of a saint on the wall of the mediaeval church that looked very much like her, with its flawless olive skin, large dark eyes and long black hair. The saint's name was Irini, and though the carpenter's daughter had been named Artemis, after a pagan goddess, very soon everyone called her by the name of the elegant, elongated Byzantine saint of their village.

A certain wealthy man whose farm bordered the village had three sons, all of them big, strong and violent. They pretty much did as they pleased, took whatever they wanted, drank too much, pestered the prettiest local girls, and bullied the other boys into angry submission. They were universally feared, hated and despised, but they had money and influence, and they lived an easy life on their father's farm, dressed in fine clothes, riding fine horses, and served by sullen villagers

The eldest son's name was Nicos, and he fell in love with Irini. He was stupid and uncouth, but because in the depths of his brutish mind there was a little, unfamiliar spark of love, he did not want to force this lovely and gentle girl. He wanted Irini for his wife. After much persuasion, because Irini had no dowry other than the finely carved chests and chairs her father had made for her, Nicos's father went to visit her parents.

When he entered their home, he noticed only that the rooms were small and that there were no cut glass lamps, no fine plates on the shelves, and no French clock or Turkish carpet. He did not see the beams, lovingly carved with flowers and birds, the bright rag rugs, the finely embroidered tablecloth, and the dyed and woven cushions on the good oak furniture. Such things had no value for him.

His lip curled disdainfully as he looked around him. He could not think why his eldest son would want to ally his family to peasants such as these when he could have had one of the fashionable daughters of a wealthy trader or merchant, but when Irini shyly came to join her parents, who seemed gratifyingly awed by their illustrious visitor, he understood his son's request. She was very lovely.

Well, the boy should have her.

Magnanimously, and very aware of his condescension, he proposed his son for Irini's husband without asking for a dowry. Further, he would give her parents a sum of money which would ensure a comfortable old age for them. Without sons, they might otherwise be destitute when they became too old to work, and this would take a great fear from their minds. Watching her mother and father as they listened to this proposal, Irini could see that they would greatly love to have such security. She could not bring herself to think of Nicos with anything other than revulsion, but she loved her parents dearly, and so she accepted him for their sake.

They were married in the dark little church where she had been baptised, under the saint's solemn gaze, and they were crowned with flowers. They were toasted in good strong red wine, and the villagers had a wonderful party with whole sheep roasted in pits, as much *shammishi* and *loukoumades* as they could eat, and unlimited brandy and zivania flowing freely from three great wooden barrels brought up from the coast.

This was a fine beginning, but it was not long before Nicos showed his true colours and he began to treat Irini very badly. She did not know that this was his real nature, and she did her best to please him and to make him happy, thinking it was some fault of hers. She greeted him each morning with a smile and brought his food to the table with her own hands, though they had servants for every purpose. She brought water and sweet-scented soap, removed his dirty boots, washed his sweaty feet and dried them with a soft towel when he came in each evening, and she gratified his every wish, but even though Nicos was stupid he knew instinctively that she did not love him.

As time went by he became more and more angry with her because of this, and he blamed her for his anger. He exercised a husband's right to beat his wife so often that even the servants began to feel sorry for her and at last they forgave her for being no better than themselves and pitied her fruitless attempts to please her husband. They knew too well from their own experience that he would never be satisfied with anything she could do. Their service to her gradually became more than just a duty and they vied to win a smile from their good and gentle mistress.

Her maid secretly brought ointments for her bruises and applied them to her injuries with tender care. The cook made special dishes to tempt her appetite, which had decreased in proportion to the frequency of Nicos's cruelty to her, and the gardener made special tiny bouquets of sweet-smelling flowers for her dressing table and brought her the best fruits from the gardens.

Irini appreciated their little gifts, but though she tried her very best, she was unable to smile and to be as light hearted as she once had been.

She thought things might improve when, after a year, she was able to tell Nicos that she was carrying his child. At first he was delighted. He had proved he was a real man, a virile man, and he would have a son to please his father and to carry on the family name. The next night he went to the village taverna and surprised the regular patrons by buying drinks for everyone. There he basked in the congratulations of his cronies and for a little while he was contented, but Nicos could not be other than the brute he was before they married, and he forgot about all this when next he lost his temper and he beat Irini so furiously that she fell. When he kicked her for good measure, she miscarried his little son.

She recovered, but she mourned for her lost child and she asked timidly if she might stay with her mother for a while. Nicos was furious at her failure to carry his son to term, which he told himself was her fault, and so he let her go. He was pleased to be a bachelor for a few weeks. He consoled himself in her absence with the women of the nearest town, and with drinking too much and gambling his father's money, and he enjoyed himself so much that for a time he did not care if she never came back.

When Irini returned to her childhood home her mother soon discovered what had happened, and she bitterly regretted that she and her husband had sent their wonderful daughter to such a bad husband. Lovingly, they helped her to take up her life where she had left it, and in these familiar and safe surroundings and with the tender care of her parents Irini began to recover her youthful bloom and beauty. However, she had learned a hard lesson and she covered herself carefully when she left the house, and kept her head down, stooping a little and walking slowly so that Nicos would not look at her and desire her and demand her return.

The Agha's Children

As the summer drew on, Irini's cousins from a nearby village came to visit their aunt and uncle, and they were shocked at the change in her. Her uncle's boys were named after two beautiful Greek heroes of ancient times, and Adonis and Paris amply justified the choice of their names. They were tall, handsome and golden-skinned, and they had become fine young men since Irini had seen them last. Shy at first, she blossomed in their admiring but strictly platonic friendship.

A village is a small place, and in every community there are malicious people who will see the worst in any situation and repeat it to cause trouble. After a week or so, a scurrilous tale reached the jealous Nicos, the tale that Irini was consoling herself with her handsome younger cousin Paris, and that Nicos was a cuckold, and was wearing a fine pair of *kerata*. The villagers were delighted to have something unpleasant to tell about the rich man's hated son, and they much enjoyed this tale. Some of the bolder ones sniggered and made the sign of the horns behind him as he passed. Nicos could hear them whispering and talking softly behind his back, but because it always stopped as soon as he walked into a taverna or kafeneion, he could never hear exactly what they said and so he had no excuse to pick a fight, and his rage and frustration could find no outlet. No one had *ever* dared to laugh at him before.

His anger and humiliation built until he could no longer bear it, and he called his brothers to his house to help him to plot retribution and revenge on this presumptuous peasant.

The next day, Nicos sent a message to to Irini's cousin Paris, supposedly sent by her and begging him to meet her at an abandoned *mandra* a little way from his village in the mountains. Assuming that she was in some trouble and needed his help Paris went alone and unsuspecting to see what he could do for her, but when he arrived he found Nicos and his brothers lying in wait for him. They ambushed him easily, and when he asked what he had done to anger them, they mocked him and pushed him about, saying only that the time had come for him to pay for his misdeeds and he should be very frightened. Ignoring his terrified pleas and his protests of innocence of any wrongdoing, they stripped his clothes from him and tied him to a tree. They took turns to hit him with fists and feet and sticks, covering his smooth golden skin with bloody stripes and great dark bruises and laughing at his screams. When he could no longer stand, they untied him and let him fall to the ground, where they surrounded him and kicked him with their heavy boots until at last he lost consciousness and finally, he died.

Even this was not enough. Nicos planned a further cruel deed.

The next morning, Irini opened the door of her mother's cottage to sweep the step, as was her custom, and she found a wicker basket there, covered with a linen cloth. She carried it into the kitchen and removed the cloth, expecting from the smell of it to find a cut of meat ordered by her mother from the butcher, or some such thing.

Inside the basket was the bloody, almost unrecognisable head of her cousin Paris. Irini stared at his awful, battered face, once so beautiful, till she was blinded by her hot tears. Her outraged and disgusted parents had recently warned her about the malicious gossip circulating in the village about herself and her cousin and she had feared what Nicos might do, and so she knew at once that only he and his brothers could have done this evil thing to her cousin. But Paris was innocent! And so was she.

Irini had never imagined that such viciousness and cruelty was possible. Her head swam and she could not breathe properly. She was forced to hold on to the kitchen table to control her shaking and to prevent herself falling to the floor, but after a while she was consumed by a cold rage and she was able to move. With a terrible calm, she tenderly covered the basket to hide the dreadful face of Paris, and she called for her mother to come down to the kitchen.

Only an evil and twisted man, rotten to his very core, could have beaten poor Paris to death and then arranged that his head should be delivered to her in order to cause her the greatest anguish, and by this dreadful act her husband had lost all right to her loyalty. She now felt no duty to him whatever, and she resolved to exact full payment from him for his lack of humanity, for his selfishness and arrogance, and for his murder of an innocent man. She would do this herself, for she knew that no villager would give evidence against him under threat of losing his livelihood or for fear of his family's vengeance. It would be easy: who would believe that a gentle and helpless girl like Irini could plan and carry out an act of vengeance?

Irini smiled in a way which would have frozen Nicos to his marrow, had he seen it. He would soon regret that by his stupidity he had freed her of her obligation to him.

Nicos was surprised but most gratified when Irini contritely returned to his home, and was apparently docile, repentant, and eager to please. How true it was that all a woman needed was a firm hand and an occasional good beating, he thought complacently. The morning after the drink-fuelled murder of Paris, he had come to his senses and realised that it was most unlikely that Irini would really be able to have an affair with her cousin in her own home and under the noses of her parents. But by then, of course, it was too late. Still, he and his brothers had immensely enjoyed beating that peasant to death and it still gave him pleasure to think of it.

The weeks went by, and Irini once again went about her duties as his wife, washing his feet, bringing his meals, smiling, obedient and docile, and obeying his every wish. His servants were also gratifyingly quick to follow orders, and he did not notice their stony faces or their sullen looks as long as they obeyed him. It seemed that to be feared brought good service, and he wished that he had frightened them properly sooner.

Irini's mother, the midwife, had an extensive knowledge of herbs, from those that cured or eased pain, to those that could kill or produce a miscarriage, but she had never misused her skills, nor given anyone reason to mistrust her.

1930 Irini's Revenge

It was strange that in the space of a single year, even though Irini and her mother tended them devotedly, Nicos's brothers began to sicken, one after the other, and they died in great pain, clutching their bellies and howling as their bowels turned to water. No one could have done more for them, or tended them more caringly, and the villagers said how lucky they were to have such good nursing in their time of need. Next, his father collapsed and died unexpectedly of a heart attack, having shown absolutely no sign of previous ill health.

Nicos himself lived long enough to see the birth of a child that looked quite unlike him, while strangely resembling Irini's cousin Adonis, but by then he was completely paralysed by his own unexpected illness and he was far too weak to beat his wife. He could only glare with rage-filled eyes at her and at the beautiful child which bore his name.

While the great powers were occupied with destroying enormous numbers of their young men, the second World War mostly passed the island by. There was a fear at one time that German paratroopers might invade, but it did not happen, and sadly, the blood shed in Cyprus during the last century was mostly caused by the hatred between one Cypriot and another, fomented by those two old enemies, Greece and Turkey, and fostered by the 'divide and rule' policy of their current masters, the British.

Hanemie was Uncle Boghos's aunt. She lived her life peacefully, and made no great impact on the history of the Eramians. She was, however, much loved.

1940

In the Midst of Life

HANEMIE ERAMIAN was sixty-eight years old and she was dying. She had known for a week or two that she would soon embark on her last adventure, and with her usual calm competence she made her preparations.

It was very pleasant to find just how many friends and beloved relations she had. She put aside a small gift for each of them, and she took it to each recipient herself. Why should she lose the great pleasure of seeing their delight by leaving the distribution of her things to the impersonal hands of a lawyer?

There was a brooch, a pin, or a small piece of jewellery for each of the girls, and a gold coin for the boys. She gave her Japanese lacquered trays to one friend, her silver dressing-table set to another, and her opal earrings to a third. Each person had something which she knew they had at some time admired, or which she knew they would like but perhaps had not the money to buy. She did not burden them with the news of her impending death, and told them only that she was clearing out a few of her things and thought they might like to have this or that trinket as a keepsake.

She had a great many friends. She was everyone's aunt. Her picture was in a hundred photograph albums, her plain, pleasant face wearing her usual good-natured smile or an expression of appreciation and interest, and her arm around a friend or a child.

She was interested in a great many things, she enjoyed good food, and the give and take of conversation under the shade of her balcony in the hottest months, or a cup of tea by the comfort of a fire in the winter. She liked to ride in the country (less often now that she was rather heavier and suffered from arthritis) and she dearly loved an excuse for a party or a celebration. She had done most of the things she had wished to do. She had been to Constantinople and sailed on the Bosphorus. She had ridden camels in Syria and Egypt, seen the splendour of Lebanon's classical ruins, visited the Pyramids, Petra, and Palmyra, and she had sailed the wine-dark sea to Greece. That rather strange description of the Mediterranean had remained in her memory since reading the classics in her girlhood, and she had hoped to make sense of it when sailing that sea herself, but in the end she concluded that perhaps Homer may have been colour-blind before he lost his sight altogether.

She had spent balmy spring days by the ocean, and summers in the cool and peaceful mountains. There were trips to see the glorious crimson and gold of autumn in Platres and Pentadaktylos, and wonderful Christmas walks with friends in the pure, crisp snows of Troodos, and she was almost content.

Her only regret was a mistake she had made early in her life, but she had gone on to make the very best of the remainder. All her brothers and sisters were married, and she was the only daughter of Boghos Effendi still to bear his name. Her sweet sister Zabelle obediently married an eligible *parti* and headstrong Elbisse had the stubbornness and courage to go her own way, but Hanemie had hesitated too long, and she had made the foolish error of indecision.

It was not that she disliked men, in fact she liked them very well. She understood them very well, too, and made affectionate allowances for all of them, from the youngest to the oldest. She found her fellow human beings endlessly interesting and she could always be depended upon to lend an understanding and sympathetic ear to the problems or joys of her many cousins, friends and acquaintances.

She made her will, detailing a few last small bequests, and left her house and her money to the Church. Then she allowed her failing body to have its way. She was taken to the General Hospital in Nicosia, where she was put to bed in a clean, bright room, which soon filled with flowers and well-wishers. There were so many of these, that the nurses found it necessary to ask her callers to arrange things with each other so that she would not be overly tired by the crowds which were constantly attending her.

It was the beginning of September, and still very hot, so that she was awake and glad to see two late arrivals when they called after visiting hours had officially ended. Her sister-in-law Shenorik and her cousin Evekenia put their heads round the door to see if she was asleep, and received her usual delighted smile and an invitation to come in.

"What brings you so late to this side of town?" she asked Shenorik. "No matter, it's lovely to see you both," and she sat up for a kiss from each of them.

Shenorik brought a bunch of violets, still cold from the spring at Deftera, beside which they had grown, and Evkenia gave her a small pot of her infallible and exquisitely scented ointment for joint-pains and general aches. Hanemie was delighted by both gifts, and asked them to stay a while and talk.

"We came with Asdig," Shenorik told her, "her labour has begun, and she is here in this hospital too. She is not at all happy, and things haven't even really started, poor girl." She and Evkenia exchanged knowledgeable glances. Hanemie noticed this, and laughed.

"Don't leave me out just because I'm an old maid. What's the joke?"

Shenorik sighed. "Asdig doesn't like it when things go beyond her control. She detested being pregnant, and now she *resents* her pain and the indignity involved, and she is hating every minute she has to bear it, and of course it just makes things worse for her. She's not even frightened, just very very annoyed."

"And the more you fight it, the longer it takes and the harder it is," Evekenia added, "I don't think she'll allow herself to go through this more than once, and I believe Vahan wanted several children. He's going to be very disappointed."

Shenorik snorted in a rather unladylike manner. "He won't have anything to say about it! I know my daughter, and in this she has my full understanding and even my hearty support. I only went through it a second time myself because we wanted a son. After that, no more! I'm just glad I didn't have five daughters first. It's a positively ridiculous way to perpetuate the race, when you think about it. All that fuss and mess and pain, not to mention the dangers! And she's right, it *is* undignified."

Hanemie did think about it. Would she have been willing to undergo the pain and danger of childbirth in order to have her own little son or daughter? Probably. It would have been wonderful to have held Arakel's child in her arms. She managed to feel both envy and pity for her much-loved Asdig, and she hoped she would have a short labour and a beautiful, healthy baby.

"She'll be happy once she has her little princess, surely?" she asked, reaching for a box of sweets to share with them.

Cousin Evkenia smiled and shook her head. "She'll be disappointed. Her baby's a little pasha, not a little princess," she said.

"Are you sure?" Shenorik laughed. "Asdig is determined that it will be a girl. And she *always* gets her own way."

"She won't with this, I'm afraid. He's a boy. You have to take what God sends you, and He has decided that this baby has a pestle, not a mortar."

Neither of her listeners questioned this statement further. Cousin Evkenia was never wrong.

"Oh dear. Asdig will be beside herself." Shenorik shook her head, then started laughing. "It's even possible that she just won't accept that he's not a girl. She has a name chosen and all the pretty baby clothes ready for a girl! He'll be lucky if she doesn't call him Sylvia, just the same, and she'll probably keep him in petticoats and little lacy dresses till he starts protesting."

Evkenia smiled reassuringly and patted Shenorik's hand. "Don't worry, he'll be another tough little Eramian boy. He'll be fine, and he's got you, too, don't forget."

Hanemie suddenly felt completely exhausted. It was a most unpleasant and upsetting feeling. She carefully relaxed against her pillows, easing her aching back and thinking that perhaps she could sleep, after all.

Her observant visitors rose to leave. "Can I bring you anything?" Evkenia asked. "I'll be passing your house tonight, perhaps you need something from there?"

Hanemie considered this, and one self-indulgent wish came to her. It might be her last chance to enjoy such a treat. "There *is* one thing. I would really, really like some ice-cream from Iraklis' shop in Ledra Street. Prickly pear perhaps, or mastic, or rose flavour, chocolate, or any flavour, really. Whatever they have will be fine. No one in the world, not even the Italians, make ice-cream nearly as wonderful as theirs. It always makes me quite greedy."

"Of course I'll bring some for you, but it will have to be in the morning: they'll be closed now. Is there anything else?"

"If you're passing my house, I left a small photograph album on the table by the front door. It's covered in pale green velvet. I'd like to have it – I can't think why I forgot it."

"I'll bring it," Evkenia told her, and the two women kissed her fondly.

The Agha's Children

In another room in the hospital, in the delivery suite some little distance from the bustle of the general wards, Asdig closed her eyes against a wave of pain, gritted her teeth and clenched her fists tightly. She wished with all her being that it was tomorrow and that her little girl was born, so that all the humiliation and unpleasantness would be over and this horrible experience finished with.

Hanemie slept a little, and woke to find her photograph album on the table beside her bed. It must be very late, or possibly very early, because there was no noise, no sound of voices, no footsteps, no rattle and clash of bedpan or trolley or wheelchair. It was very soothing, this quiet. She had always risen early and she enjoyed the feeling of being awake while the world around her slept.

She reached for the album, and found it oddly difficult to lift the book and set it on her lap. She quickly suppressed a momentary alarm at this unfamiliar weakness, ashamed of her racing heart and her involuntary gasp of fear: after all there was no point in being afraid of the inevitable and she had been given plenty of time to prepare for her departure. She told herself that what was going to happen would happen, and that she should not dwell on it. She firmly turned her thoughts elsewhere.

How kind people were. Cousin Evkenia must have made a second trip to the hospital just to leave the album for her to find when she woke.

She opened the book. She had not looked at these pictures for many months.

There was a familiar rush of love and regret when she looked at him. She had not had the courage of Elbisse nor the sweet obedience of Zabelle; she had kept him waiting, avoiding the inevitable confrontation with her father. He had waited for years, that dear and faithful man, and then he had died. Beloved and patient Arakel.

Here he was in that silly boater and sailing outfit, looking rather foolish. Next, with herself and her cousins Huliané, Elise and Marie, sitting on the steps of the Melikian house after the funeral when Artin was buried. Then a wistful portrait of him looking at her picture in an album. Further on, he stood solemnly in uniform. He was an officer in the French Army fighting in the World War, in danger, surrounded by horror and death every day. Even so, he had managed to send her the photograph, and the letters, and his love.

He looked sad.

How could she have been so foolish?

He sent postcards and long affectionate letters, pictures of himself and the places he had been, and he sent poems in his beautiful, flowing hand, noting conscientiously that he had copied them for her, and had not composed them himself. Still she had thought she had all the time in the world. Here was picture after picture. Arakel, faithful, gentle, loving, always there.

And then, shockingly, one day he died.

His face blurred through her sudden tears. She wiped them away and she closed the book, holding it tightly in her arms. She knew that some people believe that you see your loved ones again when you die.

She realised that she was about to find out, and she hoped desperately that it was true.

When Cousin Evkenia brought Hanemie's ice cream in the morning, she found the room empty, the sheets stripped and the flowers removed. She sat down in the chair by the bed and took some time to regain her composure. She would miss Hanemie terribly.

After a few minutes, she blew her nose hard, dried her eyes, and tried to look cheerful. She would not spoil Asdig's special day. No one should tell her that her favourite aunt had died, not today. Bad news could wait.

She took the ice-cream to her exhausted and greatly relieved cousin, who had successfully delivered her healthy, handsome baby boy.

Uncle Boghos has enjoyed a long and productive life. He came into his responsibilities young, but he has always done his duty to the best of his abilities, and he is that rare find today: a courteous, gallant, old fashioned gentleman. His bloodline is that of Aleksan and the mighty Boghos Effendi, and he found that this legacy of physical strength stood him in good stead.

1942

Boghos and the Thief

BOGHOS FROWNED at his Keo beer. It is a very fine beer and it was in a chilled glass, frosting nicely. It had a proper amount of head, and was the right colour of liquid sunshine, so his frown was not for the drink.

"When I was a young man there was much work to do at the farm," he began, taking a draught of the beer, "and we had servants to help. Some were from families who had worked for us since the days of my earliest ancestors at Deftera, and these deserve our respect and fair and honest treatment. A man has a responsibility towards such good men."

Boghos's expression became fierce, emphasizing that his next words were very important. "If a family servant asks for our help to redress a wrong, it is important to do what we can."

We nodded and waited for him to go on. We were having a leisurely lunch in the mountains, at Mariam's restaurant 'Kopiaste', which means 'Enjoy!'. Most people still call it Mariam's, anyway. Boghos had known the owner since he was a young man hunting in the mountains with his guns and his dogs, and she had begun her famous restaurant by serving eggs with sausages to him and his fellow hunters.

She had a smile for him that spanned the years, and Boghos's nephew said quietly to his wife, "Hmmm, maybe there is a history there. Still, the things a man does before his marriage can't be held against him, can they?" His wife smiled sweetly and dug a knuckle in his ribs.

Boghos continued: "We had a servant from one of the families who had been with us for generations. Her name was Elpi and one day she came to see my mother, who was at that time living at Deftera. Elpi went to the kitchen where my mother was distilling her special rose-water, and she sat in a chair, covered her head with her apron, and cried and wailed. My mother was very sorry to see this, so she sat down beside her and asked what was troubling her so. Elpi told her that there was a bad man in the village, a handsome and charming, but very bad man, and that he had made her daughter pregnant. Now he refused to marry her. Worse, he had abandoned her and would not even acknowledge the child as his, so that the girl's good name was gone and it would be impossible for her to find a husband once everyone knew about her shame.

"To have a child with no father was a terrible, terrible thing for a girl in those days and some girls killed themselves rather than live with the misery of such dishonour. Elpi told my mother that she had no way to punish him, and that she needed our help.

"We knew this man well. His name was Petros and he had been turned off from the farm more than once because he pretended to work with great diligence, but in fact he spent more energy avoiding his tasks than he would have used in doing them. He was a thief and a liar, and a man you could not trust. My father had died a few years before and the farm was now my responsibility, so my mother agreed with Elpi that it was my duty to punish Petros for ruining her daughter. You must understand that things were very different then and that this was a bitterly shameful thing for the daughter of a respectable family. It would normally have been the responsibility of her father or brothers to deal with him, but Elpi's husband had died and she had no sons to take her part. She only had us to turn to and so it seemed that I had no choice.

"I was young and muscular and very strong then, so that people sometimes thought I was a wrestler, which in those days was not a man on steroids, pretending to fight and fall over for television cameras. These wrestlers were roaming strong-men who travelled from village to village taking challenges from any man with the courage to stand against them, and giving shows of power and endurance to make a living. Although Petros was a strong man too, I knew that I should be able to teach him a lesson and make him a little sorry for his callous treatment of Elpi's daughter. Elpi should not feel that her daughter's sorrow and shame would go unpunished.

"Petros had the habit of walking across one of our fields to the village each day, so I waited for him beside a tree and when he came strolling along, a carefree man, I jumped on him and I gave him a good beating. When he stopped fighting back, I stopped too and told him why I had done it, and then I had to let him go," Boghos shook his head sadly, "but I knew that he would not forget and that some day I should have to deal with him again."

He paused, remembering that day long ago. He was 90 years old, but those days when Elpi's daughter was young were still fresh in his memory. With evident pleasure, he reduced the level of beer in his glass by another inch. "Some months after this, one of our men came to the farmhouse and gave me some news. '*Affendigo*,' he said, 'everyone knows that Petros is stealing your figs and selling them. It is time that you did something about it.'

"In those days, there was work to be had at the new airport which was being built a few miles beyond the village, and some of our people went early in the morning each day to earn some money there, working as labourers or some such thing. It seemed that Petros was at least doing some work for a change, but unfortunately it was not good work.

He was taking some baskets, filling them with figs from my trees and standing beside the road to sell them to the workers as they set off at first light.

"I got up before sunrise and walked through my fields to wait for him at the fig trees. Around dawn, he came walking along carrying his baskets and ready to steal my fruit, but when he saw me he dropped them and ran. Now, I told you that he was a strong man, but I was stronger and I ran and ran, and eventually I came alongside him and passed him. I had with me a heavy stick, and I struck him twice on his arm as I passed by. I struck very hard, with all my strength, and at once he fell down and did not want to get up.

"This was a long time ago, and it was in the days before we had toilets inside our houses. We would put them a little way from the main buildings so that things would not be too unpleasant in the summer heat, but still close enough not to be too inconvenient in the cold and wet days of winter. We used to set some men to dig a hole and we put a seat over it and a small wooden house round it for our privacy, and then we would just dig another hole and move the little house each time it became necessary.

"I had finally caught Petros as he ran past these toilets. When I went back to him, he would not get up, and I could not leave him there, so I stood and wondered what I should do with him to keep him safe till I could call an officer of police.

"At that moment, to my surprise, a man rushed out of the toilets to see what had happened, and he fell over, saying a very bad word. It was the local policeman, who was a sergeant, and in his haste he had not pulled up his pants properly and they had tangled his ankles and tripped him.

"After he got up again, dusted himself down and made himself tidy, I asked him if he could arrest my captive.

"He looked at Petros, who was scowling up at us from the ground. 'Oh, I think I can arrest him,' he answered, pointing to the two stripes of bruising that my stick had made on Petros's bare arm, and showing me the three white stripes on his own sleeve.

"'He's only a corporal!'"

Uncle Boghos ran the farm at Deftera very well, and he took his responsibilities seriously. He loved his life there, and took great pleasure in the day to day work and the yearly achievements of field and fold. He brought the first herd of Friesian cattle to Cyprus and he increased the milk yield spectacularly, he planted many acres with fruit trees, and he bred beautiful race horses. He grew almost everything the farm needed on his own land, and he brought his little nephew there for the wonderful, endless days of the summer holiday and gave him the priceless gift of wonderful memories.

1946

The Little Pasha

IT WAS THE first day of the holiday. The little boy woke in his narrow iron-framed bed and kept perfectly still, savouring the wonder of the moment. His grandmother, with whom he shared the plain, whitewashed room during his stay, had wakened long before and was downstairs beginning her early morning routine of farm duties. Her brass four-poster bed was neatly made up, the lavender-scented sheets smoothed, and the crocheted quilt was bright with many colours in the sunlight sifting through the half-open louvers of the shutters and spilling across the polished wooden floor. He lazily watched the shadows of leaves on the lace curtains for a while, then turned his head to greet the portrait of his three-times-great grandfather, which hung on the wall beside his bed.

At first he had been worried to find that the steady and disconcerting gaze of the stern, dark man in the picture followed him wherever he went, and he had spent a fruitless hour or two trying to find a place where he was out of its view, but whenever he slyly poked his head out from behind the bedclothes or the curtains, he was still being watched.

Later he had decided that it was a good thing. The eyes did not close in the dark like his own (he had checked that several times) and he thought that being watched by this unblinking stare would deter even the odd things that sometimes made bumps in the night and creaked threateningly on the stairs.

He would have known he was at the farm even if he had kept his eyes closed. He could hear a rooster announcing its supremacy among the hens, a goat complaining loudly somewhere nearby, and his uncle's voice calling a greeting to someone as he walked across the farmyard at the front of the house. He could smell bread baking downstairs, and the kitchen clock sounded a melodious double chime for the half-hour.

Quickly, he got down from his bed and padded with bare feet across the cool, octagonal stone tiles of the long hall to the dining room. He climbed on to a chair and looked out of the window. The huge eucalyptus tree in the paved yard tossed its aromatic leaves in the breeze, shading the courtyard where his grandmother had set crockery outside on the table for his breakfast, and his uncle was standing beside it and talking to one of the labourers. Everything was just as it should be.

He ran back to the bedroom and shook out his sandals. Last year his mother's cat had taught him this lesson and now he always checked inside them before putting them on. He was getting ready to go out and play when the fat, lazy old animal had leapt from under the bed with astonishing speed and batted his hand away as he reached for his shoes. She growled when he tried again, and kept on making worried cat noises until he took proper notice. He had found a small scorpion inside, and now he was careful.

Hastily he buckled the sandals onto bare feet, pulled on shorts and shirt, and dashed down the stairs to the kitchen.

He was at a stage when he was growing fast, and his long, tanned legs had grown a little more quickly than the rest of him, but he would catch up soon. He had smooth olive skin, large dark eyes with long lashes, an innocent expression which served him well, except with his mother, and his hair was as thick and dark and curly as a girl's. He knew this would not last long. His grandmother believed that shaving his head every summer would make his hair grow more strongly and prevent it thinning later in life, so an appointment with a razor would soon be made for him.

Until he was three years old, his mother let his hair grow long in girlish ringlets and she dressed him in little frocks. She did not intend to undergo pregnancy and childbirth more than once, and he would be her only child. He would be a boy soon enough, she thought, so she had enjoyed this little time with him as the daughter she had always wanted.

The boy knew that she would rather not have had a son, but now he was old enough to notice and protest at wearing girls' clothes, and he was very glad to be a boy.

Boys had much more freedom than girls.

He finished his breakfast quickly. There was much to do at the farm, but he had first to make sure that everything was just the same.

He toured the outbuildings and the near fields, looked at the horses in the stables and the long-legged foals in the paddocks, watched the workers in the dairy for a while, jumped from stone to stone in the river bed, practised throwing his pocket knife at a tree, and found once again that he still could not run quite as fast as a chicken. He did catch an enormous brown zizziro, which deposited a warning spray on his hand before it flew away, he watched some small grey birds washing themselves in the wooden horse-trough, he got a thorn in his foot and another graze on his knee, and the pockets of his shorts soon held a good sized collection of unusual stones, a bit of wood polished into an interesting shape by the river, a piece of string, a coiled, pale snake-skin and some locust beans.

Next he reacquainted himself with the farm dogs, prudently holding a good big stick with a knot at the end in case any of them had forgotten him. They circled him, sniffing and yelping, then tumbled him over as they all tried to lick his face at once. Only Tamana sat outside the undignified scuffle, his big yellow eyes half-closed against the sun, his leathery black nose twitching as he took the boy's scent.

The lesser dogs made way as Tamana came forward and graciously allowed his ears to be scratched. When he had let the child see that he was safe and accepted, he stalked away and lay down by himself under a plane tree, giving a too-friendly pup a harmless but painful nip on the way. Tamana was boss dog and not to be trifled with.

The boy spent a little while detaching ticks from the other dogs while they panted happily and leaned their hot, dusty sides against him, then he ran inside for his lunch.

He ran everywhere. He was very happy at the farm, it was the best place in the world and he loved being there. There was always something wonderfully interesting to see or do, and even food was nicer here.

He ate everything on his plate, and then had second helpings. There was freshly made bread, a home-made yoghurt with cucumbers grown in the big kitchen garden behind the farmhouse, a rich and tasty stew of farm-bred meat, and enormous beans cooked in olive oil, tomatoes and herbs. There was breathtakingly icy well-water to drink, served in thick, frosted glass tumblers. The grown-ups had home-brewed beer. The boy liked the golden colour and the bubbles, but he found it much too bitter for his taste when he surreptitiously sipped some from the jug while carrying it to the table.

After lunch he resumed his inspection of his domain, but when his grandmother walked past the bush in which he was hiding from imaginary bandits who were treacherously attacking the farmhouse, he abandoned his game and ran to catch her up. It was always fun to go to the village with her.

She took his hand, kissed him, and ruffled his hair, and he knew that she was thinking again that it was time his head was shaved. He didn't like it, but he thought it was a small price to pay for a glorious month at the farm.

1946 The Little Pasha

Everyone they passed on the road knew her and greeted her. Sometimes she stopped to chat, moving to the shade of a tree to talk and proudly showing him to everyone..

They were always impressed. *Panayiamou,* how big he had grown, *O Bebis,* how tall and strong, may the saints protect him! He would be a strong man like his uncle for sure, just see what long legs he had. Someone should buy a blue bead for him to wear to keep away the evil eye, for certainly other mothers would envy such a big, strong, handsome boy.

He scuffed his feet and refused to look up, embarrassed to be the centre of such attention.

At this time, and until his uncle had a son, he was the Eramian heir, and so far, he was the only boy in his immediate family. In town he was constantly attended: he had his own much-loved nanny at home, and a girl to wheel him out in his gleaming baby carriage, and she was there to play with him and take him out for walks when he was older. However, she had little to do. All his mother's many friends and cousins vied for the pleasure of taking him to the park to listen to the band or to walk among the trees in the old moat gardens, and they called often at his house, offering to look after him for a while or wanting to play with him in the big garden behind the town house.

He took all this as his due and was at home anywhere. He was a self-sufficient and contented child, happy, confident, and endlessly interested in the wonderful and fascinating world around him.

His grandmother lovingly called him her little Pasha at home, but in the village he was '*O Bebis.*' This just meant 'The child.' More than a century and a half ago, their ancestors had done the same when speaking of the man whose portrait was on his bedroom wall. It was as if he were the only child in existence, and like the boy Artin Boghos, he thought the world revolved around him and, again, mostly, it did. It was fortunate that his sunny nature prevented him from becoming insufferably conceited.

He listened to the village gossip with interest, particularly when the women looked at him and lowered their voices. This usually marked the beginning of a bit of adult conversation which they thought he could not hear, but usually they underestimated the sharpness of a child's ears, and he would startle his grandmother later when they sat by lamplight in the yard and he asked the meaning of some word which she was sure no one had used in his presence.

He could already swear in three languages. Luckily, she did not know this, either.

At the centre of the village was a crossroads, and at each corner was a taverna. As chatelaine of the Eramian farm, grandmother was exempt from the usual exclusions, and she sat where she pleased and was served a tiny cup of thick black coffee, hot and sweet, and a glass of spring water. She gave the boy a cup of his own and a big, sticky sugared plum to eat while she discussed the crops, the weather, the price of corn, and the scandalous rise in taxes with the men. In this way they were able to pass on their concerns or grievances in a friendly manner, knowing that she would take notice and attend to them wherever possible, and bring them to the attention of her son when it was not in her power to act.

She did not stay too long, she knew the rules and she varied her visits to patronise each of the four tavernas equally, so that there should be no favouritism.

Next, she went into the church and lit a candle for her husband Stepan and her parents, Apgar and Huliané. Here she would sometimes find the women who could not approach her in the taverna, and who did not want to ask her in public for advice or help on a more private subject which should not be aired in the arena of the street. Today, however, they had the church to themselves.

It was very dark and cool inside, a welcome contrast to the superheated atmosphere outside. This was uncomfortable in July, and almost unbearable by mid-August. The air was scented with incense and burning olive-leaves, there was a great round tray of little candles stuck into sand, and the painted walls showed solemn saints in colourful robes standing round in the smoky gloom with disapproving, distant, narrow faces, their long fingers making the shapes of blessing, and holding bibles or the instruments of their martyrdom. The boy was particularly fascinated by the depiction of a saint who, though portrayed as whole and healthy, nevertheless held a second head in one hand. Grandmother told him that this was Saint John the Baptist, and she said that it would have been disrespectful as well as ugly to show him headless, so they had given him a spiritual head as well as a real one to remind the observer of his manner of death. He examined them carefully, and asked which was the real one and which was the spiritual one. She laughed and told him he was so sharp that one day he would cut himself, but she did not answer.

This church was quite different from the Armenian one in town, and belonged to the Orthodox Greeks. Grandmother said this was perfectly alright. God was the same wherever one worshipped Him, and He would not mind if she came to services here sometimes when she could not go to their old church in the city. She did not intend to miss her worship altogether while she was at the farm, simply because devout Greeks praised Him a little differently.

Next to one of the tavernas was the village butchery. Every couple of days or so, a sheep, goat or steer was killed, skinned and gutted, and hung up from a rail in the street for people to point out the cuts of their choice. Blood dripped on to the earth below, and the slippery, rather disturbing insides of the animal were thrown to the local dogs, which fought over them in a battle of snarling and snapping ferocity.

As the two went by this place, one of the dogs trotted past with a bit of the guts which he had managed to snatch from the brawl, and the boy reached out and gave his ear a friendly tug. The dog immediately turned on him and snapped its bloody jaws an inch from his nose. It intended no harm, it was merely warning him off and it looked at him for a moment, then picked up the scrap which it had dropped to make its point and ran off before one of the other dogs could dispute its ownership.

The boy moved behind his grandmother and watched with big eyes until the dog disappeared from view. He was not particularly frightened, just sensible, and he did not like the smell of the blood.

The scene had been witnessed by the patrons of the tavernas and by the crowd waiting at the butchery, and seeing the opportunity to enjoy a welcome and interesting change to the sameness of life, they gathered round to discuss the incident and the noise of debate and wise advice swelled around the old lady and the child. They all talked at once, with much arm waving and explanatory gestures. It was customary to speak loudly when making an important point, and the noise quickly grew. The boy could only hear those nearest to him, the ones who were pushing close, leaning over him, and shutting out the sun.

"Panayiamou, what a close escape!"

"Saints be praised the innocent one is unharmed. But look, he is frightened, the poor child!"

"You must put some of the blood on his head, *Jeera,* or he will always be afraid."

"Holy Mother be thanked for his escape, but he is pale. He has been terrified!"

The boy was still not frightened, but he did not like the idea of the strong-smelling blood being put on his forehead. He moved further behind grandmother.

"Mana mou! See, he *is* frightened!"

"*Jeera,* you *must* do something, or it is true that he will be timid all his life."

Heads were nodded all round. "Yes, yes, it is true. At his age a scare like this will make him a coward. This is well known."

Grandmother drew herself up to her full four feet six inches, managing by force of personality alone to seem imposing. The crowd drew back a little.

"Thank you for your advice: you are all very kind. Yes, indeed. You may be assured that I will certainly do something. My grandson has never been a coward, and he never will be." She smiled around the circle, which made a space for her. "Thank you all. *Kalimera sas!*" and she moved away, holding the boy firmly by the hand.

"I'm *not* frightened, grangmother," he told her, reverting to his baby name for her in his anxiety not to be seen as a coward. "I just didn't want them to make me all bloody, that's all."

"I know, my little pasha, I know." she said, lovingly. "We're going to see cousin Evkenia"

The boy did not mind this. Cousin Evkenia was a member of their huge and interesting extended family, and he thought her house a very exciting place. Her rooms were rather dim and she had fringed lamps and beaded tablecloths. There were lace antimacassars and tables with fat twisty legs, gilded dadoes and chandeliers with lots of sparkly crystals, and there was an extraordinary clock, taller than him, and it had a smiling face and the sun and moon on its pendulum. It ticked louder than the one at the farm, and it chimed a little tune. There were velvet cushions and hard, fat bolsters embroidered with beads and sequins, the carpets were richly coloured and patterned with birds and flowers, and best of all, she made wonderful, tiny sesame cakes which she supplied in unlimited numbers to small boys with healthy appetites.

Cousin Evkenia came to the door herself to let them in. She was short, plump and somehow not at all alarming even though she wore only black from head to foot. She produced some of the expected sesame cakes, sat the boy on a low stool to enjoy them, promised him a glass of lemonade shortly, and then sat down herself to hear what had brought them to see her.

In mediaeval England cousin Evkenia would have been in danger of an accusation of sorcery, and could have been burned as a witch. She was a very special lady with a very special reputation. She could charm warts so that they waned with the moon and disappeared, she could write a little prayer and sew it into a tiny cloth bag and it would keep a traveller safe on his journey or give a good night's sleep to a chronic insomniac, and she could bless away a curse. She could empower a blue bead so that it would protect a sleeping child from nightmares or the evil eye of an envious stranger, and she had a large, permanently sleepy but friendly white cat, who would allow visiting children to inflict almost any indignity upon him or his tail without protest or retaliation other than a lazy blink of his golden eyes. She was a mother confessor, an agony aunt and a natural psychoanalyst, and she never revealed a secret or showed in any way that she was shocked or disapproving.

She was a treasure indeed, and the community was healthier and happier than it would have been without her wise advice and help.

Grandmother explained what had happened. "I really don't think he was frightened," she said, "but there *was* something wrong. Probably that crowd, pushing round and shouting."

Cousin Evkenia looked at the boy. He looked back, mouth full of sesame cake, and smiled.

"Not much wrong there." she said. "*Were* you frightened?"

"No," he said, stoutly. "I'm *never* afraid."

"Never?"

"We...ell", he began. There was something reassuring about Cousin Evkenia, something which inspired confidences. "I don't like the dark very much. But I'm not frightened of it."

"Hmmm. Do you have bad dreams?"

"No. I've got the man in the picture. He never shuts his eyes, so nothing can get me."

Cousin Evkenia raised her eyebrows at grandmother.

"I think he means the portrait of my great grandfather, Artin Boghos Agha. It's in his bedroom."

"You're right not to be afraid, my little Pasha." Evkenia smiled, "but I'll make sure for you, so that your grandmother can tell the villagers that you are safe."

She bustled around on her little plump feet in their black satin pumps, leaving a faint scent of lavender as she passed. She brought two white wax candles, lit them, and placed them to either side of an icon of the Holy Mother. She set olive leaves to make fragrant smoke on glowing charcoal, poured some cold water into a silver bowl, and put a crystal jar of dark green olive oil, and a dish of salt next to it. Next, she took a sprig of bay leaves and dipped it in the water, touching the boy's brow and hands with it, then she repeated the actions with a little oil and a dab of salt. She murmured words which he could not quite hear.

He watched all this quietly, not understanding, but sure of her good intentions. When she asked him to look into the water, he obediently did so.

"What do you see?" she asked.

He was about to say that he saw nothing, when it seemed that the water clouded over as if mists were moving slowly within it. As he watched, completely fascinated, it cleared and there, seemingly suspended in the water, he saw the picture which hung on his wall.

He told Cousin Evkenia. "It's a picture of the dark man. Only he's smiling."

"Good," she said, and she took the silver bowl away.

She held both his hands and looked into his eyes. "You'll never be frightened, my dear child. You will have a strong body and a strong mind."

The boy believed her, and so it was true.

Grandmother gave Cousin Evkenia a bottle of her famous rosewater, another of pickled plums, and promised to send her a round of Anari when the next batch of cheeses was ripe.

Back at the farm, and allowed an hour to play before tea, the boy ran off to think. The sesame cakes already seemed far in the past, and he picked some figs to sustain him till mealtime, before heading down to the river to his private place in a thicket under a shady grove of trees on the near bank. He passed Hanemie's fatal stepping stones at his usual run, then wriggled through the bushes and tall grass to his secret hideout in the bushes. They hid him completely from view and he was sure nobody would disturb him here.

In fact, his uncle and two of his cousins knew this place well: many Eramian children had discovered it through all the years since Boghos-Berge built his first three arches by the river, and all of them had found it a refuge and solace from the sometimes unfair and incomprehensible world of adults. The adults who remembered it employed a little selective amnesia on the boy's behalf, when necessary.

He sat cross-legged on the ground and took out his store of treasures. He carefully inspected the figs for worms, splitting the fruit and examining them minutely for anything that wriggled. The worms were exactly the same colour as the inside of the fig, which made them difficult to spot even with his sharp eyes, and he took his time. The plump fruits were dark and velvety outside, and rosy and syrupy inside, just at their moment of perfection and nothing moved there as far as he could see, so he ate both fruit and rind with great enjoyment.

His immediate needs taken care of, he lay flat on his belly and rested his head on his crossed arms. He considered the incident with the dog which had snapped at him. He understood that dogs had different and simple ways of seeing things, and he had truly not been much frightened. He thought some more, and came to the conclusion that it was really the adults who had been frightened, and that they had expected him to feel the same way. He thought too, that Cousin Evkenia knew this, and because he thought her very wise he wondered if her little ritual had been more to reassure his grandmother than to protect him from a fear he had not felt. He wasn't certain exactly what being a coward involved, but it must definitely be something to be avoided.

Grownups sometimes behaved very oddly.

After a while in which no further insight came to him, he took out a toffee which he had half-eaten and saved for later use, unstuck it from the stones and marbles which had also been in his pocket, detached the fluff it had accumulated, and sucked it contentedly. Then, guessing that it must be near teatime, he put his treasures away and started along the dusty track towards the village.

He had been to a Western film in town last week with Diggin Marie Melikian, and now he became a cowboy, walking bow-legged, swaggering, hands hovering over imaginary six-guns. Whirling, he shot an Indian raider pretending to be a prickly pear, and another masquerading as a mildly curious goat.

Suddenly, he remembered that there was *baklava* for tea, and forgetting his six-guns, he broke into a trot. The setting sun was in his eyes as he hopped and skipped towards home, and his long, long shadow jumped and leaped along behind him.

Although there are hundreds of descendants of Boghos-Berge who have settled and thrived in other countries, Uncle Boghos and his son and grandson are the last of the Eramians in Cyprus to bear the family name.

In him, and in the peaceful existence of all his cousins everywhere, the decision of Boghos-Berge Eramian Agha, made on behalf of his children nearly two hundred and fifty years ago, is justified.

2005

Respect

The Shenorik farm at Deftera

UNCLE BOGHOS was enjoying half a cigarette after dinner. This was not because he was mean, but because he was companionably sharing it with his wife, who had also not wanted a whole one. He started smoking when he was eighty-seven years old, and when we looked surprised and said how unhealthy it was, he raised his eyebrows. "Why should I worry?" he laughed. "Do you think I still have time to die of cancer?"

He studied his plate thoughtfully, and said: "You know, it is a difficult task to give advice. Sometimes, however, it is a necessary thing." He pointed the cigarette at his nephew, who had just finished eating a very good trout.

His nephew did not immediately see any connection between the cigarette and the difficulty of advice, or any connection at all with the trout, but he knew that if he was patient, all would become clear.

"A while ago, a cousin of ours whose husband had died some years before was sending her son to France to study. He was a quiet young man and so far he had led a sheltered life, and she was afraid that he would be led astray by more worldly and sophisticated students, so she asked me if I would have a little talk with him before he left and give him some advice as to how to go on.

"When I was a young man myself, we did not have radio or television, and there was little to do in the evenings except eat and drink, or read or talk. Some of us could play the piano or sing, and we had very good parties at Christmas, New Year, and on our birthdays. But life was much harder, and we worked harder too, so we did not feel anything was wrong with going to bed early and getting up early to do our work.

"Now, though, things are different, very, very different." He looked at his cigarette. "Not everything in a cigarette these days is tobacco, you know, and there are other hazards for a young man too, drugs, diseases and so on. Things are easier for young people in some ways, and very much more complex in others, so I really did not know what to say to him.

"Still, his mother *is* our cousin, and this was a duty. So I thought I should do my best, and I asked him to come to the farm to see me.

"It was a hot day in June, and I put some beers on ice and set the kitchen chairs out in the shade. Away from his mother the young man seemed much more confident, and we had a bottle of beer and then we had another, and I told him that I had been asked to give him some advice. He gave me a sideways look, but he said nothing and was obviously waiting for me to speak, so I started.

"I said: I know you do not drink too much, and you do not smoke or go to the red light district, and that you probably already know all about marijuana cigarettes, and the stupidity of gambling, and the bad things you can catch from easy women, but your mother is worried about you."

He stopped and gave us a wry look. "The young man still said nothing, so foolishly I went on. I said: It is easy to say 'no' to these things when you are alone, but surely, when your friends are with you and they say you must try this or that, or tell you that you should go to the casino with them, and you do not want to sound foolish or inexperienced, things will appear in quite another light. Sometimes a petty girl will come and sit on your lap at the cabaret and tell you what a fine boy you are, and everything will seem very nice, but you must remember to be sensible and say no, and do nothing to cause sorrow to your mother.

"The young man listened politely, but still he said nothing, and I suddenly thought that I should at least admit my ignorance about some of these things to protect my good name and to keep his respect, so I said: 'I can only warn you that drugs and gambling are wrong, my boy, because of course I have never done these things myself....'

"The young man had drunk several beers by now, and he had lost all of his shyness. He grinned at me and opened another bottle. 'So let me get this right,' he said, 'you don't gamble or take drugs, but if, like you, I drink and fight and enjoy the company of women I will live to be 90, as you have done?'

"What could I say? I couldn't lie to him. I decided he could probably look after himself quite well in France, and together we finished all the beer. I think he'll go far, that one."

We all laughed, and Uncle Boghos stubbed out his cigarette and ordered a second coffee.

We had eaten a fine meal on the terrace at Mariam's restaurant, and we had drunk the good wines of Omodhos. The wine bottles were empty and we were happily contemplating our tiny cups of strong, sweet Cypriot coffee, which had arrived accompanied by little plates of 'sweets of the spoon' with the owner's compliments.

The plates each held a piece of sugared melon and a pickled walnut, shiny with syrup. These walnuts are taken while they are still green and soft, the bitterness is drawn out and they are finally 'pickled' by immersion in tooth-achingly sweet sugar syrup until they are velvety black, and they taste nothing like walnuts. They taste wonderful and should be nibbled a little at a time in order to appreciate fully this miracle of transformation from mouth-puckering bitterness to ambrosial perfection.

Uncle Boghos looked thoughtfully across the valley to the mountains where in his youth he had so often walked and hunted. A brisk wind was chasing cloud shadows across the wooded slopes, which were as wild as they had been in the days when he was young, except that now there was no longer anything to shoot. It had all been shot, and in some places in the Troodos mountains the crunching noise underfoot is not made by brushwood, but by hundreds of spent cartridges.

In the wilderness of the Akamas, which is a nature reserve, big bold hunters come swaggering down through the villages with their trophies hung on their belts for all to admire, and they carry high-power guns with telescopic sights and wear special jackets, gloves, hiking boots and arm braces. Uncle Boghos wore leather riding boots, cord breeches, and a woollen shirt when he went hunting. He shot only what could be eaten, and he used a good plain shotgun, for which he made his own cartridges, but now the trophies of most of these so-called 'hunters' consist of one or two sad little singing birds, so tiny that they have almost been blown to pieces. These are not real hunters, and most years one or two of them manage accidentally to shoot each other, though not always fatally. The government has proposed that each of them should now wear a bright orange waistcoat with his licence attached to the back to avoid further accidents.

Uncle Boghos swirled the last of his coffee in the little cup and upended it so that the muddy dregs could make patterns as they ran down the inside into the saucer, ready for a spot of fortune-telling later.

He was still gazing towards the mountains, but now he was seeing them as they were many years ago. "You know," he said, "all my days I have walked on the earth, and I was never a man whose feet walked only on carpets. When my father died, I was only twenty-two years old and in all my life till then he had allowed me no responsibility. He was a careful, meticulous, painstaking man, and I remember that each evening he would sit at the table after dinner and count the change from his pocket, checking every coin before he put it away in his cash box. Then he would count his money once more and if even one small coin was unaccounted for, he would count it again to make quite sure, and then he would frown, and think, and go over his actions of the day one by one until he could remember what he had done with it.

"Ours was a big farm. We employed many workers and we had no worries about finances, but till my father died I was never given any money of my own, not even a small allowance, so that often I was ashamed because I could not stand my round to buy drinks for my friends or entertain them." He looked a little embarrassed and said slowly, "I confess that late one evening after my friends had bought my drinks for me yet again, I once stole a few shillings from that box when he left it unlocked, because I was in such need. I think he knew I did it, because he gave me a hard look the next day, but he said nothing.

"When he died, I was very young. Suddenly I was in charge of this large farm, responsible for the day to day running, planning for the future, and responsible too for the welfare of my workers and my family.

"However, now I had some money of my own for the first time. The very first thing I bought was a car to replace our horse-drawn carriage, which was something I had always wanted, but I also got a motor bike. Having that car meant that I could drive my mother to and from the city whenever she wished, and having some money in my pocket meant that I could at last stand my own round and not be ashamed, and I could invite some of my friends to dine with me at the farm. It is a good thing I have never been a gambler, because it would have taken hold of me then, but I have not been tempted by the casino ... and I have never even placed a bet on my own horses at the race track, even when I was sure one of them would win.

"Certainly we had servants, and I had men to do the manual work of the farm, but they knew that if necessary I could do it as well as they, and I have never asked a man to do work that I could not do myself.

The men of the village were hard, plain men and they were mostly our friends, but there were some who would have noted any sign of weakness in me and then they would be quick to take advantage. Things would have become very, very difficult. This meant that I had always to be strong and sure and never seem weak or to be uncertain of what I should do.

"I loved our farm, and I enjoyed the work, and it was very nice indeed to be able to invite people to visit me, but best of all I enjoyed buying that car." He smiled to himself, and returned his attention to the view across the valley. "I have walked over all of these hills and mountains, and truly, I think there is not a place where my foot has not been. I have loved to ride here, too, and I have had some fine horses."

Uncle Boghos bred Cyprus quarter-horses for racing, and his famous mare Favorita had won the Cyprus Derby one year. He had many other proud successes, but those were in his later years and he was talking of a time long before that.

He took a sip of water and a bite of melon.

"I went hunting often in those days, and I had much pleasure and contentment from being in the mountains, alone or with friends. We had many dogs at the farm, some guard dogs and some hunting dogs, and most of them were good only to make a noise at strangers and look fierce. They all had names, those dogs.

"Do you remember Tamana?" he suddenly asked his nephew.

"Yes," Berge said, "Wasn't he the enormous one, the boss dog? I remember them well, and when I was a little boy I was impressed that they ate anything, even onions or figs and apricots when they dropped from the trees! And none of them messed with Tamana."

"Tamana was the boss dog, certainly. He weighed thirty-five kilos and I once saw him kill another of the dogs with a single bite to its neck. The foolish animal got between him and a bitch that he wanted. That big dog was certainly a good fighter, but he was no good at all for hunting. He had plenty of puppies though, and one of them looked to me as if he could be a good hunting dog, so I took him apart from the others and trained him. He turned out very well indeed and was beginning to be a good worker, even though he was still young, and we often went out on the mountains together.

"One fine morning, I had arranged to go hunting in the Troodos mountains with one of my friends, but when we reached the place we had chosen, he said he had changed his mind and that he would go further along the slopes to hunt because he had heard that the game was better there. I decided that I would go along our original route, and we agreed to meet up at dusk, so I called my young dog to me and took up my gun.

"My dog stood still. He looked at me, and then at my friend, who had already started along his path. I called him once more, but he decided that the other way was more interesting and he ran off after my companion. He had forgotten all his training and he did just as he pleased. I had made a mistake with him.

"I knew I could not trust him to go hunting with me now because he might run away at any time. He could not be a guard dog because he was far too friendly with strangers, and he could not be a pet because he was much too old to train for the house. Our dogs were all working dogs of one kind or another, and I knew that now I would have to put him down. No one else should be asked to do this for me, or it would be assumed I was too weak to do it myself. It was not a pleasant task, and it was best to do it as soon as possible, so I took him away and did it as soon as he returned that evening. It was a sad thing.

"Mostly though, it was a very good life at the farm, and while I did have trouble there sometimes, I always dealt with it as best I could. I do not think I have done too badly over the years, and if I had to live my time again I would change nothing."

We finished our coffee and 'sweets of the spoon,' after which Boghos' wife Ashkhen signalled to the waiter, intending to pay for the meal.

His nephew neatly intercepted the bill before Mariam's handsome waiter could hand it to her, and he looked at her mischievously, avoiding her attempts to take it away from him.

"I'll pay for this," he insisted. "Bearing in mind the fate of that dog, you'd better not smile too lingeringly at that waiter!"

Uncle Boghos tweaked his nephew's ear and laughed with us, but his gaze was still on the mountains, remembering his friends and his horses and dogs and his life at Deftera. "It has been a good life," he repeated softly to himself, "and if I had my time again, I would change nothing."

Boghos-Berge's descendants travelled on to many countries, some by choice and some fleeing to a place of refuge, and they bear many names and speak many languages. Their blood is mixed with that of a score of other nations, and they have thrived and multiplied thousands of miles away from their ancestral home in the mountains of Armenia and the ancient principalities and kingdoms of Cilicia, which is now Turkey.

Those who told the stories and tales which form the bones of this book have passed on their memories so that they will not be forgotten, and to ensure that their children will know what drove their forbears to leave their wild, dramatic mountains, the stony windswept hills, the soft, green and fertile valleys, and the wide and lovely lakes of their ancestors' lands.

There are doctors in Canada, lawyers in America, businessmen in France, captains of industry in England, students in Australia and New Zealand, farmers in Cyprus and accountants in Syria among the Eramian descendants, and hundreds more cousins carry on a multitude of other professions and trades all over the world.

Today, there are more than three hundred living cousins, each with a common ancestor in Boghos-Berge.

They are the survivors, and they are all the Agha's children.